Kate Johnson was born in the 1980s in Yorkshire and now lives in Essex, where she belongs to a small pride of cats. She has a second cousin who made the Guinness Book of Records for brewing the world's strongest beer and she also once ran over herself with a Segway scooter. These two things are not related.

Kate has worked in an airport, a lab, and various shops, but much prefers writing because mornings are definitely not her best friend. In 2017 she won Paranormal Romantic Novel of the Year from the Romantic Novelists' Association with her novel *Max Seventeen*.

katejohnson.co.uk

 twitter.com/K8JohnsonAuthor
tiktok.com/k8johnsonauthor
facebook.com/catmarsters

T0035255

Also by Kate Johnson

Hex Appeal

HEX AND THE CITY

KATE JOHNSON

One More Chapter
a division of HarperCollins*Publishers* Ltd
1 London Bridge Street
London SE1 9GF
www.harpercollins.co.uk
HarperCollins*Publishers*
Macken House, 39/40 Mayor Street Upper,
Dublin 1, D01 C9W8, Ireland

This paperback edition 2023
2
First published in Great Britain in ebook format
by HarperCollins*Publishers* 2023
Copyright © Kate Johnson 2023
Kate Johnson asserts the moral right to be identified
as the author of this work

A catalogue record of this book is available from the British Library

ISBN: 978-0-00-855115-5

Printed and bound in the UK using 100% Renewable Electricity
by CPI Group (UK) Ltd

For my mum. Who always remembered about the mushrooms.

Chapter One

The Coven was here.

Iris always said it wasn't a coven, because the only people who believed in covens were the sort of people who got over-excited about witches dancing naked under the full moon, and it was too bloody chilly for that in Highgate, thank you.

Whatever they were called, there was a hell of a lot of cackling when they came round.

Poppy loitered in the upstairs hallway, clutching Malkin as if he alone could protect her from Iris's friends. Given that Malkin was, whilst technically a witch's familiar, also just an overweight tomcat, this didn't seem likely. But she appreciated the company.

She had to go into the kitchen for tea and toast and to find her phone and … and, well, to see if there were any clues as to what had made her wake up this morning not just with a crashing hangover but a horrible sense of foreboding.

'What did I do last night, Malky?' she whispered to the cat, who purred hopefully at her, his thoughts entirely focused on second breakfast. If she'd done anything that affected the household last night, Malkin would know, and he wasn't shy about telling her. But currently all he was interested in was his next meal, and Poppy's hair, which was in a combative mood this morning. As she made her way down the stairs, the cat batted and swiped at the curling strands, dislodging a couple of large hairpins as he did. Poppy winced as they clattered on the wooden treads.

Maybe she'd lost her phone. Maybe that was why she felt this sense of dread. Poppy had a pretty sweet deal when it came to cheap rent in exchange for housework, but her wages at Hubble Bubble didn't exactly cover the amount of phones she lost. Iris said she'd never known anyone so chaotic—

Malkin grumbled and hissed at her hair, and she shushed him a bit too loudly.

'Well, the dead arose and appeared to many!' cried one of the Coven, and Poppy winced.

'I wouldn't say that around here, Sylvia,' said Iris placidly. 'What with it being so close to Samhain and the cemetery only just there.'

'It's a figure of speech,' Sylvia said.

'When you're a witch nothing is a figure of speech,' said Fiona, with feeling, as Poppy entered the kitchen.

It was a large room, made larger by the grand Victorian conservatory that overlooked the excessively verdant garden. And yet it still wasn't large enough to contain Iris's friends. There weren't many of them, but each one had an ego about the size of Jupiter, so it was a bit of a squeeze when they decided to meet up for coffee.

This morning, they appeared to be trying to do the crossword whilst also holding a loud conversation about bees, and eating all the brownies Poppy had made whilst complaining they were really terrible. Which, in fairness, they were. Poppy had attempted to learn to cook from her parents, from uni friends, from boyfriends and girlfriends, and even from actual witches. It remained one of the many things she was terrible at.

'Morning,' she croaked, and tried to hold onto Malkin as some kind of distraction, or maybe shield, but the ungrateful bastard wriggled to get down.

'Ten letters, escorts souls to the underworld,' said Iris, as Poppy reached for the cat's food.

'I dunno, grim reaper?' Her head swam a bit as she straightened up, still avoiding the eyes of Iris's friends. Oof. There had been wine last night. And then there had been cocktails. Possibly shots too. Thank God for Iris's Patent Rehydration and Restoration Remedy, or 'hangover cure' as they called it in the shop.

'That's two words, and also too easy. It's one of those Greek words.'

'Latin,' said Fiona, who had discreet highlights and nice nails and constantly complained about how hard it was to raise a family in north London. 'The twins are always getting words like this in their homework.'

'I thought the twins were seven,' said Poppy disbelievingly.

'Eight. They're very advanced for their age,' said Fiona smugly.

Sylvia, who liked to argue with Fiona about pretty much every aspect of raising children even when they were in total agreement, snorted and reached for another brownie. She was a woman of comfortable proportions and somewhat forthright views on whatever you happened to disagree with.

'You overcooked these again,' she said.

Poppy sighed. 'Yes, I know, but I undercooked them last time so I thought—'

'My brownies are always in demand at PTA meetings,' Fiona said. 'The trick is—'

'Good night last night?' asked Iris, and the others fell very silent.

Poppy glanced at Iris from under her hair, which was being beastlier than usual this morning. Her landlady sat by the kitchen table in the big bay window, grey hair in a neat bun, blouse unwrinkled, the picture of calmness. Across from her Fiona and Sylvia were equally composed.

They all looked at her in a way Poppy had only ever experienced with witches. As if what they saw wasn't just your outer self, but all the layers of secrets and history you were trying to hide.

They were so ... self-possessed. Poppy usually felt as if she was possessed by the devil, a roulette wheel, and some very argumentative weasels.

'Yes,' she said cautiously. Their faces gave nothing away. Poppy put some bread into the toaster, telling herself they were just trying to spook her.

'Your friend have a nice birthday?'

Iris sounded so innocent. Fiona and Sylvia were watching like hawks.

She couldn't let them know she'd done something stupid last night. Or at least, *probably* done something stupid. Not remembering it made it even worse. Iris already thought Poppy had the self-control of a hurricane. She had no intention of adding fuel to that particular fire.

Poppy attempted nonchalance as she nodded. 'Yeah, I think so.'

'She like the necklace you got her?'

Aha! 'I made her a bracelet, which you know because you helped me pick out the stones for it,' said Poppy.

'Oh, yes. I remember.' Iris sipped her tea. 'I'm just surprised you do, lovey. Happy hour at the Lamb & Flag, was it?'

Dammit. Did they know, or did they *know*? Poppy's gaze flew guiltily to the sink, where she might or might not have left her glass after she'd helped herself to a nightcap. Or three. But the sink was empty, and Poppy really hoped that was because she'd sorted it out last night, and not because Iris had done it herself.

'Er, yes something like that,' she muttered, emptying a whole sachet of food out for Malkin, who purred appreciatively.

'There's a cocktail umbrella in your hair,' Sylvia said helpfully, and when Poppy reached up and pulled one out of her mane, added, 'Other side.'

Poppy smiled awkwardly as she divested her hair of

two cocktail umbrellas, some purple curling ribbon and a wilted gerbera. Her hairbrush was probably still in there.

'And you bumped into Claudia?' said Iris, without looking up.

Poppy froze with the gerbera in mid-air.

Claudia, with hair like polished obsidian and lips like bruised cherries. Claudia, who smelled like jasmine and wickedness and couldn't dance for toffee. Claudia, who had listened to Poppy's heartfelt declaration of love and then taken another girl home and hadn't even bothered to lie about it.

'The thing is, Pops,' she'd said, when Poppy confronted her all those weeks ago with another woman's very expensive underwear in her hand, 'you're not really the kind of girl I could take home to my parents.' She'd eyed Poppy's snarling hair and jangling bracelets and the purple eyeliner running down her cheeks, and added kindly, 'You're just a bit ... weird, that's all.'

Claudia, who had been full-on snogging another woman in the doorway of the bar opposite Hubble Bubble last night just as Poppy was leaving for the pub. A woman in a designer dress and sky-high heels. A woman with a briefcase. A woman whose sleek hair almost certainly never attacked people of its own accord. The right sort of woman.

'Uh,' she managed, and the flower in her hand fell to the marble counter.

Iris calmly filled in another clue on the crossword. 'Jezebel,' she said with satisfaction, and Poppy felt her cheeks heat.

'That's not fair—'

'Seven letters, wife of King Ahab. She broke your heart, darling, you're allowed to be angry with her.'

Fiona nodded. Sylvia said, 'Happy hour at the Lamb & Flag is an excellent way to get through things.'

Iris paused with a biscuit in her hand. 'When I found out my Herbert had been carrying on with another woman, I popped a little herbal remedy into his tea every afternoon. She didn't get any satisfaction out of him after that, I can tell you.'

Poppy blinked. She'd become used to Iris's non-sequiturs over the years, but to get one combined with a possibly apocryphal tale from her past was halfway to bingo. Poppy had no idea how old her grey-haired landlady was, but if even half of Iris's tales were to be believed, she'd lived an extremely colourful life.

'I did that when my college boyfriend told everyone I'd given him the clap,' said Fiona, nodding sagely, as if this was a completely normal conversation.

'You two are lightweights,' said Sylvia, leaning forward. 'When I found out— No,' she amended, glancing at Poppy. 'We won't scare her.'

The other two laughed.

'Well, I'm not putting anything into Claudia's drink,' Poppy said firmly, buttering her toast. 'No curses of any kind,' she added before Sylvia could suggest something else. 'Didn't you tell me that what I do comes back to me sevenfold?'

'Did I?' said Iris absently, apparently counting on her fingers. 'How extraordinary of me. Psychopomp.'

'What?'

'Psychopomp,' repeated Iris, filling it in with satisfaction. 'Escorts souls to the underworld. Like Paddington. Speaking of, lovey, best get a wiggle on if you're taking the bus.'

'No, I'll—' Poppy began to say she'd cycle to work as usual, then remembered she'd left her bike at the shop last night and got a cab home. Which was probably just as well given how much alcohol she'd apparently put away. 'Crap.'

'Why don't you try one of those bikes you hire?' said Fiona. 'There's even electric ones, so you can cheat.' She gave Poppy's thighs a critical look. 'If you *really* want to.'

'Ooh no, Poppy tried one of those once, didn't you, love? Forgot to return it properly, so it charged her three hundred quid.'

Fiona sucked her teeth. Sylvia cackled.

'I didn't forget,' Poppy said, gazing around wildly for her satchel. 'The machine wasn't working. Or my phone. Something didn't work.'

'Why is it always chaos with you?' said Sylvia, and there was a very short, very full silence Poppy didn't understand the significance of.

'It's bad planning,' said Fiona. 'I'm always telling the twins, failure to plan is a plan to fail.'

'How's that work out for you?' said Sylvia, which saved Poppy the trouble of a response.

'It's fine, I'll get the bus,' she said, and snatched up the toast. The bus took twice as long, especially if she missed the first one, which she usually did. Where were her shoes? Did she need a jacket? October in London was an absurd month for weather. 'Where's my Oyster card?'

'Use your phone, dear.'

'Where's my phone?'

Fiona closed her eyes for a moment, then said, 'In your coat pocket.'

'Good job you went back to the shop for your coat, eh?' said Iris. How did she *know*? 'This St Luke's Little Summer doesn't last into the evenings.'

'Er, yes.' Poppy shoved a piece of toast between her teeth, grabbed her satchel and her coat, and ran for the front door.

Then she ran back, swearing, and shoved her feet into her trainers.

'Bye, everyone,' she yelled through her toast, and raced down Swain's Lane just in time to see the 88 bus drive right on past.

Poppy stood for a moment, wondering if she had time to grab a coffee or if she'd just spill it down herself on the bus. 'Great start to the day,' she said.

It started to rain.

Alex Raine folded his arms and gazed up at the ten-foot poster of himself outside the Mysterio Theatre. Shirtless – that had been non-negotiable. Muscles defined and gleaming. Hair backcombed and braided and Vikinged up to the extent he was only amazed they didn't rub lye into it. The eyeliner was real but the phosphorescent eyes had presumably been photoshopped. He felt pretty sure he'd remember that.

The whole thing glowed in shocking violet and moody

black. *Axl Storm*, boomed the bold font choice. *His jaw-dropping new show: opening tonight!*

'What d'you think?' said Jonno, peering at some of the luminous runes Axl Storm appeared to be conjuring from thin air.

I think I still haven't put Percy Beaker behind me yet.

Alex looked into his own smouldering gaze and rubbed his chin. '*Oozes raw sexual magnetism*' swooned a review from Edinburgh, printed right across his nipple. He side-eyed Jonno.

'I dunno,' he said doubtfully. 'I just think it needs to be a bit sexier.'

'Sexier? Mate, you could get passers-by pregnant with this poster.'

Alex felt his mouth twitch. Jonno winced.

'Wait, sarcasm?'

'Sarcasm. It's absurd, Jonno. Look at the way they've faded out the bottom half. I look like I'm naked.' He'd been on protein powder shakes for weeks before the shoot and hadn't been allowed to drink any water on the day so his muscles really popped, and it had been very hot under the studio lights.

'You do look like you're naked.'

'And I distinctly remember wearing leather trousers for the shoot. They were very squeaky.'

'Yes, I remember. They added a certain something to the proceedings.'

'Fart noises, mostly,' said Alex. He glanced around the street. He probably shouldn't be standing right next to his own poster like this. He'd spent too long creating Axl Storm to have someone see through the glamour. Axl Storm smouldered in leather and eyeliner. He didn't slouch about in a hoodie with his hair in a ponytail.

If no one knew Axl Storm was Alex Raine, then they'd never know Alex Raine used to be Sandy Grubb and they'd never remember Sandy Grubb used to be Percy Beaker.

But you know, his own image mocked him. *You'll always know.*

He turned away from the absurdity of his own image and looked at the cramped entrance to the theatre, crowded with yet more posters and lights. 'Do you think it's safe to go back in?' he said.

Jonno pushed at the bridge of his glasses and peered in through the foyer. 'Maybe if we go this way. I'd avoid backstage for a while if I were you.'

'That should be easy,' said Alex drily, 'what with it being opening night and all.'

They went into the theatre's foyer, a place that always filled Alex with huge excitement. The ornate wooden panelling and Victorian tiles. The box office illuminated with stained glass. The little brass signs. It was all magic.

The souvenir booth was lined with his posters and programmes for tomorrow night, and there were T-shirts with some of his catchphrases on. *How the hell did I end up with catchphrases?*

From the stairwell leading to the stalls came the sound of someone screaming in Polish.

'Should we start auditioning for another new Valkyrie?'

Jonno said doubtfully. 'Maybe one of the girls from the corps could fill in. Who's Yelena's understudy?'

'We're not firing Yelena,' Alex said, with more confidence than he felt. A terrifying screech came from the auditorium, and he winced. 'She might quit and save us the bother,' he added hopefully.

They both stared at the door to the stalls. There was some really lovely Art Deco work on the signage there. Alex tried to concentrate on that and not the screaming.

'Jesus, Alex, we can't go on like this. She's your third Valkyrie this year.'

'That's not my fault,' Alex said, which was not exactly the most truthful thing he'd ever uttered.

'I mean,' Jonno began diplomatically, 'it's kind of your fault.'

'How is it my fault?'

Jonno gave him a disbelieving look. Alex attempted to look innocent. But his manager had a bit of a point. All this attention from women had seemed unbelivably exciting, once upon a time, and now he couldn't seem to put the brakes on.

'It must be terrible for you, Alex, having all these beautiful women accidentally fall naked into your bed when you don't even ask them to.'

'Sarcasm?' said Alex weakly.

'Sarcasm.'

Alex spread his hands. 'I can't help it.' Another direct lie.

'You can definitely help it.'

Alex pointed at one of his smouldering posters. 'I have raw sexual magnetism, Jonno. We all know it.'

'Ugh.' Jonno mimed retching.

'It's on the posters outside.'

'The heavily photoshopped posters.'

'It's paying your salary,' Alex reminded him, and Jonno sighed.

'And yet I manage to resist you.'

Alex shrugged. 'That's because I haven't turned the smoulder on you.'

Jonno held up a hand. 'Please don't.'

Alex grinned at his friend. 'I promise to only use my powers for good.'

'Look, just apologise to Yelena.'

Alex opened his mouth to protest that he hadn't done anything to apologise for, and shut it again, because he knew this wasn't how it worked. He hadn't promised Yelena the moon and stars; in fact, she'd been one of his backing dancers when he was seeing Monika, and probably when he was stepping out with Shanae too. Not that much stepping or indeed being outside had been involved there, but *the point was*, Yelena had seen how this sort of thing went before.

From inside the auditorium came one of Yelena's famous screams, which he thought was overdoing it a bit.

'Could you try something for me?' Jonno said. 'Just as a … an experiment.'

Alex sighed. 'Go on.'

'Could you – and I know this is a difficult concept to

grasp, so I'll go through it slowly with you – could you try, okay, *try* … not sleeping with people you work with?'

'I do try,' Alex said, but he wasn't even convincing himself.

'Once more, with feeling!'

'Okay, I'll try. No more sleeping with people I work with.'

'Good.'

'It's too messy.'

'It is.'

There was silence for half a second, and then Yelena shouted something in the auditorium, and Jonno's eyes slid back to Alex.

'Look, I never promised anything, it was just a one-time thing,' Alex protested. And then his stupid ego had him adding, 'Well, one night. You know.'

'I really don't want to.'

'She made the assumption it was more, that's all I'm saying,' he said.

'Did you correct that assumption?'

Alex bit his thumb.

'Look, she wanted to come to this awards thing next week, and I said she couldn't. I said I'm just presenting, I don't get a plus-one. She said she was my girlfriend so she should have got an invite…'

Jonno winced. 'And you said?'

'Er, I said she wasn't my girlfriend, that we'd just had a one-time thing.'

Jonno groaned.

'It's not even up to me! Even if we were married I wouldn't get to take her, but she said she'd already bought a dress.'

Jonno covered his face with his hands. 'Did you say the married bit?'

Alex felt his gaze slide guiltily to his friend, who groaned. 'Should I not have?'

'Alex, Alex.' Jonno sighed and patted his shoulder. 'It's a good job you're pretty.'

Well, what the hell else have I got? 'That doesn't feel like a compliment.'

'Mate,' said Jonno, 'it wasn't meant to be.'

'Sorry sorry sorry, some kind of protest going on in Camden, bus got diverted, ended up on the Tube and I swear to God I got the Morden line but it took me to Kings Cross anyway, so I ended up on the Piccadilly and thought I'd get out at Covent Garden because it was closer and, like, what do you learn your first week in London? Never get out at Covent Garden. Well actually it's don't change at Bank, but Covent Garden is a good one too and, hello? Elspeth?'

Her colleague didn't even seem to have noticed Poppy had arrived for work nearly half an hour late. She was leaning against the large prosperity mural Poppy had painted on the wall behind the shop counter, and gazing at a man who was browsing their display of silver circlets and diadems.

'Who's that?'

'My future husband,' said Elspeth dreamily.

Poppy blinked at him. He was large, and that was about all she could tell from the back. Nondescript jacket and a dishwater blond manbun. Elspeth's taste in men slightly baffled Poppy, but she'd only been saying wistfully last night how long she'd been single, and Poppy had woven a lucky-in-love charm into her birthday bracelet.

'Okay,' she said. 'Look, I just need to check on something, okay? Don't let him … like, walk away without paying or something.'

'Maybe,' said Elspeth, still gazing at him.

'Right.' Poppy darted into the back room, which made her head throb a bit. She hated taking the Tube because something always went wrong, and she wasn't a massive fan of buses for the same reason. But her bike was still here in the back room – at least something was going right – and the bottles of luminous sports drinks she'd picked up as she flew through Camden had helped her hangover a bit too.

Enough so that she could feel something properly magical in the shop. Her own magic too, and not just the bracelet she'd given Elspeth.

Poppy made a lot of the jewellery they sold in the shop, and helped Iris with the teas, skin preparations and scents they sold. But neither of them put actual magic into the things they sold to civilians. That sort of thing would only lead to disaster. A carefully worded charm woven into a bracelet for a dear friend was one thing; random spells being abused by random Londoners was quite another.

But something in the shop felt like magic. It was there on

the edge of her senses, like something just out of sight or on the edge of hearing. She'd done something last night, probably when she came back to the shop after hours for her jacket. And given her state of mind, not to mention her blood alcohol levels, it probably hadn't been something good.

She had to track down that spell, or charmed item, or whatever it was, and neutralise it before it did any damage.

Bet non-witches don't have to deal with this shit.

A search of the back room revealed nothing. Dammit. That meant it was something out in the shop itself, which would be harder to check thoroughly. Although if Elspeth was mooning over Manbun then at least she wouldn't notice.

Poppy sidled out into the shop and lurked amongst the broomsticks, which proved to be a bad idea since her hair got stuck on the bristles.

'Can I help you with anything?' called Elspeth hopefully, and Manbun turned to glance at her.

'I'm just browsing, thanks.'

Well, he had a nice voice. A lovely deep baritone. The sort of voice Poppy had heard the drama students at Central St Martins practising for weighty, serious roles.

'The diadems are lovely. The rose quartz one, there, for instance. Very helpful in manifesting new love, is rose quartz,' Elspeth said in an offhand sort of way. Poppy rolled her eyes as she tried to tug her hair free.

Manbun put down the rose quartz diadem quickly. 'Ah. Yeah. Not what I was looking for. What stones are good for … clarity? For seeing the truth?'

None of them, if you don't really want to see it, Poppy thought to herself, as she grabbed a hank of hair in one hand and a broomstick in the other.

'Well, aventurine, that's the greenish one there. No, that's aquamarine,' Elspeth laughed and moved around the counter to assist him. 'Now, with crystals, what can be very important is seeing what you're drawn to. Is it for yourself?'

'Will you get –' Poppy hissed at the besom that seemed to be making sweet love to her hair '– off! Go! Be free! I will you to separate from me!'

With a crash, it did as she asked, and she ricocheted backwards against a stack of cauldrons. Iron cauldrons, that clattered and banged so loudly Iris could probably hear them all the way in Highgate.

She winced, reaching to steady the nearest with one hand whilst still holding a hank of her hair with the other.

Elspeth and Manbun were both staring at her, and as Poppy met his disbelieving gaze she realised two things. Firstly, that he was staggeringly good-looking, with full lips and a strong jawline and blazing blue eyes, and secondly, that the head of the broomstick had come off and was slowly being consumed by her hair.

Poppy felt her face burst into flame.

'Are you all right?' he asked doubtfully.

'Yes! Yes.' Poppy tried to tug some of the broom head free, but at least half of it was gone. Oh well. It could make friends with the hairbrush she'd lost this morning.

'You've got a horseshoe in your hair,' said Elspeth, and Poppy looked up to see she'd dislodged one of the iron shoes nailed around the backroom door. They had been bespelled by Iris to keep wandering customers at bay, and Poppy could already feel her hair starting to spit the iron out.

'Oh yes. So I have,' she said, retrieving it. 'Er, you might want to try lapis lazuli, for clarity?' she added, for cover. 'For those seeking wisdom and enlightenment?'

'Enlightenment,' said Manbun, a smile flashing pure sunshine at Poppy. 'Yes! That's what I want.'

You and me both, Poppy thought to herself. She was feeling drawn to the lapis herself right now. Probably because some enlightenment about whatever she'd done last night was sorely needed. Chaos seemed to be following her even more than usual this morning.

When she closed her eyes she saw the way Claudia's hand had clenched in that other woman's skirt.

'We have some lovely pendants,' said Elspeth, guiding him to the display. 'Perhaps set in silver, for purity of vision? Is it for someone in particular? Perhaps someone you want to see the truth, even though it might not be very pleasant?'

Poppy turned away from Elspeth's dreadful flirting. The cauldrons were all over the shop, literally, and so were the brooms. She really ought to note the broken broom in the shop's incident log too. Sylvia, who owned Hubble Bubble, was largely philosophical about minor breakages, but sooner or later she was going to dock Poppy's wages.

She tidied up the cauldrons and the brooms, went into the back room to find the incident book, which was full of her own messy handwriting, and by the time she returned to the shop Manbun had thankfully left.

'Right, well, that's that sorted,' she said needlessly, as Elspeth stared dreamily at the shop door. 'Els? Did he buy anything?'

'Hmm? Oh, yes. One of the pendants. The lapis one with the gold flecks. In the eye of Horus.'

'Eye of Odin,' Poppy corrected absently. 'Which he sacrificed in order to gain wisdom. Wow, that guy really did want to gain clarity about something, didn't he?'

'That guy? That guy?' Elspeth goggled at her. 'Don't you know who *that guy* was?'

Poppy shoved back her hair and said, 'No, but I'm pretty sure you're about to tell me.'

'Oh my God. He was only Axl Storm!'

Poppy waited. The name rang the very vaguest of bells, but it would probably be quicker for Elspeth to remind her. Probably.

'Axl Storm!' Elspeth repeated.

'Repeating his name isn't helping. Who is Axl Storm?'

'Oh my God, Pops. Where have you been?'

Elspeth was about five years younger than Poppy, but on occasion it felt more like fifty. 'Just sitting in my rocking chair, gazing through my cataracts at my cats,' Poppy said.

'That bracelet you gave me is totally good luck,' said Elspeth, fiddling with it on her wrist. 'I can't believe it brought Axl Storm here. It's... All my plans are working.'

'Plans?' said Poppy, but Elspeth wasn't listening. She grabbed her phone from the pocket of her fashionable jeans and scrolled through an app.

'Here! Axl Storm.'

Poppy peered at the screen, where a lot of dry ice and

thumping music seemed to be taking centre stage, and eventually realised there was also a man in the middle of it. He wore some kind of leather and metal outfit she could only describe as 'rockstar Viking' and his blond hair had little braids and lots of backcombing going on.

'Oh yeah, haven't I seen some posters for him somewhere?' Poppy said, and Elspeth shh'd her.

'In the mythic halls of Valhalla,' he intoned, in that same baritone but with a more sonorous accent, 'the souls of the dead were flown to eternal paradise by the terrifying and beautiful shield maidens known as the Valkyrie.'

He smouldered into the camera. Elspeth swooned. Poppy said, 'Is he wearing eyeliner?'

Through the smoke and strobing lights, a woman dressed as a sexy Viking descended from the heavens, appearing to carry a fully-grown man in, yes, more sexy armour. His was artfully bloodstained and helpfully stuck with an arrow.

The Valkyrie also did a lot of smouldering to the camera, which concentrated on her smoky eyes and exposed cleavage and not on how she released herself and her passenger from their harnesses.

'Gotta admire the stagecraft, I suppose,' said Poppy, who had taken a few aerial ballet classes when she was dating a gymnast at uni.

'Poppy! You know that's not the point,' said Elspeth. 'Look, here's the best bit.'

Poppy couldn't help but notice the video had a little 'favourite' icon in the corner. Elspeth had watched this a *lot*.

Axl Storm was now doing a lot of hand waving, and

emitting glowing streams of light from his palms. That was a nice trick. Poppy, who was an actual witch, couldn't do that. She could light candles with a glance, but glowy hands were beyond her, no matter how many times she'd tried in the privacy of her bedroom.

'I wonder if it's lasers of some kind?' she murmured, as Axl Storm began chanting in some language that was presumably meant to resemble Old Norse or something. The sexy Valkyrie sashayed forward with a goblet of smoking liquid, which she presented to the warrior with the bloodstained armour. He drank it, and dramatically stiffened, his arms flying wide and the goblet crashing to the floor in a splash of glowing liquid.

'Watch,' breathed Elspeth, as the dead warrior began to rise into the air apparently unaided. Axl Storm's hand gestures urged him upwards, the music surging as Axl strained and pouted. Poppy stifled a giggle.

Eventually, the warrior vanished out of sight, presumably into the fly loft of whatever theatre this was being performed in, and Axl Storm pronounced, 'He has ascended!' to great applause.

It was a flying trick, no more. Invisible wires and the like. You saw similar on stage in the West End every night and twice on Saturdays.

'I don't,' she began to say, but Elspeth said, 'There's more!'

'But not every warrior ascends,' said Axl Storm portentously, and the Valkyrie reappeared –when had she vanished? – with another dead warrior. This one had black armour, so you knew he was evil. The music shifted to a minor key.

Thankfully, then the shop door chimed, and Poppy said, 'Okay, put it away,' with some relief.

'But that's the best part,' Elspeth lamented.

'I'll look it up later,' Poppy promised. To the customer, she said brightly, 'Is there anything we can help you with? Our broomsticks are particularly lively today. One of them just tried to fly into my hair.'

The customer, a woman wearing a velvet coat and lots of jewellery, smiled at Poppy. 'Your hair is amazing. What do you use on it?'

'I feed it a regular diet of natural bristles,' said Poppy, and the woman laughed as if this was a joke. 'We also have a lovely preparation with coconut oil and rose hip, which I think would be good for your curls...'

She moved out from behind the counter to sell the woman some hair products, and forgot all about rockstar Vikings. More customers came in, and Poppy sold them room diffusers and soup cauldrons and silver jewellery – and only when she was explaining the uses of lapis lazuli to an American tourist did she remember about the charmed item she'd been looking for earlier, and how she couldn't feel it any more at all.

In fact, she hadn't felt it since...

With a sudden flash of clarity that had nothing to do with the lapis earrings she was holding, Poppy remembered careening into the shop last night, retrieving her coat and knocking over half the pendants on the rack opposite the counter. And she'd been grumbling about Claudia under her breath. And she'd…

Had she accidentally cursed one of the pendants?

And had it been the lapis and silver eye of Odin that Elspeth had sold to Axl Storm?

'Oh fuck,' she breathed, which probably cost her the sale of the earrings.

Chapter Two

I t had been nearly ten years ago when Poppy saw an advertisement in the Student Union for a home share in a house in Highgate. 'Older lady, loves to nurture plants, cats and people, seeking fun younger person to share house that's far too big for me.'

What Iris hadn't said was that she was a witch, and that she'd targeted Poppy specifically with that ad.

'No one else has seen it, dear,' she said, when Poppy ventured to wonder why Iris wasn't inundated with offers. Her house was massive, ornate and fascinating, and it had a large private garden and even off-street parking. Poppy had tried to work out its value online, but it didn't appear to have been sold for decades. It was at least twice the size of any nearby houses, the prices of which had made her eyes water.

'I posted that advert just for you,' said Iris calmly, pouring Poppy some more tea in the lovely, light-filled conservatory. 'Put a charm on it so nobody who wasn't a witch would even really notice it.'

Poppy smiled nervously, prepared to humour this mad old woman. Sure, Iris looked very polished, and her house was certainly in no need of any able-bodied student's help to keep it clean and tidy, but she was clearly a few spanners short of a toolkit.

'Witch?' she said.

'Yes, dear.' Iris looked at her expectantly, then sighed. 'Oh dear. I had a feeling you didn't know. Religious upbringing, was it?'

'Er, my mum's a vicar, but—'

'Is she now? Very modern, I must say. I suppose this might come as a bit of a shock then.' Iris took a sip of her tea, then ran her hand over the vase of flowers on the table. Each perfect lily and exquisite rose seemed to bloom brighter as she did, and all the unopened buds unfurled.

'How did you...?"

'I nurture things,' said Iris, as a plump kitten wandered in. 'Kittens, plants, grudges.' She flashed a smile at Poppy. 'You like cats?'

'I like all animals,' said Poppy, as the kitten regarded her with its head on one side. It was thinking her hair looked fun and it wanted to play with the tassels on her top.

'They probably would be fun, Malkin,' said Iris, 'but don't go snagging the fabric, you hear?'

Poppy smiled, and then her brain caught up with her ears and she stared at Iris.

'Communication with animals is a prime witch trait,' Iris said, sipping more tea. 'I tend to hear them as a sort of stream-of-conscious, but my friend Sylvia says it's more like being shown a montage of images. What about you?'

'I, er, I just sort of … know what they want,' said Poppy. 'It's just body language, isn't it?'

But she knew it wasn't. She knew most people didn't understand animals the way she did. She also knew most people didn't have hair that literally had a mind of its own, and that they hadn't spent their childhoods playing with the ghosts in the churchyard.

Her mother said she had an overactive imagination. Her father wondered if it was ADHD. Her teachers had mostly told her off for not paying attention and always forgetting her homework.

Iris was the first one who'd said anything that made any sense.

She looked up and met Iris's steady blue gaze. 'If I'm a witch, shouldn't I be able to fly? On a broomstick? And…' She cast about for memories from books and films. 'Make glowy lights with my hands!'

Iris shrugged. 'You can try, but it's not very useful. Lighting a candle is, though.' She nodded at the tea light on the table and it bloomed into a steady pale flame. 'Broomsticks are not a particularly viable thing in London, but maybe we can go and visit our sisters in Essex and you can try there. What else? I suppose you want to know about potions?'

Poppy shrugged helplessly.

'Some witches are very good at them. Some terrible. You're quite creative, so you might have a knack. Cauldrons are optional,' she added before Poppy could ask. 'I prefer a saucepan. Cats, we have covered. Wands and staffs are not much use, unless you feel the need to wield a phallic symbol. What's your gender identity?' she continued, as if querying Poppy's favoured brand of lip balm.

'Uh, cisgender. She/her,' said Poppy, who had only left her provincial town a few months ago and was still very much getting to grips with concepts such as gender identity. 'I, er, might be bisexual though.'

'All the best people are,' Iris said. 'Now, most witches tend to have a particular affinity with one area of witchcraft – not all, but most. As I said, I nurture things and help them grow. Such as you, if you'll let me. I'm sure we can find out where your particular talents lie, can't we?'

Poppy had smiled and nodded at that, and ten years later had still never discovered a talent for anything but making a mess.

A very big mess.

Alex hadn't intended to buy Yelena a present that afternoon. He'd gone for a walk to clear his head before the opening performance tonight, and tried to think of what to say to her that didn't sound like he was breaking up with her. Which he wasn't, because they weren't a couple and he thought that had been clear. In fact, he was sure he'd said something like, 'This is just for fun,' right at the start, but maybe 'fun' meant something different in Polish.

The day had turned dull and overcast, which figured. His opening night performance was going to feature a Valkyrie who hated his guts. *We should have done previews instead of going in cold from Edinburgh.* But then what? The press would have seen a sulky Yelena, and then written about it, and then people would come just to laugh at him. And laughter was the death of a show like his.

And then, as he was mooching through Covent Garden and wondering if he had enough calories left in today's allowance for a tiny gin and slimline, a little magic shop had glowed out of the gloom, enticing him in.

What can be very important is seeing what you're drawn to… He'd gone in to look at the card decks, the trick ropes, the magic hats just like in The Great Magnifico's treasure chest, and then the brightly drawn tarot cards had caught his eye and the next thing he knew, he was having a conversation about the merits of lapis lazuli vs aventurine.

His mind drifted back to the mad woman with the Rapunzel hair who had knocked over half the inventory. He'd never seen hair like it. It had to be fake, because no mane in nature was that thick and long. A lion would be jealous. A lion probably wouldn't have bits of broomstick and horseshoes stuck in its mane, though.

She'd been very … distracting.

And now he carried an exquisite little gift bag, with real silk ribbons and flower petals and all that, and he still had no idea what he was actually going to say to Yelena when he gave it to her. *Rapunzel told me this would bring you enlightenment.* No.

'Shirley,' he said to the floor manager. 'Do you have a pen and paper?'

Of course she did. Alex wrote a little note, 'To my friend Yelena,' and emphasised how much her friendship meant to him in terms he hoped were pretty unambiguous even in her second language. *You're a cop-out, Alex Raine,* he told himself as he folded the note and tucked it into the bag.

But a cop-out who had a show to put on and needed everyone on their A-game. He should probably be giving them a pep talk. That was really Jonno's job, though, and he was good at it. And Alex had to make sure his hair hadn't gone flat in all the gloom and mist this afternoon. And he had to avoid Yelena.

'I have to go and … er, meditate,' he said, and Shirley gave him a knowing look as he dashed off.

The house where Poppy lived with Iris was somewhat appropriately named Ivy Cottage. Somewhat, because ivy festooned the place. But also not, because the house was about the size of seventeen cottages all stuck together. It was fronted by an outrageously gothic gatehouse, bearing stone nymphs and gargoyles and inscriptions in Latin, the iron gates wrought in writhing ivy and spiky holly.

The effect was slightly spoiled by the wheelie bins outside, awaiting Poppy's attention to tidy them away inside the courtyard.

She tried to rehearse what to say to Iris as she lugged them inside one by one. 'Funny thing, I might have accidentally put a spell on a necklace we sold in the shop today.' Yeah, that'd go down well. 'You know how I was really upset about Claudia last night, heartbroken even –' pause for sob '– well, heartbreak affects us all differently, and … wait!' Poppy stopped with her hand on the shed door latch.

'You know how you put something into Herbert's tea when you found out he'd been cheating on you? Well, I did something similar. Only not to my ex. To a random stranger. Who has probably gone and given it to his ridiculously hot girlfriend and now she'll, like, get hit by a bus or something—'

'Who will, dear?'

Poppy swore, stumbled, and tripped over her own feet, pulling the recycling bin down on top of herself.

'Well, at least it was empty,' said Iris.

Iris was of middling height and absolutely indeterminate years. Her long grey hair was usually coiled into some elegant style Poppy could never have achieved in a million years, and dressed with jewelled or tortoiseshell combs. Today she channelled Katharine Hepburn in her outfit choice, and her eyeliner was immaculate.

Poppy sprawled on the damp flagstones of the garden path, rain seeping through her skirt to soak her bum, and wondered if she would she ever achieve a fraction of Iris's poise, even if she lived for the rest of eternity.

'Bad day?' said her landlady.

'Something like that,' said Poppy, as her hair began to make friends with a yoghurt pot that had got stuck to the bin lid.

'Did anyone die?'

Poppy winced. 'Not yet.'

'Well, then. I'll make us some tea,' said Iris, and sauntered off back to the house.

There is nothing wrong with being chaotic. Iris had said that to her shortly after Poppy moved in. *Chaos is necessary and healthy for growth, it brings creativity and breathes new life into stale order.*

It was just … sometimes Poppy could do with a tad less of it.

When she was thirteen, a cute boy called Lee had kissed her behind the bike sheds at school, and Poppy had been walking on air – always an issue if you were a witch – for the rest of the school day, until she overheard Lee's friend Ryan congratulating him on 'scoring with the weirdo' and handing over what looked very much like a fiver.

At university, she'd developed a crush on a glamorous post-grad called Sadie, and been absolutely thrilled when she asked Poppy along to a party at her digs. Poppy had screwed her courage to the sticking place and asked her out, only for Sadie to laugh in a pitying manner and inform her that 'Girls like me don't go out with girls like you.'

There was Craig, whose social media revealed him to have been seeing three different girls at the same time as Poppy – although none of them had seemed to mind. There was Edward, whose father was a baronet, who had messed around with Poppy and then told her he was marrying a stunningly beautiful model. There was Stacey, who went on a few dates with Poppy and then told her she was 'just too … weird' and promptly started shagging some girl who kept her own blood in a vial around her neck.

Poppy had tried hard not to lash out at any of them for hurting her, and apart from thirteen-year-old Lee spilling his can of Fanta all over his lap so it looked like he'd wet himself, she'd largely succeeded. She'd tried to keep her chaos to herself, and channelled it into the jewellery she sold in Hubble Bubble.

And she'd tried not to be devastated every time someone she fancied let her down. Most of them were just silly crushes anyway. Nothing had really been serious until Claudia, and Claudia…

Well, Poppy had fallen in love with Claudia, and Claudia had fucked some woman who looked like she'd gone out on week three of *The Apprentice*, and now there was a cursed pendant causing God only knew what kind of havoc.

The bins safely stored, Poppy chucked her rain-soaked clothes in the laundry and put some comfy leggings and a sweater on instead. Her hair agreed it would allow her to tie it back with a scrunchie, which was a relief since it had been doing its utmost to get in her face all day.

Downstairs, she found Iris in the massive greenhouse, carefully and gently coaxing seedlings to climb a twisting frame.

'Look, it makes the shape of a witch's hat!' she said. 'Leroy at the allotments made it for me. Isn't he clever?'

Poppy, who could have definitely made it for Iris if she'd asked, smiled. 'Very. I reckon he's a bit sweet on you, Iris.'

'Leroy?' Iris scoffed. 'Don't be ridiculous. At his age.'

Since Poppy had no idea what Leroy's age was, and had never been able to even guess a decade for Iris, she just shrugged.

'There's tea in the pot,' Iris went on, waving at the tea tray, 'and I brought the gin, too. Now. Tell me why someone

33

might be hit by a bus, and if it's going to get upsetting do stay away from the plants, dear. You know what happened last time with your hair.'

Poppy took a seat on one of the little wrought-iron benches and drank her gin-laced tea while she told Iris what had happened that afternoon, and what she thought had happened the night before.

'Got drunk, accidentally cursed an object, forgot about the object,' Iris summarised as Poppy tailed off. 'We've all been there. Now. This man you think Elspeth sold the pendant to—'

'I don't think,' Poppy said. 'I know. I couldn't feel the magic after he'd left. I just didn't realise it to begin with.'

Iris nodded. 'But you know who he is?'

Poppy shrugged helplessly. 'I know his name. At least his stage name. Nobody can actually be called Axl Storm, can they?'

Iris made a so-so motion with her hand as she pruned a cutting a fraction of an inch. 'You say that, but I once knew a fellow by the name of Castle, called his daughter Windsor. I suppose Axl Storm can't be very difficult to find, can he? Perhaps we can do a location spell. Been years since I did one of those for a person, and not for your phone or keys.'

'We night not need to.' Miserably, Poppy brought out her phone and showed Iris the picture she'd taken of an advertisement on the side of a bus.

'Axl Storm is Spellbinder,' Iris read in a dramatic tone of voice. 'Five stars … Edinburgh Festival … internet sensation… Raw sexual magnetism, I say.' She peered closer. 'He does remind me of someone. Do you think those are his real eyes?'

'His eyes were blue,' said Poppy, trying not to think about how much more attractive he'd been in person than on his absurd over-posed posters.

Iris peered at her over her glasses. 'I see,' she said. She straightened up. 'Well, that's simple then. We go along to the Mysterio tonight and retrieve the necklace.'

'Tonight?' Poppy had cycled past the Mysterio on her way home. People had already been queuing outside for returns, under the smouldering gaze of Axl Storm himself.

Iris nodded at the screen. 'That's when his new show opens.' She glanced at her watch. 'We've just enough time to get there before curtain-up. We could slip in backstage and steal it.'

'Iris,' Poppy said.

'Ooh, yes. I could distract them – a bit of real magic! – and you slip in. Wear something black. Like in those Tom Cruise films.'

'Iris.'

'Or maybe I'll do the stealing. Nobody ever suspects an old lady. How's your femme fatale?' Iris said. She eyed Poppy, in her leggings and hoodie, her hair already full of twigs. 'Well, maybe I could rustle up a glamour...'

'Iris,' Poppy said. 'No.'

Iris heaved a dramatic sigh and pointed her secateurs at Poppy. 'You're no fun. I suppose we just buy tickets then. Be a lamb, call us an Uber.'

Poppy stared at her. 'Tickets? An hour before opening night? To a show with that many five-star reviews? For a guy with so many online fans they've even got a name for themselves?'

'What is it?' Iris wanted to know. She carefully snipped another bit of ivy.

'The Stormchasers.' Poppy made a face. 'Besides, I already checked, and it's sold out for weeks.'

Iris just snorted. 'Lovey,' she said, 'we're witches. We can get tickets to anything we want.'

'How's the crowd?' Alex asked Jonno, as they strode past a flock of goth Vikings doing warm-up stretches.

'Oh, great. Full. Excited.'

'Critics?'

'Only the nice ones.'

Alex side-eyed him, but the truth was he didn't want the truth right now, and Jonno knew it. They passed a cubby with a sink, and Alex paused. Was he going to be sick? Not this time. It wasn't always easy to tell on opening nights.

They'd run out of skimmed milk earlier so his afternoon shake had been made with semi-skimmed and Alex was pretty sure he could feel the fat settling. On opening night. That was going to lose him one of his five stars, probably.

'Do you have your lucky socks on?' Jonno checked as they headed back towards Alex's dressing room.

'Yep.' They had little black cats on them and a hole over his right little toe.

'Lucky pants?'

'Trick question,' said Alex, and Jonno sighed almost imperceptibly.

'Because opening night pants are no pants,' he recited, and added, 'which is still a weird thing for an Aussie to say, because if you went out there with no pants on we'd need an entirely different kind of licence.'

'We're in England. Pants go under trousers,' said Alex, who'd had this conversation with Jonno a thousand times and still appreciated it, because it took his mind off the myriad things that could go wrong out on stage. Especially since he now weighed a whole … Alex tried to do the maths on how much more he'd weigh from drinking milk with one per cent more fat.

The shake had been way nicer though. Which wasn't actually saying much.

'Whatever. You're not wearing undies and I don't care because I don't do your laundry. Do you have your lucky ring that your great-grandfather passed down to you along with his occult wisdom?'

'The one I bought for a dollar fifty in a really dodgy pawnshop in Atlantic City?' said Alex, and flashed his left hand. 'Always.'

'That's what audiences love about you,' said Jonno as they reached Alex's dressing room. 'The authenticity.'

'Ten minutes to places,' said the stage manager as she whipped past.

'Thank you, ten.' Alex tensed as he listened for the repeated 'Thank you, ten,' from the next dressing room, but Yelena's voice rang out clearly, and his shoulders relaxed.

'I really thought she was going to walk out this afternoon,' said Jonno.

'But she didn't,' said Alex. He leaned over the dressing table and peered at his eyeliner. Maybe he needed more.

'You worked your magic,' said Jonno.

'It's what I do.' He looked himself over critically.

The man looking back at him was gorgeous. Alex had devoted the last decade or so to making sure of that. His abs, pecs, and biceps were perfect. His jawline was sharp and square. There was no trace of Percy Beaker, or Sandy Grubb, and there was less and less of Alex Raine, too.

'What did you write in that note?'

Alex opened his mouth to explain, felt the bile rising, and made it to the sink just in time to get rid of that extra one per cent. *It's fine*, he told himself. *Everyone gets nervous before an opening night. The fact your number one supporting cast member still hates your guts isn't a factor. Everyone in theatre hates each other.*

He ignored the voice in the back of his mind that said most people in theatre weren't doing stunts that could get them killed if their partner was in a snit.

'Valued teammate,' he gasped. 'Trusted friend.'

'And that did it?' said Jonno, with less than his usual tact at this point in proceedings.

'Five minutes to places!'

'Thank you, five,' they both shouted back.

'It had better,' said Alex, standing up and reaching for the mouthwash. 'Besides, I gave her a present, and it had what all the best presents have.'

'What's that?' Jonno said.

Alex checked his hairpiece was secure and his harness

clips were all in place and straightened his fake fur cape. 'Authenticity.'

Watching Iris work was always an education. Her particular skillset was in making things grow, but she could turn her hand to almost any facet of witchcraft. Right now, she was going for some kind of persuasion.

'That's right,' she said, holding out a blank piece of paper to the usher. 'The best seats in the house. Centre front of the stalls, is it? Wonderful. Come along, Poppy.'

Poppy smiled nervously at the dazed usher and hurried past her into the packed auditorium. People got out of Iris's way as she approached. Poppy expected none of them knew they needed to move elsewhere, they just did it, and Iris sailed right through to their seats – which did seem to be the best in the house.

The stage was visible, no safety curtain apparent. Smoke swirled around what appeared to be a stone monolith, inscribed with runes that were almost certainly nonsense, and lit dramatically with a shifting array of blues, purples and greens.

'Shouldn't we be trying to get backstage?' Poppy hissed to Iris, who was already settled in her seat and reading the programme.

'Hmm? Oh, in the interval. I do like the theatre, Pops.'

'Yes, but we're here to get the pendant and I'm not sure there is an interval.'

Iris appeared not to hear. 'He really is a looker, isn't he? I'm sure I knew his grandfather, you know.'

That distracted Poppy enough to look over at the programme. 'What, really?'

'Mmm. Before the war. Café de Paris. Gorgeous chap. Spit of this lad. Even with the eyeliner. Ever so exotic that was, in those days. O'course, now you just see lads on the King's Road with – yes? Can we help you?'

That was to a couple who were edging towards them, holding tickets and looking puzzled.

'I think those are our seats?' one of them said, somewhat hesitantly in the face of Iris's certainty.

'I don't,' Iris said, and turned her attention back to the programme.

'Perhaps there's been a mistake,' Poppy apologised.

Iris said without looking up, 'Perhaps you've got a terrible headache and need to go back home right now.'

Immediately the man put his hand to his head. 'My head's killing me, love,' he said.

'Mine too. Maybe it's the lighting.'

'Maybe we should…?'

'Yeah. Sorry to bother you.'

Poppy gave Iris a hard look. 'That was cruel. These are probably expensive seats they booked ages ago.'

Iris sighed and closed her eyes for a moment. 'Full refund and rebooked tickets on a date of their choice,' she said, and opened her eyes. 'Happy now? Look, it says here he won best magic show at the Adelaide Fringe. Do you think they'll come round with the ice creams?'

Whether or not they would was a question she didn't get answered, because the lights suddenly dimmed and a voice boomed out from all directions at once.

'Eorls, ceorls and thralls,' it said, and Poppy recognised the resonant voice of Manbun, only deeper and with added effects. 'Welcome to my festival of the arcane arts. Where seeing is believing, but believing is not necessarily seeing, and nothing is as it seems.'

'That doesn't even make any sense,' Poppy muttered.

'Please, remain in your seats for your own safety. For interfering in a dark ritual can have devastating consequences.'

Poppy felt, rather than saw, Iris's penetrating gaze fall on her. She sank a little lower in her seat.

They should have gone to find the pendant straightaway, instead of sitting through the show. Poppy didn't know what she'd enchanted the damn thing to do, but given her feelings about Claudia last night, it almost certainly wasn't going to result in puppies and kisses all round.

A collective murmur from the audience drew her attention to the stage, where the rockstar Viking himself had appeared, all leather trousers and exciting make-up and a fur cape that must have been a nightmare under the stage lights. He did some posing, to great applause, then waffled on about arcane arts for a bit, whilst sexy dancers writhed around him. Poppy wondered what the empty box off to their right was going to be used for. Probably some dramatic disappearance and reveal sequence.

'I cannot take this seriously,' Poppy murmured to Iris, who looked enraptured. She'd conjured up some popcorn from somewhere.

'Ooh, look at that chest, lovey. You can't say that's not a nice chest. And abs. Is that what they call a six-pack?'

Someone nearby shushed them. Iris narrowed her eyes, and the shh turned abruptly into a cough.

On stage, Axl Storm was proclaiming that his great magic had angered the gods and he was imprisoned, but he had escaped—and would they like to see how?

The audience roared that they would, and Poppy watched as a cage was brought on, and Axl was chained inside it with great ceremony. In a nice twist, the cage was then lit on fire.

The music that had been throbbing in the background now began to swell. Poppy glanced around the stage, where various dancers were writhing and gesturing, and Axl was contorting inside the flaming cell. She wondered if anyone else had noticed the moment during the chaining-up part when Axl had been beaten dramatically to the ground and obscured from view.

'Trapdoor and body double?' she murmured to Iris.

'Don't spoil it,' Iris hissed. 'But also yes.'

Sure enough, after a torturous few minutes when it looked as if Axl would be consumed by the flames inside the cage, a dramatic flare rendered him invisible and, when the light faded, all that was left was a furred cloak and a charred skeleton.

The audience gasped. Poppy wondered why Axl's body was supposed to be burnt but not his fur cape. Then a spotlight shone on a sexy Viking hanging from – yes, the empty box on the right. She laughed.

'But the gods could not confine me,' he said, and

appeared to float down to the stage, whence he carried out an elaborate execution sequence where he seemed to survive a beheading. Someone off to their left screamed when the blood spurted across the stage, and Poppy had to stuff her hand in her mouth to keep from giggling.

Then came the Valhalla sequence she'd seen on Elspeth's phone. The sexy Valkyrie appeared, descending to the stage on magnificent wings, carrying the fallen warrior in his historically iffy armour. And Poppy's smile melted off her face, because the Valkyrie was wearing her pendant.

It glowed under the stage lights, which wasn't something lapis lazuli usually did. Poppy could feel the magic coming off it in waves, like a sonar that battered her concentration.

Beside her, Iris went still, her hand clutching Poppy's.

What should we do? Should we do something? But what? Leap up and shout, 'Take off that pendant, it's magical and evil!' in the middle of the show? If people didn't laugh, they'd just think it was part of the act.

But what was the pendant going to do? Poppy didn't think she'd outright cursed it. It just wasn't the sort of thing she did. She might have blessed it to give the wearer what they deserved, perhaps. But Manbun – Axl – had bought the pendant in search of enlightenment. Would the Valkyrie suddenly be enlightened as to something she deserved to be punished for? It seemed like a stretch.

She watched on tenterhooks as both Valkyrie and warrior made it to the ground, and a lot of chanting ensued as he was given the smoking chalice of whatever, before magically flying off into the flies. The audience gasped.

'Very smooth,' murmured Iris, and Poppy began to relax.

Of course her pendant wasn't going to cause anyone harm. It was just a bit of metal and crystal. The worst it could do was what it promised – bring enlightenment. Perhaps the Valkyrie would realise she was wasting her time in this silly hokey show and go and get a proper job in the West End, or in movies, or—

A slight gasp from the audience jolted Poppy's attention back to the stage. The Valkyrie was flying in with her next warrior, the one dressed in black, but she appeared to have stopped in mid-air. A consummate professional, the unfortunate woman continued pouting and tossing her mane of braided and stiffened hair, whilst on stage Axl repeated the last verse of his chanting, his hands glowing in a way Poppy hadn't figured out yet. The warrior dressed in black gave a theatrical groan.

And then they were moving again, and Poppy saw them all relax a bit, right before something exploded in a shower of sparks and the warrior crashed into the monolith with a scream. The audience applauded. Poppy froze in horror.

The Valkyrie, one of her wires evidently severed, swung in a graceful arc across the stage, before the second wire snapped and she plummeted helplessly to the stage, tumbling over down the steep rake until she crashed into the footlights.

Poppy realised she was on her feet only when someone said loudly, 'Sit down!'

For a second nobody on stage moved, then Axl began shakily, 'My Valkyrie, what evil has this warrior done to you—' and then faltered and stopped when the Valkyrie began screaming.

Poppy put one foot on the binocular clip of the seat in front, the other on the seat back, and ran over the few rows ahead, leaping between audience members. *Thank you, aerial ballet classes*. She was on the stage before any of the stagehands or security could stop her, and kneeling by the fallen Valkyrie.

Her right arm was bent at entirely the wrong angle, and one of her legs had an extra corner in it. As the pulsing, patterned colours of the footlights strobed over it, Poppy realised she could see blood and bone and turned away in shock.

Her gaze abruptly met Axl's, and she said, 'Stop the show. Call an ambulance.'

He swallowed, and for a moment appeared frozen in place. 'Yelena,' he murmured.

'That's her name? Yelena? Call her an ambulance.' Suddenly feeling perfectly competent, Poppy turned to the audience and projected her will into her voice.

'This is not part of the show. Somebody call an ambulance, please.'

A nervous laugh rippled out from the front row. Poppy could see Iris making her way towards the stage, managing as she did to purposefully hinder the progress of the theatre staff.

'It's all right, Yelena,' Poppy said as soothingly as she could. She gently smoothed her hand over Yelena's shoulder, her collarbone, the chain of the pendant... 'It will be all right. Lie still, help is coming.' Damn it. The clasp she'd fitted her own self was too secure and the damn thing wouldn't come off. Poppy tugged at it, but Yelena whimpered, so she stopped.

'Lights up,' called Axl, and she glanced over to see him leaning over the man who'd crashed into the monolith. 'My friends,' he addressed the audience in his booming voice. 'I regret that this is not part of the show. Please consider this a –' he was glancing offstage '– an impromptu interval and make your way to the theatre bar where refreshments will be provided. Thank you.'

It was right after those helpful words that the stage curtains caught on fire.

Chapter Three

'**D**o you want to get out of here?'

Alex watched the ambulance carrying Yelena depart, and didn't turn immediately. The police had cordoned off most of the street, although it hadn't stopped people from cramming up against the windows of bars and restaurants to see if the theatre was going to explode or burn to the ground. Alex didn't think this was massively likely, since the deluge system – basically a sprinkler system on steroids – had doused the fire immediately. Unfortunately it had also flooded the stage and half the stalls, and a quick peek around the front of the theatre had revealed many a drenched and angry theatregoer.

Theatregoers whose phones didn't seem affected by the water, as they snapped pics and jabbed vindictively at their screens. At least one was filming herself and gesturing behind her at the chaos. Great. The internet was going to turn on him.

Percy Beaker, what a creeper…

He took a few deep breaths to calm the bile rising in his throat. That was a long time ago, when he'd been a different person. Literally. This time wouldn't be like that. It couldn't be.

Oh, and the police wanted a word too. But they didn't scare Alex half as much as the general public or, most dreaded of all, the insurance investigators. He knew all the safety checks had been done on the stage equipment – it was sheer stupidity not to – but the possibility that Yelena's fall had somehow been his fault ate at him like acid.

Do you want to get out of here?

Alex shaded his eyes from the flashing lights of the departing ambulance and looked down at the speaker. It was the girl who'd run forward from the audience, the only person in the theatre who'd realised Yelena's fall wasn't part of the show. Her hair blanketed her shoulders like a cloak. He remembered that hair.

'Rapunzel?' he said.

'Manbun,' she replied. One eyebrow arched. 'There's a lot of people around that corner who aren't terribly happy with you right now. And I hate to tell you, but you're hella noticeable in that get-up. I can get us out of here, if you like.'

I'm the hella noticeable one? Alex wanted to say. She had hair to her waist, streaked with various colours and strewn with flowers and twigs and what might be a living butterfly or two. As he watched, a few tendrils of hair appeared to shake themselves, and she gave a sort of twitch, like someone signalling to a naughty child to cut it out.

He must have imagined that. Shock or something.

Maybe he should go over and ask the medics to check him out.

'I have a shop just down there,' she said, jerking her thumb behind him. 'You came in earlier today. Crystals and the like.'

'Cauldrons,' he said dumbly. Her eyes were very big and appealing. In the flashing lights from the police vehicles they looked like different colours.

'Stacks of them.'

'Broomsticks.' Her hair. 'Horseshoes?'

'All that and more. Plus a bottle of vodka stashed in my locker.' She glanced past him. 'Is that guy your manager? He looks angry.'

Alex winced and didn't turn around. 'Bleach blond, glasses, pink shoes? Yeah. How far is this shop?'

She smiled. 'About three minutes. Bit more if we avoid the crowds.'

'Crowd avoidance. Yes.'

She nodded. 'Give me your hand.'

He gave it to her, and she took it, her own hand stronger and rougher than he'd expected.

As he followed this decidedly strange woman away from the theatre, Alex was aware he was not behaving entirely normally. He felt woozy, as if he was drunk. Maybe he'd inhaled some smoke. No, he'd be coughing more. Wouldn't he?

'Oh, that's the Opera House,' he said, like a child on a car journey pointing out cows. The Royal Opera House was completely massive, colonnaded and grand and occupying a whole block of its own, plus a bit on the adjacent street.

'Have you been?' she enquired politely.

'Uh. No.'

'It's very good. Iris and I went to see *Tosca* last year. She said it wasn't as good as the original, but given that it premiered in 1900 I'm assuming she's exaggerating a bit. Well, maybe. You never know with Iris.'

'Iris?'

'My landlady. The one who was eating popcorn.' Casually, the stranger holding his hand added, 'The one who came up on stage and calmed Yelena. She's very good at that sort of thing.'

'Yes,' said Alex. He walked a few more paces with her, past the stage door of the Opera House, and said, 'She was sleeping with Jose, you know. The fallen warrior guy.'

'Who, Iris? Wouldn't put it past her.'

'No. Yelena. He told me.' As he lay there on the collapsing stage, possibly in fear of his own death, Jose had grabbed Alex's hand and confessed. 'She was in a filthy mood with me all today and I thought it was my fault but it turns out she was also seeing Jose and—'

He broke off, and his footsteps faltered. For a moment, Rapunzel tugged at his hand as if he was a recalcitrant toddler, and then she stopped and regarded him, chewing her lip.

'Jose was the one she dropped?'

'Into the rune stone. Yes. I think his collarbone was broken.' Alex felt like he was explaining the plot of a disaster movie, not something that had happened right in front of him – and 2,000 paying customers – not half an hour ago.

'Yes. Nasty business, that.' She looked like she was going to say something else, then changed her mind. 'Come on. Nearly there. Vodka awaits.'

She led him to the covered market at the centre of Covent Garden, and unlocked the back door of a shop.

'You see? A magic emporium. Go and sit down and I'll bring you a drink.'

Dazed, Alex did as he was told, wandering into the shop he'd visited just that afternoon, when it had been bright and busy and alive. Now, half-lit and shuttered, everything in it looked strange. The stack of cauldrons, the stand of broomsticks. Was this a silly crystal shop, or something more sinister?

He suddenly jumped as an apparition appeared at the window. Wild-haired and wild-eyed, face smeared with dirt and ash, wrapped only in a red toga. Had he summoned some ancient Roman ghost?

'You can probably put the blanket down now,' said Rapunzel, emerging from the back room with two mugs in her hands. 'I'll try not to swoon at the sight of your manly chest.'

'What?' Alex blinked at her, then looked back at the apparition in the window. Which was a mirror. 'Oh God.'

His over-styled hair had been drenched and then shoved about by his panicked hands, and now looked like he'd lost a fight with a helicopter. The carefully applied make-up had washed away in patches, so that his face and neck were now streaked with grey and black blotches. His low-slung leather trousers had soaked through, and now that he realised this, the sudden discomfort was becoming impossible to ignore. His boots squelched.

He was clutching a red emergency blanket around his shoulders like a frightened child. He didn't even remember acquiring it.

'Yeah. I'd recommend getting those leather strides off. I'd offer you something to wear, but ... I don't think any of my spare clothes would fit you.'

Alex glanced at the front of the shop, which was shuttered from public view, and then back at Rapunzel. She appeared completely dry.

'Come on, you go on stage half-naked, what's the rest of it?' she said.

'Uh,' said Alex. *Opening night pants are no pants.*

Her eyes widened, and then she started to laugh. 'Commando?' she said. 'Is that it? Saints preserve us. All right, um...' She sighed. 'I'm going to owe Sylvia so much this month it won't be worth paying me. Go and have a wash back there and I'll lend you a robe.' She gestured to a rack of sumptuously embroidered clothing. 'You can pretend to be Gandalf. Go on,' she said, when he hesitated.

The little staff toilet off the storeroom had a sign next to the sink that said, 'You don't have to be magic to work here, but it helps.' Alex washed up as best he could, stripped off the trousers that were becoming quite uncomfortable now, and gazed mournfully at his sodden lucky socks.

'So much for you,' he said.

They'd taken Yelena and Jose to the hospital, where she at least would be going straight into surgery. There was no point in Alex following, he'd been told. He wasn't the next of kin anyway. He could call later and visit tomorrow.

He should have talked to Yelena. Cleared the air. Apologised for misleading her, even if it had been entirely unintentional – and, he wanted to add, almost entirely on her part – but that wasn't the point, not right now. She could have died tonight. Could have broken much more than her leg.

But you had to go and seduce her, didn't you. Not content with bedding half the cast, he had to add Yelena to the list. Probably the most crucial cast member, and he'd fucked things up with her. He'd done this.

He looked at himself in the mirror for the second time that night, and the person looking back at him wasn't Axl Storm. It was barely even Alex Raine.

You're a fake. Stop trying to impress everyone. And keep it in your damn pants.

'Well, I would if I was wearing any,' he told his reflection, and turned out the light.

Rapunzel had left a robe for him outside the door. It was green velvet, lined with satin that was patterned with astrological symbols, and trimmed with silver embroidery. The sleeves were long and hanging and the hood pointed. Even on someone as tall as Alex, it nearly reached the floor. But it wrapped over at the front and tied with a belt, so he could at least go back into the shop without causing sexual harassment.

Rapunzel sat on a cushioned bench beside a rack of shoes that appeared to be made mostly from leaves and flowers. She was writing something in a ledger and sipping from a mug bearing the legend *Resting Witch Face*.

'Hey. Feeling more human? Have a drink,' she said. 'It's just vodka right now, but you can put some Vimto in it if you like.'

Alex had no idea if she was joking or not. 'Er, no. Neat is fine,' he said, which would have had Jonno spluttering with laughter. If Axl Storm was ever seen drinking in public, he sipped sophisticated-looking cocktails made from designer spirits, not vodka from a litre bottle poured into a mug that said *Hexy And You Know It*.

He sat down beside her and took a sip. Yep, that was cheap vodka. He could practically feel the hangover already. When was the last time he'd had more than a single designer cocktail? How many calories were in vodka, anyway?

Oh look. The mug was somehow empty. 'More?' he said. He could work out more tomorrow.

'More,' she agreed, and poured him some. Her eyes, shrewd over the bottle, did appear to be different shades. One purple, one green. Maybe she wore contact lenses.

Her hair was still that mad wild tangle, but it didn't seem to be all that wet, even though she'd been under the same deluge system he had. And her mauve dress and lavender shawl were dry too. She must have changed while he was in the bathroom. Yes, that was it.

'You look like a fairy,' he said without really thinking, and she looked slightly taken aback.

'I'm going to guess you don't know many fairies,' she said, 'or you'd think twice before saying that.'

'I mean like…' he waved his hand. 'Tinkerbell or something.'

'Tinkerbell was a psychopath,' said Rapunzel, putting the ledger to one side. 'All fae are psychopaths.' She drank a bit of her vodka and said, 'I am a witch though.'

'Are you? Cool. I'm a magician.'

'Hmm. How do you do the glowy hands thing?'

'Magic.'

One side of her mouth turned up. She had a little mole just above her jaw on that side, he noticed.

'Magic, huh? Not … lasers? Holograms? Little LEDs implanted just under the skin of your palm?'

He held out his hand to show her. 'Nope.'

She took his hand and inspected the palm. Her hair fell around her face in a thick, multi-shaded curtain. Was he imagining that it glimmered slightly?

Then her fingers traced his palm and he forgot all about her hair. The tips of her fingers were cool and slightly rough, but their touch was delicate, gentle, and far too much of a turn-on for a man only wearing a velvet robe.

He pulled his hand back, and she glanced up, a touch of contrition in those eyes. One violet, one jade. Couldn't be natural.

'Sorry.'

'Don't be.' He'd enjoyed it. But then he'd enjoyed things with Yelena, and Monika and Shanae, and none of those had exactly worked out well.

'Hmm.' She nodded at a candle nearby and the wick burst into flame.

'Very nice.' Probably some kind of trigger he was too tired to look for. 'Look, Rapunzel – what is your name?'

Her brows quirked. There was a piercing in one of them. 'How do you know it isn't Rapunzel?'

'Is it?'

She smiled. 'No. It's Poppy. What's yours?'

Alex sipped his vodka. *Complicated question.* 'Not to sound pretentious, Poppy, but you were at my show, so … don't you know who I am?'

At that she laughed. 'I know your stage name is Axl Storm, but … if that's your real name, then I'm Rapunzel.'

'All right.' Alex went to flip his hair out of his eyes and grimaced at the tangled mess it had become. 'So long as you promise to keep this a secret?'

She held out her hand, little finger crooked. 'Pinky promise.'

Well, that was a little too cute. 'Are you sure you're not a fairy?'

'Absolutely sure.' She wrapped her little finger around his and said, 'I promise not to reveal your real name. Is it Neville?'

That startled a laugh from him. 'No.'

'Derek? Wait, I know. Roger.'

Her finger was still curled around his. Alex looked into her mismatched eyes and said, 'Alex.'

'Only one letter different.'

'Barely cheating at all.'

'Stage names aren't cheating,' said Poppy, letting go of his finger. 'They're … marketing. Enhancement. Like putting on make-up. Is your hair real?'

He raised his eyebrows. 'Yes. Well – most of it.' He felt around for the pins and removed the Viking braids that were much easier to add than have re-braided every night. 'Is yours?'

She had these little coloured tendrils that curled and sort of floated, as if they weren't subject to gravity. Some of them appeared to glow a little bit. Couldn't be real.

'It's very real,' she said, with some feeling. 'Do you want me to brush it for you? You've got a lot of product in there. The tangles will set in as it dries and I don't suppose you can just ask it to behave, can you?'

There was something weird in the way she inflected that last part. As if he couldn't ask it to behave, but she could.

Did he want her to brush his hair? Yes. Yes he did. This weird fairy witch woman was putting some kind of spell on him. Although he conceded it could be the vodka. Either way, he moved to sit on the floor as she produced a hairbrush from nowhere and began teasing out the tangles.

'The woman on stage who fell. She's your girlfriend?'

Alex shuddered, and not because she was finger-combing his hair. 'No.' *Unless you ask her.* 'Um. Well. Complicated question.'

She said nothing, just combed his hair a bit more. Her touch was gentle, her lightness with the brush astounding.

'You were sleeping with her?'

'Yeah. Well, I mean – that implies it was an ongoing thing and it only happened once. Well.' He winced. 'One night.'

Rapunzel sounded like she was grinning. 'Did she fall for your raw sexual magnetism?'

He groaned. 'I did not put that on the posters, okay?' *But you didn't veto it either, did you?*

'Did she?'

He held out his mug. 'Is there more vodka?'

'Sure.'

She poured some into his mug like a butler pouring tea, and he drank some before he said, 'Yeah. Let's say we fell for each other's raw sexual magnetism. What can I say, she's very... bendy.'

'I'd say that was in poor taste given the extra bends she had in her limbs this evening, but I'll let it pass. Did you know she was seeing the other guy?'

'No.' The image of Jose sprawled, shocked and broken, on the crushed monolith would stay with Alex for a long time. The way he'd whispered his confession, tears rolling down his face. The way Alex had realised it didn't hurt him in the slightest.

'Do you mind?'

'No. Except,' he groaned again, 'now it'll look like I did something to them both out of spite or something. Which I didn't!' He turned to her earnestly. It was very important she knew this. 'I'd never hurt anybody. All the safety equipment is checked and double-checked. I watched it being done.'

Her hand on his shoulder was calming. 'I believe you. Have another drink.'

He did. The vodka was going down smoothly now, and the way she combed his hair was strangely hypnotic.

'When you came in here earlier,' she said casually. 'That pendant you bought...'

'The one with the blue stone?'

'Lapis lazuli set in silver in the eye of Odin, yes – she was wearing it, wasn't she? During the performance?'

'Was she?' Alex hadn't noticed. Once he was in character on stage he more or less trusted everyone to play their parts without him having to check every detail. 'It wasn't part of her costume.'

'She was wearing it. When she fell. I saw it.'

'You noticed that?' Yelena had been broken like a rag doll, and this woman was noticing her accessories?

'Yes. She was still wearing it when she went in the ambulance, wasn't she?'

'I don't know.' Her fingers in his hair felt so good. Calming. Soothing.

'Do you know where they took her? Which hospital?'

Alex leaned back against her hands, stretching like a cat. 'Mmm. Can't remember.'

'Alex.' Her voice was amused. 'You're not falling asleep, are you?'

'Me? No. Just keep doing that.'

She wasn't even combing his hair any more. Just playing with it. Sinking her fingers in deep and gently massaging. It was magic.

'You like it?'

'I like it a lot.' He turned his head to look up at her, and as she leaned forward he got a spectacular view down her dress. 'I really like it.'

She laughed, a lovely warm sound. It did things to the contents of her bodice that made Alex light-headed.

No, Alex. Resist. Stop seducing women you barely know. Oh, you're not even listening, are you?

'Why Mr Axl Storm,' she said. 'Are you looking down my dress?'

He exhaled hard. 'Yes. Sorry.' He made to turn away, but her hands turned him back.

'I didn't say I didn't like it.'

Alex stilled himself. He carefully put down his mug of vodka. Then he twisted more fully to face her. 'What else would you like?'

Her hands were still in his hair. She leaned down and he stretched up and their lips met.

It wasn't the smoothest kiss, since he was on the floor and she was behind him on the bench, but it didn't need to be. It just needed to be enough to know she wanted more, and then he pulled her down into his lap and they were kissing properly, her hair falling around them like a curtain, her lips tasting of vodka and magic.

Okay, she was sitting in Axl Storm's lap and snogging him.

This wasn't exactly where Poppy had expected the evening to go.

Go to the theatre, retrieve the pendant, de-curse it, be back in time for *Bake Off*. That was the plan. All right, it was a vague plan, but it hadn't included any snogging.

And now here she was, sprawled in Axl's lap – or more to the point, Alex's lap – and her tongue was down his throat and his hands were under her skirt. The robe she'd lent him gaped open, and if she'd thought he had raw sexual magnetism on stage it was nothing to up close and personal. He was just so … *brawny*. He could probably pick her up and toss her around like a pancake.

The thought of what else he could do made her feel a bit dizzy.

She hadn't intended any of this. He'd been lost and confused, and she'd just tried to take care of him. And then he'd put on that damn silly robe that ought to have looked like a Hallowe'en costume, but somehow turned him into some kind of primal god, probably of fertility or something, all bare chest and tangled hair and shadowed eyes. The sort of deity who swaggered into the mortal realm and plucked his choice of comely maidens and feasted orgiastically until sunrise.

And Poppy had very suddenly been absolutely ready to be plucked.

Right now his big, capable hands were on her backside, urging her closer and well, goodness, that robe didn't conceal anything below the belt, either. Those leather trousers of his certainly hadn't contained any padding.

Her hair swirled around them, silken and caressing, binding him to her. The same hair that had once wound itself around Claudia's neck and pretended it was an accident was basically stroking Alex.

So my hair approves, Poppy thought giddily as Alex kissed her neck. *I don't think that's how normal people judge relationships.*

Right then her phone pinged, right there where she'd left it on the bench. She ignored it – it would just be Iris, asking how she was doing – but then it pinged again, and again. Iris tended to text like she thought, in disjointed fragments.

Breathless, Poppy pulled away from Alex a fraction. 'Sorry,' she said, 'I'll just—'

The messages were right there on screen, but her vision was blurry with lust and it took a second to focus. And then she did, and she couldn't snatch the phone up fast enough.

'*Did you get the cursed pendant back?*'

'*Don't tell him it's cursed obviously.*'

'*Civilians get nervous about that kind of thing.*'

She literally couldn't snatch it up fast enough.

Beneath her, Alex had turned into a statue. An extremely hot statue with a sculpted bare chest and tousled blond hair and an absurdly chiselled jaw, but those eyes that had been blazing hot a moment ago had turned into chips of ice.

'Cursed pendant?' he said.

'What? No, she just meant like, this cursed pendant, bloody thing, you know, will no one rid me of this turbulent, uh, necklace, kind of thing,' Poppy said, turning the screen off and turning it face down, but not before a fourth, fatal message lit it up again.

'*Sorry you're probably seducing it out of him right now.*'

Well, that killed the moment stone dead. There was no way Alex, who had bloody eagle-eyed vision, *curse him*, had missed that.

Still, she tried. 'Where were we?' she said hopefully.

Those cold blue eyes were narrowed now. 'Seducing what out of me?'

'Um. Nothing. Iris is old, she doesn't… Look, this isn't what it looks like.'

Alex tilted his head. 'Isn't it? Because what it looks like from here is that you're seducing me to find out about this pendant, this *cursed* pendant, which my girlfriend was wearing when she plummeted to the stage, in a harness I had personally witnessed being safety-checked an hour before, and which you happened to be there to see. Front row, centre.'

'Actually it was row three,' whispered Poppy, because everyone knew the actual front rows had an impeded view of the stage, and then a bit louder, 'and you said she wasn't your girlfriend.'

'Oh, that's the important thing here?'

'Well, given you've just had your hands inside my knickers, yeah, kind of,' snapped Poppy, even though she knew it wasn't important at all. Not when that pendant had just caused a perfectly safe harness to snap and nearly kill someone.

Only … only here she went again, getting involved with the wrong guy. Barely knew his name and she was halfway to naked with him, and she knew he was seeing that other girl. *Stupid Poppy, stupid.*

'Would you mind getting off me?' Alex said icily, which Poppy thought was pretty rich since he'd been the one pulling her onto his lap in the first place, but she was perfectly happy to scramble away from this angry stranger.

Her hair had begun to twine itself around his wrists, and she yanked it back impatiently, and got inelegantly to her feet. Alex did the same, the effect slightly tarnished by him realising quite how exposed his robe had made him, and wrapping it more firmly around himself.

'Tell me what Iris meant by cursed pendant,' he said. 'And me being a "civilian".'

Poppy thought about lying. She thought about making up some rubbish about Iris being senile, or about the pendant being an important heirloom, or about being a spy or something, and then her shoulders slumped, and she said, 'I accidentally put a spell on that pendant. I didn't mean for it to be sold.'

'A spell,' Alex said, his voice heavy with sarcasm.

'Yes. I'm a— Iris and I are witches. I don't usually do actual spells in the shop, because –well, you never know who's going to use them and what for, and then you end up with a disaster like tonight, but this was an accident. I swear it was an accident. We came to the show tonight to try to get it back before it caused any trouble.'

His brow was drawn down into a fearsome scowl. 'Well off-hand, Rapunzel, I'd say you failed.'

'Well, yes. And I'm sorry. It was never my intention to hurt anyone. I just wanted my ex to get what she deserved.' Which was why revenge was a dumb idea and she'd never tried it before. Excepting Lee and the can of Fanta, obviously.

'Your ex deserved a compound fracture and a dislocated shoulder?' Alex said. He shook himself, and turned away, towards the back room where he'd left his sodden clothes. 'Look, whatever. I'm leaving. You stay the hell away from me and my show.'

'What show? The theatre's waterlogged.'

Alex snarled at the reminder, which Poppy supposed hadn't exactly been tactful. But she was in a panic.

'Yeah, thanks to you. You'll be hearing from my lawyers,' he said.

'Oh yeah? You going to tell them I sold you a cursed pendant? You're supposed to be the magician here!' she shouted after him as he crashed around in the back room.

'A pretend one!' he said. 'I'm a bloody actor! But at least,' he snapped, emerging with a bundle of his belongings, 'I'm not making up some shit about curses instead of telling the truth!'

'That is the truth!' Poppy yelled.

'Oh sure it is, Rapunzel, sure it is. You know what,' he said, glowering down at her, 'if you wanted to get in my pants you could have just turned up at the stage door like every other groupie.'

'Groupie?' gasped Poppy, and her outrage made the lights flicker. 'I'd never even heard of you until today.'

Alex strode to the shop's front door and rattled the shutter. 'I find that hard to believe,' he said. 'I'm an illusionist and you run *this* place.' His gesture took in the spangly robes and scented candles and crystalled tiaras as if they were the most tawdry of goods.

'I'm a witch, and you're an actor,' she snapped back. 'And leave that door alone unless you want to set the alarm off. Go out the back. Go on. Piss off.'

He gave her a mocking bow, which he actually managed to pull off even in that stupid embroidered robe, and said, 'Gladly, you mad… witch,' and swept off out into the rain.

As the door banged behind him, Poppy called, 'And you can pay me for the robe!'

He waved a hand but didn't look back as he strode

away, barefoot, in what she was pleased to note was the wrong direction for the cab rank. The rain turned the cobbles into an oil painting, Alex an artistic shadow against the reflected lamplight. God damn him, he even made flouncing out look beautiful.

'And you're not that great a kisser,' she yelled, which was a lie so bad it made the lights in the shop flicker out completely. In the dark, she tripped over his stupid hair braids and her knee crashed into the prickles of her hairbrush.

'Great. A perfect end to a perfect day.'

She went back inside, and this time she drank the vodka directly from the bottle.

Chapter Four

Alex was woken by the smell of coffee and the manic clatter of that most terrible of things: a morning person.

He made to pull the pillow over his head, only there wasn't a pillow. His head rested on the arm of a sofa which, he discovered as he woke up a bit more, was very much shorter than he was. Whose sofa was this? Who had he gone home with last night? And why had she kicked him out to sleep on the sofa? He didn't snore *that* badly.

He had no duvet either. He was covered by a velvet robe, embroidered with gold, and as he stared at it in bemusement last night came back to him in vivid, horrifying detail.

Yelena's fall. The destruction of the stage set and probably half the auditorium. Rapunzel trying to seduce him for some cursed amulet. Stumbling home barefoot through the rainy streets of Soho towards his rented flat, only to remember he had no key and no phone and no wallet, and had to concentrate very hard to remember where Jonno was staying.

He groaned, and rested one arm over his eyes before he attempted to open them. His skin smelled of smoke and sweat and some floral scent that could only be Rapunzel's.

Poppy. She'd given him her name. Poppy, like opium, and just as dangerous.

'Morning, sunshine!' trilled the voice of his best friend and manager, who was rapidly sliding down the scale of Alex's estimation. Why so cheerful? Why so perky? It had to be the middle of the night. 'It's just before one and the hospital said you can visit from two.'

'One a.m.?' said Alex doubtfully.

'What do you think, princess?' Something landed on his stomach. His street clothes and phone and wallet. 'I got your stuff from the theatre. I don't want to know,' Jonno said firmly, 'what you were up to last night in,' he waved a hand at the spangled robe, 'that get-up. Just please tell me we won't have another vengeful ex on our hands?'

Alex scrunched up his face as he recalled Poppy yelling after him that he wasn't that good a kisser. 'Uh, probably not,' he said. His ego was too fragile right now to contemplate whether she'd actually meant that or not.

'Good. Now, don't you ever disappear like that after a complete disaster without even telling me where you're going, or I will find you and I will castrate you,' said Jonno, just as Alex happened to move his arm and see his friend standing there wielding a breadknife.

He swallowed. 'No. Absolutely not. Promise.'

'Good.' Jonno smiled at him, but there was a definite edge to it. 'Now. It goes without saying you're paying personally for the cleaning surcharge on this place, right? Your feet,' he shuddered, 'are unspeakable.'

All of Alex felt unspeakable. As he sat upright every bit of him ached, and he was fairly sure his feet were bleeding. He'd walked barefoot through Soho, wearing just a velvet robe, in the rain, in October. It was a wonder Jonno had even let him in.

'The bathroom is that way,' Jonno said pointedly. 'I brought your shampoo and conditioner.'

'Much obliged,' Alex sighed, and went to do as he was told.

The shower felt amazing. Alex realised he hadn't even allowed himself to think about the terror of last night, but clearly he'd stored it all in his muscles, because his neck felt like concrete. His hair, surprisingly, wasn't too bad, but then he recalled Rapunzel brushing it, and some terrible mixture of lust and fury stole over him.

Her soft hands and merry eyes. Her warm laughter. Her hair, which had seemed to Alex, through the shock and vodka, to be semi-sentient.

And she'd been sent by her – whatever that old woman had been – to seduce him. For some amulet.

Alex paused in the act of towelling his hair. She'd seduced him to retrieve a cursed amulet?

No. He must have been imagining things. That was insane. The shock had clearly affected him worse than he realised.

Clean, dressed, and a lot more fragrant, he allowed

Jonno to ply him with eggs, and gingerly put a pair of thick socks on over his sore feet.

'It's because you're a Pisces,' Jonno said sagely. 'My nana was a martyr to her feet and her birthday was the week before yours.'

'It's because I walked around London barefoot,' Alex said. It was a minor miracle he hadn't been mugged, but then on the other hand he was built like a Viking. *And dressed like a lunatic.* 'Don't you start with that astrology bullshit.' It sounded perilously close to crystals and candles and – wait, had Rapunzel lit a candle without touching it last night? He must have imagined that, too.

'Whatever. You go and see Yelena, do the pretty with the apologies,' Jonno said, and before Alex could protest added pointedly, 'and I'll see the insurance people. Unless you want to swap?'

'Remind me when visiting hours are?' said Alex.

Troubled, hungover and exhausted, he allowed Jonno to get him into a cab and send him to the hospital, where he mustered up a bright shining morning face for the nurses on Yelena's ward.

'Oh, I'm sorry, she already has visitors,' said the woman at the desk. She had long bleached blonde hair in a plait, and the pen in her top pocket was leaking. 'We can only allow two people at a time.'

Alex kept his smile in place. 'She does? Wonderful! Her family has come?' he suggested, despite having no clue whether Yelena even had family in the country.

'Er, yes, I think so,' replied the nurse, frowning a little.

Then it cleared. 'Yes, they're speaking Polish to her, so they must be.'

'There can be no other explanation,' agreed Alex with a cheer he definitely didn't feel. He tried to peer past her without making it obvious. Probably it was just some of the other dancers who'd come to visit Yelena. That made sense. There was no need to be suspicious.

He leaned forward. 'Can I ask,' he said in a lower tone, 'how you keep the ends of your hair so shiny? I condition mine and keep it trimmed and the split ends still drive me insane.'

'Oh!' Her cheeks pinkened. 'Well, I use a deep conditioner on it once a month. I should do it more often, I suppose...'

'Really? Which brand? I've tried hot oil, everything.' Alex flipped his blond mane at her and wondered if he was overdoing it.

But as she listed the treatments she used on her hair, she fiddled with the end of her plait, and that meant her eyes weren't on the computer screen as Alex – who had very fast vision indeed, and had perfected reading at strange angles at many an audition – clocked Yelena's room number.

'Really? And that's it? Well, it looks fantastic on you,' he said inanely as she paused. 'I must remember to look that up. Really? Just once a month?' he said, as he sauntered casually away.

Then he paused at the corner, and got out his phone. He pretended to read and respond to something until the nurse had moved away, and then he loped off down the corridor to Yelena's room.

He heard the voices before he got there, speaking in what seemed to be Polish. He heard laughter, both Yelena's and, yes, the warm tones of Rapunzel.

Poppy. Whatever.

He paused, took a breath, and put on his brightest, most charming smile before he opened the door. Whereupon three women turned to look at him, and not even Macbeth's witches could have been more terrifying.

The older woman who'd been with Poppy last night sat by the bed, holding out a box of chocolates to Yelena, who was in the act of choosing one. His formerly glamorous assistant was bruised and splinted and looked exhausted, but there was a brightness to her eyes that made him wonder what had been in the chocolates whose wrappers were strewn over her bed.

And then there was Poppy, whose ridiculous Rapunzel hair seemed to fluff up like a cat about to attack, before she turned and gave him a look so skewering it actually robbed Alex of breath for a moment.

All of a sudden, it was as if she could see right through him – through Axl, through Alex, right down to the core of him. Deep inside where he was still that frightened, miserable kid, huddled in the dark and trying to smother the unhappiness with food. *Percy Beaker, what a creeper…*

'*Ach, Panie Storm!*' said the older woman. Iris, presumably. 'Or should I say Mr Raine?'

Alex pulled himself together and closed the door behind him very quickly. *Be charming, Alex. Be handsome. Be dazzling, and then they won't look for anything underneath.* 'I'd be obliged if you didn't,' he said, smiling through clenched teeth.

Yelena said something in Polish and the other two laughed. Alex smiled as if he was also in on the joke, and moved closer. He wanted to take Yelena's hand, but Poppy sat stubbornly in the way, and he had no desire to brush up against that hair and smell that scent and be transported back to that little shop in the rain—

He reinforced his smile and said tenderly, 'Yelena. How are you feeling?'

She eyed him suspiciously and said something else in Polish.

'I see,' lied Alex.

'She said she's in excruciating pain and it's all your fault,' said Poppy, without turning round.

'Poppy,' admonished Iris. She smiled indulgently at Alex and said, 'Well, aren't you just a handsome young thing. Have a sit down, lovey. Dear Yelena here isn't up to English right now, are you, *kotku*? How's your Polish?'

Alex found himself in a chair without entirely knowing how he got there. 'I'm afraid I have sadly neglected it,' he said.

'That's not the only thing,' muttered Poppy.

'Now I'm sure I remember your grandfather, dear. Was he on stage, too?'

Alex gratefully turned his attention to Iris. 'My grandfather? No. Very much not.' Grandpa Raine had been an insurance clerk and keen bowls player who had a morbid fear of public speaking. Grandpa Markham had been a factory foreman at the time of his death, when Alex was three, and had often been spoken of as a sturdy man who didn't hold with any nonsense.

'I doubt you'd have known either of them,' he smiled at Iris. 'They were not the most glamorous of men.'

Too much? Poppy's eye roll said it was. But Iris seemed to enjoy the flattery.

'Great-grandfather, then?' she said, and Alex laughed, because this was part of the Axl Storm story.

His great-grandfather *had* been a stage magician, which made for a nice easy story to tell the press about how he'd first learned magic. Especially since The Great Magnifico had never used his real name, and after the horrors of World War Two he'd put away his magic box and never spoken of it to anyone. If Granny hadn't found it in the attic after his death nobody would have ever known, and now she was gone too, there was barely anyone to associate Axl Storm with the real man behind The Great Magnifico.

To Iris, he said, 'Ah, you've read my website! But you couldn't possibly have known my great-grandfather. He'd be a hundred and nine by now.'

'I'm older than I look,' said Iris with a hint of self-satisfaction.

'But not a hundred and nine,' he laughed.

Poppy muttered something under her breath.

'Now *he* was a magician,' Iris said, with a sigh of nostalgia. 'Café de Paris, matinee idol looks, we all swooned over him. Terrible shame he gave it up,' she said.

Alex, who was doing rapid sums in his head to try to

work out how old Iris could possibly be if she had even been a child when The Great Magnifico was on stage, nodded on autopilot. 'War changes everyone,' he said vaguely. 'But here we are, neglecting Yelena. Can you understand me, *katku*?'

'*Kotku*,' murmured Poppy.

'Is what I said,' Alex added smoothly. 'Perhaps one of you can translate, if Yelena is feeling too tired?'

He kept his helpful smile in place and rudely leaned right past Poppy to take Yelena's hand as he told her how very sorry he was that she'd been hurt, and that the insurance people were investigating right now to see what could possibly have caused it, and that he knew she was vigilant about training and safety at all times.

That last part might have been laying it on a bit thick, but Jonno had impressed upon him the legal importance of making it clear that he, Alex Raine, must not take any blame for her accident, even in a sympathetic way. 'Don't even buy her a gift,' he'd said. 'It could look like an admission of guilt.'

Bit late for feeling guilty about gifts, Alex thought ruefully. The pendant was not in evidence right now.

'I know I checked the harness,' Yelena said fretfully, translated by Iris. 'I always do, and the stunt coordinator. And Jose. We check each other.'

Her face crumpled at that, and Alex said, 'He'll be all right, Yelena. Don't you worry about him.'

She began crying, and Iris hesitated before translating the next bit. But Alex more or less got the gist of what

Yelena was sobbing anyway. Swept away by passion, didn't mean to ruin everything, might be in love, etc. Even Poppy began to look uncomfortable.

'She, er, said,' began Iris, but right then the door opened and a different nurse came in. Not the one Alex had charmed. This one looked like she ran an orphanage in a penny dreadful.

'All right, who's making my patient cry?' she said, and even Iris cringed a bit. 'Why are there three of you in here? The rules do say two.'

'Well,' Alex began, as Poppy said, 'You see,' and Iris murmured, 'My dear…'

But the nurse was not to be moved. 'Everybody out, please. For the good of my patient.'

Alex was not inclined to argue, and it didn't seem the others were either. He gave Yelena an apologetic look, smiled as charmingly as he could at the nurse, and held the door for Iris and Poppy.

The two women exchanged a look that contained an entire conversation, and then Iris moved off to the nurses' station, and Poppy folded her arms and glared at Alex.

Under the bright hospital lights, and without the fog of shock and alcohol, she didn't look quite so otherworldly as she had last night. Her hair was still a health hazard, and her eyes were –she had her coloured contact lenses in, he amended – but she looked like a normal young woman. Albeit one in a sort of peacock-coloured dress and trailing multicoloured scarf and – good grief, even her shoes were mismatched. He supposed that went with her eyes at least.

From the nurses' station came Iris's voice, kindly passing on her compliments to the staff about how well they were looking after her friend, and hadn't it been the same staff who took such good care of her dear George when he'd been so ill, and…

'George?' murmured Poppy, looking faintly surprised.

'So, you speak Polish?' he said, and her brows drew down again.

'No. Iris speaks Polish.'

'But … I heard you—'

'What are you doing here?'

Her folded arms unfortunately pushed up her breasts, and Alex could not have stopped his eyes following the movement for all the money in the world. He'd felt those breasts pressed up against his chest last night. Had cupped the swell of one in his hand, ran his thumb over the exposed skin, felt the soft flesh give as she shuddered—

He forced his gaze back upward. Surely he'd only been looking for a split second. She couldn't have … of course she'd noticed.

He cleared his throat. 'What am I doing here? What are *you* doing here?'

'The decent thing,' she said piously. 'Iris and I wanted to follow through on our help last night.'

'Well, aren't you a saint,' Alex said sourly.

'At least I'm not just here to head off a lawsuit,' she snapped back. 'Been to see Jose, have you? Handshake and reassurances all round, was it?'

'The insurance investigators will determine how the

accident happened,' Alex said, and her expression said she knew perfectly well his manager had made him memorise that phrase.

'Sure. Sure. And when they find out it was caused by a cursed amulet, you'll say what?'

Alex rubbed his head, which still hurt. Possibly because of the vodka she'd poured down his throat, possibly because of the stage collapse last night, or possibly because the last twenty-four hours had been a nightmare of Elm Street proportions.

'I'll say that's nonsense, because it is.' He didn't know what had caused the accident. The best outcome would be something that wasn't anybody's fault that his insurance would cover. He had no idea what that was. Right now he didn't care. But he suspected that 'cursed by a magic amulet' wasn't going to be included in his policy.

'Not that it's an amulet, or cursed,' Poppy amended quickly, 'because – oh, what now?'

Her phone was ringing. She glanced at it, and made a noise of frustration.

The door to Yelena's room swung, and the terrifying nurse exited, her gaze zeroing in on them.

'No phones on the ward, please. You can take a call in the corridor, if you have to.'

Poppy looked torn for a moment, then she exhaled quickly and said, 'It's my mum. I really should… Don't go anywhere,' she added to Alex as she hustled towards the exit. 'Mum, hi...'

'Where the hell would I go?' Alex murmured, because it wasn't as if he had rehearsals or anything to get to.

His show was on indefinite hold. The theatre was in no fit state to operate, and everything was under investigation. Apart from what he expected to be a frustrating few sessions with police and insurance people, he had absolutely no plans.

He blinked at the hospital corridor. No plans. When was the last time that had happened?

'Axl Storm?' the nurse said.

Fighting an urge to promise he'd washed his hands and done his homework and protest he hadn't been the one smoking in the toilets, Alex found a nervous smile for her. 'On my better days, yes. I'm Axl Storm.'

'Yes, I've seen your posters. Shame about the accident. Yelena wanted you to have this.' She held out the lapis lazuli pendant, somewhat dirty and twisted now. 'She was making some kind of apology, I think. Her English is failing her right now, but then again she is on quite strong painkillers. Anyway. She definitely told me to give this to you, because you deserve it.'

'Deserve it?'

The nurse shrugged. 'Like I said, could have been lost in translation. Now. Visiting hours are almost over, and I believe you have another cast mate to see?'

It was a clear instruction. *Get off my ward.* Alex tucked the pendant into his pocket, and obliged her.

'...No, sorry, Mum, I just had to move outside.' Poppy stood in the corridor outside the ward and tried not to peer back through the windows in the doors too obviously.

'Are you at work? I thought it was one of your days off, that's why I'm calling. Are you still part-time?'

Poppy took a breath and reminded herself that her mother loved her and wanted her to succeed in life, and that she wasn't making a deliberate point about only working part-time in the shop. For which Poppy also made jewellery and candles, whilst practising her witchcraft as well. Not that she'd ever told Mum about that last one.

'No, I'm not at work, I was just … visiting a friend. In hospital,' she added, for bonus points.

'Oh dear! I hope it's nothing serious.'

No, people just go to hospital for funsies. 'She'll be fine. How are you?'

'Well. Very excited, actually. Your cousin Sarah is getting married!'

Poppy felt the fake smile stretch out her face even though her mum couldn't see her. The reaction was automatic. She'd been doing it all her life.

Sarah was two years younger than Poppy but had been skipped ahead as a child. She'd got perfect grades all through school and even found time to take extra subjects. Naturally, she'd gone to Oxford, where she'd got a first-class degree in Law, been headhunted by several prestigious firms and was now a human rights lawyer in Brussels where, *naturally*, French was among the languages she was fluent in.

Poppy had smiled politely at the news of each of these tremendous events, and got on with being slightly rubbish at everything that wasn't an art class, getting a degree in jewellery design, and working part-time in a novelty shop whilst doing housework for an old lady with lots of cats.

And doing witchcraft, she reminded herself every now and then. Poppy could do things Sarah could only *dream* of. She just couldn't do them in public.

Poppy's parents had never compared her to Sarah. They'd never expressed any disappointment with her life choices in any way. They'd shown nothing but pride in her degree and her mother often wore the jewellery Poppy made. And yet...

And yet, Poppy's family was full of people with proper professions, teachers and lawyers and doctors and accountants. They considered her mother to be the wacky one and she was a bloody vicar.

Meanwhile, I've accidentally made a cursed amulet and my hair keeps eating sweets it finds on the pavement.

'That's great,' Poppy said. 'Who's she marrying, the Crown Prince of Jordan?'

'Don't be silly, love, they broke up ages ago.' Poppy had no idea if this was a joke. 'No, she's marrying Kaspar, you know, the equestrian?'

The Olympic equestrian. Who was also transitioning into politics with excellent hopes of joining the Dutch parliament at the next election. Poppy, who tried to be a good person but couldn't bloody help being a human being, personally always thought his ears stuck out too much and his laugh was annoying.

'How lovely for them,' she said politely.

'And! Do you know what?'

Sarah and Kaspar have also cured cancer? They've

solved world hunger? They've invented a teleportation device? 'What?'

'They've asked me to officiate!'

'Mum, that's great.' Poppy was pleased for her mother. She was always trying to remind various friends and relatives that their friendly family vicar was on hand for weddings, christenings, and the inevitable funerals.

'Your father is already worrying about helicopter parking and security arrangements.'

'Well, that's Dad for you,' Poppy said vaguely, trying not to be spiteful about the need for helicopter parking. 'How's everyone else? Did Lizzie get back together with her girlfriend? That would be an excellent wedding to officiate at.' Her cousin Lizzie worked in computer game design and was Poppy's favourite, not to mention an excellent distraction.

'She did, but I don't know if they'll ever get married. I'm still holding out hope one day I can do it, but her stepmum will probably come around faster than the CofE.'

'Ugh,' said Poppy, stepping out of the way of an orderly with a wheelchair. 'I still don't know what Uncle Jeff sees in her. She's been so vile to Lizzie.'

The family drama swept her back up, as family drama always did. Mum updated Poppy on cousin Amanda's children, and Aunt Di's many chihuahuas, and asked where she was in the saga of Uncle Bob's messy divorce.

By the time Iris wandered into the corridor, looking surprised, Poppy was deep into the intricacies of why her cousin Zack wasn't talking to his in-laws, and all thoughts of pendants and rockstar magicians had flown out of her head.

'Well, they should have known he's sensitive about that sort of thing. I mean, don't they listen at all?' she said, as Iris stood with her hands on her hips. 'Wait, hang on a sec, Mum.'

She looked enquiringly at Iris, and as she did the warm gossipy chat with her mum drained right out of her and she remembered: she'd come to the hospital for one good reason.

And given Iris's stony countenance, she'd failed.

'Fuck,' she whispered, and her mother sighed. 'Sorry. Look, Mum, I've got to go. There's stuff I have to do. I'll call you back later, or tomorrow, yeah, and you can tell me what Sarah's going to make her bridesmaids wear, okayloveyoubye,' she finished, speeding up under Iris's glare.

'Sorry, that was my mum. She sends her love,' Poppy added hopefully, putting her phone back in her pocket.

'And you can send it back,' said Iris crisply. 'Where is Axl Storm?'

Poppy looked around, as if a very large Viking with supermodel looks was hiding behind the vending machine.

'Um,' she said. 'He's not on the ward?'

Iris raised an eyebrow.

'All right, I'm sorry, I haven't spoken to my mum in ages and family is important. Okay. Are visiting hours over? Can we mojo the nurse to let us back in?'

'We could,' Iris said, 'but the pendant has gone. I asked. Yelena gave it back to Axl.'

'And he… I didn't see him go past me,' she said. 'I'd have noticed.'

'There appears to be more than one door.' Iris sighed. 'We'll have to do a finding spell. And we can't do that here. Far too…' She waved her hands at the clinical cleanliness of the hospital as if it personally offended her. 'What have you got in your pockets?'

Poppy had learned most of her magic from Iris. And the first thing she'd learned was that crystals and candles were useless if you didn't have any power or any intent. A real witch, Iris sniffed, could do magic without silly props, although she acknowledged the props helped.

Poppy felt in the pockets of her skirt, turning up a fuzzy throat sweet and a lip balm that had nearly run out, and began to rummage in her satchel.

'Er, candle stub, handful of zirconias to finish that tiara I started last week… Oh! I have the programme from last night,' she said, brandishing it, and Iris nodded approvingly.

'Excellent. Now,' Iris looked around, 'they won't let us light a candle in here, I suppose. Come on, then. This bit of London is awash in garden squares.'

Most of the garden squares in this part of London were privately fenced off, but that sort of thing never stopped Iris. She held the candle stub whilst Poppy used one of the zirconias – *fake, just like Axl Storm* – and the theatre programme to concentrate on him.

When Poppy had first been told by Iris, nearly a decade ago, that she was clearly a witch, she'd expected to learn spells and incantations, to mix potions with specific and gruesome ingredients, and to maybe have her hands glow occasionally. Iris had said she could do all that if she liked – minus the glowy hands bit – but really all she needed was something to focus her will.

Words were just words. Crystals were just stones. But if they represented something to Poppy, they sharpened her intent.

'This crystal to find Alex Raine,' she muttered, holding it in her cupped hand. 'This crystal will find Alex Raine.'

'The sound of his voice,' Iris prompted her. 'The colour of his eyes.'

That deep baritone, so warm and velvety, stripped of the archaic cadence of his Axl Storm persona. The vivid, intense blue of his eyes, blazing with anger at her. The roughness of his jaw, stubble that abraded her hands and lips. The breathless shiver that ran through her when his tongue touched hers. The scent of him, rising hot from his skin as she pressed her whole body against his—

'Ow!'

Poppy's eyes flew open as Iris blew out the small flame that had erupted from the little crystal. She tossed it from one hand to the other as it cooled, glowing gently.

Hah, bet perfect cousin Sarah couldn't do that.

'Never seen that happen before,' Iris observed. 'What were you thinking?'

'Uh, just … intense thoughts,' Poppy said, attempting a smile she knew wouldn't fool Iris for a second.

The crystal in her hand was drawing her towards the south edge of the garden, and she hitched her satchel onto her shoulder to follow its lead. But two steps later she paused, and turned back.

'You aren't coming?'

Iris smiled, and adjusted her hat. 'No, dear. You'll need to move fast, I expect, and my hips aren't what they used to be. Besides, I can't hold your hand through everything, can I?'

'But – the amulet – I mean pendant – how do I, er, un-curse it?'

Iris shrugged. 'If it isn't obvious, bring it back home and we'll see. Now, off you go, he's probably moved off a distance already.'

Poppy badly wanted to ask Iris if she was sure, but Iris was always sure. So she fastened her coat, pocketed the candle stub, and set off.

Poppy knew finding spells. She lost things frequently enough that she could practically do them in her sleep. She knew the pull of the crystal would get stronger the closer she was, and probably warmer and brighter too. Right now, it already seemed pretty warm, but then it had just burst into flame. Would she be able to walk the distance? Would she need a bike? A cab? A train, a plane...

The crystal didn't care much for street patterns, which meant it led her right through the middle of University College, the post-grad bar and the Institute of Advanced Legal Studies, and cut across Russell Square. By the time she passed the Duke of Bedford statue it was getting even warmer in her hand. Poppy got her phone out and pretended to keep consulting it. She didn't think advanced legal students would have much truck with a girl following a magic crystal.

Past the back of the British Museum, through Bloomsbury Square Gardens, and then on towards the sudden busyness of High Holborn. But that was too far. It wanted her to go back … and down what looked like a private entrance to a service yard. The crystal was pulsing pretty strongly in her hand now, the glow showing through her fingers. Poppy was clearly in a residential area. Where was she going to find Alex? At home? At someone else's home? In bed with someone else?

'You're very pretty,' Yelena had said to Poppy, before Alex arrived in the hospital. 'Don't let him seduce you. He's good in bed, but he won't stick around. He doesn't have the attention span. He probably went home with another girl last night while I was in here.'

'Haha what kind of girl would do that,' said Poppy, and quickly changed the subject.

Now she stood in a little Dickensian backstreet, staring up at the building the crystal clearly wanted her to go into. A perfectly ordinary brick terrace with a shop on the ground floor and a door next to it listing several flats.

Several flats. How the hell was she supposed to know which one? 'Hey, crystal, any ideas?' she muttered, but it just pulsed harder in her hand.

Right at the point where she resolved to magic open the lock and see where the crystal wanted to go after that, she heard a scream from above. And then a lot of swearing. And then—

Then something flew through the upstairs wall. Not the

window, the *wall*. Right through it, without disturbing a brick.

'Ghosts?' said Poppy, staring up at it in confusion.

Poppy had grown up next door to a church, and still lived next to a graveyard. From her bedroom window, she could see the peaceful, ivy-covered tombs of Highgate Cemetery, its residents long ago turned to bones and dust. Some of them, inevitably, had left their spirits behind, wandering the mortal realm, and – as in life – some of them were real arseholes.

At the age of ten, she'd befriended a sad little girl called Emmeline, whom no one else could see, and who never left the churchyard. At the age of sixteen, she'd developed a phobia about a certain bus stop on the way to school, because there was an angry and bloody spectre of a teenage boy lurking there.

At the age of eighteen, she'd met Iris, who offered Poppy a dirt-cheap room in a huge and beautiful house five minutes from uni … which just happened to be opposite a graveyard. And one of the first things Iris had taught Poppy, therefore, was how to block out ghosts. With enough practice, it was like closing an eye, and these days she mostly kept it closed. But sometimes, something really strong could force it open. The kind of spirit anyone could see, even if their magical sensibility was so far past zero it was beyond Poppy's comprehension.

It appeared that the thing flying out of Alex's flat and landing on the road so hard it made the ground shake was one of them.

'But you're incorporeal,' Poppy said, frowning at it. 'How did you...'

The ghost noticed her then. Most of them did. Iris said it just came with the job. *If it was a job I'd get paid.*

Poppy stood horrified, unable to move as the spirit came closer. To her left a door opened and someone said, 'What the hell just came through my shop?' but her muscles were frozen. The spirit stalking towards her was female, and naked but for a loincloth and elaborate headdress, which consisted of a braided and beaded wig and a large crown of gold. And her face...

Her face was the stuff of nightmares.

Eyes that were black holes, a mouth that opened as a chasm into darkness, dark symbols chasing each other across her skin. The wind howled around her, wind like the screaming of dying souls, wind like the scouring sand of the desert, wind that took Poppy's hair and twisted it around her throat—

And then Alex shouted, 'Rapunzel! Move! Move, for fuck's sake!' and something hit her shoulder and she shook herself out of her terror.

At an upstairs window, Alex stood with a bunch of dripping flowers in his hand. The shards of a vase were clinging to Poppy's hair.

'You threw a vase at me,' she said in disbelief.

'The ghost mummy was about to eat you,' he called back in much the same tone.

'Eat? No, it...' Poppy looked around, but the howling, screaming, terrible spirit had vanished, and she was standing in a small backstreet surrounded by shards of glass.

'What the hell was that?' said the man in the shop doorway. 'Is this some kind of … performance art?'

'I…' Poppy began, turning in a circle. There was no sign there had ever been anything strange here.

'Yes,' called Alex from the upstairs window. 'Performance art. Sorry about that. We'll sweep up the glass later. Poppy,' he snapped. 'A word?'

Chapter Five

In the cool blues, greys and whites of his rented penthouse, none of what had just happened seemed real to Alex. The abstract art on the walls in soothing blue, the glass doors to the roof terrace, the recessed spotlights in the ceiling. It was all so bland and modern and normal. It was not the sort of place where a ghost mummy thing should exist.

'It came up through the floor,' he said to Poppy, who still had shards of glass on her sleeve. 'I was just reading my emails and it ... came up through the floor.'

She blinked at his laptop, which had fallen off the sofa arm and onto the floor. It was still displaying an email from Jonno, about when and where the insurance people wanted to see him. An ordinary, everyday thing.

Alex righted the coffee table, which was on its side, and put his laptop on it. There. Almost normal again. *Apart from the screaming ghost mummy*. It was as if he could still hear it.

'And,' Poppy said, sounding somewhat distant, 'what were you doing at the time?'

'Reading my emails,' he repeated. He peered at her. Those mismatched eyes looked glassy. Was this how he'd seemed to her last night? Well, at least he could take the high ground here, and manage not to seduce her. 'Maybe you should sit down.'

She nodded, and sat on the kitchen table, which wasn't quite what he'd meant. Alex fetched her a glass of water, but when she reached to take it, something fell out of her hand.

'You dropped your … rock?' It was a dirty grey, like a diamond with smoke damage.

'Zirconia,' she said. 'It found you. Alex, where exactly are we?

'My flat. Just off High Holborn,' he said. 'You're the one who found me.' *And by the way*, he wanted to add but didn't, because she was in shock and he wasn't a bastard, unlike some people, *how come that … thing only turned up when you did?*

'High Holborn,' she muttered. She felt in her pockets, and only seemed to realise the thing she was looking for was in her other hand when she tried to put it down to look for it. Her phone, which was open to the maps app. 'The British Museum…'

'About five minutes that way.' He waved at the window he'd thrown the vase from, and shuddered. That thing had seemed so real, and so horrible.

She stared at her phone, and then at nothing.

'Poppy?'

'If you want to get the Tube to the museum these days,' she said, gazing at the wall, 'you generally go to Holborn, Tottenham Court Road, maybe Russell Square.'

'Yes?' said Alex. Holborn Tube station was within falling-down distance of his flat.

'But there used to be another stop. On the Central. Before they linked up to Holborn. The British Museum stop. I remember Iris telling me. It's around here.' Her head snapped up. 'Really close to here. Maybe right underneath us.'

'Yes?' said Alex again. The Central Line followed the route of High Holborn at this point, but it was so far beneath the surface you didn't even feel the rumble of the passing trains. *Apart from just now. When the ghost that flew through the wall hit the ground.* But that had to have been a train. Had to.

'There used to be a rumour,' said Poppy, getting up and moving over to the spot on the floor where the ghost had suddenly appeared not ten minutes ago, 'that there was a tunnel from the station to the Egyptian Room at the museum. And that the station is haunted by a mummy.'

Alex's mouth opened to tell her that was absurd, because ghosts weren't real and people were gullible, and he should know, but he'd seen the damn thing with his own eyes. And apparently so had the man in the shop downstairs.

But worse than that, worse than having seen the thing, having screamed and cowered from it, having thrown a vase at Poppy to get her to move away from it, was the realisation that she was currently kneeling with her hand on the exact spot where the thing had appeared through the floor, and he *hadn't told her that.*

He took in a deep breath and let it out. 'You think that … thing was the ghost of an Egyptian mummy?'

She shrugged. 'Looked Egyptian to me.'

'But that kind of thing is an urban myth. Poppy, you don't believe in ghosts, do you?'

Poppy looked back over her shoulder with a raised eyebrow. 'Okay, Mr I'm-Just-An-Actor, you tell me what you think the screaming transparent thing that can fly through walls and windows was?'

She had a point. But Alex still tried to say, 'A special effect?'

She snorted. 'Nice try. Anyway – look. I came here for the pendant.' She got to her feet and looked at him expectantly.

'The pendant?' His heart sank.

'Yes. The lapis pendant Elspeth sold you yesterday, which has an *accidental,*' she emphasised carefully, 'spell on it, which is clearly causing chaos.' She held out her hand. 'Which will continue until you give it back.'

'Right,' said Alex. He rubbed the back of his neck. The smile he dragged up wasn't very dazzling at all.

'Right,' said Poppy, slightly threateningly.

'The pendant,' Alex said.

'Yes.'

'Which Yelena gave me this afternoon at the hospital.'

'*Yes,*' said Poppy.

'And which was sitting on the coffee table just there when the ghost mummy came through the floor.'

Poppy's breath seemed to escape her, and he didn't see her breathe back in again for far too long a time. She looked down at the coffee table, which held only Alex's laptop. There was a conspicuous absence of any jewellery, or indeed anything else at all, on or near it.

Her eyes squeezed shut. 'And where is it now?' she asked, braced as if for a slap.

'Ha,' Alex said, trying for a laugh and failing. 'Funny story.'

The noise Poppy made was closer to a sob. 'The ghost mummy took it?' she said.

'The ghost mummy took it.'

She flopped down on the sofa and drummed her heels for a moment, like a child throwing a tantrum. Then she sighed and looked up at him.

'Well then, Manbun,' she said, which didn't even make sense since his hair was in a ponytail right now. 'Do you know what we do now?'

'Have a nice cup of tea and call it quits?' Alex offered, with far more hope than expectation.

'No. We find an entrance to an abandoned Tube station that may or may not have a link to the British Museum, track down a terrifying and very angry ghost who is corporeal enough to make the road shake, and ask nicely for the bloody pendant.'

'We?' said Alex weakly.

'Oh yes, Manbun.' The look in her eyes was nothing short of savage. 'We.'

. . .

'And that's why I'm never touching vodka again,' Poppy muttered as she stalked through the seventh level of an underground car park that must surely have been what Dante had in mind when he described the levels of hell.

'Hey, Rapunzel, I didn't make you kiss me,' Alex said.

'What? No, I wasn't talking about you,' Poppy said irritably. She both did and didn't want him here. Didn't, because she'd have to explain her magic to him, and he'd think she was mad, and also because she fancied the pants off him and hated him at the same time. And did, because she really didn't want to go hunting a ghost mummy by herself.

'Oh.' That had probably hurt his ego. *Good.* 'Was it, ah, did you say you meant to give the pendant to your ex?'

'No. I don't curse people,' Poppy said firmly. 'I meant absolutely no harm to anyone. I was just … in a bad mood when I handled the pendant, and sometimes my magic is a little bit, uh, uncontrollable, and…' *And I'd had a lot of wine and also vodka because Claudia had been snogging that other woman and—*

'Whoa,' said Alex, as the sickly yellow lights flickered. 'Was that you? Or the, er, the mummy?'

'Maybe it was the electricity, you ever think of that?' snapped Poppy, who hundred per cent knew it was her.

Alex raised an eyebrow at her.

'Fine,' she snarled. 'It was me. Careful, or I'll plunge us into total darkness.'

And the darkness down here would be complete. Seven storeys below Bloomsbury Square Gardens, the oldest garden square in London, there was nothing but heat, trapped in the infernal spiral of internal combustion engines.

Heat, and the odd ghost.

The Gordon Riots of 1780 had claimed their first victims in Bloomsbury Square. Poppy knew this because as she and Alex had headed for the car park beneath it, their ghosts had angrily accosted her. These older ghosts had been joined by more than one angry young man in shirtsleeves, their beautifully embroidered waistcoats burst open with terrible pistol wounds and sabre slashes. Who knew that the site of the bus stop on Vernon Place was where so many duels had taken place? Poppy, that was who, at least since about fifteen minutes ago.

Now they were so far underground, the car park was silent but for the odd vehicle somewhere above, and the rumble of passing trains. At least she hoped they were passing trains. That ghost mummy had managed to make the ground shake as she hit the road outside Alex's flat, her presence so strong Poppy was able to follow her without needing a tracing spell. At least, up to a point.

'Okay,' she said, as they came to the back wall of the car park on the lowest level. There were utility type doors around here, and she suspected they'd have to go through one of them. 'At this point we need to do a spell.'

'There you go with the "we" again,' said Alex nervously.

'You were last in possession of the amul— pendant,' she said, 'so it will be more effective if you're involved. Hold this.'

She handed him the candle she'd taken from his blandly expensive flat. It was Diptyque, and probably cost half a day's pay for Poppy. 'And this.' She gave him some twists of silver from the scrap bag in her satchel. 'And … this.'

The final thing was the programme from his show, but first she thumbed through it to find Yelena's picture in the cast listing. 'Oh hey, she was in *Holby City* once.'

'Who was?'

'Your girlfriend.'

Alex's smile was thin. 'I don't have a girlfriend.'

'Look, whatever. You bought a silver and lapis lazuli pendant for your "friend" and now we need it back, so think about her, and why you bought it for her, and just … focus on the necklace itself.'

She glared at the candle in his hand and it burst into light, which made Alex jump out of his skin. Poppy caught the candle before he dropped it on the floor, which reeked of petrol.

'Fine, I'll hold the candle. Just concentrate on the necklace you bought Yelena. Look at her picture. Think about her.'

Alex stared at the calm flame of the candle, which smelled pleasantly of rose and blackcurrant. In the dull yellow lights of the car park, it looked warm and pure. 'You — How did you—'

'The necklace, Alex,' she snapped, 'or do I have to do everything myself?'

She held the candle, and in her other hand another zirconia – lapis lazuli not being something she happened to carry in her satchel – closed her eyes and took a deep breath. Yelena. The necklace. The blue stone with its threads of gold. How it had felt beneath her fingers as she'd crafted the pendant in her workroom in Iris's house. The smooth warmth of it, the way the gold flecks had caught the light. The gleam of the silver as she coaxed it into the shape she wanted, the eye of Odin taking shape beneath her patient fingers.

'I will this to be,' she breathed. 'That I will find the pendant.' She tightened her fingers around the crystal. 'This stone to find that stone. Guide me to it.'

'Should I—' Alex began, and she said, 'Shh. Put your hand over mine. Don't worry if it gets warm. I will this to be, that I will find the pendant...'

His hand was large and strong, closing over her cupped fingers with a warmth that bloomed through Poppy. 'This stone to find that stone. This stone to find that stone...

Beneath her fingers the crystal began to warm. Nodding with satisfaction, Poppy repeated her words a few more times, and opened her eyes.

'Whoa,' said Alex again, very softly. Light spilled from beneath her fingers, glowing up through her skin.

'Yeah,' said Poppy, and found herself smiling at him. Even under the horrible car park lights, he was so bloody handsome, especially with his eyes wide and his lips parted, and when he looked up from her hand he was smiling, and she—

—made herself pay attention, extinguished the candle and shoved everything in her satchel, and tried not to feel cold when Alex let go of her hand.

Yelena told you he's a manwhore. He had his tongue down your throat while she was in hospital. Don't go falling for it, Poppy. Don't go falling for all that charm.

'Right then,' she said. 'It wants us to go this way.'

'It?'

'The crystal. It will lead us to the necklace.' Poppy set off in the direction the crystal led her, which happened to be towards a rather nice Range Rover with blacked-out windows. Beside it was an empty space, and as she rounded the bulk of the tall car, she saw a grate in the concrete wall.

'Uh, we're not going, uh, through … there?' Alex said. It was just about large enough for an average person to go through, which meant Alex might have a problem with it. What with his American football shoulders and frankly ostentatious height.

'You can stay here if you want to,' said Poppy, for whom darkened passageways held little fear. She'd never encountered anything in one that worried her. She stepped forward and laid her hand on the grate.

'I will this lock to yield to me,' she muttered, and focused her energy on visualising it happening. Poppy lost her keys all the time; sometimes, magicking open a lock was easier than looking for them.

'Are you trying to melt it or something?' Alex said, and she sighed impatiently.

'Would you shh?' she said. 'I'm trying to concentrate.'

'It's just,' said Alex from behind her, 'it looks like it's just a simple latch and the concrete is crumbling, so…'

He stepped past her, grasped the grate in those strong hands of his, and glanced around behind them.

Then he grunted slightly, and the grate came away in his hands. A chunk of concrete fell to the floor.

He gave her a sunny smile as he set it down. Poppy narrowed her eyes at him.

'You could call it magic if you like,' he said, 'but I call it a gym membership.'

Just because he was being smug, Poppy whipped out the candle and lit it with her actual magic.

'All right, fine,' he said, 'but I still think it's a trick.'

However much of a trick it was, the candle lit their way through a darkened passage far better than any flashlight could. A single scented candle with a single standard wick somehow managed to light the darkness as well as a flaming torch, and with about as much drama.

Alex could really have done without the dark tunnel. It wasn't that he was afraid of the dark, or of small spaces – there was literally no room for that in a theatre – but this kind of spooky underground caper was enough to set anyone's nerves on edge. A well-lit and busy Tube station was one thing, but a damp, dark concrete tunnel lit by a flickering flame about a foot tall – which came from a candle the size of a whisky tumbler – was the stuff of horror films.

And if he allowed himself to remember they were following the trail of a cursed amulet stolen by a ghost mummy, dear God, his vision started to go foggy.

'I reckon,' said Poppy, 'this is probably an access tunnel from the old station. Cos, like, the actual station entrance was just off High Holborn, right? But we're further north than that. And the car park was probably the old platform, because why else would you dig down seven storeys under a seventeenth-century garden square, but they've obviously diverted the line, which –' she turned to him and smiled briefly '– was probably what made the earth tremble when the ghost hit it, right?'

'Right,' said Alex, wishing his voice hadn't broken in the middle of that single syllable.

'But there's probably some kind of access tunnel linking the old line with the new one, which is probably, like, staff access or emergency or ... I dunno, where they house the electrics or the plumbing or something...'

Visions of what could happen if electricity met plumbing in a narrow tunnel underground flooded Alex's brain in a most unnecessary manner.

'...and look, it's not that filthy so somebody must come down here every now and then. I bet the ghost...'

Right on cue, *right on bloody cue*, an unearthly wailing filled the tunnel.

'That's probably just the train from Tottenham Court Road,' Poppy said but her voice wavered a bit.

'Yeah,' said Alex, and cleared his throat. He'd never wanted anything more than he wanted to turn back from this. 'Uh, so, the candle thing. How do you do that?'

Poppy glanced at the tall flame as if in surprise. The light didn't waver much as she moved, and her cloak of hair never seemed to be in danger of being set alight. 'It's just sort of ... projected, I suppose.'

'What is?'

'The candlelight. I wanted it to burn brighter, so it is.'

'Candles burn brighter because you *want* them to?'

She shrugged. 'I told you. I'm a witch.'

Right. Only, in Alex's experience, most people who called themselves witches burnt a lot of white sage and said things like 'blessed be' a lot, and would have run a mile from a candle burning like a flaming torch.

'A real witch?' he said, somewhat lamely.

'No, Alex, a chocolate one,' she said. 'Did you not see the spell I just did? In the car park? With the crystal?'

He swallowed again. 'Yeah. How did you do that?'

She sighed. 'Same as the candle. Focused will. How do you do your glowy hands thing?'

'Glowy hands?' There were things scuttling on the ground. *Scuttling.*

'Yeah.' She swished her hand around in the air in a parody of his stage act. 'Like a dude on the cover of a paranormal romance from the mid-noughties.'

'Oh, you read a lot of paranormal romance, do you?' he said, trying to find an upper hand somehow.

'Yes,' she said plainly. 'How do you do the hands thing? On book covers and movies it's digital postwork, but on stage? I can't figure it out.'

'Magic,' he said automatically.

'Try again, *Alex*.'

'Uh, LEDs?' he said, and he hadn't meant his voice to rise at the end, but it did, chiefly because that horrible wail sounded again, and this time it was closer and it was also definitely not a train.

'See, I wondered about that, but are they subcutaneous or what, because I could not feel them under your skin,' Poppy began, and then broke off, and cleared her throat, and said, 'I think we're getting closer,' in an entirely different tone.

'So, uh,' Alex said, and made himself take some calming breaths, 'uh, what's the plan? When we … uh … get there?'

'Plan?' Poppy said. 'I don't know, what's your usual plan for dealing with ancient ghosts who've stolen your magic amulet?'

'Sarcasm?' quavered Alex, as the thing wailed again.

'Sarcasm doesn't usually work. Look, Plan A is asking politely. I can send the ghost back whence she came, if need be.'

'Like an exorcism?' Alex said.

'Sure. Like an exorcism.' Poppy glanced back at him, and her gaze flickered up and down. 'You want to hold the candle?' she said.

'Uh…' It would be nice to have control of the light. And maybe he could throw it at the ghost. *Like that would be useful.* 'Yes. Thanks.'

She handed it to him, and it was no warmer or heavier than a candle of that size ought to be. The flame was bright but not blinding, and the heat he expected simply wasn't there. Somehow, it was just a normal candle with a normal flame, and she'd made it seem bigger and brighter.

But even knowing that, Alex took comfort from it, and it was only later he realised Poppy had given it to him for that exact reason.

'Hold my hand,' she said, and when he frowned, she added, 'It'll strengthen the spell.'

He never quite knew if that was a lie or not, but he did it anyway.

As they moved forward, slowly now, the torch-candle illuminated an opening ahead. A curved, almost circular opening, lined with cracked tiles. Across it was a rusted gate, standing partly open.

From it came a faint bluish light. And a slightly less faint wail.

'Looks like the Tube to me,' said Poppy, with false cheer in her voice. She edged sideways through the gap, which was probably made harder for her by Alex not letting go of her hand. Unfortunately, this also meant he had to follow her.

When he hesitated, she looked back, and her expression softened. 'You don't have to,' she said.

Which obviously meant Alex couldn't possibly back out now. 'I do,' he said. 'I will. I'm not afraid, you know,' he said, as he turned sideways to get through the gap.

'Really? I'm fucking terrified,' said Poppy, and led him forward.

Chapter Six

The ghost was drifting around in the abandoned Tube station, emitting a pale blue light that filled the place with a horribly eerie glow. It was still recognisable as female, but Poppy really, really didn't want to think about the details of why that was, on a body that was barely clothed and had been dessicated to the texture of beef jerky many centuries ago.

Poppy had seen many gruesome things since she discovered she was a witch. The ghost mummy was right up there in the top five.

But more than being horrible to look at, it was the sense of complete wrongness that came off the thing. Some ghosts were friendly and charming and some were total arseholes, but none had ever felt like they were sucking all of the light and good out of the world the way this one did.

The eyes were just ... holes into blackness. The mouth a chasm of horror. And in one translucent claw nestled the lapis pendant. Its solidity somehow served to make the ghost look even less solid, even more wrong.

It turned as they entered the platform, a drifting movement as if it was floating in water. The air was very cold, and that was not normal for the Central Line. That was the opposite of normal for the Central Line.

Poppy was very aware of her own breath misting in the air, and the rapid breathing of Alex just behind her. He was terrified, and no wonder. She was terrified herself and she'd spent half her life living next door to dead people. Her hair wrapped itself around her like a protective cloak, and as she tucked the spent crystal into her pocket, the light from the candle winked out. *Super*.

Poppy instructed the muscles of her face to form up into a smile, and said, 'Hello. It's nice to meet you. I wonder if—'

The ghost turned and screamed at her.

Into the freezing air of the underground station blasted a sudden hot wind, straight from the desert, full of scouring sand and dust. Poppy's hand tightened on Alex's, and his squeezed back. Her hair flew up to cover her nose and mouth, and as she turned to tell him to cover his face, he drew her to him, shielding her with one strong arm.

Well, not that this wasn't a totally hideous situation or anything, but it was quite nice to be pressed right up against Alex's chest like that.

The screaming stopped, and the wind died down, and Poppy looked up at Alex, who'd had his eyes screwed shut and his face pressed against her hair. And – was her hair protecting him, too? Her hair liked him. Go figure.

'All right,' she said, and began to turn back to the creature, but it screamed again and she flung an arm up in front of her face again.

Alex pulled her back against him, and she took as deep a breath as she dared and stamped her foot.

'All right!' she shouted, her mouth full of – nothing. All that sand and dust melted away like snowflakes. Had it been real? How could it have been?

She swiped her hair back from her face and narrowed her eyes at the ghost. 'I've had just about enough of this, thank you,' she snapped. 'You can stop that screaming right now. You're not impressing anybody.'

'What are you doing?' murmured Alex, horrified, behind her.

The ghost cocked its head at Poppy.

'I don't know if you can understand me,' she went on. 'Because I'm afraid I don't speak ancient Egyptian, and I've absolutely no idea if you've picked up any English from all your time at the British Museum, but I'm pretty sure you can understand the tone of my voice. No,' she added firmly, as the ghost opened its mouth wide again. 'No screaming. No.'

She was pretty sure Alex could feel the way her hand trembled in his. Her heart was pounding so loud she could barely hear herself. But she glared at the ghost until it retreated a little, hovering above the train tracks.

'That's better. Now. We'd like that pendant back, please.'

She held out her hand, and behind her Alex whispered, 'Oh God, we're going to die.'

The ghost regarded them for a moment, and then its

horrible mouth split in a wide grin and it made a dry cackling sound.

'Do you think that's funny? It isn't yours, you know. You stole it. Alex paid for it, fair and square. Didn't you?' Poppy said, tugging at his hand.

He tugged right back. 'Do *not* bring me into this.'

'Too late,' Poppy said cheerfully. To the ghost, she said, 'So if you wouldn't mind, I'll be taking it back now.'

She held out her free hand again. The ghost hissed something in a language Poppy hadn't a hope of understanding. *Boy, I could really use Iris's translation help here.*

'What did it say?' Alex said in a distinctly side-of-the-mouth kind of way.

'What am I, a babelfish? I don't know.'

'Can it understand you?'

'I was hoping tone of voice would do the trick,' Poppy said. 'Like with dogs. The pendant, please,' she added, more loudly. 'I won't ask again.'

Be firm, Iris had always told her. *You've got the upper hand. You can send them away, and you shouldn't be afraid to carry out that threat.*

The spectre of the mummy drifted down to the platform and the paving cracked under its feet. Poppy tried not to shiver at that. Not many ghosts were powerful enough to affect the physical world around them. But then this ghost had a long and terrifying reputation. People said the man who'd brought the mummy back from Egypt died horribly, and so did any subsequent owner, their families and servants, and anybody who photographed or investigated the cursed thing.

Poppy was pretty sure it was all nonsense, but that didn't matter. People told the story. They believed the story. They imbued the ghost with power. And now that ghost was stalking towards them with hieroglyphs swarming across its leathery skin, muttering something threatening in a language that sounded very good for cursing.

'I can send you away, you know,' Poppy said, and the ghost stopped. See, it could understand her perfectly well. 'Exorcise you. Send you on to … wherever it is you go.' Under her breath she muttered, 'Do Egyptians have a hell?'

'How should I know? I do Vikings,' muttered Alex in return.

'Well. Everyone has some kind of hell, right,' said Poppy. 'Something bad. When the scales don't balance and you get sent to the bad place.'

'Scales,' Alex said. 'Wait a second. I went on a school trip once … your heart weighed against a feather?'

The ghost eyed them suspiciously.

'And then what happens?' Poppy said.

'Er, then you're, er, I don't know, you get eaten? By a hippo or something? Your soul dies,' said Alex. 'Maybe.'

Great. Her deep dark threat relied on the memory of a bored child at a museum.

'Soul death,' said Poppy to the ghost, as sternly as she could. 'That doesn't sound very nice. You want me to send you there? To the place where they judge souls?'

'Hearts,' muttered Alex.

'Hearts,' Poppy repeated. 'You want that?'

The ghost mummy looked down at the pendant in her clawed hand. Then back up at Poppy.

She laughed.

Poppy took in another breath of cold, cold air. Then she squared her shoulders, disentangled her hand from the warmth of Alex's, and said, 'Right then.'

The ghost waited. Her terrible face looked amused, as if waiting to see what new empty threat Poppy was going to deliver.

But this one wouldn't be empty.

'Raise that candle,' she said to Alex, and when he did, she willed the flame into life.

The ghost looked startled.

'I'm sorry,' Poppy said. 'I asked you nicely. I explained the alternative. You've been frightening people a long time. You've outstayed your welcome.' She walked forward slowly, her heart hammering. 'It's time to go.'

The ghost screamed at her again, but Poppy was ready. She kept her concentration on the candle flame, and when it didn't go out, the ghost stopped screaming. She began muttering instead.

Poppy cleared her throat of the imaginary dust and sand, and said in a loud clear voice, 'Your time here is ended. It is time to move on.'

Poppy had attended art school. She'd dated drama students and taken acting classes. She could project her voice as well as Alex could on stage. And she'd banished more than one ghost. Granted, they were usually of the variety that wanted to move on, and if they were buried in Christian cemeteries Poppy had more than a passing knowledge of the terminology. But angry ghosts were angry ghosts no matter where they'd come from, how old they were, and how powerful they had become.

'By my will, I bind you,' she called to the ghost. 'I bid you to leave this earthly realm.'

The ghost screamed again, and the force of it blew Poppy's hair right back. She heard Alex gasp as it whipped him.

'By my will, I bind you,' she repeated, and again, 'By my will, I bind you. I bid you leave this earthly realm. No more will you haunt London. No more will you frighten the living. No more will you touch the world or be seen or felt by it.'

The ghost was shouting at her now, and Poppy didn't need to understand its language to understand its meaning. The mummy was trying to curse her. She felt the force of it begin to swell against her.

'By my will, I banish you,' Poppy shouted. 'You will leave this earth! You will go to your place of judgement!'

The blue light grew blinding. The desert wind howled around her, drowning out her voice, whipping her hair into a frenzy.

'By my will,' Poppy screamed, 'I banish you!'

The screaming grew to unbearable levels. The ghost flew at Poppy, mouth open like the gateway to hell, foul breath enveloping her.

'By my will, this will be done,' Poppy howled, and with the most dreadful screech she'd ever heard, the ghost was suddenly torn apart, and something cold blasted into Poppy.

All of a sudden the wind dropped, and so did Poppy's hair, falling heavy against her shoulders. She stumbled a little under its weight, and felt Alex's hand steady her.

The eerie blue light had vanished. The cold faded. The westbound Central Line train hurtled past, all light and sound, and when it had gone, the station was dark and empty.

'The pendant,' Poppy said.

'What? Poppy, are you okay?'

She looked round at Alex, against whom she seemed to be leaning quite heavily. 'The pendant,' she said. 'Did the ghost take it with her?'

He peered at her in the darkness. The candle appeared to have gone out again. 'I don't know. She sort of … exploded.' He sniffed. 'All over us. Ugh.'

He recoiled, and as Poppy's senses returned she recoiled too. Only there was nothing to recoil from. The stink was coming from herself.

Her hair flapped limply against her shoulders, coated in something sticky and black which stunk like … like it had started out as an unholy combination of sewage and formaldehyde and vomit, and fermented for a few millennia.

Poppy's hand went to her mouth as she gagged, but that just made it worse because her hand was covered in it too. Everything was covered in it.

She tried to take a few breaths, and when that didn't work she said out loud, projecting as much will into it as she could, 'I will this stink to fade from my senses.'

That didn't eliminate it, but it made things bearable. She

grabbed Alex by the shoulders, and repeated the same thing in his favour. He straightened abruptly.

'What did you do?'

'Made you nose-blind. It won't last. Come on. Let's get out of here.'

'Wait,' said Alex. 'The pendant?'

Right. The reason they'd come in the first place. Poppy fished the finding crystal out of her pocket and let it guide her to the pendant, but when she reached the edge of the platform, she groaned.

'Can you bring the candle?' she said, but Alex shone his phone light, which was probably more effective.

The pendant lay smashed on the tracks, obliterated by the passing train. A few shards of lapis shone sadly in the light, amongst the shreds of silver that were all that remained of Poppy's handmade necklace.

'Did it work?' said Alex. 'Did destroying the pendant destroy the curse?'

Poppy concentrated. She felt absolutely bone-weary. 'I think so,' she said. 'I can't feel the magic any more. It's gone.'

'Halle-fucking-lujah,' said Alex, and she was inclined to agree. 'Let's get the hell out of here.'

She agreed with that, too.

However nose-blind they were themselves, the spell didn't work on anyone else. The few people they met in the car park on the way back to daylight recoiled in disgust, and out in the open air people crossed the street away from them. As Poppy stood gulping in blissfully clean air, a small child asked its mother what was wrong with those two people.

'I don't know, love,' said the mother, casting them filthy looks. 'Some people are just less fortunate.'

Oh God, and she'd got to get all the way home before she could take a shower. Her hair was drooping badly. Poppy didn't think she could take this stink on a train or bus and a cab was obviously out of the question. She could hire a bike, but the thought of cycling all the way to Highgate made her want to cry. Banishing the ghost had really taken it out of her, and the adrenaline was draining away from her fast.

'Come on,' Alex said. 'My place isn't far.'

'Your place?'

He gave her a crooked smile. He wasn't covered in mummy goo as badly as Poppy, but he was a lot taller and broader than she was, and she hadn't been much of a human shield.

'Relax, Rapunzel. There's two bathrooms. I'll lend you some clean clothes.'

No short walk had ever seemed longer. When they finally squelched up the steps to Alex's flat, he showed her to a bland spare room with its own shower, and she nearly cried.

The hot water was plentiful, the little guest bottles of shampoo and conditioner got thoroughly emptied, and Poppy had never used so much soap in her life. When she emerged, blissfully clean, she found a T-shirt and sweatpants on the bed, and her own disgusting clothes removed. She didn't know what Alex had done with them.

Preferably he'd burnt them. Shame, that had been a nice coat, but—

That was her phone ringing, wasn't it? Damn, she'd left it in her coat pocket. Hopefully Alex hadn't done anything drastic with her clothes just yet. Poppy wrapped her towel more firmly around herself, opened the bedroom door, and came face to chest with a nearly naked Alex.

And *what* a chest. If she thought she'd seen it live on stage the other night, it was nothing to the real thing six inches from her nose. He had abs like a ladder she badly wanted to descend, and those indents above his hipbones that made her throat go dry. She wondered what the bold, stark tattoos on his chest and shoulders would taste like. He wore a towel low on his hips, and the fabric clung as lovingly as Poppy wanted to.

Her blood pounded. Her skin prickled. There was a ringing in her ears.

'Poppy?' A bead of water trickled from his long wet hair down over his pectoral.

She was definitely staring. She might have been panting. She wanted to climb him like a tree.

'Yes,' she whimpered. Yes to anything. To everything.

'Your phone's ringing.'

Oh, so it wasn't her ears. Poppy blinked, her face heating up, and reached for the phone he held out. Her gaze darted guiltily to his, and he was smiling, damn him. When his fingertips grazed hers, she shivered all over and dropped the phone she'd just taken from him, fumbling and swearing and nearly losing her towel as she bent to pick it up.

'Is everything okay?' said Alex, looking down at her from above his excellent chest and amazing stomach and sinful hip indents, and dear God she had to move, or she was going to cop an eyeful of whatever he had under that towel, and given what she'd felt last night it was pretty impressive, and—

'Yep, yeah, sure, fine,' she babbled, clutching her phone desperately.

'Poppy?' The voice was coming from the phone screen, and to her horror it wasn't just a voice but a face too. A video call! What kind of psychopath did that to an unsuspecting person?

Her cousin Sarah, that was who. Poppy must have accidentally answered the call when she picked up the phone, and now a super-polished Sarah was looking up at Poppy from the least flattering angle in the world, all double chins and over-excitable hair.

'Am I interrupting you two?' Her cousin looked amused.

'No,' Poppy yelped, as Alex said, 'Not at all. Hi, I'm Alex.'

'Well hello, Alex,' said Sarah, rather too flirtily for someone who'd just got engaged. 'I'm Poppy's cousin, Sarah. I can call back later if you'd like…?'

The question was so leading it should have come with reins. Poppy scowled and said, 'No, Alex was just going to get dressed,' and then felt her entire body blush as she realised how *that* sounded.

Alex stepped back, laughing, and Poppy tugged miserably on her towel as she crawled back into the bedroom. At least that hadn't fallen down. Not that Sarah would have noticed with His Magnificence standing there, gleaming like a god.

Sarah whistled. Her lipstick was immaculate. 'Wow, Pops. He's gorgeous.'

'Uh,' said Poppy incisively, and managed to add, 'Yes.'

'Go on then. Drama student?'

'What?'

'That's your usual type, isn't it? Oh wait, is he a drummer? I remember you telling me, drummers have the best upper body definition. Even when no one knows who they are.'

That was Sarah all over. She could make you feel like a piece of shit even as she was paying you a compliment.

And sure, yes, Poppy had dated a bunch of drama students – when she was a student herself. But making jewellery wasn't the sort of thing Sarah considered a proper degree, and the same extended to the sorts of students Poppy had been out with.

A few years ago she'd had a fling with a student whose father was a baronet. She'd thought that might have impressed Sarah. But of course, her cousin was already seeing an Olympic athlete.

And then it had turned out that Edward was marrying a supermodel, because that was what one did when one was going to inherit a baronetcy, apparently, and girls like Poppy were just for fooling around with.

Poppy had told them she was the one to dump Edward, and she knew nobody believed her.

'He's just a friend,' she said repressively.

'A friend, eh? Well, are you bringing this "friend" to the party on Friday?'

Poppy blinked, and stared at the wall for a moment as she flicked through her mental calendar – which was, at best, a stack of scrawled shorthand notes on the back of some crumpled receipts. 'Friday?' she ventured, when nothing came up.

'My engagement party? You never RSVP'd, so I thought I'd check. It's your neck of the woods.'

'Highgate?' said Poppy, and for a moment she tried to picture Sarah, with her nude heels and Kate Middleton blow-dry, hosting a party in Highgate Cemetery.

'No, of course not. What is there in Highgate? It's at the *Cutty Sark*.'

Memories of fire and panic flickered across Poppy's brain. The venerable ship going up in flames, the public dismay, Iris telling her it wasn't her fault. 'That's in Greenwich,' she said dumbly.

'Yes, I know, I booked it. Got so lucky. Cancellation. Have you been since it reopened? It's so nice. There's this event space underneath, like right under the ship, and…'

She prattled on, and Poppy tried to think of an excuse, any excuse, not to go. The fact that she'd been given only three days' notice ought to have done it, but after the day she'd had, her brain just refused to come up with any creative solutions.

She was just trying to muster a coherent excuse to do with Iris, when a knock came on the door. 'Poppy? Are you decent?'

Sarah broke off and gave Poppy's damp hair and towel a

knowing look. 'I'm sure he's seen you in less,' she purred. Louder, she shouted, 'Why don't you come in, Alex? Poppy's got nothing to hide from you.'

Poppy tried desperately to signal to either of them that this wasn't the case, but the door was already opening and Alex – fully clothed this time, thank God, her heart couldn't take much more of that golden skin – looked in. His damp hair was loose on his shoulders and his feet were bare, and the smile he gave her was warm.

Nope, turned out fully clothed was no help either. The man could put on a cow onesie, complete with udders, and still seduce a nun without breaking a sweat.

'Oh, the way you're looking at him, Pops.' Sarah put her hand to her heart. 'I haven't seen you this smitten since that barmaid with the tongue piercing.'

'Moving swiftly on,' said Poppy, as Alex's eyebrows rose.

'Yes, to business,' said Sarah briskly. 'Just confirming numbers with the caterer. Will you be coming alone, Poppy, as usual? Or bringing Alex here?'

Alex glanced quickly at Poppy, and something passed over his face that she didn't entirely understand.

'Of course,' he said. 'Wouldn't miss it.'

What had possessed him to say that? Poppy looked appalled, and he couldn't blame her. She'd made it very clear she didn't like him in the slightest, and here he was, muscling in on some family event. He'd wait until she finished her call then tell her she didn't need to take him.

Only … only, the way she'd looked when she saw who was calling, and the dejection audible in her voice even when he couldn't hear her words, and the way her cousin had said 'alone, as usual'… Suddenly Alex wanted to be a knight in shining armour, rushing forward with cohorts gleaming to save her from overbearing relatives.

He wasn't entirely sure what a cohort was, but he'd polish his when he found out.

Besides, there was the small matter of how Poppy looked wearing only a towel, and how clear a reminder that was of her writhing in his arms last night, and most importantly, how she'd looked at him as if she wanted to lick him all over. Which he would be more than fine with. Very, very much more than fine with.

Get it together, Alex. It was his job to be hot and sexy and make women fancy him. Poppy was clearly just reacting to the carefully sculpted torso he and his trainer worked hard on, and the smoulder he'd practised in the mirror until it was second nature. She didn't even like him. She'd made that abundantly clear.

A small voice inside him ventured that they never actually *liked* him. Women threw themselves at Alex, sometimes literally, and he enjoyed what they offered. And then they got dressed and had nothing more in common. Even Yelena, for all her hysterics, had never seemed to actually enjoy his company outside of the bedroom. She treated him with no more warmth than she did Jonno.

Alex was a trophy, and he knew it.

So why not be Poppy's trophy for a night?

On the phone, Sarah was trilling about her engagement

party, for which she'd organised a jazz combo and a low-calorie menu. 'Because Kaspar is finding things rather difficult now he's not training every day,' she added. 'Used to eating massive bowls of spaghetti, and once he stopped riding he just piled the pounds on. The press were very cruel.'

'He's stopped riding completely?' Poppy said, as Alex stood in the doorway trying to remember what he'd come in for in the first place.

'Yes. Well, competitively. Doesn't have the time these days, but he's still out on Vincent a couple of times a week.'

'Wait,' said Alex, as her words caught his attention. 'Vincent? Kaspar?'

'Kaspar is Sarah's fiancé,' Poppy explained, 'and Vincent is his horse. He was an Olympic equestrian.'

Alex goggled at her. 'Kaspar de Bruin? Your cousin is marrying Kaspar de Bruin?'

'Yep,' sighed Poppy.

'Oh, are you a fan?' said Sarah.

'Um, *yes*.' Alex moved around so he could see the phone, and Poppy reluctantly made room for him to sit beside her on the bed. 'He's amazing. His fitness routines are just off the charts. I've been following his YouTube workouts for ages.'

'I'm sure he'll be pleased,' said Sarah, in the manner of someone who did not approve of YouTube workouts.

Alex was still going. 'That perfect round he rode at the Rio Olympics? Six weeks after dislocating his shoulder? It was immense. And the music – I mean, with a horse called Vincent you've got to go for "Starry Starry Night"—'

'The song is actually called "Vincent",' Sarah corrected him, and Poppy muttered something that sounded a little like 'But the horse actually isn't'.

'Oh, I was in floods,' Alex told her. 'My manager thought I was mad, crying over horse dancing on the telly.'

Sarah's face froze a little at the use of the phrase 'horse dancing', and he suddenly remembered the dejection in Poppy's voice as she talked with her cousin. Her polished, suspiciously well-lit cousin, who had an expensive haircut and was marrying an Olympic athlete and national hero, and made fun of Poppy for being single.

Poppy hunched up tight beside him, her hair lying flat and meek against her bare shoulders, fingers pulling nervously at a thread in her towel. Poppy, who had just banished a centuries-old ghost with nothing more than a candle and the force of her personality. Poppy, who was kind and clever and funny, and who kissed like a goddess.

'And here I am, talking about your fiancé,' he said, putting an arm around Poppy, 'when I have the most amazing woman in the world right here beside me. We don't need gold medals, do we, my love?'

Poppy's eyes went very big, and then she suddenly turned on a smile and said, 'No. Of course we don't. Darling.'

'Right,' said Sarah, sounding unconvinced. 'Yes. So... I'm sorry, Auntie June didn't mention you, Alex, so...'

'Oh, well, you know Mum, she doesn't like to brag,' said Poppy. 'Doesn't like to make it all about her.'

Alex cheered internally at that. He gave Poppy's shoulders a squeeze, and she looked back at him adoringly.

'And besides,' she added, still gazing at Alex in a manner he could get quite used to, 'I'm not going to share all the details of my love life with my mum. I mean, she doesn't need to know all the...' She glanced down at herself, wearing nothing but a towel in the middle of the afternoon, and then let her gaze travel lingeringly over Alex's body.

He lost his breath for a moment, then made himself focus as Poppy said coyly to her cousin, 'I'm sure I don't need to tell you what it's like, right? Can't keep our hands off each other.'

'Absolutely,' Alex said, leaning into her. Was it his imagination, or did her hair feel like it was stroking his arm? 'Get us alone in a room together and whoa, it gets very X-rated.'

'Totally X-rated,' Poppy agreed. 'Like this afternoon, right? Literally nothing that's happened since I walked in here could be shown before the watershed.'

Alex grinned at that, because she wasn't lying in the slightest. 'No, not a thing,' he said. 'Remember that thing you did with the candle?'

'Oh yeah, you loved that, didn't you?'

'I'll remember it 'til the day I die,' Alex promised. Her violet-green eyes sparkled at him.

'And we just couldn't get back here quick enough,' she said.

'No. Clothes off the minute we walked in.'

'Mine are totally ruined,' said Poppy, and Sarah cleared her throat loudly. Alex blinked.

Right. Yes. This wasn't real. Or at least, the spin they

were putting on it wasn't real. *But it's so much fun.* Alex really couldn't remember the last time he'd had that much fun with – well, with anybody.

'Sorry, Sarah,' Poppy said, cuddling into Alex's body in a way he liked far too much. 'Got carried away there. You know how it is.'

From the brittle smile Sarah gave, Alex wondered if she actually did.

'Yes, well,' she said. 'Oh dear, I've got to go. So busy, you know. Got a call with The Hague in ten minutes. I'll text you the details about Friday,' and then she was gone.

Poppy sat with her phone outstretched for a few moments longer, then she deliberately closed the app and laid it facedown on the bed.

'Right then,' she said.

Alex realised he was still sitting there with his arm around her bare shoulders, and she was still snuggled right up against him. And while he was fully dressed, she was not, and her towel really didn't cover much at all. And her hair was silky against his arm, and her eyes were big and lovely, and her chest heaved, and—

'You're a better actor than I realised,' she said, and the way she moved away from him was so very subtle but so very clear.

Alex cleared his throat and moved the opposite way. Wondered if he dared stand up or if it would be really obvious how his body had reacted to her.

'Yeah,' he said lamely. 'Well, it's what I do.'

Her laugh was unconvincing. Alex risked standing up, and made it to the door before she said, 'Thank you. For …

playing along like that. Sarah always gets the upper hand, and I guess it's nice to...'

'I bet Sarah hasn't banished any ghosts and ended any curses today,' Alex said, glancing back as she smiled a tiny bit. Then it faded.

'No, she's probably just put a human rights abuser behind bars or something,' she said. 'You don't have to come on Friday, by the way. I'm sure you're busy.'

I should be. 'What, with rehearsals and the seven thirty show? My schedule is wide open,' Alex said, and Poppy winced.

'Oh. Yes. Um. Sorry.'

He shrugged. 'It's not your fault.'

Poppy screwed her face up. 'Um.'

Alex held up a hand. 'I'm not getting into this. Cursed amulet, whatever. It's all over now. Yelena will recover, the theatre will dry out –' and dear God, he hoped the insurance covered it '– and we'll come back with the show as soon as we can rebook. Maybe you can even give me some pointers.'

'Pointers?'

'Yes. You're a witch,' said Alex, and it still felt surreal to admit that. But how could he ever deny it after what he'd seen and felt today? Axl Storm employed every trick in the book and several that weren't, and he could never have replicated what Poppy had pulled off in that abandoned Tube station.

Or ... could he? Alex had done some street magic, back in the day when street magic was cool, and he knew there was a remarkable amount you could fake on a seemingly random street with seemingly random passers-by. She'd need a lot of planning and a lot of crew, but maybe…

'Yes, I'm a witch,' said Poppy tiredly. 'A witch who has never perfected a laundry spell, so if you don't mind, I'll take my disgusting clothes and get them home before the smell sets in.' She paused. 'Do you want me to take yours?'

Alex cocked his head. 'I can probably figure out the washer here,' he said. 'I wasn't always a rockstar magician, you know. Once upon a time I had to do my own laundry.'

'The horror,' said Poppy drily, getting to her feet and clutching her towel carefully. 'I'll send your clothes back. Or drop them off. Or—'

'Why don't I wash them for you?' said Alex. The flat had a washer/dryer. He could probably manage to wash her clothes without shrinking them or turning everything pink.

'Um,' said Poppy, and looked panicked again. 'Uh, best not. I tend to have an effect on technology when I'm feeling … rattled. I'd probably make it explode or flood the street or something.'

Alex wanted to say that would be worth it for a few more hours of her company, but he could tell she was desperate to get away. Did she really dislike him that much?

'Sure,' he said. 'I'll get you a bag for them.'

Poppy rubbed at her face. She looked terribly tired all of a sudden, and Alex wondered how exhausting banishing a ghost was.

'Alex,' she said, as he turned to go. 'Thank you for –' she waved at her phone '– that. You didn't have to do it.'

He smiled. 'No. No, it was fun. I had fun.' He hesitated, and said, 'Look, can we start over? I feel we really got off on the wrong foot yesterday. I would actually like to come to your cousin's party with you.'

'Because you idolise her fiancé?' Poppy said drily.

'No,' said Alex defensively. Then added more honestly, 'Well – I mean though, he did win a gold medal with a dislocated shoulder. Come on. That's pretty impressive.'

Poppy rolled her eyes. 'Ugh. Such an overachiever.'

Alex laughed. 'I bet he couldn't banish ghosts though.' She gave a tired shrug. 'I'd like to go with you, Poppy. I actually would.'

He watched her take a breath and let it out slowly. 'Sure,' she said, with a very distinct lack of enthusiasm. 'Why not. You'll fit right in.'

Alex had no idea what she meant by that, but it was clear she wanted him to leave her alone now.

'Do you want me to call you a cab?' he said, and she nodded. 'I'll get out of your hair then,' he said, and left her in peace.

Chapter Seven

I t was a truth universally acknowledged that if Poppy had anything exciting, important or embarrassing going on in her life, the Coven would be there to witness it.

She didn't think Iris specifically called them up to witness her humiliation, they just seemed to have a sixth sense for it. Fiona had just popped round to get some border plants for the new raised beds she'd had put in, and Sylvia had given her a lift because she wanted to try out the new Polish deli around the corner. Or maybe she wanted to try out Uber. Poppy didn't really listen to the excuses the Coven came up with any more.

Her phone pinged for the tenth time that evening. Her mum wondering if she needed a shawl for the event, because it might get chilly on the deck of the ship.

'Oh no, dear, you want something sexier for an engagement party,' said Sylvia. She flapped her hand a bit, and Poppy's nice green dress somehow – without actually changing in any way at all – clung to all her curves.

'No! Stop that. Change it back. I like this dress,' Poppy said anxiously. It was comfortable and flattering and green was a calming colour. And she'd have to face Sarah and all her other relatives, to whom Poppy was not so much the black sheep as the pathetic little lamb who constantly needed to be rescued by the farmer.

She tried not to glower at her three farmers. Fiona wasn't using any sort of magic to tweak Poppy's dress, simply getting up and tugging at the neckline with her hands like a total civilian.

'The thing about engagement parties, Pops, is they're amazing places to meet eligible men. All the groom's single friends will be there. And he's an Olympian *and* a politician. And your cousin went to Oxford! Imagine the standard of friends they have!'

Poppy had imagined it. For three days now she'd imagined who Kaspar and Sarah would invite along, and every single image that popped into her head was of some self-obsessed dickhead in a suit. The political ones would brag about their education and drop names of people Poppy would feel embarrassed about not having heard of. The sporty ones would bore on about their training regimes and mention things like 'PBs', which always sounded vaguely scatological to Poppy for some reason.

'I'm not sure any of them will be my type,' she said. Her phone pinged again, and Poppy glanced at a message wondering about cab fares before she muted the damn thing.

'Nonsense, Poppy. Successful is everyone's type,' said

Fiona. She peered critically at Poppy's cleavage. 'Sylvia, could you…?'

'No,' Poppy shrieked, as something happened in the region of her bra that went right against nature. 'Stop it.'

'It's no different to wearing a padded bra,' said Sylvia.

'Then I'll wear a padded bra,' said Poppy, 'if I want to, which I don't.'

'No, you're right,' said Fiona. 'Big boobs are vulgar.'

Poppy immediately resolved to go and find her most padded bra. Maybe add a couple of chicken fillets to it.

'Perhaps,' began Fiona, reaching out towards Poppy's bust, and Poppy's hair reached back and slapped her wrist.

To Poppy's surprise, Fiona laughed. 'I wish I knew how you did that,' she said. 'Sentient hair! I've never heard of such a thing. Did you enchant it?'

'No,' said Poppy. She tugged at her dress and went to the fridge in search of some wine to fortify her for the evening ahead. She checked her pockets and her tiny handbag – because Iris had said she couldn't take her satchel to a fancy party, and Fiona had agreed and done something to it that made it capacious enough to fit a shawl, pair of flat shoes, and emergency sandwich for the journey home.

With any luck, she thought as she downed one glass and began on another, the Coven wouldn't find out about Alex. She definitely could not take the teasing, and the poor man would be utterly overwhelmed by them. Better that she meet him there, and then he could come and be bored silly by her family for a polite half hour before buggering off to go somewhere more interesting, probably with girls who wore dresses that showed their cleavage a lot more.

Ugh, why did the party have to be at the *Cutty Sark* though? Why couldn't Sarah have hired a hotel like a normal person? Even as Poppy had been leaving Hubble Bubble earlier, Elspeth said, 'Wasn't that the ship that had that great fire ten years ago?'

And Poppy, who was concentrating hard on not telling Elspeth she was going on a date with the very man she lusted over, had replied, 'Sixteen,' without thinking. And cursed herself. 'I, er, I was there the day before,' she said. 'The Maritime Museum. School trip. Sticks in my mind.'

The news reports had said the fire on the historic ship was caused by an appliance that had overheated. It had started hours after Poppy was safely home in bed a hundred miles away. But for months afterwards she hadn't been able to look at a naked flame without shuddering, which was super fun when your mum was in charge of lighting them at church.

Dammit, she should reply to her mum. Apparently using the Tube app to plan their own journey was beyond her parents.

She was upstairs, replying to her mum's texts with one hand whilst looking for some earrings with the other, when a sound came from downstairs that she could only describe as a commotion.

'Oh my goodness, he's handsome,' bellowed Sylvia in what she thought of as her inside voice.

'Oh no,' said Poppy. She tripped over a scarf, a small

cauldron, and a single high heel she had no recollection of purchasing, and ran downstairs with one earring in.

'Good lord, my Uber drivers never look like that,' said Fiona, as Poppy reached the turn of the stairs.

'I thought you were taking the train,' said Iris, as Poppy flung herself into the hallway.

The three witches were standing in the hallway, gazing at the front door. Since this led only to the courtyard garden and not to the street, Poppy had no idea how they could possibly see who'd arrived, but it seemed Sylvia was using some hocus pocus to let him in through the gate that was usually locked.

'I have no idea what you're—' she began, completely fruitlessly, as the doorbell clanged and echoed through the house. 'No, don't—'

But Iris had already opened the door, and the other two were crowding in behind her, and right then a light Poppy had never seen before came on in the portico, illuminating Alex as if he were some sort of celestial being.

The Coven let out a collective sigh.

'Good evening,' said Alex, in that deep voice of his, and Poppy was the only one who managed to keep her reaction internal. It wasn't easy, since Alex in a suit was quite the sight. He smiled warmly at the Coven, then let his gaze travel beyond until he found Poppy, standing with her hands outstretched like a weeping angel statue, and his smile widened. His eyes twinkled like lapis lazuli.

'Poppy. You look…' His gaze warmed, especially as it lingered on her cleavage. 'Lovely,' he said, and such an ordinary word had never sounded so luscious before.

Poppy told herself dispassionately that he was just doing it for attention. And that he was probably wearing blue contact lenses. 'What are you doing here?' she said.

'Poppy! Don't be rude. Won't you come in for a drink?' said Iris, in full matriarch mode.

'How do you even know who he is? He could be a total stranger,' said Poppy.

'A total stranger who called you by name? Hi, I'm Sylvia.' She shook Alex's hand, giving a little sigh of pleasure as he smiled at her.

Fiona fluffed up her hair. 'Fiona,' she said. 'Is that Saint Laurent?'

Alex looked down at his immaculately tailored suit and replied, 'TK Maxx.'

'Besides, we met at the theatre,' said Iris.

'I sent you a text,' Alex said, eyes back on Poppy, who guiltily recalled the muted notifications.

'How do you know where I live?'

'I ordered you a cab the other day,' he said.

'The other day?' said Fiona, turning wide eyes on Poppy.

'When nothing at all happened,' said Poppy quickly. She grabbed her bag. 'Gotta go! Bye!'

'Oh, when I felt that massive surge?' said Sylvia.

'I don't want to hear about your massive surges,' Iris said.

'Don't forget to network,' Fiona called after Poppy as she grabbed Alex's arm and manhandled him out of the house.

She closed the door and leaned against it. As if a door

could contain them.

'Your family is interesting,' said Alex, into the welcome silence.

'They're not my family. Trust me, my family are … very different.'

Poppy's house was insane.

Alex had looked up Ivy Cottage on Streetview before he drove there, and assumed the GPS had somehow given him the wrong location, because there was no way Poppy, who appeared to work in a shop that didn't mind her taking full days off to go ghost hunting, lived in a massive Gothic monstrosity with its own gatehouse.

And yet here he was.

His first clue to how weird it all was had come when he'd been able to park directly outside. Then, as he'd got out of the car to check the house name, the gates had swung open at his approach, creaking so theatrically he expected the sound to come from a speaker.

Obviously, he told himself as he walked under the dark stone arch, watched by gargoyles, this huge house was subdivided into many apartments, which Poppy probably shared with half a dozen students or something. The courtyard garden he walked through would be shared, in the daylight, by dozens of people.

But the massive, arched, studded oak front door had only one doorbell, an ancient metal thing with a handle, and no list of flats. And when it was answered, the hallway inside clearly belonged to just one residence, occupied by a somewhat eclectic trio of women who inspected him as if he was a fascinating rare specimen.

Wrong house, wrong house, he panicked, and then a whirl of movement caught his eye and there was Poppy, clattering down the stairs in a green dress, looking like a mad fairy and making the fake smile he'd given the trio into a very real one.

'Is your suit really from TK Maxx?' she asked now, as she led him across the courtyard, which was now suddenly charmingly lit by lots of romantic little lanterns.

'What? No. It's bespoke. I have this awards thing next week,' he added, just in case she thought he spent that much time thinking about clothes.

'Right. I didn't think the high street catered to Viking giants.'

'It's a terrible oversight,' he agreed, gesturing her through the gate ahead of him.

From the corner of his eye, he could have sworn he saw a gargoyle move to watch him, but when he looked, it was just a stone carving.

Poppy stood looking at the street. 'Is this our car? Where's the driver?'

Alex grinned. 'You're looking at him.'

Poppy blinked at the car, then at him. Alex moved forward and opened the passenger door for her.

'Your carriage, milady.'

'You have a car. In central London.'

'I'm not always in central London.' In fact, when he'd bought this car he'd still been touring, every night a different city. He still had the inflatable mattress for sleeping in the back with the seats pushed down.

Poppy didn't look like she believed him, but she got in, and he went around to the driver's side as she carefully tucked in her long, flowing skirt. Her dress was green and silky, billowing around her as she moved and settling lovingly against her curves when she didn't. Her shoulders were tantalisingly bare—but for the ever-present cloak of hair, this time streaked with blue and purple and dotted with tiny flowers.

As he started the car, he saw in the windscreen reflection a strand of hair seem to snake out towards him all by itself – but when he turned to look, it was lying innocently against her sleeve.

Right. And the gargoyle had just been made of stone, too.

'Axl Storm,' said Poppy, as they drove away, 'drives a Kia?'

'No. Alex Raine drives a Kia. Axl Storm drives a … hmm. Probably some kind of flaming chariot.'

'A flying chariot,' Poppy corrected.

'Of course. Drawn by winged horses?'

'Six-legged ones.'

'Naturally.' He was smiling again. Funny how when he wasn't mad at her, the smiles came really easily.

'Or – what do they have in the movies? Some kind of magic…' Her voice faded. '…hammer…'

'You're thinking of Mjölnir,' Alex began, but she wasn't listening to him. She was looking off to her left, where trees and iron railings sheltered crooked lines of leaning tombstones. 'Is that Highgate Cemetery?' he asked.

He'd have missed Poppy's nod if he hadn't glanced her way.

'It's lively tonight,' she murmured.

Lively? 'Is there some kind of event going on?'

'No,' said Poppy, somewhat distantly. 'I mean, maybe. But not with the living.'

Alex shuddered, the memory of that awful screaming spectre still fresh in his mind. He had nightmares about it.

'Ghosts?'

'Yes.' She closed her eyes and clenched her fists, then looked back at the cemetery and shook her head. 'I can't seem to... They're all looking at me.' She shuddered. 'Can we go any faster?'

It was a North London road in the early evening. Alex doubted it. 'How about you just turn and look at me until we've got past it?' he said.

She gave a weak laugh. 'Any excuse for attention, eh, Manbun?'

'You got it, Rapunzel.'

He felt her regard as she turned to look at him. Serious, assessing. Alex let the ordinary doubts about his appearance surface, instead of letting the personal ones take charge. Should he have shaved? Left his hair loose instead of tying it back? Was his suit too formal, or not formal enough, did he have something in his teeth—?

Am I handsome enough? Am I buff enough? Am I charming enough? Have I dazzled everyone into forgetting yet?

'Have you always had long hair?' she asked, surprising him.

'Uh, yeah. Well – I mean, for a few years now. It hasn't been short since...'

Since Percy Beaker. He'd grown it long, a lank, greasy curtain to hide behind. It hadn't been until he'd been scouted by a modelling agency that he'd had it cut into a Zac Efron shaggy layered style, and then *Surf Rescue* had asked him to grow it a little longer, and then when he started doing magic someone had commented he looked a bit like a Viking so...

'Since?' Poppy prompted.

'Uh, since I've been Axl Storm. What about you, has your hair always been long?'

Maybe Poppy recognised that for the deflection it was. But she still answered, 'Oh, yes. Since I can remember. Can't cut it.'

'Can't?'

'No. It breaks the scissors.'

He laughed. She didn't.

'Well, it looks great,' he said lamely. 'You look great.'

'Thank you. The Coven said my dress was too...' She flapped her hands. 'Floopy, I think was the word Sylvia used.'

'Coven?' said Alex, mildly alarmed.

He still wasn't really sure he believed her about the witch stuff. The ghost thing, sure, he couldn't deny that. A trick with a candle? Okay. But magic hair? A coven? Moving gargoyles?

'That's what I call them. Iris says they're not a coven,

because that's all nonsense, but they're her friends and they're all witches.'

'All of them?'

'Yeah. Anyway, look, I don't want to talk about them.' They were past the cemetery now, heading down normal, everyday residential streets. 'How come you came to pick me up? I was expecting to meet you there. It's miles out of your way.'

Because I was curious about where you lived. Because I wanted to see more of you before I had to share you with your family. 'Because I really needed an excuse to get out of an interminable meeting with the insurance people,' Alex said lightly.

Poppy made a sympathetic face. 'I'm sorry.'

'It's not your fault.'

There was a short pause, then Poppy said, 'Well, it kind of is. Will the insurance cover it?'

Alex nodded firmly. 'Jonno is very hot on these things. He's especially good at being so picky and pedantic even the loss adjusters give up and give him what he wants.'

'An impressive skill,' agreed Poppy. She hesitated. 'Look, my family don't know about the whole witch thing. If they did, they'd think it was just another silly Poppy idea and mutter about when I'll get a real job.'

'You mean witchcraft doesn't pay?'

Poppy snorted. 'Why do you think I work in a shop? I come from a long line of people who began planning their pensions when they were still at university.'

'Ah,' said Alex. 'Me too. My dad was an actuary, and

now he spends his days gardening and carefully checking the share prices on his pension fund.'

'Mine's a compliance officer. For the council.'

'Impressive,' said Alex, who had very little idea what that actually was. 'What about your mum? Mine's a database administrator. Worked all the way up from data entry clerk. We're very proud.'

'Hmm,' said Poppy. 'I can probably beat that.'

'Really?'

'My mum's a vicar.'

Alex risked the traffic to stare at her for a moment. 'Get right out of town! A vicar? Really?'

'Yep. Since I was thirteen. It's super fun moving to a new school when you have weird hair and a tendency to forget your shoes, and then everyone finds out your mum is the new vicar.'

'Yikes.' He paused at a red light and looked over at her. 'Was it tough?'

Poppy shrugged. 'I was pretty used to being the weird kid by then. Tell you what, it was a relief to come here.'

Alex glanced around. 'Er, to King's Cross?' The area had been cleaned up in recent years, but it still had a shady reputation.

'To uni. I went to Central St Martins.' She waved a hand at the buildings to their right. 'Everyone's weird at art school.'

Alex glanced at the bright modern buildings. Hanging around outside them were students with tattoos and interesting piercings, and he felt a sudden stab of regret that he'd never been one of them, and never would be now.

'They don't look weird,' he said, and tried to keep the wistfulness out of his voice. 'They look … fun.'

'Were you a student?' asked Poppy, but right then the lights changed and a bicycle wove in front of them, and Alex swore and braked hard, and never got around to answering her.

He regretted this an hour later, at the engagement party on board the *Cutty Sark*. And not just on board it, but under it and inside it too. The old ship, once the fastest tea cutter in the world, now rested in a dry dock sheltered by a glass canopy, so that one could stand right underneath the hull and eat canapés and drink champagne. At one end of the large event space was a collection of figureheads, brightly coloured wooden people and animals that had once adorned the front of ships like the *Cutty Sark*. It was an impressive space. It was just a shame it was utterly lost on Poppy's relatives.

It wasn't that Poppy's family were bad people. They were all just spectacularly dull. It seemed that Poppy's mother, who hadn't just attended church on a Sunday like a normal person but gone the whole hog and chosen it as her vocation, was regarded as an exciting oddball. A vicar, the most respectable pillar of the community, the exciting one.

He could see why Poppy hadn't told them about the witchcraft.

So far, nobody had asked him what he did for a living, and he was trying to gauge the situation – and Poppy's mood – as to whether he should tell them the truth. Or something within ninety degrees of the truth, anyway.

Poppy clung to his arm, appearing to listen to her Uncle

Bill's extremely boring story about his journey from the Travelodge and how the DLR was quite confusing because of all the different directions you could take, and there wasn't even a driver, it was automated – as if Poppy, who'd lived in the city ten years, would find this interesting information.

She smiled up at Alex, her eyes apparently trying to communicate something he didn't quite understand. But he thought he was getting her intention. She wanted a repeat of their performance on the video call with Cousin Sarah.

'We drove here,' she said, when Uncle Bill paused for breath. 'Alex doesn't take public transport, on account of getting recognised so much, do you, darling?'

He smiled. Yes, he'd been right. 'You're right, my love. I used to try, you know, keep it humble, but when your face is on the side of a bus it's just a bit embarrassing.'

'Always getting stopped for selfies, weren't you?' Poppy said.

'Yes, took me hours to get anywhere. Now it's Ubers, with a request not to talk,' he said.

'Uber?' said Uncle Bill's wife, whom Alex had been introduced to as 'her indoors'. 'Is that one of those Twitter things, Poppy?'

'It's an app,' said Poppy patiently, 'that calls a car for you.'

'But what on earth for? We just call Den's Taxis,' said Uncle Bill, 'if we need to go to the airport or something, which reminds me, Poppy, did I tell you about our trip to Crete? Marvellous, it was, although I didn't like the food, did I, dear?'

'Alas,' said Poppy quickly, 'it'll have to wait, Uncle Bill. I'm so sorry. I've just seen Sarah and Kaspar over there and I haven't talked to them yet.'

She dragged Alex away, rolling her eyes at him.

'I did warn you,' she hissed.

'You weren't kidding,' he hissed back. 'Wow. I'm not surprised they don't know about the witchcraft. You'd never get a word in edgeways.'

'What's this about witches?' said a voice behind them, and Poppy froze for a minute, before she sent Alex a very quick signal he definitely understood, and turned to face the speaker.

It was a middle-aged woman, dressed so neatly and respectably that she could have illustrated both words in the dictionary. Beside her was her exact male counterpart. They were so ordinary it was actually weird. If Alex had ever needed to describe them for a police line-up, he'd have said, 'They were white people,' and then been unable to think of absolutely anything else.

'Hi Mum,' said Poppy with absolute inevitability. 'Hi Dad.'

Her mother looked over Poppy's outfit with a lightning glance that took in her vintage shoes, flowing dress, and her hair with its inevitable collection of blossoms and pins. Alex thought he saw a living butterfly in there.

'Darling,' said Poppy's mother. 'Don't you look … exciting.'

Poppy still had hold of his arm, so he felt her stiffen at that, before she leaned in to give each of her parents a kiss.

'And you must be … Alex? Sarah said you were bringing someone, Pops. Why didn't you tell us?'

Poppy glanced up at him, and he could see her wavering in her role. Then she rallied and said, 'Well, it's all so new, Mum. So exciting. Alex and I are just so…'

She gazed up at him with what, if he hadn't known she was faking it, would have looked like complete smouldering heat. And even when he did know, his breath still caught and his groin tightened.

Her hair caressed his arm.

'Well, I can see that.' Her mother looked slightly taken aback. 'Alex, then. What do you do?'

Alex glanced at Poppy, who gave him the tiniest nod.

He squared his shoulders, drew himself up, and in his most Axl Storm voice said, 'I'm an illusionist.'

That did it. Both of Poppy's parents blinked at him. Her mother said, 'Oh,' in the most surprised tone he'd ever heard.

'For children?' asked her father.

'No,' said Alex, smiling. 'Definitely not for children.'

'Unless you want them to learn about Viking executions,' Poppy said. 'You got five-star Edinburgh reviews, didn't you, darling?'

'Well, one doesn't like to brag,' Alex said, shrugging nonchalantly.

'Sold out West End shows, every night,' Poppy said. 'And how many online followers?'

'Sold out shows?' said Poppy's father, before Alex could answer. He frowned and glanced at his watch. 'But you're here on a Friday night.'

'Oh,' Alex began, not sure what he was going to say next, 'well—'

'Wait, I know you,' said Poppy's mother, studying him. 'Vikings, yes. One of my parishioners was showing me your videos. You're very good, aren't you? All the misdirection and –' she waved an elegant hand '– sparkle.'

Alex felt his smile become slightly frozen.

'Thank you very much,' he said, although he was pretty sure she hadn't meant it as a compliment.

'Oh yes, the one who takes his shirt off all the time,' said Poppy's father. He looked Alex over, as if trying to see through his shirt. 'You must spend an awful lot of time at the gym,' he said.

'Goodness me, I wish I had that much time to exercise!' said Poppy's mother, with a little laugh.

'It's part of his job,' Poppy said, her smile a little frozen too.

'Yes, I remember now. It was in the news. Your theatre burned down, didn't it?'

'No,' Poppy said forcefully. 'It didn't burn down. There was a fire.'

'It's very different,' said Alex, who had spent a lot of time with insurance people this week.

'A fire? Was anyone hurt?'

Alex winced. 'Not … by the fire.'

'But you've had to shut down?'

'Temporarily,' he said, no longer attempting to smile.

'Oh dear,' said Poppy's mother.

Alex rallied. 'But I tell you what, Poppy was amazing when the accident happened. Just leapt up onto the stage to help my cast member who was injured. You were so brave, and reassuring, Poppy,' he said, and this time he didn't have to fake his smile.

'It's what anyone would have done,' she said.

'It isn't. Most people thought it was part of the show. You should be very proud of her,' Alex said to Poppy's parents.

'Well, of course we are, aren't we, Pops? You know that,' said her father.

'But – does that mean you were in the theatre when it happened?' said her mother. She looked appalled.

'Uh,' said Poppy.

'Why didn't you say something!' said her father.

'You could have been hurt.'

'But I wasn't,' said Poppy. 'Not even a hair singed, see?'

Privately, Alex thought Poppy's hair could probably withstand a falling building.

'Well, I'm surprised, given how much it's always getting in the way. Oh, Poppy,' said her mother. 'Why is it always chaos with you?'

Poppy's arm clutching his went very rigid.

'Well, I love the chaos,' said Alex. 'It's exciting, eh, Pops?'

She gave a very small, very brittle smile.

'Oh look,' he said, peering into the distance, past the ship's hull. 'That looks like Kaspar. I must go and say hello. Big fan,' he said, and towed Poppy away.

She tried to tug herself free of his arm, her eyes not meeting his. 'Can you let me go? I'm going to find the loo.'

'Sure,' said Alex, releasing her, 'but I haven't seen

Kaspar at all. I just thought you needed an escape route. Look – Poppy.' He led her to a slightly quieter area, where the staff were setting out canapés. 'If you want to get out of here just say the word and we'll be off. Maybe find a greasy spoon or get some chips or something, yeah? These canapés don't look like much of a meal.'

'I can't go,' Poppy said. 'At least not until I've seen Sarah and said hello, or there'll be another tale of how Poppy fucked things up again by going to an engagement party and forgetting the bride.'

Another tale. How many were there? Did Poppy really get into that much trouble or were her family just so boring she was the only thing they had to talk about?

'Right, so we'll go and find her and say hello and then go,' he said. He ducked his head to peer into her mismatched eyes. 'Poppy, I know this is your family, but they're making you miserable.'

'They mean well,' she said, still not looking at him.

'Maybe, but they're crushing your spirit. Who cares if you're chaotic? I like chaos. It's exciting.'

'You like chaos? Like when it nearly burned down your theatre and cancelled your show indefinitely?'

'Well,' he conceded, 'that part I could do without, but look on the bright side. If I was performing tonight I wouldn't get to hang out with you.'

'I thought you didn't like me,' she said. She shook back her hair and glared up at him.

Oh, I like you a lot. 'Well, that was when I thought you were trying to seduce me to get a magic amulet,' he said, and her expression softened a bit. Alex moved in closer. 'In fact—'

Right then his phone rang. Of course it did. He hesitated for a moment, but then Poppy stepped back and said, 'Go on, answer it. Could be important.'

It would probably be Jonno with another mind-numbing update about the theatre insurance. Alex was already preparing excuses when he answered. 'Hi, mate. Listen, I'm kind of busy—'

'Have you heard from Yelena?' Jonno cut across him.

Alex frowned, guiltily aware he hadn't been back to visit her since that first day. 'Uh, no, but I wasn't expecting to. Is she okay?' Had her condition worsened? Were there unforeseen complications?

'I called earlier to see how she was, and the staff told me she'd discharged herself two days ago. No forwarding address. So I tried calling her, and nothing. Went round to her digs, and nothing. Her flatmates said they haven't seen her. Nobody's heard from her.'

'That's worrying.' At Poppy's concerned look, he explained, 'Yelena has discharged herself from hospital. We don't know where she's gone.'

'Are you with someone?' Jonno wanted to know.

'Uh, yeah. A ... friend.' He hadn't actually told Jonno about Poppy. How on earth would he explain how they'd met?

'Maybe she went to a hotel?' said Poppy.

'I don't think we pay her hotel money,' said Alex guiltily.

'Or home. Maybe she went back to Poland.'

'That's a good point. Maybe she went back to Poland,' Alex said into the phone.

'Can you even fly that soon after breaking a bone? The hospital weren't very pleased with her leaving. Do you think we should tell the police?'

'Why? Is it illegal to leave a hospital?'

'No, you drongo, I mean because she could be considered vulnerable and she's gone missing. Quite apart from anything, the insurance people want a statement from her.'

Ah. That was the real reason for the panic. 'Then the insurance people can find her,' said Alex. A clinking sound came to his attention, and he looked around to see Sarah and Kaspar on the stairs under the glass dome, tapping a teaspoon against a glass. 'I'm sure they're good at that kind of thing. Getting airline manifests and so forth.'

'I suppose,' said Jonno reluctantly. 'Okay then. Hey, where are you? Sounds like a party.'

'It is,' said Alex. 'So if you'll excuse me, I have to go.'

'Don't forget you have the awards ceremony next—' Jonno said quickly, but Alex had already ended the call.

'Good evening everybody!' called Sarah, as Poppy sent Alex a questioning look. He shook his head and put his phone back in his pocket. Yelena had almost certainly gone to stay with some family or something, and would be fine.

He directed his attention towards the staircase, which was an impressive double affair with a platform in the middle, perfect for making speeches from. Below it was the display of figureheads from various ships, including what appeared to be a duplicate of the *Cutty Sark*'s own. She was fierce and bare-breasted, which he imagined had been a source of entertainment to lonely sailors on long voyages.

'Thank you all so much for coming,' said Sarah, who unsurprisingly had a carrying tone of voice. 'It's so lovely to see so many family and friends here tonight, especially the family…'

At this, Alex gave Poppy a quick smile, because Sarah actually did appreciate her.

'…who have come all the way from the Netherlands. *Bedankt dat je tijd voor ons hebt vrijgemaakt…*'

She continued in Dutch, as Poppy gave a sour smile and said, 'See, it's them she wants to thank. Bet she wouldn't have invited any of us if Mum hadn't let the cat out of the bag.'

Sarah said something that made the Dutch speakers laugh, and then another thing, and then they all toasted her with their glasses.

'Or as they say in English, cheers!'

'As they say in English,' mocked Poppy under her breath. 'You grew up in Northampton.'

Alex grinned. 'So the slight Dutch accent isn't natural?'

'Like buggery it is. Any money she occasionally lapses into Dutch just to show off.'

Alex laughed, and grabbed two glasses of champagne from a passing waiter.

'Thought you were driving?'

He shrugged. 'Maybe we'll get a cab.' *And maybe it'll be back to my place, and maybe—*

A murmur began running through the crowd, surpassing even the volume of Sarah's voice.

'...I said, when I met dear Kaspar he said to me, *nu komt de aap uit de mouw*—'

But the sound had grown louder, and now people were pointing. Alex, who was usually taller than most people, had to crane to see over the heads of Kaspar's Dutch relatives, but it turned out what they were looking at wasn't at head height.

At least, not at human head height.

The figureheads under the staircase were … moving.

'That's a nice effect,' he said to Poppy, but she had gone very pale.

'That's not an effect.'

'Are you sure? Some fairly simple animatronics, maybe motion-activated—'

'That's magic. I can feel it. Shit. Shit.'

And with that, she was off and running.

Chapter Eight

The figureheads were moving.

There were dozens of them, some human and some decidedly not. A huge golden eagle shook its wings. A terrier barked and growled. What appeared to be Abraham Lincoln straightened his shoulders and looked around in some surprise.

'Okay, so this is mad,' Poppy muttered as she shoved through the crowd to get closer. Her mind raced with ideas and solutions. Who had done this? How and why? How could she stop it?

As she passed a couple holding champagne glasses, they sniffed them and said something in Dutch, which Poppy was almost certain would translate as 'What did they put in our drinks?'

'What is going on here?' called a strident voice from the front, and someone screamed.

'Excuse me. Excuse me!' Poppy shoved her way to the front, vaguely aware of Alex shouldering through the crowd behind her. 'Right, what's … happening … hereohmyGod.'

'I'll thank you,' said one of the figureheads, a formal-looking gent with huge sideburns, 'not to blaspheme, young lady.'

His painted mouth formed the shapes of words. His brow drew down. He was made of wood and he didn't exist below the waist, but his face was moving, and when he spoke it was with a distinctly creaky sort of edge. Poppy began to feel a bit queasy.

'And for heaven's sake, cover up,' said a Victorian figure in a high-necked frock. She looked over Poppy's fairly modest green dress with a sniff of disapproval. 'You can't go around in just your shift.'

'An' whit's wrong,' came a strident voice from above, 'wi' gaun aroond in just yer sark?'

The figureheads all drew in a collective breath, which was even weirder considering absolutely none of them had lungs. Some were merely heads on sticks.

'Holy shit,' said a voice just behind Poppy. Alex. For some reason, his large presence was a tiny sliver of comfort.

As Poppy looked up, she realised that Sarah and Kaspar were still at the top of the stairs, behind the largest and most impressive figureheads. They were flattened against the back wall, Kaspar clutching Sarah's arm. And well they might, because the figureheads creaked as they moved, their gaudily painted faces turning to look at the happy couple.

'It's a rather silly trick,' Sarah said. 'Haha, everybody,

don't be alarmed. It's just some kind of clever … anima … troni—'

Her voice abruptly rose in a shriek as a horrific splintering noise came from above, and through the glass roof they saw the figurehead attached to the bow of the ship itself wrench free and climb down to stand on the glass. This was made all the more terrifying by the fact that she didn't appear to have any legs, just a solid wooden skirt that ended in wooden curlicues.

Behind her, Poppy heard someone whimper and someone else say, 'She's fainted. This isn't funny!'

'It really isn't,' Alex said. 'Poppy? What do we do?'

Poppy was watching the figure above them make her way awkwardly across the glass roof. The figurehead rocked from wooden point to point, the way a child would make a solid doll walk. Only that was a cute thing, and this was beyond awful, the solid thuds of the figure akin to the sounds coming from outside a cabin in a horror film.

'Aye, that'll be the fresh me,' said the white figure crowning the collection inside the glass dome. She had gold trim on her white gown, and both breasts bare. In one hand she held out something that looked like a horse's tail. 'She gets tae hae yin tit covered, th' jammy besom. A've bin chankin' mine aff for years.'

'Please, what language is this?' said one of the Dutch relatives behind Poppy.

'Tis Scots, ye skellum,' scoffed the inside figurehead, as the one outside reached the sloping edge of the roof. She hopped in place for a moment before leaping off the glass structure and hobbling away. And Poppy would have followed her, but that last hop had done something to the glass roof and now a large crack had appeared in it.

A shriek came from Sarah's direction.

'Sarah, you need to come down,' Poppy called. 'Stay near the wall and come down the stairs.'

'We wilnae hurt them,' said the figurehead inside.

'Yes, but the glass might,' said Poppy. *I'm talking to painted wood.* 'Sarah? Kaspar? Either come downstairs or get outside.'

'Where that ... that ... *thing* is?' cried Sarah.

'Sarah, please. She's already gone. Go outside now. Please.'

'I won't!' cried Sarah. 'This is my engagement party! You can't ruin it, Poppy!'

'I'm not trying to ruin it,' Poppy said evenly. 'I'm trying to save it. In fact, why doesn't everyone go outside right now?'

'Poppy, what's going on?' said her mother, materialising behind her. 'That lady's fainted.'

Fantastic. 'Nothing,' said Poppy. 'This is all totally planned.'

'It's not bloody planned,' shouted Sarah.

'It's all completely fine,' said Poppy through gritted teeth. 'Mum, why don't you tell everyone to go outside? For some ... fresh air?'

The crack in the glass was probably fine, but she didn't want to take any risks. And she wanted to try and fix the situation without Sarah and her mother and everyone else interfering.

'It's a bit chilly out there, Pops,' said her father.

It's about to get a lot chillier in here. 'It really isn't that bad. Look, we need the space to set something new up,' she tried desperately.

'No, this is some trick gone wrong,' said Kaspar, from behind the figureheads. 'Where are the staff?'

Poppy glanced around, but all the waitstaff appeared as horrified as the guests. One woman in a suit hurried forward. 'I, er, don't know what's going on,' she whispered to Poppy. 'Is this a flashmob? Or a stunt? Like in *Love Actually*?'

'Sure,' said Alex, before Poppy could say anything. 'Only it's all gone a bit wrong, so why don't you get everyone outside for photographs?'

'Well, they've already done the photos,' said the woman in the suit doubtfully.

Poppy took a breath and projected her will into her voice. 'More photos,' she said, and raised her voice. 'Everyone needs to go outside and have more photographs taken. Right now. Everybody outside.'

'But—' began Sarah.

'Really, Poppy, what are you planning?' said her mother.

Poppy's temper snapped. 'Everybody outside,' she shouted, with the sort of force she'd used against the Egyptian ghost. 'By my will, you will all go outside right now!'

The woman in the suit nodded and turned to her staff. 'Everybody, the party's moving outside now,' she said. 'Everybody please follow me outside!'

She needn't have told them. All the guests, including the lady who had recently fainted, began calmly walking towards the stairs, carrying their drinks and chatting as if this was all part of the party.

'Not you,' Poppy said to Alex, as he began to follow them. She had a feeling someone as large as Alex might come in handy. Plus … well, his presence was kind of reassuring.

He blinked at her. 'What? But you said…'

'You, stay with me,' she said. 'Alex.' She grabbed his chin and made him look at her. 'Stay with me.'

He nodded, and shook himself a bit. 'Right. Yes. What do we do now?'

His voice sounded different, Poppy thought. She couldn't quite put her finger on it.

'Well,' she said. 'We, er…' *Pull yourself together, Poppy. You're a witch. This is magic. You can handle it.*

A tiny little voice underneath the pep talk whispered, *I'm so tired of handling it.*

She squared her shoulders and said to the bare-breasted figurehead, 'Excuse me?'

'Aye?' said the figurehead.

'My name is Poppy. What's yours?'

'Are you serious?' muttered Alex.

'They call me Nannie,' said the figurehead. She seemed to straighten a little, which was no mean feat for a figure permanently tilted at 45 degrees. Her carved face wore a fearsome expression, but as she spoke – and was spoken to – the forced scowl faded away.

'Nannie. Pleased to meet you. The, er, figurehead who just climbed off the ship. Is she going to be a danger to anyone?'

'Naw. She's gaen tae find her coven o' hags,' said Nannie.

'Hags?' said Alex, alarmed.

'Witches,' said Poppy. 'Right.' She had a very vague recollection that the *Cutty Sark*'s figurehead was a witch from a Rabbie Burns poem, which would definitely explain the way Nannie spoke like a ... well, like a Rabbie Burns poem. Poppy had never actually heard a Scottish person talk like this in her life. 'Yes. You're a witch, aren't you?'

Wood creaked as the figurehead smiled. 'Aye, lassie. Taks yin tae ken yin. Did ye dae this?'

'I really did not,' said Poppy. 'Do you, er ... have you...'

'Hae we ever come tae life afore? Naw, lassie. And 'tis just as weel. There wis ae time oot at sea Ah wis beheaded by a storm. A'm glad ah wasnae alive for that!'

'So – you remember who you were? Are?' said Poppy.

The figureheads all nodded. 'Yes, young lady,' said the one who'd addressed her first. 'I am William Gladstone, at your service.' He bowed his head, which was pretty much the only part of him available to bow.

'William Pitt, ma'am,' said a ginger figure with horrible glass eyes.

'Benjamin Disraeli, Earl of Beaconsfield,' said a figure with a little soul patch beard, and Poppy heard a grumbling from Gladstone.

'Earl of Beaconsfield,' he mimicked. 'Least I have arms,' he added more loudly, waving said limbs at Disraeli.

'Gentlemen, please. This is no place for politics,' said an American accent, and Poppy was somehow unsurprised to find it belonged to Abraham Lincoln.

'People put weird shit on their ships,' Alex muttered.

'You're telling me,' said a gold-painted cherub with no legs.

'This is all fascinating,' said Poppy, 'but what I'd like to know is why you're all, um, sentient right now.'

The figureheads all glanced around at each other, with much creaking, and made vague noises that indicated they didn't know. One figure, who was little more than a bust – bust being the word that definitely came to mind when looking at her – rattled off something in a language Poppy hadn't a hope of understanding.

'I'm sorry?' she said.

Another figurehead, this one in the style of a Roman soldier, spoke in what seemed to be Latin.

'Ah, he says,' that was Pitt, 'that she speaks a heathen dialect of the Celts, but he believes she is talking about some kind of sorcery.'

'Well, yes, we know that,' said Poppy impatiently, and the Celtic woman glared at her and rattled off something that was unmistakeably an insult, no matter what language it was in.

Alex had wandered over to one of the information boards. 'I think she's Boudicca,' he said, and the woman nodded proudly.

'An honour,' said Poppy, which seemed to please her. 'Do you know who did the sorcery? Because it wasn't me,' she added firmly.

'No, Poppy,' said a familiar and yet wholly surprising voice from the top of the stairs. There was a terrible creak as the figureheads turned to look at her. 'And that's the frightening thing.'

Poppy gaped at the elegantly dressed figure standing there. 'Fiona?'

The youngest member of Iris's coven nodded, her perfectly styled hair barely moving with her. She always looked like the epitome of North London middle-class affluence, all discreet highlights and expensively casual clothes. Her idea of a bright colour was teal, and her most whimsical accessory was a muslin scarf printed with giraffes. Her children wore co-ordinated outfits that never got grubby or wrinkled, and refined sugar did not pass their lips. Fiona was one hundred per cent the mum at the school gates who said things like, 'Well, I would never let *my* child do that...' and had them speaking Mandarin by the age of four.

Poppy was terrified of her.

She cleared her throat. 'What do you mean, that's the frightening thing?'

Fiona began descending the stairs. 'I mean that if you had done it, you could undo it. Or we could, at least. But I've no idea what's causing this. I just felt it—I was at an event at the Trafalgar Tavern, you know.' She waved her hand vaguely towards the left.

'You just happened to be a few hundred metres away?' said Alex. He had his hands in his pockets and was regarding Fiona with his head slightly cocked.

There was a creak as Nannie the figurehead leaned forward. 'Whaur is this tavern?'

An austere lady in black on the left replied

disapprovingly, 'Let us not speak of taverns. A great amount of ill comes from the dependence upon drink—'

'Weesht, Elizabeth Fry, woman!' snapped Nannie. 'We cannae gang there anyway.'

'But the figurehead on the mast got up and walked away,' said Poppy. 'Well, hobbled. She's a weird shape.'

'Pure weird shape! Keek at lassy legs doon there,' said Nannie, scowling at Poppy.

'We are unfortunately confined,' said a lady who might have been Florence Nightingale, 'by means of metal bolts and a, er, pole arrangement.'

'We've got metal poles up our arses,' said the large, rough-looking figure beside Nannie.

'Yes, quite,' said Florence, her painted cheeks appearing to pinken.

'Aye, and she's a living figureheid,' said Nannie. 'We're just lumps o' wood.'

'If you're quite finished?' Fiona said. She'd reached the bottom of the stairs now. 'If you must know, I was at a fundraiser for a children's literacy charity.' She cocked an eyebrow at Elizabeth Fry, who gave a sort of shrug as if to say this might *just* be an acceptable reason to enter a tavern.

'You got changed quick,' said Poppy, eyeing Fiona's elegant evening dress. She'd been wearing expensively casual jeans and a Breton top the last time Poppy saw her, in Highgate.

Fiona rolled her eyes. 'Number one, Poppy, I have four children, I can do everything faster. Number two, I am a witch.' She glanced at Alex, and for the first time since Poppy had met her, appeared to hesitate. 'Er, does he...?'

'I know Poppy's a witch,' Alex said, sauntering back to Poppy's side. 'I helped her banish a ghost mummy.'

'Well, you held the candle,' Poppy said.

'Which you couldn't have done without. It was thousands of years old,' Alex added.

'The mummy, not the candle.'

'The candle was Diptyque,' Alex explained.

'I could have done it without the candle,' Poppy said, flashing a smile at Fiona to let her know she was both an adult and a competent witch.

'Then why did you make me carry it?'

'It's just easier with a candle,' Poppy snapped.

'You see? I helped. We met earlier,' he said to Fiona. 'This still isn't Saint Laurent.'

She cast a very practised eye over his handsome blue suit. 'No. Savile Row?'

Alex sighed, conceding the point. 'You got me.'

'Aye, he's a braw jimmy,' sighed Nannie.

'I don't know what that means but I'll take it as a compliment,' said Alex. 'Now, ladies, gentlemen, and those of you who choose not to define, there are a couple of important questions here.'

'Wait, why are you asking the questions?' said Poppy.

'Because you're not,' he replied, with annoying perspicacity.

'And what questions are these?' said Fiona.

'Well, firstly, do you know who did the, er, spell that brought you to life?'

The figureheads glanced around at each other with that

unnerving creaking sound. 'Well, you're the witch, Nannie,' said Florence Nightingale.

'Aye. But Ah dinnae ken. Ah just heard a voice telling me tae wake up.'

The others nodded, and murmured versions of the same thing.

'A male voice? Female?'

'Ach, Ah couldnae say! Ah tell ye yin thing though, 'twas Sassenach.'

'Sassenach?' queried the Roman soldier.

'English,' said Fiona.

Alex grinned. 'You speak Scots? Or was that from *Outlander*?'

'I'm a witch, young man, that's all you need to know,' said Fiona, in tones so freezing Poppy was in no doubt whatsoever that the answer was definitely *Outlander*. 'Whoever did this was English. Given we're in London, that really doesn't narrow it down much.'

Poppy knew she'd already ruled out Iris and Sylvia. There was simply no reason for them to have done this, and besides, they'd surely have given her a heads-up if they had. 'Who else is there?' she asked.

'Well, there's Maggie Silver, but you don't see her about much these days. Lettice Lane, maybe, but she doesn't usually go far from Limehouse. Could be the Essex lot, but they generally let us know if they're witching in town. I could have a call around, I suppose.'

'Can you undo it, if you don't know who did it?' asked Alex.

Fiona shook back her hair. 'Quite probably,' she said.

'Because that brings me to my next question. Do you,' he addressed the figureheads, 'want this to be undone? Do you want to go back to how you were?'

'Back tae bein' made o' wood?' said Nannie.

'Gladstone always was a blockhead,' Disraeli said waspishly.

'Gentlemen, please,' said Florence Nightingale.

'This is like being on drugs,' muttered Alex. Louder, he added, 'We'll let you think about it.'

He turned away from them all, as a murmuring grew amongst the figureheads.

'We'll let them think about it, will we?' said Fiona, in what Poppy imagined was the tone she used with her children if they dared to misbehave.

'It's only fair,' said Alex. 'They might like being like this, and then we're condemning them to a life of being made of wood again.' He rubbed his forehead. 'I can't believe I'm having this conversation.'

'He's right though,' said Poppy. 'We should at least ask for consent.'

'Consent is sexy,' said Alex, grinning at her, and right then consent really wasn't the only thing that was sexy.

'And if they don't give it?'

Alex shrugged. 'What's the worst that could happen? The museum gets a really cool new exhibit?'

Poppy considered it. 'I mean, it would liven things up a bit,' she said.

'Are you mad?' hissed Fiona. 'We are not leaving enchanted figureheads here to just talk to … anyone!'

'Why not?' said Poppy. 'Would've made my school trips more interesting.'

'Ho ye, hags!' called Nannie, and the three of them turned. 'We hae decided.'

Poppy's heart raced a little. 'And?'

'None o' us wants tae spend th' rest o' oor lives made o' wood, bein' keeked at by strangers.'

'With metal poles up our bums,' said the hunter beside her.

'Aye, wi' metal poles up oor bums. Change us back, if ye please.'

Poppy glanced at Fiona, who looked a touch smug. 'You're really sure?' she asked the figureheads.

'Aye, lassie. We're nae real.'

Fiona nodded. 'I do have a restoration spell,' she said, and added quickly, 'Please don't tell the children I can clean up their messes with magic. But I really would like to know who did this in the first place.'

'We cannae tell ye,' said Nannie. 'Guidbye, hags.' One wooden eyelid creaked as she winked at Alex. 'Guidbye, braw jimmy.'

To Poppy's surprise, a flush of colour stained Alex's cheeks.

'Och, yin mair thing. Th' fresh me on th' ship. She's a living figureheid, ye ken? She'll nae ken she's made o' wood. Ye might wantae gang after her, afore folk start callin' cantraip.'

'Cantraip?'

'Magic,' said Fiona. 'She's right. I'll sort this lot out, and you go after the other one.'

'I'll help you with this first,' said Poppy. It wasn't that she didn't trust Fiona, so much as she didn't trust her not to take all the credit.

'Suit yourself. Now.' Fiona touched the locket around her neck with one hand, and with the other touched her thumb to her wedding ring. 'You, Alex, be quiet. Poppy, focus, and repeat after me: What is broken, be mended. What is enchanted, be restored. Let order prevail. You figureheads who move and speak, be you restored to wood.'

Poppy ran her hands through her hair and duly repeated this, pushing all the force of her will into the words. She stared hard at Nannie, whose gaze dulled and lost focus, and whose animated face returned to wood.

'You figureheads who—'

'That's it, I think,' said Fiona, touching her arm, and when Poppy blinked and stood back, she realised the other witch was right. All the figureheads were inanimate again. Painted eyes, or in the case of Mr Pitt, glass eyes, stared blankly. The hands that had been frozen reaching out stayed that way. Only the horse tail in Nannie's hand fluttered slightly, before it stilled.

Although… was it Poppy's imagination, or did the carved lips smile a little more than they had before?

'Are you sure?' said Alex.

Fiona peered up at the crack in the glass, which had vanished now. 'Yes. All done. Spit spot.' She settled the locket back in place, and Poppy realised she'd never let slip that it was a magic talisman. 'I've got to get back to my event before they wonder where I've gone. Do you need any help getting the guests back in, Poppy?'

'I'll do it,' said Alex. He gave a cocky grin. 'Charming people is my speciality.'

'Well, it's nice you have something,' said Fiona, and Alex jogged away up the steps.

Poppy couldn't help watching him go.

'He's definitely easy on the eye,' Fiona said, and Poppy felt her cheeks heat.

'Well – yes. He's not— We're not— This wasn't an actual date,' she spluttered.

'Oh no?' said Fiona. 'I saw the way he looks at you, Pops. Just … be careful, all right?'

Poppy tore her eyes away from Alex as he exited the glass dome. 'What do you mean?' How much did Fiona know about her disastrous dating history?

'I mean, sweetheart, the handsome ones are always trouble. Look at him. He could have any girl he wants, and probably has. Not that you aren't captivating, but I wouldn't go falling for a man who could never love anyone as much as he loves himself.'

And that was the problem. Alex was gorgeous and boy, did he know it. She could see it in the way he moved, the way he smiled at people. Ordinary people didn't walk around as if they were being awarded points out of ten for sexiness. Alex clearly expected full marks from all the judges every time he smiled.

Charming people is my speciality.

Irritated, Poppy said, 'And how do you know he loves himself?'

Fiona just shrugged. 'I've got eyes, that's how. Now, tell me honestly. Do you have any idea how this –' she waved at the still figureheads '– actually happened?'

'No. I told you,' said Poppy, somehow reduced to the role of a sulky child in the face of Fiona's condescension. 'I didn't do it. I didn't do anything.'

Fiona frowned. 'You do cause chaos wherever you go, is all I'm saying— All right, all right. That zombie ghost you banished – what happened there?'

'Mummy ghost,' Poppy corrected. 'I just exorcised it. I've done it loads. It was a stubborn one, but I did it.'

'And there were no ... complications? It's just that something's felt off this week, and I can't quite put my finger on it. Almost as if...' She trailed off, frowning.

'Oh,' said Poppy guiltily. 'Er, did Iris mention the pendant?'

'What pendant?' said Fiona patiently.

'I accidentally cursed a pendant in the shop. But we got it back and it's destroyed now.'

'Destroyed? Poppy ... you did remove the curse before you destroyed it, didn't you?'

A coldness crept through Poppy's veins. 'Um. We didn't mean to destroy it,' she said. Noise from above heralded the guests beginning to come back inside the glass dome. Lowering her voice, she continued, 'Is that bad? It had already done its cursing.'

Fiona pressed both her hands together and looked as if she was silently counting to ten. 'Is it bad?' she said. 'Poppy ... you trail chaos wherever you go, but you have to admit that a set of bloody ship's figureheads coming to life for no good reason when you *just happen to be near* is a bit of a coincidence! What kind of curse did you put on it?'

In a very small voice, this time actually feeling she might deserve being spoken to this way, Poppy said, 'I don't know.'

'You don't *know*?'

'I was, um. I was a bit drunk,' whispered Poppy.

Fiona pressed her hands to her eyes, heedless of her tasteful make-up. 'Drunk,' she said, and Poppy definitely had flashbacks to her teenage years when the churchyard ghosts had egged her on to try the other kind of spirits.

'But I went after it to clean up the mess,' she said hopefully.

'A mess like this?' Fiona said, sweeping her arm at the figureheads, and incidentally Alex, who was jogging down the stairs again. He gave her a thumbs-up, smiling, as behind him the guests started coming back in.

He really is easy on the eye. 'I'll fix it, okay?' Poppy said, moving off to meet Alex before her mother could find her. 'We've got to go and find the other Nannie, bye, thanks for helping, bye now!'

'What was that about?' said Alex, as she hustled him away.

'Nothing. Doesn't matter. Have you got your keys? We'll need the car.'

Chapter Nine

Alex found Sarah skulking behind the visitor centre, a tell-tale plume of smoke rising from behind her back. And from the smell of it, she hadn't been smoking tobacco.

'Don't tell Kaspar,' she said immediately.

Alex held up his hands. 'Not a word. But won't he smell it?'

Sarah gave a bitter laugh. 'He thinks my colleagues smoke. He's always lecturing them about it. I'm going to quit by the wedding. I definitely am. Besides, everyone in Amsterdam does it.'

'Sure,' said Alex, who was fairly sure Poppy had said her cousin lived in Brussels. 'Listen, I've come to round everyone up to go back inside. They've finished setting everything up now.'

Sarah nodded and snuffed out the spliff, hiding it in her pocket before trotting after him. 'Set up what?' she asked after a moment.

'Search me,' Alex said cheerfully.

Sarah rolled her eyes. 'Are you really Poppy's boyfriend?' she asked.

Alex couldn't stop the warmth that spread through him at the thought of that actually being true. 'Why would you think I'm not?' he said.

'Oh … I don't know. You're kind of out of her league,' Sarah said, and that should have felt like more of a compliment.

He laughed. 'I'm really not. If anything, it's the other way around.'

'What? Poppy? Oh, you are funny. Poppy's sweet and everything, but she's completely hopeless. No job, no prospects—'

'She has a job,' Alex said. 'She works in a magic shop.'

'Yes,' Sarah said pityingly. 'Exactly. She works in a magic shop. And she will for the rest of her days, if she's not careful. I suppose that's what you get for going off to learn about jewellery making for three years and calling it a degree.'

Anger flashed through Alex. 'She makes beautiful jewellery,' he said.

'Yes, but it's not a career, is it?'

He stopped and glared pointedly at the silver and amber necklace she wore, which didn't really suit her colouring. 'Where did you get that?' he said.

'Oh, this artisan jeweller in Brussels,' she said, so automatically he knew she'd rattled it off a million times before. 'He's very exclusive, he—'

'Almost certainly started out like Poppy,' said Alex, starting walking again.

'Yes, but he's very successful, and she, you know. She's never really applied herself,' Sarah said, hurrying after him.

Because she's also had to learn how to be a witch, Alex wanted to snap. Plus, what did it matter if Poppy wasn't successful? She was happy, and wasn't that more important?

The revelation hit him like a smack. He was successful. Was he happy? Was he – if he was totally honest with himself – not a bit relieved his show had been cancelled?

'...tell her to go to Amsterdam and apprentice herself there, but she'd never do it. Too much like hard work. Poppy prefers to coast through life, I've always thought. Never had any ambition. I blame Auntie June. She's always spoiled Poppy. Massively overcompensating for the adoption.'

That word dragged Alex out of his stupor. 'Adoption? Poppy is adopted?'

Sarah's eyes grew wide. 'Christ,' she hissed, grabbing his sleeve. 'Do *not* tell her I said that.'

'She doesn't *know*?'

'No. I'm not supposed to know. Mummy got drunk one Christmas and... Don't tell her. I always thought her parents would and they never did. Mummy says Auntie June was so desperate for a baby she'd have stolen one.'

As Alex felt his jaw go slack, Sarah added hastily, 'Not that she did! It was all properly legal! Just ... she was so desperate for a baby that when she got one, she spoiled it rotten.'

Alex thought about the way Poppy's shoulders hunched

defensively when she was around her family, and wondered what Sarah thought spoiling really was.

'You won't say anything, will you?' Sarah's eyes were a bit too wide. Great, she was high at her own party. 'She doesn't know. She's always been the black sheep of the family, it'd break her heart to find out she's the cuckoo in the nest too. You won't tell her, will you?'

Alex sighed. 'Of course not. It's not my secret to tell.'

'Oh good.' Sarah sagged as she hung on his arm. 'Thank you. You really are lovely, Alex. And you're so handsome. Were you always this handsome?'

If you only knew. 'No, I just woke up like this one day,' he said lightly. 'Quite the surprise, I can tell you.'

He escorted Sarah back to Kaspar and escaped back inside, where the slightly bemused guests were beginning to return with no real idea of why they'd left. The figureheads all appeared to be made of inanimate wood once more, but Alex still gave them a wide berth as he jogged down the stairs and met Poppy.

God, she was lovely. Her hair was like a fairy crown, all gleaming in the lights, adorned with tiny flowers. He wanted to plunge his hands into it, feel it twine around him, wrap him in silken softness as he kissed her until they both forgot their own names.

He wanted to take her in his arms here, right in front of her boring family, and show them that even if they didn't think Poppy was good enough, he thought she was magnificent.

But his romantic notions were dashed by the woman

herself, who grabbed him by the arm and marched him back towards the exit.

'We've got to go and find the other Nannie,' she said. 'Have you got your keys?'

He did, and as soon as she got in the car she was drawing things out of her tiny handbag that couldn't possibly have fit in there. A lump of wood, a storm lantern, a tartan serviette holding God only knew what.

'How—?' he said.

'I pack for all eventualities,' she said. 'Force of habit.'

'What do you mean?'

'Oh, I forget things, I lose things – am I going to set off a smoke alarm or anything if I light a candle in here?' she said, as Alex exited the car park.

'Why don't we have fun finding out?' he said.

He drove aimlessly around the nearby streets as she fiddled about with things on her lap. 'Hold that,' she said absently, and he drove one-handed for a while with a napkin-wrapped bundle in the other hand. The red and green tartan appeared to have holly leaves on it. Why did she have a Christmas napkin?

Chaos.

Just about at the point where he was going to have to make a decision about one-way roads, Poppy cried, 'Aha!'

'Aha?'

'Yes. Go … that way.' She pointed, something in her hand glowing between her fingers.

He obeyed, and after a moment said, 'Do I still need to hold this?'

'What? Oh God, sorry. Snack for later. You want some sausage roll?'

Alex just started laughing.

She directed him in a somewhat haphazard fashion through the evening streets, which were busy enough, trying repeatedly to get them to cross the river regardless of whether there was a bridge or tunnel. And once they were north of the Thames, the glowing thing in Poppy's hand definitely wanted him to go east.

'Not north?' he said.

'What am I, a compass?' said Poppy.

Alex glanced at her glowing hand. 'Well,' he said, 'yes.'

'All right, fair enough,' she conceded. 'But why north?'

'Er, she's Scottish? Didn't the wooden, er, lady say she'd be going to find her, um, witches? And we're in London, ergo, all of Scotland is north of all of here. We head north and then … um, recalibrate.'

'We are not going all the way to Scotland,' Poppy said. She craned over to look at the fuel gauge, which meant her breast pressed against his arm and he had to concentrate pretty hard on the road. 'You'll run out of fuel.'

Not with you, he wanted to say, but that would sound weird and creepy. Besides, at this point he wanted her so badly he didn't think he'd be running out of anything, unless it was time, and only then if the world ended.

'We'll be fine,' he managed, and Poppy leaned over him to look at a street sign.

'Next right,' she said, and he really had to concentrate on driving.

This part of London was the old City, which had once

been walled in, where the streets were still on a mediaeval plan. They twisted and bucked, abrupt turns and narrow corners coming out of nowhere. These days, of course, the City was home to banks and multinationals, its narrow streets lined with impossibly tall buildings of concrete and steel. On a Friday evening, the offices were empty but the bars were full, and the streets crammed with black cabs and buses. Any available gap was filled with courier bikes, and Alex figured he might need a miracle to avoid hitting any of them.

'Who builds a financial district on streets that haven't changed since the Black Death?' he muttered, narrowly avoiding a delivery bike.

'People who didn't see cars coming,' Poppy replied. 'Left!'

'Like me if you keep shouting,' Alex said, but he made the turn anyway.

'Anyway, the City isn't in the City any more,' Poppy said. 'It's in Canary Wharf now.'

'What's really bad is I actually understood what you meant there.'

'Right. We need to— Bloody one-way streets! All right, under the railway bridge here.'

'Surely there's got to be a better way to do this,' said Alex. 'On a main road. Aren't we near the…' He glanced around, and saw a familiar turret rising beyond the modern buildings. 'Yep, the Tower of London. Are you sure she's not headed there? Were witches burnt at the stake there?'

'No, and witches weren't burned,' Poppy said. She blew on her hand, tossing whatever it held from side to side.

'They were hanged. We're really close. We should get out and go on foot.'

'Are you joking? Right next to the Tower of London? They planned ample parking here a thousand years ago, did they?'

Poppy was already glancing around madly as he turned right past a small enclosed garden. 'Just get me past that,' she said, abruptly turning her back to the window. Her face was pale.

'Why?' It looked like a perfectly ordinary little green, the sort you got all over London. Some kind of memorial in it, maybe.

'Why? Jesus God, Alex, we're on Tower Hill! Where they executed people!'

'Ah.' The car slowed as he reached a pedestrian crossing, and he saw Poppy's eyes squeeze shut. Her shoulders hunched, and her breath fluttered, as if she was trying not to be sick.

She'd reacted badly enough to the ghosts in Highgate. What would these spectres be like – the terrified spirits of people beheaded and hanged after the horrors of the Tower? He could only imagine the fear and anger, not to mention the gore. No wonder Poppy was the colour of spoiled milk.

'Hey,' he said, wishing he could hold her. 'It's okay. We're nearly past it. Just look at me instead.'

That got a weak smile out of her. 'You just love being looked at,' she managed.

'Especially by you.'

He could see nothing outside the car on her side. Just

ordinary people doing ordinary things. But something suddenly made her flinch, and every muscle in her body seemed to clench itself tight. He thought he saw tears in her eyes.

Her hair wrapped itself protectively around her, like a cloak.

'Poppy?'

A car horn made him jump too, and he realised the lights had changed. The car lurched forward, and Poppy didn't open her eyes until they were around the corner and out of sight of the little garden.

'You okay?' he said, and she nodded and let out a shaky breath.

'Yeah. I think ... yeah. It was just a lot. I can't turn it off tonight. There were a ... lot. Jesus, Alex. There were so many and they were so ... angry...'

He reached out with one hand and took hers. 'I'm sorry,' he said. 'If I could do anything I would.'

She sniffed, and straightened in her seat. Her hair smoothed over his hand as if stroking him.

'Well, one thing you can do is pull over,' she said. 'This thing is close. It'll be easier on foot.'

Alex glanced in the rear-view mirror at the receding glimpses of the Tower behind him, and that innocent-looking garden. 'You sure you're far enough away?'

'Oh yes. They can't leave the Hill. And I need some air.' He slowed again for another light, and Poppy said, 'Let me out.'

'Poppy!' Was she mad? It was definitely a no parking kind of road. 'I can't park here—'

But she was already unfastening her seatbelt. 'Catch me up,' she said, and then she was off.

'How will I—? You've got the sodding spell!' Alex yelled.

'I've also got a phone,' Poppy said, and slammed the door as the car behind Alex beeped at him to get a move on.

Images of what she might be facing, chasing down a living wooden figurehead with a haunted slaughter site behind her, nearly had Alex crashing the car. He had to drive another few hundred yards before he could even pull off the road, and even then it was into a tiny alley leading to the river, where he was absolutely sure he was going to get a fine. But that was tomorrow's problem. He leapt out of the car and raced back the way he'd come.

As it happened, he didn't need to call her. Her green dress was just vanishing around a corner, and as Alex waited impatiently to cross the road he saw people standing around looking puzzled and entertained.

'...can't figure out how they do the legs?' one person said as Alex jogged past.

'Living statues, man, I just don't understand why,' said another.

Yep, that sounded like it. Alex hastened down a couple of backstreets, and came to what seemed to be a ruined church.

'Right, of course,' he said, as he passed an older couple complaining to each other that they really shouldn't allow those sorts of people in such places.

'It's not respectful,' said one.

'That language!' said the other.

'Couldn't understand a word.'

'Maybe it's that modern art?'

'Ugh.'

Alex paused to catch his breath, then went up the steps into the garden.

It had been a church once, and the tower still stood, surrounded by some of the walls. The bones of the windows stood glassless, the roof probably sacrificed to a German bomb. He'd never seen anything like it before in London, a city with little sentimentality about replacing things it didn't need any more.

Maybe it was a peaceful place with the sunlight dappling through the trees, but not tonight, and certainly not with Nannie the figurehead wobbling about in the middle of it.

The figurehead was muttering and waving her arms around angrily. Alex looked around, but there was no sign of Poppy. A cold wind blew the leaves around in circling eddies, and he realised, despite all the people he'd seen outside the garden, there was no one else in here.

'Alex?' The voice came from the shadows, but it was Poppy's, thank God.

'Yeah?'

'Good. Close the gate.'

He did, and as he closed the one he'd come through, there was a sort of whooshing effect, as if a seal had formed around the garden.

When he turned back, Poppy was sitting on one of the benches that ringed the centre of the garden, her head in her hands, muttering.

Alarmed, he rushed over. 'Are you okay?'

She waved him away impatiently. Right. She was doing another spell.

Dating a witch was proving to be a complicated business.

Wait, was that what they were doing? Dating? Well, this *was* a date – he'd picked her up, they'd gone to a party, they'd chatted with some enchanted objects and chased one of them across London, just like any date – but what was going to happen after this?

Alex certainly knew what he wanted to happen after this. Or at least what the contents of his excellently tailored trousers wanted him to do. But even if Poppy was amenable to driving back to his place and getting very naked and very sweaty, what after that? Did he want to be her boyfriend? He couldn't remember the last time he'd wanted a relationship. Way before he became Axl Storm, definitely. Before Alex Raine, for sure. Back when all his prospects were hopeless and he might as well dream—

'Alex! What are you daydreaming about?'

He blinked at the object of his affection, who was getting to her feet and glaring at him from under her wild mane. Her hair had swept up even more leaves and detritus along the way. He thought he could see some cigarette butts and bits of broken glass in there too. *London, never change.*

'And don't interrupt me like that when I'm concentrating. It's hard to get people to stop noticing you.'

'Impossible, I should think,' he said, gazing at her.

She frowned at him. 'I've sealed off the garden,' she said, rummaging in her bag. 'No one should come in here now. Okay. When I light this –' she brandished a large candle '– it should show you what I'm seeing.'

'What are you seeing?' said Alex, but the candle was already bursting into light. It was a bright, eerie, cold light, and he was so fascinated by her lighting it without the aid of a match that he didn't immediately notice exactly what was being illuminated.

Then he did, and he stumbled backwards, falling onto a bench. Glowing in the darkness all around the peaceful garden were the pale, translucent shapes of … well, they had to be ghosts. A man in clerical robes, a World War Two soldier, a nurse. A trio in long white nightgowns, a woman in a corseted dress, a man in baggy breeches.

Every one of them so hideously disfigured in death that it didn't take long to work out why they were still here. None of these people had died peacefully or painlessly. They'd been bombed, they'd been burnt, and in the case of the three in the nightgowns, it looked like they'd died of the plague.

Worse still were the children, four of them, one still clutching a rag doll.

'Alex?'

That was Poppy – warm, beautiful, alive Poppy – leaning over him with concern. 'Are you all right? I know it's a lot. But I thought it would help if you could see what we're dealing with.'

'Witchcraft!' spat the ghost of the woman in the long dress.

'As it happens, yes,' said Poppy. She took Alex's hand in

hers before she turned to face them, and he appreciated that more than he could ever say.

'She admits! A witch!'

''Tis witchcraft kept us here these long years!'

That was mostly the older ghosts. Alex figured, somewhat deliriously, he could categorise them as Fire and Plague.

''Tis witchcraft did murder us,' pronounced the woman in the long dress, who'd clearly made herself the leader of the ghosts. 'What d'ye think caused the plague?'

The ghosts in the nightgowns nodded.

'And the fire that raged? Witches! Witches!'

'Nay, 'twas the Dutch,' said one of the children. Alex couldn't look at them.

The woman cuffed him around the head, as if he was still alive. 'Dutch? Whyever would the Dutch burn London with them still in it? Halfwit. 'Twas witches,' she proclaimed, in a self-satisfied manner.

'Now now, settle down,' said the nurse, who had a distinctly more modern look about her. But not by much, because she still wore a starched cap and apron. 'Everything is witches with them. I tried to explain about penicillin once, can you imagine? Now. Plague and fire, I think that's quite obvious,' she gestured to the older ghosts, 'and over here we have the Blitz. It did for us and the church, I'm afraid.'

'Most incommodious,' said the elderly vicar, who didn't look too badly off, unlike the other two. 'I never finished my sermon, you know.'

'Except to us, every night,' murmured the young soldier.

'Is there anything we can help you with? This interesting person,' the nurse gestured to Nannie the figurehead, who was swaying gently as if at sea, 'offered to bring us all back to life, but I'm not sure I particularly want her to.'

'I would,' said the young soldier wistfully. 'See my old mum again.'

Poppy glanced at Alex, who figured the least he could do was get to his feet. As he did, she addressed Nannie the figurehead.

'Can you do that?' she said doubtfully. 'Bring them back to life?'

'Aye! For Ah'm a real hag,' boasted Nannie. 'Yon carlin there is but a wee bairn.'

Poppy sighed, and Alex realised that, incredibly, she didn't seem to be afraid at all. Not of the horrifying ghosts, and not of the figurehead who was boasting of real powers.

'Nannie,' she said, 'I hate to break it to you, but you're not a real witch.'

'Am so!'

'You're not even a real person. You're made of wood—'

'An ye're made o' shite!' Nannie hissed.

'—and you're based on a character. In a poem.'

'Gypit hoor!' yelled Nannie. 'Ah wull sae mak' them real.'

'No, you won't,' said Poppy, and gestured to the ghosts. 'Guys, a little help here? She can't make you real. I mean – alive. Wait a second.' Poppy frowned at Nannie. 'You said real.'

'Naw, Ah didnae.'

'Yes, you did,' said Alex, and Poppy squeezed his hand.

'Yes, you did,' said the nurse.

'Good people, do not heed this creature!' cried the burnt woman, and the nurse rolled her eyes. 'Can not you see that it was made by the devil himself?'

'Aye, an' tae th' de'il Ah'll send ye!' spat Nannie.

'I liked the other one better,' said Alex.

'Me too. But this one thinks she's the real Nannie, and … wait, does anyone know what happened in her poem?'

'What poem?' said the burnt woman. ''Tis witchcraft, woman, can you not see?'

'"Tam O'Shanter,"' said Poppy. 'By Rabbie Burns. Um. Might be after your time,' she said apologetically to the older ghosts.

'Oh, mm, Burns, yes,' said the vicar. 'Nannie, in her cutty sark? Mmm. Yes.' He peered at Nannie, with one breast proudly bare, for a little too long. She waved her horsetail at him saucily.

'Vicar?' said the nurse patiently. 'The poem? What did this, er, person do?' To Poppy, she added, 'What is she exactly?'

'A figurehead,' said Poppy. 'Under a spell.'

'I see,' said the nurse. 'Well, you see stranger in the trenches. Do go on, vicar.'

'Oh. Mm. Yes. Well, you see, it's been a while, and my Scots is – well, do forgive my accent…'

It took a while, but eventually they got the relevant lines of the poem out of him. Nannie, the young witch in her scandalously short shift, had chased after Tam O'Shanter with all the power of the devil in her, but Tam's plucky mare, Maggie, was too fast for her, and all Nannie could catch was the horse's tail.

'The tail,' said Alex and Poppy at the same time, as Nannie swished hers about, her arms making that awful creaking sound. That explained something, at least.

'Why was she chasing him?' Poppy asked.

'Well, mm, you see, my dear, at the time, not that we still believe in such things now, of course...'

The vicar's rambling explanation was that Tam had stumbled upon a witch's sabbath, an unholy rite involving the devil and several grisly corpses.

'Presumably she was chasing him to add to their numbers,' the ghost of the vicar concluded.

'Just to make it clear, we don't do that any more,' Poppy assured Alex.

'Glad to hear it.' Alex told himself his shiver was purely because it was getting chilly out here.

'So, you chased after Tam, failed to catch him, and then what? Is that it?'

'Whit mair dae ye need?' said Nannie scornfully. She rocked more violently from side to side on her wooden base. 'Ah am a hag o' unco skill!'

'You're not real, Nannie,' Poppy said. 'What did you do after you caught the horse's tail?'

'Whit does it matter tae ye? Whin ah hae taken their souls – Ah mean brought them back tae lee—'

'What did she say?' said the soldier.

'You see! You see!' cried the burnt woman. 'The devil! She wishes to steal our immortal souls! Oh, Father,' she implored the priest, 'save us from this eternal torment!'

'How?' said the vicar. 'I'm as dead as you are, madam.'

Alex had to pretend his laugh was a cough.

'You're going to take their souls and try to become real?' said Poppy, and when Nannie lurched at her, furious, she held up a hand and the figurehead stopped, as if repelled.

Alex suddenly realised that Poppy's hand in his was vibrating slightly.

'You will do no such thing,' she said quietly.

Nannie scowled at her, and gnashed her wooden teeth, but she did not appear to be able to move.

'You are made of wood, and to wood you will return,' Poppy said. Power thrummed in her voice.

'Wheesht, rigwoodie hag!' screeched Nannie, but there was a hollow quality to her voice that hadn't been there before.

With one hand still outflung towards the figurehead, and the other locked into Alex's, Poppy turned to the ghosts and said, 'She can't bring you back to life. She wants to use you to make herself real.'

'She will not have us!' cried the burnt woman, gathering the others around her. 'She will not my soul to take!' She clasped the children in her arms, the children with their awful blackened faces and pustulent plague sores.

She began to pray, loudly, and after a moment the others joined in, albeit less stridently. Poppy glanced at the vicar, the nurse and the soldier.

'I've no wish to become real anyway,' said the nurse. Her apron was filthy, her starched cap was askew, and when Alex allowed himself to look at her properly, he could acknowledge that this was because half her head was missing. 'I'm tired, and I want to rest.'

'I have lived more years than all these together,' said the vicar, whose glasses were askew and whose cassock was bloodied. 'Why should I wish to return to that lonely life?'

The young soldier looked at them with more hope than expectation. His ammunition belt had left a blackened hole in half his torso. 'I just wanted to see my old mum,' he said.

'I'm sorry,' said Poppy, and she sounded it. 'But it's been eighty years since the war. There's no one left to see.'

For a moment Alex thought he would rebel, but he nodded, and put his hand on the vicar's shoulder. 'Reckon some of that prayin'll help us, padre?' he said.

'I see no reason why it shouldn't.'

The nurse nodded, then she paused and said, 'It won't hurt you, will it, Miss? If we pray?'

Poppy smiled. 'Pray away. I'm no more of the devil than you are. But this one, on the other hand…'

She turned back to Nannie, and Alex felt the power thrumming through her intensify. He felt as if he was vibrating, as if he was a conduit for the power she drew up through the earth.

Was this what it felt like to do real magic? It was electrifying, as if all his nerve endings had been supercharged.

'Ye reekit carlin!' snarled Nannie. Snarling was about all she could do now, because it appeared she was turning back to wood. 'Howfin hag! Ah curse ye tae th' de'il!'

The cold wind that had been swirling around the ruined church seemed to rise, sweeping leaves and debris, cigarette ends and broken glass, into a whirlwind around them. And still Poppy didn't falter or even sway, her hand held out firmly against the swearing, cursing figurehead.

Her hair flew out like a bell, and debris pinged off it. Alex's nerve endings began to throb.

'From wood you came,' Poppy called, her voice strong and steady, 'and to wood you shall return. All shall be as it should be. The souls of these people to their rightful resting places. The hag to the pages of a poem.'

The wind grew into a howl, and Alex couldn't tell if it was joined by the ghosts or the figurehead. He could feel power pulsing through him, from the ground up through his bones and his veins, buzzing along his skin to the hand that clasped Poppy's. He was only amazed he didn't glow.

'All shall be as it should be!' she repeated, voice rising over the swirling chaos. 'By my will, this unnatural possession will end! As I will it –' she was shouting now '– So! Will! It! Be!'

With an unearthly howl, the wind slammed into them, and then everything was silent and still.

The ghosts were gone. The figurehead was made of wood. All was as it should be.

Magic coursed through Alex like electricity, and when Poppy turned to face him her green and purple eyes were glowing in the dark.

Her chest rose and fell with every breath. Her hair rose like a cloud. The air between them crackled with magic.

Alex had never wanted a woman more in his life.

When her mouth met his he couldn't say who kissed

who. His hands were in her hair, hers tore at his collar, and his back hit the hard stone of the church wall.

All the electricity that had risen up through Alex slammed into his veins, and he was on fire for her.

His mouth devoured hers, those sweet plump lips and clever tongue that had spoken with such power. He physically couldn't stop kissing her, feasting on her mouth and drowning his senses in her. His hands were full of her, and it wasn't enough.

Her fingers drove into his hair, and sparks flew from them. Alex groaned and crushed her to him, her hips against his, but he needed more, so much more.

He spun her against the wall, and she twined her legs around his waist, grinding herself against him. Yes. *Yes.*

His hand dragged roughly up her bare thigh, under the silk of her skirt. He was shaking. He'd never needed anything this much before. He needed to touch her there where she rocked against him, needed to find her slick and hot and wanting him.

Impatient, she grabbed his hand and shoved it inside her knickers, and he found exactly what he wanted. Poppy's wordless moan vibrated through him.

Wordless. Alex had no concept of words, not any more. Besides, he had better uses for his mouth.

Her lips were on his neck, and she wriggled deliciously in his arms. Her hand dragged its way down his chest, probably singeing through his shirt as it went, and squirmed inside his trousers without seeming to even have to undo them.

'Mmm,' she purred. Her mouth found his again, and her

free arm clasped him close, her hair wrapping around them both like a cocoon. As if he had any intention of moving away!

He couldn't take it any more. 'Condom,' he gasped, the first word he'd managed since her lips touched his. 'Wallet.'

Her hands delving inside his jacket were almost more than he could take, but she found his wallet, the clever witch she was, and she found the condoms he kept there, and she unwrapped one and reached down and—

He had to take it from her, because if she touched him now he'd go off like a rocket. Poppy's lips were hot on his neck, and his hands shook like it was his first time, but he got the damn thing on and then he was inside her, and oh *God*, the magic he'd felt before was nothing to this.

She made a whimpering sound in her throat that drove him demented, and he couldn't have stopped if another bomb dropped on this church. He surged into her, slamming her against the wall, and she grabbed his head and bit his lip, nodding breathlessly.

Poppy's eyes glowed and glittered, light spilling from them even when she squeezed them shut.

His skin pulsed with fire. There were sparks behind his eyes. The entire world narrowed down to the two of them, just the heat and slickness, the friction, the desperate drive for more. The absolute wonder of Poppy. Was it magic? He didn't care. Her gasps and moans in his ear, her fingers trailing fire everywhere they touched. It was too much, and it wasn't enough, and it couldn't last—

A white-hot heat burned behind Alex's eyes, and then he was holding up a trembling Poppy as she wrapped her arms and legs around him and shook and gasped his name.

'Alex. Alex. *Yes.*'

He couldn't stand. It was a good job they were braced against the wall because Alex felt like his power cord had been cut. All he could do was hold her as they both came back down to earth.

Poppy's hair twined around them both, caressing and soothing.

'Holy shit.' She spoke into his neck, huffed out a laugh against his skin. 'That was ... I don't think I can move.'

'Me neither.' Her soft, luscious body was pressed against him, her legs locked tight around his waist, her arms around his neck. 'I don't want to.'

'No.' Her breasts – her lovely breasts, still cruelly concealed inside her dress – heaved. His own heart hammered like it would burst from his chest. 'My God. I'm amazed we didn't knock the rest of this place down.'

'Mmm.' Maybe they had. He didn't care. He was looking down at Poppy's lovely face, flushed and glowing, her lips swollen from his kisses. *My kisses. I did that.*

And he wanted to do it again, so he took her ripe lips with his, and she sighed and kissed him back. Her body snuggled against him, and damn if that didn't make him want to go again.

But then a sound intruded on his consciousness, and it was such a strange sound it ripped him from his reverie.

A door creaked open, the sound echoing loud and eerie in the enclosed space, and from outside came the sounds of panic and a dull, heavy roar.

'Um,' said Poppy, looking around somewhat muzzily. 'Was there a roof here before?'

'Nay, it be not safe here,' said a voice behind Alex, and his eyes slammed wide in horror. 'The blaze has already consumed St Botolph's, and if we shelter here it will spread and bake us inside like bread.'

Dread drove out all of the pulsing joy that had filled Alex, and he turned his head to see the interior of a stone church, with its roof and pews intact, lit through the windows by an orange glow.

'Holy shit,' whispered Poppy, and this time her tone was entirely different. 'What did we *do*?'

Chapter Ten

O utside the church, the streets were full of panic. People rushed by with wooden buckets, and still more hurried the other way with handcarts and armfuls of possessions. Mothers ran with crying babies in their arms.

It didn't take much to see what they were running from. The glow rose behind the church, so huge and red it was as if the sun was setting right in the middle of central London. A strong, hot wind blew towards it, tugging at Poppy's skirt. The roar of the fire was like a solid wall of sound, and the heat coming off it could be felt several streets away.

But how many streets?

Snow fell, only it wasn't snow. Poppy had never seen ash come down from the sky before. It swirled and eddied in the wind, settling hot on her skin. Her hair shook it off.

'We have to go,' she said. She grabbed Alex's hand as he stood, dumbstruck, outside the church. The woman within had dismissed them in no short order as 'vagrants and fornicators' and spat at them as they left. Outside the church, people barged and shoved, carrying possessions to be stacked inside.

Poppy looked around madly for fire engines, police, any sort of sanity.

A man ran down the hill with a pig over his shoulders.

'What is happening?' she whimpered. Five minutes ago she'd been coming her brains out and now the city was on fire and people were running around with pigs. 'Pigs,' she whispered.

'Poppy? Poppy! Snap out of it. Nothing's on fire. You hear me? This is some kind of illusion.'

'What?'

'Look around you. The people. The buildings. This church!' He waved at the very solid stone church that had been a ruin the last time she looked at it. The church where they'd just had sex. Really, really good sex. 'This isn't real. It can't be. Look, those shops have thatched roofs. I'm pretty sure that was, like, an office building last time I looked. No thatch.'

Poppy looked where he pointed. It was true. The buildings looked medieval, all exposed timber and patched up plaster. There was nothing like that in London now, specifically because of the Great Fire that had burnt most of the old city and killed several of those ghosts in the church.

The ghosts…

She looked doubtfully at the people hurrying by. In the shadows the fire created, everything was dark, and there were no streetlights. But it was enough to see the clothing of everyone around her. The long dresses and full skirts, the doublets and breeches.

'Maybe these are ghosts?' she said. 'Like the ones in the church?'

'Yes,' said Alex. He took both her hands. 'Exactly. This is all like those ghosts. Has to be.'

Hot wind blew her skirt stickily against her legs. 'Has to be?'

'Trust me, I'm an illusionist. This is like my glowing hands trick.'

'Yes, how do you—'

A boy nearly ran into them, begged a quick pardon, then raced up the hill to a house where a man in knee breeches stood anxiously looking out.

'All the way to Whittington's College? We must go then. If the wind changes...'

The door slammed behind them.

'This is a very detailed illusion,' said Poppy doubtfully. The wind was beginning to tangle her hair, which resisted petulantly, and her eyes stung a bit from the smoke.

'But it has to be an illusion,' said Alex. 'It can't be real, because time travel isn't real. Is it?'

'Course not,' said Poppy, with more confidence than she felt. 'Right. Yes. It's not real, so it can't hurt us, can it?'

'Exactly,' said Alex. 'We just need to get away from this church. Back to the car.'

He smiled at her, and began walking down towards the main road with her, and she tried not to notice the way the heat from the completely imaginary fire scorched one side of her face, or how they had to keep dodging a flow of people pushing up the hill, laden with carts and sacks.

'Alex?' Poppy said, as a family hurried past with a handcart of belongings and a loudly crying baby.

'Yeah?'

'Did … do you think we did this? When we…?'

His hand squeezed hers. 'What, we were so hot we conjured an image of the Great Fire of London?'

'Er … yeah.'

He paused, and turned to cup her face in his hand. 'Yes,' he said simply, and the heat in his gaze had nothing to do with the fire.

'It was pretty amazing, wasn't it,' she whispered.

'Amazing? No. Poppy,' said Alex, the firelight burnishing his handsome face into the visage of a god, 'I am not lying when I say that was the best sex of my life.'

Poppy went all gooey inside. 'Really?'

'Really and truly. I'm not surprised it set the city on fire.'

He leaned in and kissed her, and it was a soft, delightful kiss but it still made her toes curl.

'Oi! Love Lane's that way!' shouted a man hustling past with a sack over his shoulder.

Alex wrapped his arms around her and held her close. He didn't seem bothered by the weirdness around them.

'We should probably go though,' she said. 'Get back to the car, and, um…' She looked up at him shyly. 'Your place?'

He beamed at her. 'My place sounds great,' he said, and led her down the narrow alley towards the main street.

This was different too, the crowded road barely cobbled. Poppy's heels weren't even particularly high, but she was glad Alex was there to cling onto. He had a very reassuring sort of solidity to him. The man was made of pure muscle. Poppy didn't consider herself particularly sylph-like, but he'd had absolutely no problem holding her up while they—

'All right, we might have a slight problem,' he said, breaking into her thoughts. The smell of smoke was getting stronger now she thought about it, and the wind blowing down the street was sharp and fierce. 'The, er, illusion isn't fading.'

What had been Lower Thames Street was thronged with people, most of them moving east towards the Tower, nearly everyone carrying goods or animals or children. Horses moved along like icebergs in the flow, and up the street she thought she saw two people carrying a bed that still appeared to be occupied.

'Maybe we're taking it with us?'

'Great, that'll be awesome for driving home. Assuming I can find the car…'

But Poppy was looking further ahead, where the wider street was giving them a view west, towards London Bridge. London Bridge, which was…

Well, three things. Firstly, London Bridge was visible, which it shouldn't have been if the proper buildings were in their proper places.

Secondly, that London Bridge was built over like the Ponte Vecchio, only much shabbier and way less sturdy-looking.

This might have been in part because, thirdly, London Bridge was on fire.

'Uh, Alex?'

'Do you think it's safe to cross the road? Like, how real is this thing? Am I going to walk into traffic?' He was waving his hand about cautiously to the left, where it nearly hit a fretful horse whose rider glared down at them.

'Alex,' said Poppy distantly, 'the city is on fire.'

'Yeah, I know, isn't it mad? Look, I'm sure this is all some weird witch sex dream – has it happened before? Or is it just 'cos the sex was, y'know, hot enough to start a fire?' He grinned cockily at her.

Poppy did not feel so confident.

Iris had mentioned someone, maybe one of the Essex cousins, who had some magic door that let her see into the past or something. What if it was more than that? Time travel was not possible. It couldn't be. Somebody would have told her.

Only… Poppy was getting the distinct feeling there had been a few choice gaps in Iris's witch curriculum.

A woman sauntered down the narrow lane on their right. She was somewhat scantily dressed, but not in a manner which suggested she'd just fled her house in the middle of the night. Corsets and petticoats were visible, and so were her tattered stockings. Her lips were stained red.

'Nay, there still be time,' she called back. 'The fire has not crossed Botolph Lane yet.' She peered down the road. 'Mayhap. I'd not take another cull, were I you.'

Love Lane. Ha, yes. Poppy wondered how much love was being sold for up there, and found herself stepping a little closer to Alex. These days, it was known as Lovat Lane, and it was a picturesque, winding little alley with a church in the middle of it, leading just off from Monument Street.

She stopped dead.

Monument Street. Where the Monument was. That huge column, built to mark the outbreak of the Great Fire on nearby Pudding Lane.

'Um, Alex?' she said. She had to raise her voice above the roar of the fire and the wind.

'It's very realistic, isn't it,' he said, a frown beginning to appear between his brows. He was sweating.

'It … is an illusion, isn't it? It's not real? We can go up to the fire and it won't burn us?'

'Yes, of course. Of course. We could probably go straight through it.'

They stared at the fire. Flames were beginning to cross the next street, little sparks jumping and flying across the narrow gaps between thatched roofs.

'Right through it,' Alex said in a voice that only cracked slightly.

They stared at the fire some more. Poppy swiped at the ash sticking to the sweat on her face.

'You maybe want to try going around it?' Alex suggested off-handedly.

'Or away from it. Away from it seems good.'

'Good call,' said Alex, as if she'd just chosen a restaurant for dinner. 'The river?'

'River is an excellent choice.'

'River?' said the young lady whose virtue seemed to be for sale. She laughed. 'Nay, good mistress. Can not you see the bridge? 'Tis full of burning timbers. There be no escape that way.'

'The docks, then?' Poppy said, glancing at the girl, and then doing a double take. 'Elspeth?'

Poppy had seen her workmate that afternoon at Hubble Bubble, what seemed a lifetime ago now. Elspeth had agreed to cover Poppy's later hours so she could go to Sarah's party. *When talking figureheads seemed to be the worst of our problems.*

The girl looked taken aback. 'I can be Elspeth for you, mistress,' she said. 'If that's your wanting.' She looked over Poppy's green dress with an air of puzzlement. 'Be thou a mistress?' she said. 'What manner of strumpet wears a green night-rail? Or be it a shift and no time for thy stays?'

'Did you just call me a strumpet?' said Poppy.

'What about you, fine sir?' The girl who looked so much like Elspeth sauntered up to Alex with a calculating look in her eye. 'I bet a fellow like you has a maypole the size of a rolling pin.'

Alex's mouth dropped open.

'I'm sorry,' said Poppy, reaching over to shut it for him. 'You just look like a friend of mine.' Really, really like her. Her brain – because who else's was conjuring all this up? – must have peopled this illusion with faces from her memory. She'd probably see her mother and Iris here too, which was on its own a terrifying thought.

'Oh, we could be friends, Mistress Greensleeves,' purred the girl, reaching out to the flutering silk over Poppy's shoulder. Poppy flinched away.

'Your timbersome gentleman here knows how to please a woman, I'll be bound,' said the girl. 'He'll have had enough of them.'

'Hey, look,' said Poppy to Alex. 'Your reputation precedes you even into illusions.' He frowned at her in a distracted sort of way.

'If you secure a boat or a coach I shall come with you and we shall play at rantum-scantum until the fire has blown away.'

'Er, thanks,' said Poppy, backing away and taking the dumbstruck Alex with her. 'I'll bear that in mind.'

'If you come back, ask for Nellie!' called the girl, as Poppy dragged Alex across the street with her and began marching him away from the fire.

'Did I just get propositioned by an imaginary hooker?' he said, stumbling a little as he glanced back.

'We both did. It's nice to know bisexuality existed three hundred years ago. Come on. We have to get to the river.'

'Why?'

'Why?' Poppy stopped and stared at him. The fire glinted off the trickling perspiration on his face. The hair escaping his ponytail clung to his neck, and his shirt was starting to go transparent with sweat. 'Alex, the *city* is on *fire*. Right up there is Pudding Lane where this whole thing broke out. It's two streets away from us as we stand. Can't you feel it? Smell it? Do you really want to risk it?'

The wind blowing down what had been Lower Thames Street was getting stronger. It felt less like a wind now, and more like a vacuum, sucking them towards the fire.

'It can't be real,' Alex said uncertainly, glancing back at the raging inferno that was beginning to consume the houses on the corner of Botolph Street. As Poppy looked at it, the spire of a church was engulfed in flames.

She stepped in something that squelched, and grimaced. 'Well, the horse shit is real.'

'People have horses in real life,' murmured Alex, but he didn't sound very convinced.

'Well, I say we get to the river and make fools of ourselves escaping a fire that isn't there. It's either that or burn to death in a fire that is.'

Alex swallowed, and nodded, and they pushed through the oncoming wind to where a crowd was cramming into the narrow alley leading to the river. He wrapped his strong arm around her shoulders, peering over the heads of the crowd.

Poppy could see little. The air was beginning to thicken with smoke, and ahead was only darkness. The moon glowed, fat and sullen, through the haze of smoke.

She'd never really thought about what the Thames would look like without its frosting of electric lights. The answer was a dark, dark void. Darkness above and darkness below, with only the menacing light of the fire casting a glow on the rippling river.

'It's rammed all the way to the water,' Alex said. 'Is there another dock further down?'

'If all else fails there's the Tower,' Poppy said, as they were jostled from behind. 'Come on. Put those muscles to use, big guy.'

Alex's smile was tense as he steered her back through the crowd. People were pressing in on all sides now, anxious people in dirty clothing, reeking of smoke and sweat. It was getting much harder to pretend none of this was real.

On the street, the crowd was getting steadily thicker. Alex's pace quickened as he led Poppy through it, and more than once she stumbled.

'I can't do this in heels,' she said, and paused to unfasten them, trying to avoid the not-so-imaginary horse shit on one toe.

'You can't run around London barefoot!'

Poppy looked up at him wryly. 'You've clearly never been out clubbing with me,' she said, and held both heels in one hand as she straightened. The ground was warm beneath her feet, flakes of ash blowing along it to coat the dried mud and – well, other things the colour of mud.

'Let me guess,' said Alex, clamping his arm back around her as they braced themselves against the wind. 'The club caught on fire?'

'Look, just one time,' she said, and stepped out of the way of a man with a goat. She peered ahead as they began moving forwards. 'Look, there's the Tower, I think. That doesn't get burned in the fire.'

'It doesn't?'

'Remember we drove past it, whole and intact, earlier today?' *Three hundred-odd years in the future?*

'Oh yeah,' said Alex. 'I miss those carefree days of half an hour ago.'

The crowd was swelling now, with refugees flooding down the hill from the City. Poppy daren't look back, but when they tried the next alley leading to the river she couldn't help it.

The orange-white of it seared her eyeballs.

This route led to an imposing building, currently

guarded by men with pikes. Poppy had never seen a pike in real life. They could probably slice a person's head off without very much effort at all.

'No one's getting in,' she said, looking at the angry Londoners arguing with the guards.

'This is the Customs House, Miss,' said a man beside her. He was holding a small child. 'They be protecting the goods.'

'From what? If the fire gets here no pikestaff is going to stop it!'

The man shrugged, and turned away to try his luck elsewhere.

'This is like the *Titanic*,' Alex said. 'Wait, that's an idea.' He shouldered his way to the front of the crowd and muttered to Poppy, 'Try to look pregnant.'

Before she could ask how she was meant to do that, Alex was saying to the guards, 'Good sirs. I do entreat you. Allow us passage to the river? My wife is with child.'

'No entry,' said the guard. Sweat ran down his face from under his metal helmet.

'Surely you would not have us burn? Our unborn child. Sir, I beg of you.'

He was very convincing, even mustering a tear. Or maybe it was sweat. Poppy's own eyes were burning even as she cradled her belly and tried to look motherly.

'No entry,' said the guard. He glanced nervously at his colleague.

'On order of— Oi, who are you?' said the second guard to Alex, looking him up and down. And there was a lot of up when you looked at Alex.

'Well,' he straightened, apparently about to try a different tack, but he was cut off.

'What's them strange raiments you be wearing? I ain't never seen no breeches like that.'

'Like they long strossers they wear in Flanders, I have heard,' said the first guard.

'Flanders?' said the second. His eyes narrowed. 'Be thou a Dutchman?'

'That depends,' said Alex, smiling charmingly. 'Would it help?'

'A Dutchman?' cried someone nearby.

'They say a Dutchy started the fire!'

'Aye, for that thrashing on St James's Day!'

'Apparently not,' said Alex, smile becoming fixed. 'Poppy?'

'Yeah?'

'Run.'

His hand on her wrist was like a vice, which was just as well as Poppy had no hope of chasing after Alex through the suddenly angry mob on her own. Fear had turned to rage, and it was only Alex's sheer brute strength that got them through the crowded alley. Somebody tried to grab her arm, and it was her own fear rather than any intention that sent a wave of magical energy through her arm, shocking them away with a cry.

Oh fuck. If they think I'm a witch we're dead for sure.

The street wasn't much better. People were crowding around the Customs House entry, some of them waving torches. Poppy's heart hammered.

'We've got to make it to the Tower,' Alex shouted over the noise.

'They want to take the Tower!' screamed one of the guards.

'Fuck's sake,' Poppy muttered. She was shaking, just like she had when she'd banished whatever had been possessing the figurehead of the *Cutty Sark*. Just like she had when all that magical energy had led to the best sex of her life.

But she wasn't exactly in the same mood now. As Alex shoved and pushed at the crowd, the fear and anger in Poppy grew, feeding on each other, bubbling over into power inside her. She'd never been much good at potions, too slapdash and impatient, but what was brewing inside her right now was probably the strongest magic she'd ever made.

'Get them! They did start it! Kill them!'

They were going to die here, victims of some terrified mob, three hundred years before they were even born, just because she couldn't control her stupid chaotic magic.

One disaster after another. One inexplicable problem chasing the heels of the last. Every day a new mess to clear up, whilst her family and the Coven muttered behind her back about how hopeless she was.

Poppy shook with the force of emotion inside her, a rage more powerful than anything she'd ever known.

Alex glanced back at her, and in the light of the fire and the flickering torches he looked like a superhero.

Then something flew at his head, and he turned to brush it away. Poppy ducked as some filthy missile was aimed at her. Alex's arm shielded his face from another blow. Hands clawed at Poppy's bare arm. Fists flew at Alex, punching up at his mighty chest. Her hair repelled something hard. A piece of wood smashed into Alex, splintering all over his suit.

A blow struck Poppy's shoulder, but even as the pain registered she saw a pike's huge, deadly blade swinging at Alex's head.

'No!' she roared, and the sound echoed out in waves that flung the pike back, twirling over and over to bury itself, quivering, in the wall of the Customs House. The crowd were blown away from them like paper dolls, flying into the air until they crashed into each other, going down like dominos.

Her hair flew out like a halo, and from it ran a second shock wave.

Alex stared at her, a mixture of admiration and fear on his face that would stay with her forever.

'Run,' she whispered, and she never quite knew if she was telling him to leave her or not. But he still had her wrist in his grip, and he didn't seem inclined to let her go. He ran, and she stumbled after him, up the hill, her shoes long gone.

The road to the Tower had never been so long, so steep, and several times Poppy thought she would fall and be trampled by the crowd. But Alex never once let her go, crashing through the crowds like a battering ram. When she fell, he simply shook her upright again and continued on, up the hill to the shining white turrets ahead.

Once, Poppy glanced back, and against the searing red-white of the fire, the crowd surging after them looked like the legions of hell.

The Tower was in sight, its torches gleaming through the thick dark air, and Poppy was ready to fling herself into the moat when a coach and four clattered out of nowhere and lurched to a stop right in front of them.

The door slammed open and a woman in a red dress said, 'You'd better get in.'

Chapter Eleven

The lady – because by her gorgeous dress and extravagantly wonderful hat she was a lady – narrowed her eyes at the mob behind Alex and Poppy.

'I see,' she said, and withdrew a pistol from the folds of her skirt. She fired one shot low on the ground in front of the approaching mob. 'Get in. Pippin, drive.'

With that, she swung herself up onto the seat beside the driver. 'Now,' she added, as the horses began to move. 'I can do a lot but I can't hold off a torch-wielding mob. Get in or stay here.'

The carriage – a massive, ungainly thing with four horses in harness – was already clattering over the cobbles. Poppy grabbed the door and clambered in, reaching back for Alex, who let her pull him in after her, and the two of them fell back against the floor as the coach lurched away.

The pistol fired again from the driver's seat.

It was a rattling, jarring ride, and with Alex sprawled on top of her, Poppy couldn't move. She lay pinned there under him as the vehicle swung and swayed alarmingly around a corner.

'Are you—?' he began, and seemed to run out of words. There was a cut on his brow, and his filthy hair had escaped its tie. Somebody stank of horse shit, and she had no idea which of them it was. Probably both.

'I'm alive,' she said. 'So are you.'

Alex managed to get himself off her, and pulled her up to sit beside him on the leather seat. Poppy was glad he'd done that, because suddenly she was shaking too badly to move. All her muscles had turned to water.

Alex enfolded her in his arms, and he was shaking too.

'We're alive,' he said. 'We're alive. Oh, Poppy.'

His beautiful suit was torn at the shoulder, and coated with ash and mud and some kind of rotten fruit. His shirt was soaked through with sweat. When Poppy pressed her face against his neck, it was thick with grime.

She'd never been so grateful to be near anyone in her life.

'This really wasn't how I planned our date to go,' he said, and that seemed hysterically funny to Poppy.

'Oh my God. Like … how many hours ago were we at the *Cutty Sark*?'

'I don't know.' Alex twisted his arm to look at his wrist. 'About … two?'

That seemed even funnier to Poppy. As she giggled and sobbed in his arms, Alex managed to dig something out of his pocket.

'You know,' he said, 'I never thought to check my phone.'

'Phone?' Alarmed, Poppy felt for her bag, but she seemed to have lost it along with her shoes. All to be burnt in the fire that was sweeping the city. *Well, at least that won't leave any historical anachronisms.* 'I've lost mine.'

'No signal anyway. Poppy ... did we travel in time?'

She lifted her head and risked a glance out of the cloudy window. The orange glow rose up above the shadows of the buildings. 'I think so.'

The coach suddenly lurched to a stop, and she heard raised voices outside. Suddenly fearful that their rescue was not going as well as she'd hoped, Poppy tried to draw up some reserve of power, of magic, of any kind of energy, but she could barely move. The carriage rocked, and she heard people shouting. Someone thumped the outside of it. A face appeared at the window, angry and yelling.

Then the voice of the woman in red pierced the carriage: 'By my will, you will let us pass,' and Poppy felt the magic ripple over her as the crowd fell back.

'Oh,' she said.

'Oh?'

The carriage began moving again, and passed under a gatehouse.

'She's a witch,' said Poppy.

Alex was worried about Poppy.

She'd pronounced their saviour a witch, as if that made everything all right, and then curled up in his arms and apparently fallen asleep. He didn't blame her, really – he was exhausted too, and it wasn't as if he'd performed several impressive feats of magic that evening.

That thing she'd done outside the Customs House. Like a sort of shockwave that blew everyone away from them as if they were autumn leaves. Alex had seen that massive axe thing swinging at him, and knew he couldn't duck in time – and then it had simply tumbled away, as if it was a dandelion head.

His girlfriend was a witch. This wasn't news to him, but he'd never really ... appreciated it until now. All the things with the candles and the ghosts – if he thought hard enough about it, he could probably figure out how to fake that kind of thing. But that shockwave? That was superhero stuff.

Not to mention the time travel. Alex was still clinging to the comforting delusion that it had all been some kind of dream, but the aches and pains of the blows he'd been dealt before Poppy did her thing kind of exposed that for the pathetic fantasy it was.

He'd seen them attack her too, even after he'd tried to convince the guard she was pregnant. The ugliness of the mob had been terrifying. But maybe not as terrifying as the way he'd seen someone throw a rock or a lump of coal or something at Poppy and then watched it *bounce off her hair*.

Her hair lay curled protectively around her now, like a cloak, all soft and silky as if it had never turned into steel armour or anything. Magic hair. She really was Rapunzel.

He closed his eyes and rested his cheek against her head, but didn't get the chance to sleep before the carriage slowed. It tilted alarmingly as someone climbed down off it, and then the door was opening and the woman in red stood there.

The flickering lights from the carriage lamps illuminated alabaster skin and a dress like ruby wine, and that was all Alex saw before she swept onto the opposite seat and banged her hand on the roof.

Poppy stirred in his arms, and he held her protectively close as the carriage began moving off again, the horses' hooves loud on the cobbles.

Wait, he could hear the horses' hooves. The roar of the fire was still there, but not as desperately loud now.

'Right,' said the woman in red. She reached up to a sconce on the carriage wall and it came to life, candles flickering in it and the other lanterns around the little box. 'First things. I made the assumption that you are Poppy Thistlewood?'

Poppy nodded.

Poppy Thistlewood? Forget Rapunzel, I'm dating a hobbit.

'Good. I am Lilith Winterscale. One of your … cousins, from Essex.'

As Poppy straightened away from Alex, he was aware of her drawing herself up a bit more. The trembling, frightened girl lifted her chin and straightened her shoulders and faced the formidable woman opposite as an equal.

'Hi,' he said. 'I'm Alex.'

Lilith regarded him with absolute disinterest. 'I'm sure you are,' she said, and turned her attention back to Poppy. 'Iris called me earlier this evening, asking for help. She's very worried about you.'

Poppy's chin jutted. 'I can take care of myself.'

Lilith let her imperious gaze travel over Poppy's torn and filthy dress, the scratches and bruises on her arms, the inevitable debris in her hair, and gave the very merest smile.

'I can take you back home, but first we have to travel to my house.'

'Why?' said Alex sharply.

'Because that's where the door is. Unless you know another way to travel back to the twenty-first century?'

'Well, we got here in the first place,' Alex said.

'Yes.' Lilith still hadn't taken her eyes off Poppy. 'Do you have the faintest idea how?'

Poppy's pale cheeks coloured. 'Um, I don't... Something went ... wrong...'

'It frequently does, according to Iris. But nothing of this magnitude. Hmm. Strong emotions were involved, I imagine?'

At this juncture her gaze did flick briefly to Alex, regarding him as if he were no more than arm candy.

'I don't think that's any of your business,' Poppy said coldly.

'When I've got to drive a coach and four into a burning city you can bet it's my bloody business, young lady,' said Lilith. 'I know chaos magic is difficult, but surely Iris has taught you some self-control?'

'Hey, I have plenty of self—' Poppy began, and then her head tilted and she said, 'Chaos magic?'

'Yes. Everyone has a specialism. Mine is time. Iris makes things grow. You ... cause chaos.'

Poppy stared apparently blankly at the far wall.

'This wasn't explained to you?' Lilith said.

'No. Iris … she said everything is always chaos with me, she just didn't… I thought she meant it was because I wasn't trying,' Poppy said.

'Not trying? My dear, you just caused a magical surge I could feel thirty miles away. You have more power than I've seen in a long time. And I've seen a *long* time,' she added, with feeling.

'But … I can't control it. Sooner or later it's going to… Look at me and Alex. They could have killed us.'

Alex took her hand in his. He wasn't part of this conversation, and in fact didn't understand half of it, but he knew when Poppy needed assurance.

'Poppy,' Lilith began, and hesitated. 'Have you…'

She trailed off again, which for such a self-assured woman was odd.

'I think perhaps you need to have a frank conversation with Iris about this,' she said eventually. 'It seems there are things she's been keeping from you.'

'What kind of things?' said Poppy.

'Things I can't tell you,' Lilith said crisply. She smoothed her skirts. 'Ah, look. We're coming up to the Bow Bridge. In about three hundred and fifty years' time, just over there in those dark fields, the Olympic torch will be lit.'

'We're in Stratford?' said Poppy.

'Nearly.' Lilith turned her attention then to Alex, and now he was in her spotlight he really rather wished he wasn't. 'Now. You.'

'Hi?' he said.

The way Lilith looked at Alex was like being in an

airport scanner, one of those ones that saw through your clothes to the muscle and bone beneath. He shifted awkwardly, suddenly aware that he was filthy with sweat and grime.

'Are you any good with a pistol?' Lilith said suddenly.

'Uh,' he said. 'No. Not really. No.'

She sniffed. 'Pity. Once we get past Stratford the likelihood of highwaymen increases.'

'Highwaymen?'

'Yes. Don't worry.' Lilith casually withdrew the pistol from her skirts. 'They won't bother us.'

The coach stopped at Snaresbrook to change the horses, for what everyone assured them would be the most dangerous leg of the journey. Poppy overheard Lilith arguing with what she assumed to be the landlord of the inn, or coachman or whoever he was, who said that driving through Epping Forest at night was suicidal.

'We're witches,' said Poppy, mostly to herself. 'We'll survive.'

'Maybe ixnay on the itchesway,' Alex muttered. They were still inside the coach, because as Lilith pointed out their clothes had nearly got them killed in London, whilst fleeing the fire. What on earth would be made of them out here in the sticks was anyone's guess, but in Poppy's dark mind that guess involved a ducking stool and a hemp rope.

She sat with her bare feet up on the seat, arms around her knees, hair cloaking her. Alex kept trying to take her hand and talk to her, ask if she was cold, offer her his jacket – and Poppy couldn't bear it.

You cause chaos.

Her mother had always said it, but Poppy imagined there was a fondness to her despair. She'd been a messy, disorganised child, but that wasn't really chaos, was it? Her parents and teachers had got used to carrying extra pencils and socks because Poppy always lost hers, but that was normal, wasn't it?

'If I had a penny for every time you cause a mess, Poppy,' her mother used to say. Her school reports were full of comments like 'Poppy is an intelligent child but she needs to pay attention and organise her time better.' She'd been sent to educational psychologists to ascertain if her scattiness had a neurodevelopmental cause, but the conclusion was always that she just needed to apply herself better.

Iris had told her every witch had a speciality, and they'd soon discover Poppy's. But ten years later they hadn't. And now this Lilith, a woman Poppy had never met but who clearly knew Iris quite well, was telling her she had a speciality, and it was chaos.

Like the villain of a superhero movie.

You cause chaos. And today, the chaos she'd caused had nearly got her and Alex killed.

The coach clattered to a halt at some time in the early hours, outside a large house that loomed threateningly in the darkness. Alex helped a silent, subdued Poppy out of the carriage, every muscle and bone he had complaining along the way. The vehicle had all the ride comfort of being thrown down a hill in a barrel full of rocks.

Lilith had procured blankets for them, and some bread and cheese, and some flasks of something that tasted sour and unpleasant but was, after the heat and panic of the fire, the best thing Alex had ever drunk.

He was in such a state of shock he ate the bread and cheese without even worrying about the calories.

Poppy ate a little, then curled under her blanket to sleep. Alex wanted desperately to hold her, but she was tense and rigid, her responses monosyllabic. What did chaos magic even mean? Had Poppy caused them to travel in time?

He hunched in a corner of the carriage, wrapped in a blanket that made him itch, and watched her until he fell asleep.

The house was in a clearing in a dense, dark woodland. A lantern burned by the door, and a dim light was visible through one of the windows. There was no other light, until he glanced to his right and saw the glow of the fire, still visible over the treetops.

'How far are we from London?' he asked.

'About thirty miles. Thirty-five.' Lilith looked back the way they'd come. 'They say you could see it all the way in Oxford,' she said.

When Alex closed his eyes he remembered the heat, the crackle, the roar. The drag of the wind being sucked in by the fire. The shouting, the screams—

'Thank you, Pippin,' Lilith said, as the coach set off around the back of the house. 'Excellent driving, as always.

Now, you two. Come with me, and don't wake the household.'

She led them inside, through a door that was merely latched, and up a winding staircase. The lantern she carried illuminated very little apart from some dark panelling, the odd spooky portrait, and some very strange items arranged on a mantelpiece.

'Please tell me those are children's dolls,' he whispered, as they were led around corners, through antechambers and up and down short flights of stairs.

'If that makes you happy,' Poppy whispered back.

She had hold of his hand, for which he was profoundly grateful. This old house was like something from a horror film, and after all they didn't know Lilith at all. What if she was luring them to some terrible doom? They killed witches in this era, right, and people had seen Poppy actually doing magic back there in London, so—

Lilith stopped at a red door with an egg timer carved into it. She laid her palm against it, closed her eyes, and murmured something. Then she turned the key, and opened the door into …

into a hallway much like the one they stood in. Dark and plain, unlit – it was hard to see what was different about it.

'Um?' said Poppy.

'That's your present day, child. Don't be tiresome. It's been a long night and I've been on the outside of that carriage, which believe me is even worse than the inside.'

Alex felt Poppy tense, but she stepped bravely ahead, and as soon as his foot hit the other side of the door Alex could smell the difference.

It was a million small things: the lack of woodsmoke, for one thing, and the scent of dust heating up behind radiators. The smell of warm plastic you got when a computer had been running too long. Furniture polish. Shampoo.

'Someone in this house uses the same shampoo I do,' he said, and then a door opened and a voice said, 'Probably me, dear.'

Both Poppy and Alex jumped, mostly because the doorway behind the figure was full of bright electric light.

'Ah, Avery,' said Lilith. 'This is Poppy, and … Andy.'

'Alex,' Alex corrected.

Avery stepped forward and shook their hands. He was of average height, lightly bearded, and wore chandelier earrings and a T-shirt with a unicorn on it.

'Are we to be blessed with an explanation?' he asked, but the door behind them was already closing, and when Alex turned, Lilith was gone. 'I see. Forthcoming as ever. Well, I'm Avery, this is Beldam House, and you look like you could do with a cup of tea and a hot shower.'

Alex dug his phone out of his pocket. They'd been gone about six hours.

Chapter Twelve

Poppy woke to an unfamiliar bed being rattled by snores.

The latter was not completely unknown to her, but usually the snorer was Malkin or one of the other animals. The former was ... not as usual as it had been in her student days.

This wasn't Claudia's bed, which had always smelled of her perfume and the peculiar vegan fabric softener she used. It wasn't the sweaty, boozy sheets of a one-night stand, or the cheap mattress and unwashed pillow of student digs. It was a pleasantly fragranced, extremely comfortable bed, with a fluffy duvet and excellent pillows.

It also contained someone who could snore for Britain.

Her recollections of the last night being somewhat tangled with a nightmare, Poppy forced herself up through layers of sleep and turned her head. The room was dimly lit by morning light through the curtains, but not so dark that she couldn't see Alex beside her.

He was handsome even now, his damp hair tangled around his face, his lashes making long shadows on his cheeks. He lay on his back, mouth open, snorting and gargling in his sleep.

Well, at least there's one flaw to prove he's human. Poppy nudged him, and when he didn't stop snoring, gave his shoulder a shove. Too late, she remembered someone whacking him with a length of wood last night, and he came awake with a strangled gasp, reaching up to rub the offended joint.

'Ow!'

'Sorry.'

His eyes crunched up, and then he opened them just a tiny bit. 'Poppy?'

'Yeah.'

'Mmph.' He made to roll over, then frowned, and tugged his arm. Poppy realised her hair had twined around it, in a manner that definitely hadn't been accidental. 'C'n I have my arm back?'

'Oh. Yes. Sorry.' She tugged at her mane, which curled back around his arm. 'Just, um, give me a…'

Alex's eyes opened more fully then. He looked down at her hair, then up at her, and he smiled. A sleepy, lazy, comfortable smile that had Poppy's insides turning to jelly.

'It's taking me prisoner,' he said.

'It does seem to, er, like you,' Poppy said, and gave up. When she lay back down, her hair curled more firmly around his arm, as if to pull her closer. 'Oi! Stop it. That hurts.'

Alex grinned at her, and turned on his side, pulling her

against his chest. Her hair settled down, and Poppy fancied if it could make noises it would be purring.

'I think your hair and I are in agreement,' Alex murmured.

Poppy shifted in his arms. She appeared to have fallen asleep last night after her shower wearing absolutely nothing, and from the feel of it Alex – who had gallantly let her go first, and hadn't even suggested sharing – had done the same.

And he was … well, he was definitely appreciative of her nakedness. She could feel exactly how appreciative against her stomach.

'Well, hello,' she said.

His cheeks pinkened a little. 'Um. Ignore that. Can't help it.'

'You probably could,' said Poppy.

'Thing is, Rapunzel,' Alex said, gazing at her with those impossibly blue eyes, 'when it comes to you, I kind of can't.'

He had one brawny arm wrapped around her back, and her hair was almost petting it. Her fingers were definitely stroking his chest, and she was in full control of those. Poppy had to admit, her reasons for abstaining were becoming hard to remember.

Then she saw the bruise developing on his shoulder, and the little cut above his eyebrow, and she remembered what had happened last night, and why.

She felt her body draw away from him, and he let her go, looking puzzled.

'I didn't mean it like that,' he said. 'I can control myself. I promise.'

'Yes, but can I?' Suddenly cold, Poppy pulled the duvet up over herself, shrouding her nakedness from his view. She couldn't look at his face, his beautiful face, so instead she focused on a bit of his hair that had developed a weird kink from being slept on. 'Alex. Last time we had sex—'

'Really good sex,' Alex corrected her, eyes warming.

'Really *hot* sex,' Poppy corrected him back, trying not to think about exactly how good it had been. 'And then what happened?'

He shrugged. 'An adventure.'

'Adventure? Adventure?' Was he an idiot? 'We almost *died*. They tried to *kill* us.'

'I'm sure we'd have figured something—'

'They threw a pike at your head! It would have been like – like *Game of Thrones*! Splatter! Brain matter everywhere!'

'But that didn't happen,' Alex said calmly, 'because you did your witch mojo and saved us.'

'Witch mojo?' Her voice was rising into hysteria. 'I don't even— That's not the point. Listen to me. A few streets away from where we were shagging like bunnies, the Great Fire of London broke out. Do you think that's a coincidence?'

Alex looked nonplussed. 'Well,' he said. 'Yes?'

'That all that power and heat and my total inability to control myself had absolutely nothing to do with the raging inferno devouring the entire city?'

'The fire started by accident,' Alex said. 'In a … pie shop or something. Right?'

'Bakery,' Poppy said distractedly. 'Don't you see? We

started the fire, Alex. You and me. Or more to the point … me, enabled by you.'

'Enabled,' said Alex.

'Yes. When you…'

Alex's eyebrows rose. 'Fucked your brains out?'

Despite that being completely true, and Alex being naked beside her in bed, Poppy felt herself blush.

'Poppy. Look. I'm not saying that wasn't amazing sex, because it was, but surely you've had great sex before?'

Not quite like that. But she couldn't bring herself to say it. His ego was already big enough.

'Did anything like this ever happen before? Even something small? Curtains on fire or something? Scorched bedsheets?'

He was laughing at her. Poppy glowered at him.

'I'm serious.'

'So am I. If it's never happened before, why assume that's what caused it this time?'

'Because I was all … juiced up. Magically speaking,' Poppy said. Her face was probably scarlet by now.

'And you never got horny after doing magic before?'

'Not … not really, no.' But she'd never felt like this with anyone before. What if they had sex again, and something even worse happened?

'Then why assume it's just with me? Scientifically speaking that doesn't make much sense.'

Poppy looked at him sideways. 'Scientifically speaking? Alex, you are an *actor*.'

'Hey, I took high school science. We should test this hypothesis,' he said.

'Hyp— What are you even talking about? We might have started the Great Fire of London.'

'What, because we were so hot?' He mimed making a telephone call. 'Hello, Kings of Leon? Our sex was literally on fire, any advice?'

'That's not funny.'

'Poppy.' He reached out and touched her cheek. 'You know that can't be true. The Great Fire of London is a historical fact. And we were streets away.'

'Yes, *only* streets! A hundred yards at best. Look, I know you're going to say I'm overreacting, but listen. What's happened whenever I've been with you? The ghost mummy, the figureheads, the bloody Great Fire of London!'

Alex looked like he wanted to argue that, but wisely didn't.

'That stage accident. Your whole show cancelled.'

He looked away at that, his blue eyes shuttered.

'You said that was the cursed pendant,' he said.

'Yes, and Fiona said we should have lifted the curse before the pendant was destroyed.'

Alex shrugged, as well as a person can while lying down. 'It's not our fault it was destroyed! Are you telling me the curse flew out and disseminated itself all over the Central Line?'

'Well, it would explain a lot!'

'About the Central Line, maybe,' Alex conceded. 'But what happened at the *Cutty Sark* was nowhere near the Central Line. It's on the DLR. And Tower Hill is on the, the…'

'Circle,' Poppy supplied. 'But you're two minutes from Tower Gateway, and then it joins the branch that goes to…?'

Alex looked utterly lost. Clearly, he hadn't been in London long if he didn't walk around with a map of the Tube in his head like proper Londoners.

'Bank,' she said. 'Where you can change for every bloody line there is, including the Central.'

'Poppy.' Alex rolled on his back and rubbed his face, her hair having agreed to spare his arm. 'Are you telling me the curse has an Oyster pass?'

'Don't be ridiculous,' Poppy said. 'I'm just saying…' But what was she saying? It sounded ridiculous even to her own ears. She turned away from him, her eyes suddenly burning in a way that had nothing to do with last night's smoke. 'You know why that pendant was cursed in the first place?'

Alex was silent a moment. Then he said, 'You said it was an accident.'

'Yes. An accident. Because…'

Because Claudia was wrapped around another woman, snogging as if her life depended on it, a woman in a designer dress, with a job that required a briefcase, the sort of woman she could take home to meet her parents—

'Something about your ex?'

Poppy's hair covered her face like a curtain. 'I saw her with someone else. And I … I was a little bit drunk, and … I don't really remember what happened. But the pendant got cursed.'

Alex sighed. 'Got pissed, did something stupid. Poppy. This is literally the story of everyone's twenties.'

'But most people don't have special chaos magic!' Poppy sobbed.

His hand touched her shoulder. Her hair shrugged him off.

'Most of the time I can stop really bad stuff happening, but don't you see? When I was upset about Claudia the pendant got cursed, and it's been unleashing chaos all over London, and then when we—'

'The chaos happened before we had sex, Poppy,' Alex reminded her gently.

'Because of the pendant! And then the worst bit happened when we had sex.'

There was a pause. 'Is that really what you think?' Alex said.

Poppy, who was sobbing now, could only make a muffled sound. She liked Alex – really liked him, his sense of humour, the way he smiled, the scent of his skin, the absolute fire he stoked in her when he put his hands and mouth on her – but she couldn't risk everything just for a nice smile and some amazing biceps.

'Where were you on 9/11?' Alex asked.

That was surprising enough to halt her tears. 'What? What has that got to do with anything?'

'I saw it on the morning news,' he said. 'It was like a weird movie. It didn't seem real. Do you remember?'

'I – well, yes. I was… Mum told me when she picked me up from school. All the teachers had been really weird and I didn't understand why.'

'And where were you?'

'At school, I told you.' When he said nothing, she rolled onto her back and glared at him. 'In Northamptonshire.'

Alex lay on his side, just watching her. 'Right. And had you just ... broken up with an ex?'

She sighed impatiently. 'I was six. And I know what you're doing.'

'Do you? What about the London Tube bombings, then? A few years later, wasn't it? Where were you?'

'At school. The teacher called us in for a special assembly.' Her mum had done a lot of praying that weekend. 'We lived in Oxford then.'

'Oxford. Broken up with anyone that week, had you? Got drunk? Angry about something?'

'Can you just make the point you're trying to make, here?'

'My point is that sometimes stuff just happens, Poppy, and it's not all because of you. And honestly, it's kind of arrogant to assume it is.'

'Arrogant?'

'Yeah. What about... I dunno, the fall of Rome? Assassination of Archduke Franz Ferdinand? The meteor that killed all the dinosaurs? Did you travel back in time to cause them when you failed an exam, or tried beer for the first time, or had your first orgasm?'

Poppy crossed her arms and glared at the ceiling. 'No,' she said sulkily.

'Then why do you think the Great Fire of London was your fault?'

She risked a glance at him then. He was so annoying,

just lying there being all ... reasonable, and logical. How dare he?

He's an actor, she told herself. *He's a fake. A pretend magician. And he's absolutely in love with himself.*

Why does that make you think he can't also be right?

'All right,' she said, 'but it's a hell of a coincidence. You've got to admit that.'

'Sure,' said Alex. 'But maybe you should go and ask some of your witch pals about it before you jump to conclusions?'

She caused chaos. It was what she always did. And since she'd met Alex the chaos had intensified. And then they'd had sex – explosive, amazing sex – and everything had gone insane.

But it was going insane before you had sex, a little voice reminded her. A little voice that sounded suspiciously like Alex's. And nothing bad had happened when they'd kissed. Or that time she saw him fresh from the shower, wearing just a towel, and had nearly spontaneously combusted on the spot.

She sniffed, and swiped at her eyes.

'This doesn't mean we can just start having sex again,' she said.

Alex's mouth turned up a little at the corners. His eyes damn well twinkled.

'I should talk to Iris first,' Poppy said.

'Of course.'

She eyed him suspiciously. He was smiling at her, and the duvet had fallen back to reveal that absurd chest of his.

All muscular and naked. Those bold, swirling tattoos, like a maze she wanted to trace with her tongue.

'Alex,' she said warningly.

'I said "of course",' he protested, rolling those big broad shoulders of his. 'I respect your boundaries.'

'Yes.' She should not feel disappointed. That was stupid. Five minutes ago she'd convinced herself she could never have sex with him, or indeed anyone else, ever again. She shouldn't be thinking about what his nipple would taste like.

She cleared her throat. 'We should get dressed and go and thank our host. Whoever he is.'

'Good plan,' said Alex, and looked around the room. 'Dressed in what?'

Poppy winced. That was an own goal. Avery had said he'd do what he could with their clothes, but they'd been pretty wrecked, and there was no sign of them now. Alex's phone and wallet were on the bedside table. That was all.

'Oh dear,' said Alex cheerfully. He threw back the duvet. 'I guess I could maybe wrap a sheet around me and go and see.' He stood and stretched extravagantly. 'What do you think?'

Poppy told herself not to look at him. He was doing it on purpose, and they both knew it, and she had self-control, dammit, she did not need to look at…

Okay, his face. He was smirking. That was a turn-off.

Dammit, then her gaze sunk helplessly down to his chest, and that wasn't a turn-off, not by any stretch of the imagination. His tattoos are silly, she told herself, but they weren't. Those strong, curving lines made him look like some kind of ancient warrior come to life.

He had a bruise on his shoulder, ripening nicely into multiple colours, and she should have felt bad about that but she was already moving onto his abs, and those, what were they called, those sort of arrows above his hipbones that seemed to point down to—

Oh.

'Holy shit,' she whispered.

'Yeah. Probably wouldn't do to walk around a stranger's house completely naked,' Alex said, as if he was actually discussing points of etiquette with her. 'Could you help me get the sheet off the bed?'

Poppy could not. She lay staring at him, helpless.

'Poppy?'

'Did you—' she croaked, and swallowed, and pointed. 'Did you have that last night?'

Alex looked down at his groin. 'Yes?' he said. 'They're not, you know, interchangeable. I didn't swap it out for my date-night penis.'

'But it's…'

Alex put his hands on his hips and waited, which didn't help because he was basically just framing the damn thing now. It was practically sitting up and waving at her.

All the words that went through Poppy's head were extremely unhelpful. Words like *massive* and *stupendous* and *could-batter-down-a-door*.

'… not physically possible,' she managed, and used her own hand to push her face away. Her eyes stayed on it though, like a dancer doing a pirouette.

'It felt pretty physically possible last night,' Alex said.

'No.' Poppy pulled her hair in front of her face. 'Nuh-uh. Nope. Can't. I'm never having sex with you again. Not now I've seen it.'

Alex was laughing, the bastard.

'How do you even get condoms on it?' she moaned, covering her face with her hands for good measure.

'I think this is the most back-handed compliment I've ever been paid,' he said. She felt the bed dip as he got back onto it, and then he was reaching for her, and she scrambled away, not sure if she was serious or not, but because her hair was all over her face she misjudged the size of the bed and toppled onto the floor.

'Poppy!' Alex was still laughing as he climbed over the bed and looked down at her. 'Are you all right?'

Oh God, it was even worse from this angle.

There was a tap at the door. 'Is everything all right? I heard—'

Their host took in Alex kneeling on the bed, Poppy sprawled on the floor, and the extremely naked state of both of them and said brightly, 'Never mind! So sorry.' The door closed with a very decisive click. The key *on the inside of it* turned.

Poppy curled into a ball and moaned.

She felt Alex taking her hands and pulling her up off the floor, and she went with him, because why not. He was going to club her to death with that thing, which had clearly doubled in size overnight, and in the unlikely event she survived, her orgasm would probably trigger the apocalypse.

Alex held her on his lap, which didn't exactly help matters, and gently rubbed her back until she felt she could lift her head and look him in the eye. Damn him, damn him. She could feel that absurd thing throbbing against her backside, and even as she told herself logically that the physics of the situation were completely impossible, her hormones decided that the opposite was true.

It felt pretty good last night, they reminded her. *We really enjoyed it last night.*

'Shut up,' Poppy muttered, trying to ignore the definite warmth in certain areas of her body.

'I didn't say anything,' said Alex, but he didn't need to, because his body was doing the talking and it had a really convincing argument.

'This is not physically possible,' she said, even as her body disagreed with her in strenuous terms and started flagrantly rubbing itself all over his.

'Not that I'm not flattered,' Alex said, his voice breaking a little as her breasts brushed over his chest, 'but do you actually mean it?'

Poppy wanted to say that she did, but it didn't appear she was in control any more. Her back arched, offering her to him, and her hair had given up all pretences and become completely prehensile, wrapping around Alex as if to keep her where it wanted her.

Poppy gave up.

'You'll probably be the death of me,' she said, swinging her leg over his and rocking against that monstrous appendage that was definitely going to kill her. *Oh God, that feels good.*

Alex looked up at her, sitting there biting her lip and trying not to moan. 'I'll try not to be.'

'We might start the apocalypse.'

'It's a chance I'm willing to take.'

She looked down at him, his absurdly handsome face and perfect body, and then she peeked down further and sighed. 'You'd better have another condom.'

Alex grinned and tipped her onto her back, laughing, as he reached for his wallet.

'Do you have to order them specially?' she said, lying there watching him roll it on.

'Keep up that sweet talk, and this'll all be over too soon,' he said.

'What sweet talk?' Poppy said, but then he was sliding down next to her and his mouth was on hers, and oh, it was so lovely to kiss him. It was as if his mouth had been made to please hers.

And not just her mouth. Alex kissed the mole on her jaw, gently took her earlobe between his teeth, and then he kissed his way down her neck to her breasts, where he lingered for a while, getting to know them.

'I've been wild about these,' he told her, 'since that first night in your shop.' His hair tickled her skin.

'You have?'

'Mmm. You were wearing that purple dress. With the neckline.' He traced it with his fingertips, and she shivered. 'And you sat there brushing my hair and all I could think about was you leaning over me, and all this,' he shaped her breasts with both hands, 'against the back of my neck.'

'That a fantasy of yours, huh?' she asked, as he did

something to her nipple with his tongue that made her breath hitch.

'It is now,' he said, looking up at her with the devil in his eyes. His hands were exploring her now, discovering the contours of her hips and belly. Poppy arched into his touch, like a cat.

'Hmm,' he said, leaning back a bit as he got to her belly button. 'What do we have here?'

Poppy shrugged. 'I went out with this dude who was training to be a piercer.'

Alex grinned. 'And is this all he pierced?'

She swatted him. 'He did my rook and daith, and those are parts of the ear,' she added, as his eyebrows rose. 'He wanted to do the, er, other stuff, but I said I wasn't letting a trainee stick metal in my erogenous zones, and I stand by that.'

'It's a good rule,' Alex agreed. His fingers slipped between her legs. 'But I feel for the purposes of clarity I really should check this for myself.'

She laughed, and then it turned into a sharp gasp.

'You're right,' he said. 'No metal at all.'

Poppy grabbed him and kissed him, and Alex simply settled in beside her, stroking and kissing her until she was squirming in his arms.

'Maybe,' she breathed against his mouth, 'we could re-evaluate whether you'll fit now.'

'Well, we could,' said Alex, and did something with his fingers that had her clutching his shoulders and hissing, 'or I had another idea.'

His other idea involved checking for piercings with his

tongue, and that had Poppy's hips flying six inches off the mattress. He simply slid his big arm beneath her waist and kept on torturing her until she genuinely thought she might burst into flames, and still he didn't stop.

He didn't stop until she'd nearly passed out, and then he loomed over her, somewhat smugly, and said, 'Anything on fire?'

Poppy grabbed him by the hips and shoved him into place. 'You, you bastard, if you don't get inside me.'

He saluted her. 'Your wish is my command,' he said, and did exactly as she asked.

Poppy moaned. Alex moaned. 'Is it,' he began, and shook his head. 'Run out of witty banter,' he gasped, and simply drove into her.

Poppy wrapped her legs around him and held on. Alex had been a machine last night, and he was again this morning. He hammered another orgasm out of her, and then his lips met hers in the sweetest kiss.

It was infuriating, how he could be so adorable at a time like this.

'Poppy,' he murmured.

'Yeah?'

'When we get back to London,' he was breathing hard now, and sweat trickled down his face, 'we're going back to my place.'

'Yes,' she said, sliding her fingers into his hair.

'And we're going straight to bed.'

'Yes.'

'And we're not getting out of it.' He groaned as she kissed his neck. 'Maybe ever.'

And Poppy, who at that moment didn't care in the very slightest about curses or chaos or fires, just nodded and said, 'Yes.'

'Yes,' Alex agreed, kissing her, and then he was moving fast and hard, and her name was on his lips as he came.

She lay there with him, idly stroking the muscles in his back as her hair wrapped around them both, and when he lifted his head she smiled at him.

'No apocalypse?' he said.

Poppy looked around at the entirely unchanged bedroom. 'No apocalypse,' she agreed.

Alex rolled the muscles in his shoulders and stretched. 'You see,' he said with satisfaction. 'Science.'

Chapter Thirteen

G ranted, the whole idea of magic being real was still new to Alex, but he was quite astonished to find Avery had left their clothes outside the bedroom door, not only cleaned and pressed but restored to perfect order. No rips, no mud or bodily excretions. His suit even smelled good.

'Do you think he takes orders?' he asked Poppy as they tried to navigate the house.

Finding the main stairs was enough of a trial. The rooms led into each other, corridors twisted and turned and ended abruptly, doors frequently opened onto walls. Eventually, a large hairy dog took pity on them and appeared to communicate to Poppy how to get downstairs.

'So, you can talk to animals?'

'Anyone can talk to animals,' Poppy said. 'It's understanding what they're saying that's the trick.'

'A trick you can do?'

She shrugged.

'Poppy.' He stopped her halfway down the stairs. 'You do know how amazing you are, right?'

Her gaze slid away from him. 'I'm not even a very good witch,' she said.

'Shut up. I've been faking this stuff half my life, and you can just do it without thinking. You're a miracle.'

Her cheeks pinkened and she nudged him, embarrassed. Alex kissed her cheek and they turned the corner, where the stairs split into two and an enormous painting faced them.

'Is that Lilith? The woman who rescued us last night?'

Alex peered at it. Lilith smouldered from the painting, still dressed in red with her hair in glamorous waves. Behind her, airships filled the painted sky. 'Why's she dressed like Rita Hayworth?'

'Because it's an excellent look,' said Poppy, and he supposed he agreed. It wasn't as good a look as Poppy's wild hair, sylph-like green dress and bare feet though.

Alex supposed she could probably wear a hessian sack and the entrails of her enemies and he'd still find her irresistible at this point. He was becoming aware he was absolutely infatuated with her.

He held her hand as they continued cautiously downstairs, to the strangest front hall he'd ever seen.

There was a fire roaring under the stairs, with no sign of a chimney. The mantelpiece was covered with dozens of little dolls, some knitted, some sewn, some clearly fashion dolls repurposed for … well, he didn't know what.

They were … they were not children's dolls. That was pretty clear.

Twining around the staircase were the branches of a

willow tree, which appeared to be growing out of the floor. An umbrella stand by the door held several broomsticks. A spiderweb up in one corner appeared to contain a portrait of Anne Boleyn.

The dog gave a yip, and one of the many doors opened to reveal a massive, truly cavernous kitchen. The sort you saw in period dramas, staffed by dozens of people in corsets, with a fireplace big enough to roast a whole pig on a spit.

Currently, however, it only held one person, who wore a pinafore dress and chignon and appeared to be consulting a very large old book whilst stirring a huge mixing bowl.

'Hello? We were looking for Avery.'

The woman looked up and smiled. Her lipstick was a frosted blue and her nails had little skulls on them. 'You found me.'

Alex hesitated. Beside him, so did Poppy.

'Genderfluidity takes on an extra dimension when you're a witch. Are you hungry? I have crumpets and raisin bran muffins.'

'How did you know?' Alex and Poppy both said at once. Alex hadn't had crumpets for breakfast for years. If Avery also had Nutella he'd be in seventh heaven.

Avery shrugged. 'It's what I do. I know what people want and how to make it happen.'

'Like a fairy godmother?' said Poppy, taking a seat at the massive table.

'If you like.'

'And—did you, like … make us new clothes, or…?'

Avery laughed. 'Do you really want to know? I got you

some shoes, too, Poppy. And a shawl, because it's nippy out there.' She paused, and said, with gentle meaning, 'Consider them a gift from your Essex cousins. Beldam House always provides whatever you need.'

Poppy nodded, but she seemed as nonplussed as Alex by that.

'I've some salve for those bruises, too,' Avery said. 'Pitchfork mob, was it?'

'Torches,' Poppy said.

'Ah. Well, you're lucky there were no burns. I'd have to whip up a new batch of ointment, and I'm right out of moon daisies.'

Avery put a plate of fresh, gently steaming muffins in front of Poppy, glanced at her and added a large mug of tea, and then set out the crumpets and, yes, Nutella, in front of Alex.

'Actual witchcraft,' he breathed. Fuck the calories. He'd done enough exercise last night and, heh, this morning.

Poppy laughed. 'He's still new to all this. So – where's Lilith? We should thank her.'

'Absolutely no idea,' said Avery cheerfully, going back to the mixing bowl. 'Did you see the portrait on the stairs?'

'It looked like World War Two?' Poppy said.

'Yes. An old favourite of hers. Despite knowing perfectly well she can't kill Hitler, she still keeps trying. How are the muffins?'

'Amazing,' said Poppy, in the same sorts of tones she'd been using naked in bed with Alex quite recently. 'I haven't had these in years. Every time I try to make them, they're a disaster.' She picked up the butter Avery set in front of her.

'It will not surprise you,' she told Alex 'to learn I am a terrible cook.'

He smiled, slathered a crumpet with Nutella, and said, 'I'm mediocre. We can order takeout.'

'Ah, young love,' said Avery. 'I've let Iris know you're safe, by the way. She says she's got a new phone waiting for you at home.'

'How did she know?' Poppy said.

'You lose your phone a lot?' Alex suggested, and she wrinkled her nose in annoyance. He bit into the muffin and moaned. Bliss. Actual heaven.

'Wow. You usually only look like that when you're naked,' said Poppy, and he nearly choked on heaven.

Avery nodded at an iPad set up on the table. 'I've been watching your shows, Alex. I mean, Axl. You're very good. How do you do the beheading trick?'

'Trade secret,' Alex said, swallowing.

'Honey, we're actual witches,' Poppy said.

'Fair enough. Right, so the important thing to remember...'

His phone pinged a few times in his pocket, but he ignored it as he explained the beheading trick to Avery and finished breakfast. Poppy's feet played with his under the table, and he gave serious thought to dragging her back upstairs to that bed, but Avery said there was a train they could get in half an hour if they left sharpish.

Alex was adding up how long it would take them to get back in his bed in Holborn, as Poppy tried on a pair of neat boots and wrapped herself in a soft woollen shawl.

'It's much warmer than it looks,' she said.

'It's not just that,' said Avery. 'Come on, I get shouted at when I delay the trains.'

The village station was a pretty little place with hanging baskets and painted fretwork, and the train came shortly after they'd waved goodbye to Avery. Compared to the carriage ride they'd endured the night before, it was like gliding on a magic carpet.

Alex was more concerned with kissing and cuddling Poppy than he was with his surroundings, and so he didn't really notice until a camera flash went off right inside the carriage that people were looking at them.

Well, he was kind of famous. Face on buses, kind of thing. And the stage disaster had obviously been in the news. Jonno told him there were memes about it. But usually, people didn't recognise Alex when he was in civvies, his hair tied back, no make-up. He did that on purpose.

'Er, Poppy?'

'Mmm?' She was nuzzling his neck.

'People are, uh, watching us.'

'Mmm. That's probably because you look like a rockstar Viking. Also you're making out with me on the train.' She swatted at her hair. 'And I think my hair just ate a coffee stirrer off the floor.'

'Some of them are taking pictures. You might end up online.'

She shrugged. 'So? I'm a Millennial, Alex. My life is online.'

'Yeah, but…' He shifted uneasily. He was going to have to tell her. 'People aren't always … kind about people who

… date people who … are kind of famous.'

She looked up at him, her mismatched eyes laughing. 'Alex, love, I'm a witch. I'll just put a hex on them.'

'Will you really?'

'No.' She snuggled against his chest, and Alex should have told her the truth then, but he took the coward's way out, and said nothing.

At Liverpool Street, she baulked at the Central Line – 'Yes, I know it's probably not cursed, but do you want to take the risk?' – and they got a cab back to Alex's flat. The route took them past St Paul's Cathedral, its dome rising majestically above the city. The dome that had famously been added after the whole cathedral burned to ashes during the Great Fire of London.

Was that only last night? Had it really happened? The ache in his shoulder and the sting on his forehead said it had, but he still couldn't quite believe it.

'What about your car?' Poppy asked, as they went up the steps to his flat.

'Oh, crap. It'll have been towed or clamped by now, won't it?' Maybe he could get Jonno to do something about it. Surely that was the sort of thing he was there for.

'Maybe. Sorry. I shouldn't have made you abandon it like that.'

'Well, it could have been worse. Imagine if we'd driven into the Great Fire of London. They'd definitely have burnt us at the stake.'

'Witches weren't burned,' Poppy said, as Alex picked up a parcel before he unlocked the door.

'I think they'd have made an exception,' Alex said. 'This says it's for you.'

Poppy frowned at the label, then laughed. 'It's Iris. She's sent my new phone here. How did she know?'

Alex grabbed her around the waist and drew her into the flat after him. Her hips nestled in against his so very nicely, and she raised her eyebrows at what she felt there, as if they hadn't been snogging all the way back. 'Rapunzel, anyone with eyes could see where this was going to go.'

'They could? Iris knew?'

Alex let his hands wander down over the curve of her waist to her lovely backside, and rocked his hips against hers. All that kissing and fondling on the train had left him in a state of semi-desperation.

'Iris definitely knew what my intentions were. I'm assuming this is her way of saying she doesn't object.'

In his pocket, Alex's phone rang. He took it out, saw it was Jonno, and silenced the ringer before he tossed it on the sofa.

'Now, I think we had some very important plans involving my bed...'

Later, as they sat in bed, Poppy set up her new phone and Alex used his to order takeout, as promised. He leaned back against the headboard and watched her fiddle with the settings, laugh at herself setting up voice recognition, and pick at the boring health food snacks which were the only things he had to eat in the place. Her hair sprawled contentedly over the pillows, her cheeks were flushed and her lips were gently swollen from all the kissing they'd been doing.

Alex would not have been surprised if bluebirds had fluttered in and begun plaiting her hair.

I am so completely in love with you.

Which was insane. This time last week he hadn't known she existed. Sure, he'd fallen into bed with girls this quickly before, but never into actual love. But pretty much ever since he'd turned around and seen Poppy standing there on the street, the rain sparkling around her like fairy dust, he'd never stopped thinking about her.

He hadn't felt this kind of excitement since he'd first picked up his great-grandpa's magic set.

At the thought, he felt his smile dim a bit. Great-Grandpa Raine, whom Alex had never met. The dusty magic set in Grandma's attic, with those photos of The Great Magnifico looking so glamorous and suave. He wanted to tell Poppy how he'd felt when he'd first opened that box, and how he'd known he was meant to be an illusionist, and how he felt the same way now, that he was meant to be with her. But how could he, without telling her everything else?

Without telling her why he'd needed to become Axl Storm. Why being Alex Raine wasn't enough. Why he'd locked Sandy Grubb away in a box inside his head he never wanted to open.

He watched Poppy's hair steal a vegetable crisp as she poked at her phone. Surely she would understand, though? It wasn't as if he'd done anything terrible. It was just a thing to explain to her, so there would be no secrets between them.

Like the one Sarah told you about Poppy being adopted. Well … well, sure, but that wasn't his secret to tell, was it? She'd be mad if she found out he knew, probably. But that was a conversation for another day.

'Poppy?' he said, and she looked up. 'I want to tell you something.'

Her eyebrows quirked. 'Sounds ominous.'

'It isn't. It's just … there's some stuff about myself I haven't told you.'

That got her attention. Poppy put down her phone and said, 'Bad stuff?'

'No! Not … well, not good stuff, but I haven't done anything bad, I promise. Just … some things I'd rather forget.'

Poppy shook her head. 'Like getting drunk and cursing an amulet that set chaos loose all over London?'

'Er … well, now you put it that way.'

But she was frowning now. 'I really should call Iris. Is this thing working yet?' She poked at her phone again.

'And we will, I just need to—'

But her attention was gone. 'I need to know what Lilith meant about my magic being chaos. Like … am I just going to be stuck making messes for ever? Stumbling from one disaster to another? I can't do that, Alex.' Her shoulders slumped slightly. 'I can't.'

'Hey.' He reached out to her. 'Even if you do, I'll still be here.'

'Yeah, sure,' said Poppy, tapping at her phone again.

'Hey! I will.' *I love you.* 'I'll always be here for you.'

Right then Poppy's phone rang, and she shot Alex a distracted look. 'Yeah, 'cos you're known for your attention span when it comes to women. Iris!' she answered her phone before he could respond to that. 'Yes, I'm at Alex's. How did you know?'

She got out of bed, and Alex watched her go longingly. She wore his T-shirt and nothing else, and he wanted to drag her back down into bed and never let her leave again.

You're not known for your attention span when it comes to women. Well ... no. He supposed he wasn't, and that was why that stung. Yelena had probably told her that. But Alex had never got emotionally involved like this before. He'd never been in love with any of the others. He'd never wanted a relationship with them, to wake up every morning beside them, argue over what to watch on TV, cook a terrible dinner, snog in public until teenagers jeered at them.

He wanted all those things with Poppy. And he could show her that, surely, just by sticking around. Hell, he had nothing else to do. While the insurance people did their interminable work he was just hanging around doing nothing. He could take the time to plan some really lovely things with Poppy, show her what she meant to him.

He really ought to be working on his act, maybe thinking up some new tricks, maybe filming some TikToks to keep interest up, but right now all he could think about was Poppy, Poppy, Poppy.

He could hear her in the living room now, talking in agitated tones. Was Iris angry with her for what had happened yesterday? Did she think Poppy had done it on purpose, or that she lacked control? Surely, as Poppy's mentor, that was at least half her fault.

Or maybe she was telling Poppy what Sarah had told Alex. Maybe this was a really serious situation, and she needed his support.

He got out of bed and pulled his boxers on. And a T-shirt. It wouldn't do to let her get distracted at this point.

Alex Raine, you are one conceited bastard.

He met her in the doorway, and immediately could tell whatever Iris had said, it hadn't been good.

'I've been summoned,' she said flatly.

She pushed past him and started searching for her clothes.

'By Iris?'

'By the Coven. Apparently we "need to talk".'

Alex winced. 'You want me to come with you?'

Poppy shuddered. 'Nooo. No offence, Alex, but the last thing this needs is an outsider.'

He couldn't help feeling a bit stung by that. Hadn't he and Poppy just gone through an intense bonding experience? Several of them, in fact? Wasn't he completely in love with her?

All right, she didn't know that yet, and it was probably best not to scare her.

She stopped, holding her bra in one hand. 'I didn't mean it like that. I just mean … it's something Fiona said—'

'Fiona from last night? Is she telling tales on you?'

'No. I mean – yes. But she said…' Poppy looked up at him, and shook her head. 'It's witch stuff, okay? You being there wouldn't help.'

'I could try,' he offered, taking her bra and flinging it back on the bed. At least, that was his intention. Poppy held onto her bra and glared at him.

'Is that your solution to everything? Sex? Look, I know it's good and everything, but there's more to life sometimes, you know?'

'Hey.' He stepped back. 'I do know that. I do have feelings.'

'I never said you didn't.' She fastened her bra without looking at him. 'But face it, Alex. You do have a bit of a reputation.'

That hurt all the more for being true.

'You were seeing Yelena when we met, and that was just last week. Every photo of you online, you're with a different girl. You're a player.'

Alex stared, dumbstruck, as Poppy went around pulling on the rest of her clothes.

'Is that what you think?' he managed.

'What? No. I mean— Yes.' She paused, boots in hand. 'I don't mean— Look, I know you're not a long term kind of guy. We're having fun, yes? But sooner or later—' She broke off.

'Sooner or later what?'

'It doesn't matter.'

Alex heard the harshness in his own voice as he repeated, 'Sooner or later what, Poppy?'

'There'll be some reason you break up with me. There always is,' she added, half to herself.

'What's that supposed to mean?'

She exhaled hard. 'I'm just … not the sort of girl guys like you date, am I?'

Alex could only stare at her. She wasn't like any sort of girl he'd dated. Or even met. She wasn't like anybody.

She fiddled with her hair and didn't look at him. 'Can we talk about this another time? I'm in enough shit as it is. I don't need to have a fight with you too.'

She made to move past him, and Alex darted in front of her. 'You think this is just about sex?'

'Isn't it?' She tried to step around him again, and Alex reached to take her arm.

Her hair shot out and shoved him away.

'Fuck's sake,' Poppy hissed, and he wasn't sure if she was talking to him or her hair. She laughed bitterly. 'Well, if that isn't the perfect demonstration!'

'Of what?' Her hair had been as strong as any limb. Alex's wrist felt bruised.

'Of why this isn't a long-term prospect! Even my hair is chaotic, Alex. Sooner or later, you'll get tired of all the constant "adventures" and just want to go and do your show six nights a week. Where you're inundated with sexy half-dressed Valkyries who know perfectly well you're only in it for the sex.'

'Poppy.' She moved past him then, and he chased her out into the living room. 'Why are you being weird about this?'

She stiffened at that, but kept on moving.

'Poppy! This is not about sex! Not for me.'

'Well, what else is it? Hmm? You want to spend your entire life being rescued from the wrong century? Or being stalked by ghost mummies, or mad living figurehead things? That's just this *week*. Lilith said my magic was chaos and she wasn't joking.'

'Lilith, who you've never even met before? How did she know?'

'I don't know! Maybe Iris told her!'

'Iris told her and not you?'

'Well, who else would she have learned it from?'

'I don't know, maybe your real parents?'

The words were out before he could stop them.

Poppy went more still than any of those painted figureheads. 'What did you say?'

Fuck. *Fuck.* 'Nothing. I didn't mean anything.'

'My real parents?' Poppy stared blindly at nothing. 'My mum and dad are not…'

'It was something your cousin said,' Alex said miserably, 'but she was high, and—'

'Sarah? Sarah was high? Sarah, the goddamn paragon of virtue, against whom all others are measured, was high? Christ, Alex, try and make up something more realistic next time will you?'

And with that she whirled out the door.

'Poppy!'

It hadn't even shut before she was back, but against all Alex's hopes all she did was march to the sofa, pick up her phone, and march back out again.

'If there even is a next time,' she retorted, and was gone.

Chapter Fourteen

P oppy was right outside the Tube station when she
realised she didn't have an Oyster card or payment
set up on her phone. If she stood outside fiddling with it
now, Alex might come after her, and this time she might not
be able to control herself. If she had another episode like she
had that night at Customs House, and knocked everyone
out—

No. She had to calm down. She was inevitably going to
face some unpleasantness with Iris, and she needed a clear
head for that. Not to be wound up and on the edge of more
chaos.

'Why didn't you come straight back here?' That had
been Iris's question, and as Poppy tried to find a polite way
to explain what she'd been doing all afternoon, Fiona's
voice had come from the background.

'Isn't it obvious? That pretty boy has seduced her. I did
warn her… It'll all end in tears. Wasn't he already seeing
someone when they met?'

Alex the seducer. Alex the womaniser. Alex who had made her forget that she couldn't control herself. Alex who would inevitably hurt her, or whom she would hurt even worse.

'Girls like me don't go out with girls like you.' *'Congratulations on scoring with the weirdo.'* *'You're not really the kind of girl I could take home to my parents.'*

'Why are you being weird about this?'

He hadn't meant it like that. Probably. But it had still hurt. Poppy had seen those pictures of Alex online when she'd looked up his show last week – and all the girls hanging off his arm had been glamorous stunners. None of them looked like the sort of girl whose hair collected cigarette butts or accidentally cursed the whole Central Line.

Alex was gorgeous, and successful, and could have any woman he wanted. Judging by those photos, he more or less had. Poppy was just … a diversion. A weird girl. Just like Edward the baronet's son had gone back to his gorgeous fiancée, just like Claudia had shagged the hot businesswoman. Just like all of them.

Bleakly, Poppy hailed a cab and told the driver she'd pay him on arrival. Iris had better be willing to stump up for this.

Dark clouds threatened the sky, and the cabbie said he hadn't thought rain was forecast.

'Well, sometimes these things come out of nowhere,' Poppy said.

One of the things she'd loved when she first came to London was the incredible array of cultural sites. The ancient Tower, the historic churches, the blue plaques signifying that someone important or interesting had lived in such a house or another. The sites of major discoveries, speeches, premieres. The battles, the riots.

The cemeteries, with their unquiet dead. The furious shades of those unjustly murdered. There were streets in Whitechapel where Poppy simply refused to go, because of the blood and terror of the Ripper's work that lingered, no matter how hard she tried to block it out.

As the cab drove her north, it passed so very many angry, wretched souls.

Her phone rang twice with Alex's number. He sent her texts.

I'm sorry.

I shouldn't have said it.

The last thing I want to do is upset you.

You mean a great deal to me.

She turned the phone face down on the seat. Maybe he meant it. He probably did. Alex was not in himself a mean-spirited person, but she genuinely didn't think he thought that much about the impact he had on other people.

Yelena had told her about the string of broken hearts Alex left behind him. He'd shagged half the cast of his show by all accounts, and any groupie who took his fancy. The man had never kept it in his pants before, why should he change now?

Because I want him to.

Because despite barely knowing him, she really liked him. She wanted more than a fling with him. But that was probably what every poor deluded girl thought, especially after she'd experienced what he had to offer between the sheets.

Her phone rang again. The name on the screen said *Mum*. Dammit, her parents were staying in London for a few days, at some Christian retreat in Limehouse. Her dad had wanted to visit the Tower and Mum had wanted to see a show—

Only they weren't her parents. Were they? Common sense told her Alex was winding her up because he was hurt, or had been wound up by Sarah. Only, Sarah didn't have a sense of humour and Poppy just couldn't imagine her getting high. And even if she had … why would she say such a thing?

Had Poppy ruined her engagement party to the extent that Sarah felt the need to be vindictive?

It did seem out of character. But then it also did for Alex.

Poppy thought back to all the times in her childhood when it had seemed like she was an alien from another planet. Her parents loved her, for sure; there had never been any doubt in Poppy's mind that she was wanted and cherished. But she wasn't actually very much *like* them.

All those glances at the school gates. Were they because Poppy was such a livewire, or because she was a cuckoo in the nest?

'Cor, this rain came out of nowhere,' said the cabbie. He was shouting above the sound of it.

'Yeah,' said Poppy, who hadn't even heard it until now.

'You got a brolly, love?'

'Uh, no. It's okay, there's not far to go, you can park right outside.'

'In Highgate?' He whistled.

'Trust me on this.'

And sure enough, there was a parking space right outside the excessively gothic frontage of Ivy Cottage. 'I'll be right back with the fare,' Poppy promised.

She marched into the house, the gates and doors unlocking themselves in front of her, and into the kitchen, where Iris sat with Fiona and Sylvia. Poppy ignored them, and went straight to Iris's handbag on the counter.

'And good afternoon to you, too,' Iris said.

'Cab fare,' Poppy said, extracting Iris's purse without looking at any of them. 'I'll pay you back.'

'Poppy, we need to talk very seriously about something,' said Iris.

'You bet we bloody do,' said Poppy, and marched back out into the pouring rain. Her hair flattened into a cloak around her.

She handed the driver his fare, and said, 'Be careful out there. I really mean that.'

She stood for a moment as he drove off, half expecting him to crash before he reached the corner. But the cab disappeared, and Poppy had to face the music.

She took a deep breath, stalked back inside the house,

and before any of them could speak, said, 'Do I have chaos magic from my parents?'

Whatever they'd been going to say to her clearly went up in smoke. All three witches – Iris in her immaculate tailoring, Sylvia in her velvet scarves and jangling jewellery, Fiona with her expensive highlights – went still, and then turned to look at each other.

'Oh Poppy,' said Iris. 'I'm afraid it's much more complicated than that.'

There was a mini supermarket just round the corner from Alex's flat. He arrived home with a six-pack of beer, a bottle of whiskey and a truly impressive amount of junk food, just as the delivery driver brought the delicious Thai food he and Poppy had ordered.

Alex glared at it, then ate it all in one go, washing it down with two cans of beer.

When was the last time he'd had a beer? He could barely remember. The odd sophisticated cocktail, for sure, carefully atoned for the next day in the gym. Sometimes a glass of wine with dinner, but it was all empty calories and Alex had a physique to maintain.

What was he, after all, without his rock-hard abs and his massive biceps? How many tickets would he sell if his jaw went flabby, how many followers would his socials have if he developed a dad bod?

He poured another beer and shoved a handful of crisps into his mouth. Who cared about any of that now? His show was dead, and the only girl he'd ever really liked had just called him a man-whore and walked out.

One of her earrings lay on the table. He'd found it in the bed, a confection of silver and amethyst with a suggestion of butterfly wings. It was so perfectly Poppy it nearly made him cry.

He cracked open the whiskey.

Thus wallowing, he was caught unawares by his phone ringing. It was Jonno.

'Oh mate,' he said. 'Am I glad it's you. I really need a mate right now.'

'Two mates in one go,' said Jonno. 'Careful, Axl Storm, you're sounding very Aussie there.'

'Who cares?' said Alex. 'I should have told her, Jonno. I was on the brink of it, and I bottled it.'

'Told who what?' Jonno said. 'Look, we've got bigger problems than that.'

'What could possibly be bigger?' Alex wailed.

Okay, he was drunk.

'Have you checked your socials today?' Jonno said. 'News sites? Anything like that?'

'No, I've been...'

'Bloody incommunicado, that's what you've been,' Jonno said. 'I don't even want to know why. Look. We have a proper problem here. Get your laptop and Google yourself.'

Alex did, although it took a few tries. '*Axl Storm: what to do about your cancelled ticket,*' he read out the top result. 'What help is that supposed to be to me, Jonno?'

'I don't mean Axl Storm. I mean Alex Raine. Or even Sandy Grubb.'

Alex actually felt the blood drain from his face. 'Sandy Grubb?' he said in a low voice.

'Yeah. Got your attention now?'

He certainly had. Alex typed the name in unsteadily, his heart hammering, and when the result came up he could only stare in sick horror.

Shock as magician hunk revealed to be HATED soap star!

You won't BELIEVE what sexy Axl Storm used to look like!

Remember Collingwood High? *You'll never guess what Evil Percy Beaker looks like now!*

Alex shut his laptop hard. He thought he was going to be sick.

'Alex?' The voice came from the phone he'd set down on the table. 'You still there?'

Barely. 'How?' Alex managed.

'Some chick filmed a TikTok of a party and said she remembered you from *Surf Rescue*.'

'*Surf Rescue*?' It had been a dire daytime soap at the time, he was amazed anyone remembered it. But it was just dross. It didn't bring up the sort of memories *Collingwood High* and Percy Beaker did. 'What's this got to do with *Surf Rescue*?'

'Someone in her comments went to school with you.

They appear to be the only person in the world who realised the hot guy from *Surf Rescue* used to be the fat kid in *Collingwood High*.'

A kaleidoscope of images swirled before Alex. Everyone he'd gone to school with, all those faces he'd tried to forget. All the jeers and the taunts and the false accusations.

'But I moved schools,' he mumbled. 'The other side of the city. I took three buses.'

'Well, it's someone who remembers you from that period. From your neighbourhood or something. They put two and two together.' Jonno's voice gentled. 'It was only a matter of time, Alex. We knew sooner or later it would happen. Someone would find an old VHS of *Collingwood High* and digitise it—'

'It never went to VHS. Once they stopped screening it, it disappeared. Remember, there was that scandal about one of the storylines being racist. The network buried it.'

'People taped stuff at home, Alex.'

'Fifteen years ago? Did they?'

Jonno sighed, and Alex knew semantics wouldn't get him anywhere.

'How bad is it?' he asked. 'Have they – have they found the message boards yet?'

'No. But you know the saying. Nothing on the Internet ever goes away.'

Alex wanted to cry. It would only be a matter of time now. He had a social media team, and PR people and all that, but there was nothing they could really do about a news story like this.

It'll be tomorrow's chip paper. That's what his gran had

said at the time, but his gran had reckoned without the Internet.

'Look, we could parlay it into publicity,' said Jonno encouragingly. 'Look at the kid from *Collingwood High*, see how fit he is now! You could do interviews with men's magazines about your fitness—'

'To promote what, Jonno? The show's dead. The theatre's ruined and the insurance investigators think we have unsafe practices.'

'But we don't, and they will conclude this, and then we'll be back on the road,' Jonno said. 'I also thought there could be a useful mental health aspect here, you know, look what happens when you bully a child actor—'

'Stop it,' said Alex.

'But what was allowed to happen to you was—'

'The worst period of my life and I'd rather pretend it never happened,' Alex snapped. 'Just drop it, okay? I don't want to think about it now.'

Jonno was silent a moment. Then he said, 'You're going to have to think about it eventually.'

'I know,' said Alex. His gaze fell on Poppy's earring. 'But not today.'

Poppy folded her arms and leaned against the counter. 'Talk,' she said.

'Poppy,' said Fiona. 'You should have come straight back here. You do understand we need to talk to you about your very serious loss of control yesterday?'

'No,' said Iris, her gaze steady on Poppy. 'We don't. Or at least, not without telling her the truth first.'

Poppy's stomach felt hollow. She dragged in a breath and tried to look like she was in control.

'The truth,' said Sylvia. 'Iris... Do you mean...?'

'I mean about who you are,' Iris said, still looking at Poppy. 'We've kept it from you, my love, because we thought it would keep you safe. We didn't want you to be burdened with it.'

'With what?' said Poppy.

The three witches looked at each other.

'My friend Zoe has two adopted children,' offered Fiona. 'They're completely and utterly her children. But she was always open with them about it.'

'And my parents weren't with me?' said Poppy. She found she was shaking.

'It was their decision,' said Iris. 'Once we'd sent you in the right direction we had to let you go.'

'We did spells, the three of us,' said Sylvia. 'All joined in, to make it more powerful. To make sure you went to the right home.'

'To people who would love you and care for you,' said Fiona.

'To your real parents,' said Iris. She sat forward slightly, and said, 'Parenting isn't about biology, Poppy. It's about who cares for you, who loves you unconditionally. Who sits up all night with you when you're ill, and helps with your homework, and picks out the mushrooms from the sauce when you don't like them. That's who we wanted for you. That's the magic we did.'

Poppy willed tears not to come to her eyes. She couldn't fault their spell, because after all, she'd had a happy childhood secure in the knowledge that she was loved unconditionally. But…

'But they're not my – my biological parents,' she said.

The Coven looked at each other again. Poppy wondered if they could communicate telepathically. She wouldn't put it past them.

'No,' said Iris eventually.

Poppy let out a breath, and with it what felt like all the breath she'd ever had. She sagged like a balloon.

'Sit down, Poppy dear,' said Sylvia.

'You really would be better off on a chair,' Fiona said.

'Fiona, fetch the gin,' said Iris.

To Poppy's astonishment, Fiona did just that. Fiona, who'd always been exasperated with Poppy's youth and inexperience, and treated her like nothing so much as the work-experience girl, was bringing her gin and pouring it into a glass. A large glass.

'Of course, it really ought to be a small batch variety,' she said, and there was the Fiona Poppy knew. 'We've been subscribing to a gin box, and – no, you're right, not the time.'

Gin in hand, Poppy grudgingly sat at the table with them. And even as she did, she realised the dynamic had already changed. She'd never sat at the table with them before. This put her on their footing. An equal.

She sipped the gin. 'Well?' she said. 'I presume you're going to tell me who my biological parents are?' A terrifying thought struck her. 'Oh God. It's not one of you, is it?'

'Good heavens, no,' laughed Sylvia. 'My children have grandchildren of their own.'

'Mine are at primary school,' said Fiona.

'It isn't as simple as that,' said Iris.

Iris had never spoken much about her life before Poppy came into it. She mentioned various paramours, some of which she called husband, but in such a way Poppy had never taken her seriously. She'd certainly never mentioned children.

'My parents are witches though?' Poppy said. 'My mother at least.'

That had to be the case. Poppy's mum and dad – her adopted mum and dad – were about as magical as an old sock. Iris had told Poppy over and over that sometimes magic was hereditary and sometimes it came out of nowhere, but surely the sort of power she had must have come from somewhere.

Again, that pause. Poppy drank her gin.

'In a manner of speaking,' said Iris eventually.

'For fuck's sake, Iris. Stop giving me riddles. Just tell me the truth. Are they dead? Are they evil? Are they in jail? Did you kill them?'

'Those are all perfectly sensible questions, and in response may I say how proud of you we all are,' said Sylvia. She reached for the gin and poured herself some.

'Proud of me? I thought I was here for a bollocking,' said Poppy.

'No, it's time to tell you the truth. Poppy, your … mother … was known to us as Else.'

Fiona and Sylvia both flinched.

'Else? What was that pause for? Is she my mother or isn't she?'

'It's … hard to explain.'

'*Try.*'

'Well.' Iris looked at the others. 'I knew Else as a female … person.'

'But she wasn't always female?' Poppy asked, thinking of Avery this morning. She hadn't asked whether Avery's appearance changed cosmetically, or physically. It hadn't felt like the sort of question you could ask someone you'd only just met.

'Else was … something of a trickster. She could change her outward appearance as easily as putting on a new coat. Presenting as male gave her no trouble whatsoever, and I believe she lived as male for quite some time. This is why it's tricky to say exactly which of your parents she actually was. Possibly both.'

'How?' said Poppy, then held up her hand as her imagination began supplying ideas. 'No, I don't want to know. So she was a trickster witch? She … played pranks?'

'Rather more than pranks,' said Fiona. 'Did you ever hear of the assassination of Archduke Franz Ferdinand?'

'Now now. Lilith said that was an immovable point in history, and there was no way of knowing Else was involved,' Iris said.

'Besides, her grasp of politics wasn't that sharp,' said Sylvia. 'She'd never have actually planned out the First World War like that.'

'Politics bored her,' agreed Iris. 'Which was interesting, because where else can you cause the most chaos? But she always preferred splashier things. Wars, usually. Disasters.'

'The Great Fire of London,' Poppy whispered.

'Yes, that was probably one of hers,' said Sylvia. 'She loved fire. Loved the crackle and the heat, and the sheer unpredictability of it.'

Poppy poured more gin, and drank it neat.

'Guess where I was last night,' she said.

There was silence. Poppy thought Fiona was sniffing the air discreetly.

'I have showered since,' she said, rolling her eyes. 'And my dress was… laundered. Do I still smell of smoke?'

Another pause, this one more tactful. 'No dear, you smell like you just rolled out of Alex's bed,' said Sylvia, and Poppy's face burned hot enough to start a whole new fire.

'He knew I was adopted,' she said, to cover her embarrassment. 'My horrible cousin Sarah told him.'

'Sarah?'

'The one whose engagement party it was. She got high, apparently. Which is unlike her.'

'Hmm,' said Iris.

The witches exchanged another glance.

'Will you stop doing that?' Poppy snapped. 'Say it out loud. I'm not psychic.'

'You could be,' said Sylvia mildly.

'Probably not,' said Iris. 'I'm sorry, Poppy. Look, here's the story as we know it.' She poured herself a gin, took a large drink, and began.

'There are more witches in London than most people realise. Not as many as in the countryside; more witches feel more comfortable in a rural setting. But many of us thrive here. Maggie Silver, Tia Bon Amie, Providence Chatter.'

'I thought Providence had gone back to Lancashire,' said Fiona.

'No, she was just visiting.'

'For thirty years, she was just visiting,' said Sylvia. 'What about Lettice Lane?'

'Oh yes. Down in Limehouse? Either way, Poppy, there are quite a few of us. And as I'm sure you can see even from a small sample, we're not the sort of people who … find it easy to form a consensus.'

'Hah!' said Fiona.

'But every one of us agreed we had to do something about Else.'

'Do something?' Poppy said uneasily. 'What do you mean?'

Iris got up and flicked on the kettle. She got out some mugs and lingered over the tea blends on the shelf, choosing a careful amount from several different jars. She refused to answer Poppy until she sat down, and neither would the others. She watched Poppy take a sip before she spoke.

'None of us took it lightly,' she said. 'It's important that you know that. Witches don't have a law, or a police force, or even a leader.'

At such a blatant falsehood from the woman who had taken charge ever since Poppy had known her, she picked up her gin and poured it into her tea.

'Within a coven … perhaps,' Iris conceded.

'Hmph,' said Fiona.

'Nonetheless. We have no formal rulings or procedures for this. For us to all come together and agree something must be done about Else was a serious, serious undertaking.'

'I've never heard of it happening before,' said Sylvia.

'Or since,' said Fiona.

'It took a very long time for us to come to the conclusion that she must be stopped,' Iris said. 'But when the time came, she'd already foiled us.'

'The one time she planned ahead,' said Sylvia.

'It wasn't a particularly complicated plan,' argued Fiona.

'Am I to be privy to this plan?' said Poppy impatiently.

'Else,' said Iris, 'had already siphoned most of her power into a vessel. There was so little left we couldn't even detect her. She was almost ordinary.'

'Almost,' said Sylvia darkly.

'A vessel?' said Poppy, imagining some kind of boat. Perhaps a chest, like Pandora's Box. Wait, was that a box? Poppy thought she might have read that it was in fact a jar…

She was aware even as she thought this that she was kidding herself. A glance at the three faces looking at her over their tea confirmed it.

'I'm the bloody vessel, aren't I?' she said flatly.

They nodded.

A vessel.

Poppy used to make jewellery out of beads and cotton threads as a child. She had a pet rabbit called Mr Magoo and was distraught when he died. Once when she was about nine, she had a dream about being a princess and woke up to find her hair had plaited itself into a corona around her head. She first kissed a boy when she was thirteen and a girl when she was eighteen. She had a mole on her jaw and twelve piercings, she liked peanuts and chocoate but not peanuts *in* chocolate, and she knew all the words to the Beatles' 'Rocky Raccoon'.

A *vessel*.

'Poppy?' said Iris cautiously, when Poppy remained still, staring at her glass.

I'm not a person. I'm a thing, created for a purpose. To hold something that isn't even mine.

'I'm a vessel.'

'You're a witch,' said Iris.

'A *vessel*. Like a boat. I'm the sodding *Titanic*. Wait, did she do the *Titanic*?'

'Possibly,' said Iris. 'I only knew I had a very strong urge to sell my ticket.'

That stirred Poppy from her stupor. 'You had a ticket for the *Titanic*? Iris, how old are you?'

'A lady never tells,' Iris said. 'Or asks,' she added pointedly.

'Are you all... old enough to remember the *Titanic*?' Poppy asked doubtfully.

'Bloody cheek,' said Sylvia.

'I'm forty-seven,' Fiona said, possibly the most affronted Poppy had ever seen her.

'Sorry. It's really hard to tell. So you were there? I'm assuming twenty-eight years ago? When I was ... born?'

Maybe she hadn't been born. Maybe she'd been spun

out of air, or hatched from Else's forehead like in a Greek myth.

'When we defeated Else, yes. As for your birth ... we didn't know exactly what she'd done. By the time we realised she'd created a baby, it was too late for us to track you. She'd concealed you so very well.'

'How?'

Fiona snorted. Sylvia rolled her eyes.

'The British welfare system, lovey,' said Iris. 'You could hide an army regiment in there.'

'They frequently have,' said Sylvia.

'Once we realised what she'd done we were appalled,' Fiona said. 'We argued like mad over whether to track you down or not.'

'In the end we thought it was better for you to have a normal childhood,' Sylvia said.

'Normal?' said Poppy. Her hair was plaiting itself into tiny braids. One of them dipped itself into her gin.

'We wanted you to have a family. We thought ... we thought maybe they'd mitigate whatever Else had done. That if you were raised with enough love, you wouldn't turn out like her.'

'And we were right,' said Iris firmly.

'But – didn't you try to find me?'

Sylvia barked out a laugh. 'I repeat: British bureaucracy,' she said.

'We trusted in the system,' Fiona said reproachfully. 'We knew you were happy and safe and loved. We had to concentrate on searching for Else. We didn't look for you until you were a bit older, and we started feeling … well, your magic, I suppose.'

Iris put down her tea and smiled at Poppy. 'I remember the day I found you. In a churchyard, somewhere in the middle of the country. A pretty little village, where there was bunting outside the local shop.'

'They put it up for the Queen's jubilee,' Poppy said quietly, 'and never took it down.'

'Thatched cottages. A row of Victorian terraces. Yours was the end one, nearest the church. A lovely sixteenth-century church, I recall, with a medieval font.'

'How do you remember all this?' Poppy said.

Iris looked at her and said, 'How could I forget it? You were playing among the gravestones. Your mother was tidying up the flowers and wreaths and things, and you were running around, playing games with the ghost children.'

Poppy said nothing. She couldn't. She remembered days like that, when the sun shone and the grass was long, when she could run around with what seemed to be absolute freedom, at least as long as she didn't go past the lych gate.

'And I saw your mother kneeling there with some sad dead roses in her hand, and she watched you running, and she just smiled. And there was so much love in her. So very much. And I knew whatever power Else had given you, however much chaos you could cause, you would never be cruel, or evil, or cause anyone any harm. Not when you were loved like that.'

Poppy swiped at her eyes.

'And we knew you were safe, so we left you alone. And

then you came to study just down the road, and I knew that couldn't be a coincidence.'

'You weren't just looking for any witch,' Poppy said. 'That advert was specifically for me.'

'Yes, lovey. We wanted to … keep an eye on you.'

'Just you three? Or do all the other London witches know about me? Providence Thingy and Tia … Maria…?'

'Please don't call them that to their faces,' said Fiona. Sylvia giggled.

'All of us,' said Iris. 'But no one else was in the market for an apprentice.'

Apprentice. Yes, because Poppy knew nothing about magic and how to control herself, and Iris was the most controlled person she'd ever met.

'And then you got me a job in Sylvia's magic shop,' she said, sitting back tiredly and rubbing her face. 'So you could keep an eye on me?'

'Because useful employment is necessary for all sections of society,' said Iris. 'Also, you can't expect me to buy all your phones.'

'Your chaos can be a beautiful thing,' Sylvia said encouragingly. 'Look at the lovely jewellery you make. Creativity can't exist without chaos.'

'Yeah, the lovely jewellery I make which ends up spreading chaos all over the city,' Poppy said.

'Or,' Iris said, 'the lovely jewellery you made for your friend's birthday. Elspeth, wasn't it?'

'Yeah. I should probably call her and make sure she hasn't, you know, turned into a monkey, or exploded into confetti or something.' Poppy sipped her tea. She didn't know what Iris had put in it, but it was calming. Poppy strongly suspected that without it, she'd be screaming. 'She was the one who sold Alex the pendant in the first place.'

'What do you mean?' said Sylvia.

'She fancied him rotten. She was the one showing me videos of him in the shop. She insisted on selling him the pendant, all flirty, like she wanted to know who it was for, fishing for a girlfriend and all that.' Poppy wondered if she should feel bad about sleeping with the guy Elspeth fancied, then decided her friend had really escaped lightly.

Sylvia still looked mystified. 'Why was your friend selling things in my shop?'

Poppy looked at the others. Was Sylvia having a senior moment? 'Because she works there?' Poppy said.

'No, she doesn't. There's you, my granddaughter Mary, Jean-Baptiste who comes in on Saturdays, and that sweet little Wiccan girl, Willow. No Elspeth.'

Poppy stared at her. To her gratification, so did Iris and Fiona.

'Why are you staring at me? I haven't met an Elspeth in years. There's just the four of you on the payroll.'

'Four of us,' said Poppy. Her stomach began to feel like it might turn inside out.

'Yes. I don't know who this Els...p...oh. Oh dear.'

'Oh dear indeed,' said Iris grimly.

Chapter Fifteen

The menu on Alex's phone was beginning to blur in front of his eyes a little bit. Someone had been drinking his whiskey.

Someone had also been ordering loads of junk food. The table held a pizza box, and half a kebab, and empty containers that had once held a burger and fries. A cheeseburger. A double one.

What was next on the menu? Pie and mash? He wondered if they could make a pie floater. Or ... what was that? Dutch pancakes! Yes. With loads of syrup. Alex could barely remember the last time he'd had syrup. He went to explore the options, but the screen mysteriously vanished, and in its place came Poppy's name.

'Poppy,' he murmured. Tears fell. Oh Poppy. He'd lost her because he was a stupid prick, and he'd never get her back because he ate carbs now.

He tried to swipe back to the previous screen, the one

with all the food on it, but instead Poppy's voice came out of his phone, and it was saying his name.

'Poppy?'

'Yes.' It was her, it was really her! 'Are you at home?'

'Yeah. Well, no, it's not really my home. It's a rental. Serviced apartment. I don't actually have a home. Isn't that funny?'

There was a short pause, and Poppy said, 'Are you drunk?'

He eyed the whiskey bottle. 'Maybe just a *tiny* bit,' he said, and squinted at his fingers as they mimed 'tiny'.

She sighed. 'Cool. Is there any left for me?'

He sat up straight, dislodging a sharing packet of Doritos he had shared with precisely no one. 'You're serious? You want to come over?'

'I'm outside.'

Alex crashed over to the front window. Through the rain battering the panes, he could see a bedraggled figure standing in the street, phone pressed to her ear.

She gave him a very small wave.

He put down his phone and opened the sash window and shouted, 'What are you doin—bleph!'

The rain splattered him full in the face, which had a somewhat sobering effect.

'Can I come up?' Poppy shouted.

Alex blinked, and shook himself.

'Yes. Yes! I'll come down.'

'No need,' said Poppy, and he'd barely even wrestled the old sash window closed before there was a knock at the flat door.

How had she done that? The front door needed a key, or a code, or something. His head felt very … sloshy.

He opened the door, and there was Poppy, absolutely soaked through. Her hair was plastered to her head, her shoulders, her entire body, and it left a dripping puddle on the hall carpet.

The first – all right, second, technically – time he'd ever seen Poppy, she'd been standing outside the Mysterio Theatre, where everyone was soaking wet from the sprinklers, and she'd been completely dry. Last night, he'd seen her step out of the bathroom wrapped in a towel, beads of water on her skin, and her hair had been no more than slightly damp.

Now she looked like she'd just been pulled from the Thames.

'I'm sorry,' she said, 'turning up unannounced like this. When the last thing we did was argue and I said some stuff about you not being long-term, but today I got told something completely horrible and the only person I wanted to be with was you, and—'

Alex enfolded her in his arms and held her close against his chest, purely happy to have her back there. And after a second, Poppy relaxed against him.

'I'm making you all wet,' she said, her voice muffled by his sweater.

'Don't care.'

Her arms sneaked around his waist. Alex sighed.

'I'm sorry I yelled at you, and you were right about my parents, and I believe you about Sarah although I still don't—'

'Poppy?'

'Yeah?'

He cradled the back of her head. Her hair wriggled feebly against his fingers.

'I'm so glad you're here.'

She looked up at him then, sniffing a bit. Her eyes and nose were red. She wasn't just wet from the rain.

He wanted to tell her all about *Collingwood High* and why he'd changed every aspect of his life because of it, and how it was all crashing down around him now, but she looked so absolutely lost and alone and so very hurt that all he could do was hold her close and try to comfort her.

'Alex? Not that this isn't lovely and everything—'

'Isn't it?' he said happily.

'—but I really am soaking wet. Could I borrow a towel or something?'

Alex was aware he was a little bit drunk, but he was pretty sure Poppy's appearance had sobered him up sharpish. He insisted on dressing her in warm, dry clothes and giving her the biggest towel to wrap her hair up in.

'It doesn't really like being wrapped up,' Poppy said. She stood in the bathroom and said, 'Stand back.'

He did. Alex had absolutely no wish to get on the wrong side of Poppy's hair.

She shook her head, and her hair rippled out ... with ten times the force she'd put into it. It flicked and shook, like a dog on the beach, only Poppy was standing quite still and her hair still went on shaking itself dry.

'Whoa,' he said.

'Yeah. Guess who always hated school showers?' she said.

'Is it really … is it sentient?'

She shrugged. 'Kinda.' It batted her arm. 'All right, yes. And has been for as long as I remember. Remember when I said I couldn't cut it?' He nodded. 'It literally threw the scissors across the room. Mum thought they were blunt or her hand had slipped or something—'

She broke off.

'Come and sit down,' Alex said, and let her out into the living room with its detritus of misery. 'Er, I'll clean up…'

'Leave it. I create chaos wherever I go, remember? It'll just come back. Now, I believe there was mention of alcohol?'

Alex settled her on the sofa, sitting there in his T-shirt and joggers and socks, her hair twisted into a rope down her back, and fetched her a glass.

'Remember that first night?' he said. 'In your shop? With the vodka.'

'When you thought I was trying to seduce you to get that necklace back,' Poppy said. 'When there's only ever been one reason I want to seduce you, Alex, and that's because I fancy you rotten. Oh, hey, funny story. Remember Elspeth, who sold you the necklace?'

Alex shrugged. He remembered Poppy knocking over a display and getting a broomstick stuck in her hair. There had been someone else there too, but he had no real recollection of them. Who could ever notice anyone else when Poppy was there?

'Well, it turns out she doesn't actually work at the shop.

It turns out no one else has ever actually met her, only me. And when we went out for her birthday that night, it was just the two of us, and that's when I got drunk and cursed the necklace.'

'I thought you cursed the necklace because you saw your ex with someone else?'

'Well, yes. But I bet she engineered that too.'

'Who?' Alex's head was swimming. He got up and poured himself a Coke. And not a diet one either, because screw dieting.

Poppy drained her whiskey. 'My mother.'

Alex sat down with a thump. He recalled Poppy's mother: a neat, ordinary-looking woman who had an air of perpetual slight anxiety, especially when it came to the chaos her daughter carried everywhere with her.

'Your mother … the vicar?'

'No. Because even though she was the one who sat up with me when I was sick, and helped me with my homework, and picked the mushrooms out of the sauce—'

'I'm lost,' said Alex.

'—she's not actually, technically my mother. Because you were right. I am adopted. And do you want to know why?'

Alex winced, because the look on Poppy's face was fierce. 'Why?' he ventured.

'Because my actual mother is some mad chaos witch who went around the world causing disasters and feeding off the power or energy or something, until all the London witches got together and banished her, only she put all her power into me and then I got adopted by a vicar, and now

Else, my birth mother, or maybe father, is back, and pretending to be a workmate of mine who doesn't actually exist.'

Alex silently poured her another whiskey.

'I'm not even a person, Alex. I'm just a … a thing. A vessel. For someone else's chaos.'

'Poppy, no.' He hurriedly put down her glass, and took her by the shoulders. 'You're nothing of the kind.'

'That's what Iris said. That Else just … created me, as something to put her power in, before the others could take it from her.'

He had to hold her. Had to. And when she was in his arms, warm and round and damp and perfect, he said, 'You don't feel like a vessel to me. You feel like a person. Whole and complete. A person who banishes evil spirits, and chats with enchanted figureheads, and has magical hair.'

'And all that is because my mother made me to do it,' Poppy said.

'Did she make you to be funny? And smart? And sexy? Did she make you to make beautiful jewellery? To make light with your fingers? To kiss like an angel?' He thought about this for a moment, then amended, 'A very dirty angel?'

Poppy straightened and gave him a watery smile. 'I think I need to catch you up on drinking,' she said.

'Good idea.' He handed her the glass.

'I probably shouldn't get too drunk,' she said, and drank it anyway. 'What if I curse something else?'

'But,' said Alex, 'that wasn't your fault. You said. Your mother made you do it.'

'And did she make us travel back in...' Poppy's mouth hung open. 'Holy shit.'

'What?'

'When we were there. Then. The Great Fire. That woman we spoke to. The, um, sex worker.'

'The one who wanted to do things with my, er, maypole?' Alex said.

'Yes. I thought she looked like Elspeth. What if she *was* Elspeth? I mean, Else? What if she actually did cause it?'

'The fire? Or the time travel?'

'Both! Maybe. I don't know. Iris said she caused all kinds of disasters. And fed off their energy. Do you remember when we were being attacked by that mob?'

'Vividly,' said Alex, rubbing his shoulder.

'And I did that shockwave thing?'

'Even more vividly,' he said, smiling awkwardly at her hair in case it was getting any ideas.

'I've never done that before. I didn't know I could. I was just so angry, and so afraid, and they were hurting you, Alex. And it just happened. I thought it was me losing control. But what if it wasn't?'

Alex tried to follow, but despite the heroic number of calories he'd consumed he was still kind of sloshy with alcohol. 'Lost again,' he said.

'What if it was me feeding off the energy of the disaster? Of the chaos? What if that gave me the power?'

'Maybe,' he said. 'But that's a good thing, right? That probably saved us. I'm pretty sure it saved me.' The way that pike had flown at his head would probably haunt his nightmares for ever.

'Yes,' said Poppy, and looked torn. 'But how can it be good to feed off fear and misery and chaos?'

Alex didn't know. And then he looked at the table, covered with junk food, and at his laptop which was full of browser tabs about bloody *Collingwood High*, and he said, 'Well, I'm pretty terrified, miserable and chaotic right now, and you're not feeding off me.'

Poppy looked around and frowned. 'Yes,' she began. 'What is happening here? You ... don't strike me as a double cheeseburger and fries kind of guy. You're more of a "don't skip leg day" kind of guy.'

Alex slumped back against the sofa. 'What's the use?' he said.

'Um. Well, it depends if you want to keep the bangin' bod, I suppose.'

Alex rolled his head to look at her. 'Would you still want me if I lost it?'

Poppy frowned. She looked more closely at the pizza box and the burger wrappers and the half-eaten kebab, and at the crushed beer cans and half-empty whiskey bottle, and said, 'Is that what this is?'

Alex gazed miserably at nothing. 'Being hot is all I had,' he said. 'Without that, I'm some chubby kid in a garbage can.'

Poppy opened her mouth. She shut it again. 'Right,' she said, 'now *I'm* lost.'

'It doesn't matter,' he said. 'Not compared to your thing. Yours is, like, actual trauma. Mine's just...' He waved a hand. 'Pathetic, really.'

Poppy sighed. 'Alex, for someone completely obsessed

with his appearance, who feeds off compliments like I apparently feed off chaos, this,' she waved her hand at the food wrappers, 'is actual trauma. Now tell me what's going on.'

'It's not even anything,' Alex said, because compared to her problems it wasn't.

'It'll be something if you don't tell me,' she said. 'Remember how I'm a powerful chaos witch? I could ... I could—'

He rolled his eyeballs in her direction. She wore his T-shirt with a picture of Gandalf on it, and her hair was quietly eating Dorito crumbs. She was damp and dishevelled, and her eyes were pink from crying, and she was just the loveliest thing he'd ever seen.

'You could what?' he asked hopefully.

'I could trash this place,' she said, 'Probably without even moving. There goes your cleaning deposit.'

'Rapunzel,' said Alex, closing his eyes and smiling, 'I lost that the day I threw a vase at a ghost mummy.'

'Oh. Right. Well, I could ... my hair could probably tie you up. Wait,' she said, as Alex's smile broadened. 'Don't tell me. You'd enjoy that?'

'I would if it was you doing it,' he said.

'I could – okay, I'm not really good at threatening people,' she said.

'You're adorable.'

'Hey, don't patronise the chaos witch.'

Alex opened his eyes, and his arms, and she snuggled into his body. Oh yes. This was right. This.

'I've missed you,' she said, and his heart swelled.

'I know. Me too. And it's been … what? Hours?'

'In my defence, they've been very traumatic hours. Speaking of. Tell me what's wrong.'

Alex stroked her hair, which leaned into his hand like a kitten. He wouldn't have been at all surprised to find it was purring.

Rain pattered against the windows. Wind shook the frames. The room smelled of beer and cold pizza. But he had Poppy in his arms again, so nothing could really be that bad.

'Remember how this afternoon, I was going to tell you something?'

'Yeah. And I wittered on about my own stuff.'

'It wasn't wittering, Poppy. I decided I needed to tell you something. About me. But it looks like the world got there ahead of me.' With a groan, he suddenly remembered. 'All those people on the train and at the station? They weren't taking pictures because I'm on the side of buses. They were taking pictures because of this.'

He reached for his laptop, and brought up a tab with the worst sort of headline.

'Remember "Percy Beaker, what a creeper"? He's back—and he's hot.'

Beneath it was a publicity still of him in full Axl Storm mode—eyeliner, Viking braids, oiled muscles, the lot—and beside that was Percy Beaker.

'I don't get it?' Poppy said. 'Who's the kid?'

Alex forced himself to look at the chubby cheeks, the double chin, the smeared glasses, the lank hair. 'Me,' he said.

Poppy's brow knitted in an adorably confused way. 'What? You? No.' She peered at it, zoomed in a bit. 'No. Seriously?'

'Seriously,' Alex croaked. His arms crossed, and then he was hugging himself defensively.

She was already scrolling through the article, skimming the salacious details. *'You know you're a Noughties kid when I say Percy Beaker and you reply, "What a creeper!" Yes, the kid we all loved to hate from teen drama* Collingwood High, *who terrorised Veronica, cut Dylan's brakes and stalked Nancy. The ultimate incel*— Alex, what is this? Were you a child actor?'

He swallowed and nodded.

'And Percy Beaker was your character in this teen drama?'

He nodded again.

'So...? What am I missing? It's a character. It's not you.'

Alex forced himself to un-hunch his body and wrapped his arms around her instead of himself. His big strong arms with his perfectly developed biceps, his broad chest with its beautiful pecs, his carefully sculpted washboard abs. The body he'd worked so hard for. The new life he'd given himself.

'Try telling that,' he said, 'to the kids at my school.'

'Oh,' she said quietly.

'It wasn't so bad being the chubby kid. Everyone knew I could act, and that got me by, I guess. I had most of my life outside school, with drama clubs and junior dramatics societies and stuff. My grandma took me to them all. My parents weren't keen. But it kept me out of trouble. And then she saw the audition notice for *Collingwood High*, and…'

'Your big break?'

'Yeah. I was so excited to be on TV. The cameras, and the huge studios—the ceilings are so high, and the lighting rigs are amazing, and the make-up and costume…'

'I see that's something you haven't lost your taste for,' Poppy teased.

'Hah,' he said weakly. He still got the same buzz now he always had. In the theatre, these days. And the occasional TV camera. But nothing compared to that first time. The excitement. The glamour. The fulfilment of his most cherished dreams.

It was probably the destruction of that which hurt the most.

'I'm sorry. Why did everyone hate Percy Beaker?'

'Well, you read the article,' he said. 'He was horrible. He started out okay, this bullied kid that Nancy—the female lead—befriended. A bit pathetic, but I gave it everything I had. And then they signed me for a second season, and I was too excited to ask about the scripts, and…'

'And they retooled the character?' guessed Poppy.

'They retooled the character,' Alex said. As an adult, he wasn't surprised. As a starry-eyed teenager, he hadn't been prepared. Percy Beaker had decided to take revenge on his bullies, and become obsessed with Nancy, the one girl who'd been nice to him. Alex had acted his little heart out, and everyone had been full of praise, and he'd gone back to school, and then the second series had aired, and…

'He was a hate figure,' Alex said. 'This was still the early days of social media, so it wasn't global. Message boards, mostly, but they're very insular, and people whipped themselves up into a frenzy. You know when you're a teenager, and your world is just so small—your school, your neighbourhood? Well, I was the famous kid in mine. And then I was infamous. Everyone hated me. And yes, I know Percy wasn't me, but there's not much distinction when you look exactly like him.'

'I'm sorry,' said Poppy.

He remembered those days, the dark days, when all he could do was scroll the Internet for hours, searching out every last mention of his name and obsessing over how much he was hated. Watching the episodes so proudly recorded by his grandma, noting every cut line, every unflattering camera angle, every editing choice that made him look more evil with every shot. The sinister music that cued up whenever he was on screen.

It was easy to hate a kid like Percy Beaker. There were essays and earnest segments on daytime television about what to do if your child was targeted by a Percy. There were memes – before memes were even a thing. And there were playground taunts. Any fat kid with glasses and lank hair was a Percy Beaker: what a creeper!

'I ended up changing schools,' he said. 'Didn't help much. Finished my final year of school mostly hiding in my bedroom, and refused to go back. I went…'

This was the worst part, somehow. Poppy had made it pretty clear how physically attractive she found him. Everyone made it clear. It was the thing Alex was most proud of, because it was the only thing he had.

'I went to the gym,' he said. 'I went on a diet. Lost the puppy fat. Lost more. Kept on working out. I think I might have had an eating disorder,' he ventured, because he'd never said that out loud before.

'Oh, Alex.' Poppy burrowed into his chest.

He gave a bitter laugh. 'It gets even better,' he said. 'I'm not even Alex.'

She twisted to look up at him. 'What do you mean? Tell me Axl isn't your real name?'

'No. Axl is because I like Guns'n'Roses. My real name is Alexander, but when I was a kid...'

He took a deep breath. Poppy rose and fell with it, but she didn't say a word.

'My gran called me Sandy.'

'Sandy?' A smile tugged at the corner of her mouth.

'Sandy Grubb.'

Poppy covered her mouth.

And Alex found himself laughing with her. Because it *was* really stupid. Who had let him be called that? Why had his parents not stopped it? Why did they think it was cute?

'I'm sorry, I'm sorry,' she said, giggling. 'It's not funny.'

'It kind of is.' He'd just never allowed himself to think of it before. 'Sandy Grubb. What was wrong with my family?'

Poppy laughed. 'It's cute.'

'Yeah, when you're five. When you're fifteen and kids already have a great excuse to pick on you? Not so much.'

'So you became Alex Grubb?'

'And in short order, Alex Raine,' he said. 'My grandma's maiden name. She was the one who'd always supported me, even when my parents said I should concentrate more on my studies. They said—' He turned his face away. And then he continued, 'They said it should teach me a lesson, about wanting to be famous and doing silly things like acting. Nobody ever cyber-bullied accountants, they said.'

'Wow.'

'Yeah. Not the best time of my life.' He looked back down at Poppy, curled in his arms with her hair twining around his fingers. 'Joke's on them, though, because I got hot, and I got a job in a trendy café, and then I got scouted by a modelling agency.'

'You were a model?' Poppy grinned. 'Was it all very *Zoolander*?'

'It was … not a million miles away,' Alex conceded.

Poppy sucked in her cheeks and pouted and smouldered.

'So you saw my headshots?' he said, and laughed. It felt so good to laugh about it. Why hadn't he realised he could do this?

'You smoulder so beautifully,' Poppy said sincerely.

'It was my trademark. Then I went back into acting… I mean, it was a completely forgotten daytime soap where I had about three lines and mostly hung around with my shirt off on the beach, but it was one in the eye for all those bastards at school.' And it got him the girls. So many girls.

'Yeah,' said Poppy. 'And now your abs are on the sides of buses.'

'And now my abs are on the sides of buses,' he repeated.

'Here in London.'

'Finest city in the world.'

'Bit far from Melbourne though, isn't it?'

Alex went cold. Had he let the accent slip? What would she—

But she knew the worst of it. He didn't have to pretend any more. Didn't have to worry that giving her a clue about where he was really from might start her down the path of learning who Percy Beaker was, and why everyone hated him.

It didn't matter any more.

'How did you know?' he asked sheepishly.

'It was in the article, dummy,' she said. 'And your accent slips when you're stressed. Or scared. It's cute.'

'Cute.' He'd worked so hard on that accent. Ever since he'd found the picture of Great-Grandpa Raine, so dashing in his London nightclubs, and realised he wanted to do magic. And if he had a different accent, and a different name, and he looked totally different, no one would ever know…

'Alex,' she said, twisting in his arms to look up at him, 'I don't know if you've noticed, but you're cute. Which is an entirely different thing to being hot,' she added, before he could say anything. 'You're as sweet and lovely as a cinnamon roll,' she said. 'You've just got this hot Viking thing going on on the outside. And that's, you know, sexy as fuck, but that doesn't last, does it? You could eat all the pizza you want, and still be adorable. I'd still fancy you rotten.'

'You say that—' Alex began.

'I do say that, and as I will it, so will it be.'

Something passed over Alex then, or maybe through him. Poppy hadn't said that lightly. She'd put that force of will into it that she did when she was doing magic. She *meant* it.

And because he was still a bit drunk and he'd had a terrible day, and because they were true, he forgot to say the next words inside the privacy of his own head.

'I think I'm in love with you.'

He froze, and so did Poppy. Shit, shit. He'd come on too strong. He'd terrify her away.

'Alex, I … It's been a week, and we barely…' She slumped in his arms, and tilted her head to look up at him. 'Who the fuck am I kidding,' she muttered. 'I might … be … starting to feel the same.'

'Really?' It was like the sun coming out.

'Yeah. Which is really stupid, because like I said, we barely know each other—'

'Come on, Rapunzel, nobody could go through what we've been through together and not know each other.'

'—and be honest with me, Manbun, how many other women have you said that to?'

'None.' He didn't even have to think about the answer.

'Seriously? Come on. You're hardly short of female attention.'

'Doesn't mean I've fallen in love with any of them.' He winced. 'That sounded bad. I never misled anyone. I promise.'

'Yeah, but did they know that?'

'Poppy.' He cupped her face with his hand. 'I'm serious about this. I've never felt like it before. I can't stop thinking about you. I miss you when you leave the room. I want to do everything to make you happy. I adore you.'

'Are you still drunk?'

'Maybe a little, but I mean it. I'm reformed. No more shagging around.'

'Just like that, you're giving up your playboy ways?'

'I promise.' He meant it. 'For you, Poppy. I pr—'

She put her finger on his lips. 'Don't repeat it. Seriously. Make a promise three times and it's binding.'

Alex looked down at her tenderly. 'I mean it though.'

Poppy kissed his jaw and snuggled in against his neck. 'I know. But you have had a lot of whiskey.'

She'd fallen asleep in his arms, in front of the TV. He liked *The Office US*, she preferred *Parks & Recreation*, but they both agreed on *Brooklyn 99*. Alex fell asleep halfway through the third episode, and Poppy didn't last much longer. She got a text from Iris asking where she was, and replied she'd be staying at Alex's.

When her phone buzzed with the reply, Poppy braced herself, but it said, '*Good. I've seen the way he looks at you. Like you hurl the moon. I had a young man like that once. Handsome as anything, and so sweet with it.*'

She must have been at the gin, Poppy thought. '*He says he's in love,*' she began typing, but couldn't tell Iris Alex thought he was in love with her. Iris would think she was daft. She deleted that, and asked instead, '*What happened?*'

'*I got old, and he didn't.*'

Poppy stared at that for a while. The screen said Iris was still typing.

'*There was a war, child. Else took him. It destroyed me. Don't let her take Alex from you.*'

'*I won't.*'

Poppy began to type that she might be in love with Alex, and that she wasn't sure, and that she was, and eventually managed, '*He says he thinks he's in love with me.*'

'*Of course he does, sweet girl. Who wouldn't be?*'

She looked over at Alex, asleep on the sofa, snoring gently. *Maybe there's an anti-snoring spell I can do.* He was a sweet man. So unlike the super-macho image he presented to the world. The smoulder and the muscles, the persona he wore like armour. And she understood why, now.

I think I'm in love with you.

Did he mean it? He seemed so sincere, but he also seemed pretty tipsy and more than a little upset by the childhood trauma that had been dug up on the Internet. He'd probably regret saying it in the morning, she thought.

But maybe not by much. Poppy fell asleep with her head on his chest, smiling.

She woke some time later, slightly stiff, and stumbled to the bathroom. Hah, funny how she'd been naked in this bathroom before she'd been naked with Alex. That day they'd banished the ghost mummy from the British Museum station, when Alex had decided he didn't trust her and didn't like her, and then he'd stood there wearing just a towel, and she'd wanted to lick him all over.

She sighed happily, and went back out to the living room, to wake him up and get him into bed. If they slept on the sofa all night they'd both regret it in the morning. Poppy knew she would, still somewhat stiff and sore from the whole Great Fire of London experience.

There was a knock at the door, which was a surprise for a couple of reasons. Firstly, it was the middle of the night, and secondly, wasn't there a lock on the outside door? Poppy knew there was, because she'd magicked it open in order to get in.

'Alex?' she said, and he barely stirred.

A key turned in the lock.

'Alex!'

'Whassat? Wha'?'

He came awake in a tangle of limbs, pushing his hair back from his face, and blinked at her.

Then he blinked at the person who'd just opened the door.

'Yelena?'

'Alex!' She launched herself across the room at him, throwing her arms around him and kissing his face all over.

'Um?' said Poppy. Alex looked stunned.

'Alex, *moje kochani!*'

Poppy didn't remember much from Iris's translation spell when they'd gone to see Yelena, but she didn't need to know that was an endearment. It was blindingly obvious.

'Do you mind?' said Alex, trying to extract himself.

'*Stęskniłam się za Tobą*, Alex.' Yelena kissed him full on the mouth.

'Okay, you need to stop that,' he said, picking her up and putting her firmly on the other side of the sofa. He looked over at Poppy as he stood up. 'I have no idea what's going on,' he said to her.

Yelena seemed to notice Poppy for the first time. Her eyes narrowed. 'Who is she?'

'I'm Poppy,' she said. 'We met. In the hospital.'

Yelena said something in Polish Poppy hadn't a hope of understanding.

'Yelena, what are you doing here?' said Alex. He looked half asleep, blinking at Yelena as she sprawled on the sofa, her leg still in its cast. She was wet from the rain, her transparent T-shirt exposing her lack of bra, her mascara smudged in a way that made her look fragile and lovely. Poppy thought gloomily that when her own mascara smudged, she just looked like a panda.

'I came back, Alex, why didn't you come to me? Have you been with this – this – *kurwa*?'

Another word Poppy didn't need a translation for. Unease churned in her gut.

'Yes,' said Alex cautiously. 'I have been with Poppy. She's my girlfriend.'

'I am?'

'Aren't you?'

Poppy wanted to say that was kind of presumptuous of him, but then given their last couple of days and the way he'd confessed his feelings this evening—

'Why are you laughing?' she said to Yelena.

The other woman shook her head, looking Poppy over from head to toe. 'Oh. Now you're his girlfriend? Shall I tell you something, Poppy?' She somehow managed to make Poppy's name sound like it was in inverted commas.

'Tell me what?' said Poppy.

'Yelena, what are you doing?' said Alex.

'I'm telling her what you told me, Alex. Only last week. Don't you remember? You told me I was your girlfriend.'

She's lying. Poppy told herself that, but she remembered how flimsy his denials had been at the time. The unease grew, more and more. Something was very wrong here.

'I never said that,' Alex said. To Poppy, he repeated, 'I never said that.'

'I think you said it was complicated,' she said. It seemed chilly in here. She wrapped her arms around herself.

'Complicated? That's your word for it, Alex? Did you tell Monika it was complicated? And Shanae?'

'Monika and Shanae were nothing,' he said. He winced. 'I mean – they meant nothing to –we didn't have a relationship.'

'He says that about all his side pieces,' Yelena told Poppy.

'I do not,' said Alex. 'I don't have side pieces.'

'No? So how come you're so cosy with her? She's even wearing your clothes! Last week we talked about marriage.'

'You talked about what?' said Poppy. She hadn't realised she'd stepped back until her heel hit the bookshelf behind her.

'We did not,' Alex said. He scrubbed his hands through his hair. His eyes were sleepy and a little bloodshot. A lot of whiskey had gone down that evening.

'What did you say?' Poppy asked.

'I don't know! That we – I said I couldn't take you to that awards thing unless we were married. I mean – not even if.' Wretchedly, he added, 'I can't remember.'

'What awards thing?'

'Next week. I don't have a plus-one.'

'Oh, sure, that's what he says,' Yelena said. 'He is just – what is the phrase? Betting on the hedges?' She gave Poppy a pitying look. 'He likes you now, *kotku*, but he'll get bored very quickly. He always does.'

They always do. Claudia and Edward and Craig and Stacey. Poppy was a novelty and she damn well knew it.

'I don't,' Alex said, but the protest was a weak one.

I've been a fool. 'You do have a reputation,' Poppy said quietly.

'Yes, but—' He seemed to stall.

'But what? You dumped Yelena the second she fell onto the stage, and you had your tongue down my throat an hour later.'

'He is such a man whore,' said Yelena. 'He was still sleeping with Monika when he did me in the rehearsal room.'

'I was not!' Alex said.

'That is what Monika says, and I believe her more than you.' Yelena addressed Poppy again. 'You know he tells lies, yes?'

'I do not,' Alex said.

'No? Where are you from, *Alex*?' When he blanched, Yelena gave him a knowing look and said to Poppy, 'Did he tell you he loves you? No – what's your phrase, Alex? So subtle, but it's not the same. "I think I'm in love with you", that's it, yes?'

Poppy felt, for the second time that day, as if her insides had been scooped out and dumped on the floor in front of her.

She'd done it again. Fallen for a pretty face who saw her as nothing more than a notch on his bedpost. A weird girl, because he hadn't had one of those yet. A self-confessed playboy – for Christ's sake, he'd told her that first night he had his pick of groupies.

And then his pièce de résistance – making out that he was the wronged one because Yelena had been cheating on him. Well, you had to have a relationship to be cheated on, didn't you?

'I... didn't—' Alex whispered, his face white.

Poppy moved mechanically to the little table next to the sofa and picked up her phone.

'Poppy, I didn't say that to Yelena.'

'Then how do I know it?' Yelena said. 'It's a very specific phrase, don't you think? It's not saying you *are* in love, you're not sure about it, it's just a maybe. And of course, you can reverse direction any time you see another pretty face you like.'

There was a pain in Poppy's chest. She thought it might have been her heart tearing in two.

'I didn't say that. Poppy, you're the only person I've ever said that to,' Alex said. He moved towards her, but she skirted around the other side of the coffee table.

'I need to get my things,' she said, and went into the bedroom.

'Was she worth it?' Yelena was asking as Poppy grabbed the damp clothes she'd left in the laundry basket. 'Those hippie girls with the long hair, they're always up for doing all the nasty stuff, you know?' *Congratulations on scoring with the weirdo—*

'Shut up,' said Alex. He followed Poppy to the bedroom. 'You can't believe anything she says,' he said. 'You don't, do you?'

Poppy stood with her damp clothes in her hand, and nearly laughed at herself, because she'd done this yesterday and then *still come back for more.*

'I don't know, Alex,' she said. 'Why shouldn't I believe her? After all – she's not lying, is she?'

'Yes, she bloody is!'

'About all the other women? About how quickly you get bored? You were actually seeing her when that crash happened, weren't you?'

His mouth opened, and his jaw seemed to get stuck.

'I thought you'd be slicker with the excuses,' Poppy said, grabbing her shawl. 'After all, it can't be the first time this has happened, can it?'

'Yes, it can, because I've never told anyone I loved them before,' he said, chasing after her as she went back into the living room.

'That's a total lie,' Yelena said, through a mouthful of crisps. 'He says it all the time. He "thinks he's in love with" every girl who takes her clothes off for him. He is good in bed though, isn't he? He's got a really impressive *chuj*, hasn't he?' She nodded in the direction of Alex's crotch.

'You've said enough,' Alex snapped at her.

'Have I? What about his childhood, Poppy? Did he tell you how he was bullied for being fat?'

Alex gaped at her. Poppy marched to the door.

'You can't possibly know that! Poppy! Don't go. Seriously, I don't know where she's getting this from—'

'From her actual experience of being with you, maybe?' Poppy said. It was funny, she thought she'd be crying at this point. Or angry. Screaming at him. When all she felt was a sort of cold numbness.

'No! I never told her that stuff!'

Poppy stopped and looked at him. 'You're lying, Alex,' she said. She was shaking. 'You've been lying since the day we met.'

'I haven't—'

'You lied about seeing Yelena. You lied about your real name—'

'It's a stage name,' he said impatiently.

'Is it, *Sandy*? You're a fake. Your accent is fake and your stage act is fake. You know what I used to find you that day, with the ghost mummy? A fake crystal. Everything about you is made up and pretend. Smoke and mirrors.'

'My feelings for you aren't,' said Alex, quietly.

He reached out to her, and Poppy stepped back. 'You barely know me.'

'Did he tell you about Percy Beaker?' Yelena said, and Poppy walked away.

She had her hand on the door handle when he grabbed her by the shoulder, and her reaction was not just immediate but devastating. Her hair flew out in a wide arc, slicing across his face, and a shockwave sent him flying back, to crash into the table laden with all its junky leftovers. It smashed under his weight, and he lay there, stunned.

'You're welcome to him,' said Poppy, and left.

Chapter Sixteen

The rain had abated as Poppy had fallen asleep, warm and cherished, in Alex's arms. There had been no soft patter against the window when Yelena knocked on the door.

As Poppy left the flat, it seemed a piece of her heart was left behind with each step, and with each one, the sounds of an impending storm grew louder and louder.

She walked out into the rain, and let it saturate her.

She should go back to Ivy Cottage. To the Coven, who thought Poppy was merely a vessel for someone else's chaos. No wonder they thought she was hopeless. She was barely even a person. Just a thing to contain the chaos that someone else used to hurt people.

Alex hadn't seen her that way.

At least, she'd thought he hadn't.

All that stuff about her being a whole, complete person, about her jewellery and her ghost-banishing and how she kissed, for God's sake, it was all just bullshit. He'd had his tongue down her throat and his hand in her knickers half an hour after they met, and within a week he was banging her in a churchyard.

How many other girls had he done this with?

Pour on the charm and the smoulder, make her laugh, use that smile and those blue eyes and that deep voice to turn her to putty in his hands, and then drop his trousers for the final coup de grâce. His bedpost must be so notched it barely stood.

The sob story about his childhood. She bet it was common knowledge, and nobody cared at all about stupid Percy whatshisface. Probably a stock photo he'd used. He'd probably been buff and shallow his whole life.

Tears streamed down Poppy's face. How could she have been so stupid? How could she have fallen for the same lines he'd used a million times? On poor Yelena, whom he'd discarded as soon as she broke her leg and therefore became a much trickier prospect to shag, and instead turned his attentions to the girl with the mad hair who'd – for Christ's sake, Poppy! – who'd given him vodka and told him to take his clothes off.

And the worst part was she should have seen it coming. How many times was she going to fall for a pretty face and imagine that this time, *this time*, it would be true love, and not just some bored playboy wasting time with her? Hadn't she been told, over and over again? She was the wrong sort of girl and always had been.

Because you're not even real.

Poppy didn't pay very much attention to where she was going. The rain hit her face hard, and she relished it. Car lights flashed and vanished, traffic parted for her. The pavements trembled beneath her feet.

A cab hit a road sign. A traffic light sparked into flames. Passers-by stumbled over their own feet, dropped their keys down drains, got into fights outside bars.

Poppy strode on, oblivious.

Her phone rang in her pocket. Only it wasn't her pocket, it was Alex's pocket, because she was wearing his sweatpants with the cuffs rolled up, and his T-shirt. Her own clothes were in a bundle in her hand, and honestly why had she even bothered taking them? So he couldn't keep them as some kind of trophy, probably. Her brain seemed to be misfiring.

She strode past the Mysterio Theatre, still dark after the accident. The shirtless posters of Alex crumbled under the onslaught of the rain and slithered to the ground as she walked on by.

She skirted Covent Garden. The shop where Elspeth had never worked, because Elspeth wasn't real, just some glamour conjured up by what was left of Else. A hollow shell who'd pretended to be Poppy's friend, who'd got her drunk and then told her not to forget her jacket back at the shop. Who'd shown her Axl Storm's videos in the shop. Who'd sold him the damned cursed pendant.

Lightning crackled from the sky, striking the peaked roof of the covered market. Poppy didn't even glance at it.

Past *The Lion King*, the evening performance just letting

out, the crowds parting before Poppy's wrath like the sea drawing back before a tsunami. Traffic screamed to a halt as she walked down the centre of the Strand on a Saturday night. Nothing hit her. Nothing would dare.

As she passed the large topiary cat outside the Savoy, he stretched his paws and flicked his tail at her.

Then a voice said, 'Oh my gosh, this is biblical!'

'Well, you'd know,' replied another, and for a second no rain at all hit Poppy as she stood and stared at her parents, standing outside the Savoy's gilded entrance.

'Poppy?'

But they weren't her parents. The neat woman in the sensible blue mackintosh, and the grey-haired man with the umbrella. They'd raised her, but they weren't her parents. Her parent was a mad chaos witch who had created Poppy like a lab-grown kidney.

'What are you doing here, love?'

'You're soaked, come in under the roof.'

'Is it a roof? A canopy, maybe?'

'A porte-cochère, now that's a fancy word.'

'We've just been to see the *Pretty Woman* musical. Ever so good, wasn't it?'

'Yes, ever so good. I'm still a bit troubled by the problematic message, but the songs were smashing.'

'We just popped into the Savoy for a nightcap.'

'Oh, it's glamorous. Shame about the rain. Perhaps we'll have another!'

They sounded merry, both of them with pink cheeks. Poppy stood in the pouring rain, while a few feet away a cat made of leaves and branches began washing his paws.

'Poppy?' That was her mum. 'Are you all right?'

In the furrow of her brow was every childhood illness Poppy ever had. Every tearful spat with a schoolfriend. Every period pain and teenage tantrum.

A huge wail escaped Poppy. 'Oh Mum,' she sobbed. 'I'm really not.'

You're welcome to him.

Alex lay stunned in the wreckage of the coffee table, staring at the door Poppy had just slammed behind her. He couldn't breathe, he couldn't move.

Yelena had lied to Poppy, but only about a couple of things. The rest was all true, and that was the worst part. Because if it was all blatant nonsense, Poppy would realise that. He hadn't called Yelena his girlfriend, and he hadn't told her he loved her, and while the word marriage had come up she was totally twisting the context. But he had been seeing her up until the day he met Poppy, and he had slept with half the cast, and he had made out with Poppy half an hour after meeting her.

It was true enough to make the rest of it plausible.

It was all his fault.

All that spun through his mind as he lay winded, unable to stop Poppy walking out the door and taking his heart with her. Was that why he couldn't move? Because she'd ripped out the thing that kept him alive?

'Well,' said Yelena, looming over him. 'Looks like you're all mine.'

Thick, dark loathing stole over him. What was she

doing? Why had she said those things? How did she even know those things?

Why was her face changing? Her hair growing. Her posture straightening.

Yelena wrenched off the cast on her foot, and rolled her shoulders as if she was clicking her bones into place. And maybe she was, because she looked like a totally different person. Tall and slender, with hair like ink floating in water.

'That's better,' she said, and even her accent had changed. Now she spoke in the rich, dark tones of someone who had deep roots in this city. Roots so deep she'd probably ruled the place with fire and blood before it had even been a city. The sort of accent Alex had been emulating for years. *You're a fake.* 'Like taking off shoes that are too tight. You have no idea how many times you nearly caught me wearing the wrong face.'

'Wrong face?' Alex wheezed.

'Yes. Running around being Yelena one minute, then Elspeth the next. You know,' she said, grabbing him by the arm and hauling him to his feet as if he was a toddler, 'I was going to just take the necklace, but it was so much more *fun* to get you to give it to me.'

She gave Alex a shove, and he landed on the sofa so hard it skidded backwards.

'She still thinks she cursed it, doesn't she? Oh dear. Dear sweet Poppy. Nice girl, not very bright. No idea I was spiking her drinks all night. No idea it was me snogging her ex in the doorway. Ah, there it goes. Now you're getting it.'

Alex was frozen now, not with shock but with horror. 'You're – you're Else?'

She gave a little flourish, as if to acknowledge that this was indeed so, and he was fortunate to be in her presence.

'You're Poppy's mother?'

Else shrugged. 'Mother is such … an antiquated word. I created her. I'm no more her mother than Henry Ford is father to a family of beautiful apple-cheeked motorcars. Now. If you don't mind, I need you just for the last little phase of my plan.'

'What plan?' croaked Alex.

'To get my power back, obviously. Those bitches tried to steal it from me, but I kept it safe. Adopted by a vicar, I heard! Oh, how I laughed. Now, I've been biding my time and recovering my strength, and it's time to reclaim what's mine.'

'You're going to steal Poppy's magic?'

The force of Else's voice twisted her face into an ugly mask. 'It's not hers, it's mine! She's barely even real!'

But Alex knew that wasn't true. Poppy was real – she was warm, vital, funny, smart, loving. She was chaotic in the best possible way. And her magic was a completely intrinsic part of her. If he allowed Else to steal it, Poppy would be losing so much of herself there would be nothing left.

'I can't let you do that,' he said, and what he intended to do was stand up and get hold of her and – well, he didn't know, after that, but it didn't matter anyway, because he couldn't actually move.

Else appeared to have frozen him in place.

'Oh, you actually do care for her,' she said, her head on

one side. 'That's sweet. She cares for you a great deal, too. Which is why I've got to kill you.'

'What?'

'Sorry, darling. Don't worry, you won't feel the tiniest bit of pain.' She smiled. 'You'll feel a lot.'

Chapter Seventeen

'Well,' said Poppy's mother. 'I suppose that is quite a lot to be dealing with.'

Nobody wanted to sit in one of the Savoy's bars, all cocktails and glamour, so they were in a pub around the corner. Poppy had ordered a very large gin, which her mother had tried to talk her out of, and then taken another look at her face and ordered one for herself too.

'Today has been a hell of a week,' Poppy said grimly.

Her father sipped his pint. He was a real ale man, her dad, when he drank at all. Could nurse a pint all night. Poppy had only seen him drunk once, at her cousin's wedding when she was twelve. He'd fallen asleep in the corner and she and her cousins had drawn a moustache on him.

'Thing is, poppet,' he said. 'None of it actually matters, does it?'

Poppy stared at him. 'How can you say that?'

He shrugged. 'Well, why should it? What if you'd been

conceived through IVF, or a sperm donor, or a surrogate? You'd still be ours.'

'Yes, but I wasn't. And did you hear the part about the chaos witch?'

'It does explain quite a few things,' said Poppy's mum.

She liked her gin with lemonade. It always caused confusion and amusement amongst bartenders, but she knew what she liked, and gin with lemonade was it. Besides, she said, it made a change from all the sherry people usually offered her.

'You don't – I mean, you actually believe me? About the witch stuff?'

'Poppy, love. When you were a child your hair threw a pair of scissors across the room. You used to light the Advent Candle from the back of the church. And remember when we found that nest of rats in the vestry and you just asked them nicely to move somewhere else?'

'They set up in Mrs Greenaway's shed,' her dad said. 'She wasn't happy.'

'I know, I had to go round and make them move again before she put down poison,' said Poppy. 'Do you mean you knew? All this time? You're a vicar, Mum. And you knew I was a witch?'

Her mum drank some more of her gin and lemonade. She was getting down to the bottom now, and Poppy's dad stood up even though he'd got loads of his left.

'Similar?'

'Yes, thanks, love. Can I get ice and a slice this time? Thanks. Look, Poppy, I might as well level with you. There was a point where I worried about possession.'

'As in a demon?' said Poppy. The candle on the table flickered.

'Well, yes. But you never seemed to have any ill intent, and it wasn't harming you, and I talked with the Dean and the diocese psychologist, and they said it was probably just a phase.'

'A phase?' said Poppy. She felt like she was going mad. How were her parents okay with this?

'I did explain about the candle thing, and they said God works in mysterious ways.'

'But,' Poppy said, 'didn't the Church used to condemn witches?'

'We also used to burn Catholics at the stake, love. Things have moved on.'

Poppy stared at the scarred wooden tabletop, sticky from a recent wipe down with that pink anti-bac spray that made her elbows blister if she leaned on the table. There was a tea light in a round holder on a beer mat advertising an IPA brewed in Camden. On the wall was a poster advertising an open mic night and a Hallowe'en party next week. It was all so ... normal.

A fresh gin and tonic landed in front of Poppy, and her dad sat back down again. He sipped at his pint and gave her a smile.

'I just can't get my head around you actually knowing I was a witch this whole time. While you were training to be a vicar and everything, Mum.'

'We always knew you were different. We just didn't know how. I used to pray for enlightenment. I asked God to show me the way. And the answer was always the same.'

Her mum sipped her drink. Poppy gave her an impatient look.

'Love, Poppy. Just to love you. And that was the easiest instruction of all.'

Damn, damn, damn. After the gin and the whiskey – and Alex, oh God, Alex – that was almost too much for Poppy. She felt tears gathering behind her eyes.

'But Mum. I have magic hair. I just made a topiary cat come to life. I recently time-travelled to the Great Fire of London.'

Her mum just said, 'Really? What was it like?'

'Fucking horrible. And what if I caused it?'

'But why would you cause it?'

'Because I can't control myself!'

Her parents exchanged a look, and then her dad said, 'Poppy, have you hurt anyone? Have you caused any serious damage? Have you ever done anything worse than your Uncle Bob after a few too many Jägerbombs?'

'Well – no—'

'Exactly. Power, control – it's all about intent. Do you want to hurt anyone?'

I want to strangle Alex Raine. No, I don't. I want to collapse, sobbing, in his arms. 'No,' said Poppy.

'Well, there you are then.'

Her parents drank their drinks, as if that was that.

'Don't you ever wish I was normal?' Poppy said.

They looked surprised she'd even asked. 'What is normal?' her mum said. 'Nobody's normal. Trying to be like everyone else will only make you unhappy.'

'Well, being a chaos witch doesn't exactly fill my life

with sunshine and puppies,' Poppy snapped. 'I can't even —' She broke off.

I can't keep a relationship going. Maybe the chaos was the reason why, maybe that was why she kept attracting and being attracted to people who had no intention of sticking around. But that didn't help, did it? She couldn't change who she was.

And Alex. Oh, Alex. She wasn't the first and she wouldn't be the last, but why the hell had she ever let herself get involved with him in the first place? He was a player, and always would be.

'Can't what?' said her dad.

Poppy felt her face crumple before she'd even said the words. 'There was a boy,' she said.

'Oh dear.'

'Are you back on boys now then?' said her dad, as if sexual preference was like deciding on your favourite band, or what kind of car to get.

'What? I was never off boys, Dad.'

'All right,' he said placidly.

'What happened with this boy?' said her mum, as the bell rang for last orders. 'Oh, we might have to continue this elsewhere. You could come back to Limehouse with us, I suppose...'

But Poppy was looking at her phone, which had just pinged in her pocket. Stupid thing to do, because it was probably Alex telling her more lies, but—

A cold shock ran through her as she read the screen.

'What is it?' said her mum.

'Your hair,' murmured her dad, but Poppy didn't even

look to see what it was doing now. Her mum took the phone from her gently and read the message on the screen.

'From Elspeth. "*Just thought you should know, if he doesn't hear from you by midnight, your boyfriend is going to—*" Oh. Oh dear,' she said. She stood up, and reached for her coat. 'Well, I suppose we'd better come with you. How far is Tower Bridge?'

'What?' Poppy couldn't think straight. Was this a threat? Or had Alex really decided to do something stupid to himself? She grabbed her phone back and was just about to try calling Elspeth when it hit her.

Poppy's mum was wittering on. 'She said, if he doesn't hear from you by midnight. That's not long. Peter, you call the police.'

Her dad nodded, and got out his phone.

Poppy's hair whipped it from his hand.

'He's not going to jump off the bridge,' she said quietly.

'But – your friend Elspeth said—'

'She's not my friend. And she's not Elspeth.' Poppy glanced at the time on her phone. *Midnight*. There wasn't a lot of time.

She scrolled through her contacts and checked for Iris and found two listings.

One of them had texted her this evening. One had messages going back years.

Why would Iris need to ask where she was? She'd know. Why would she be bringing up boyfriends? *Don't let her take Alex from you*.

Poppy carefully selected the real Iris, and called her. 'Else's made her move. Call in the cavalry.'

Chapter Eighteen

I f he had a harness and safety equipment, Alex knew he could make an epic stunt out of this.

'What do you think?' he said, as the wind blew his hair into his face. 'Disappearing trick? I could dive off here, get some mirrors, deflectors, kind of thing – and seem to vanish?'

'What? There are no mirrors,' said Else. She paced back and forth on the roof.

'No, but if there were, we could do something neat. Or is it too big? That's the problem.'

It wasn't the most pressing problem, if he was honest, but it was a problem. Tower Bridge stood high above the river at road level, and famously split open its road to let ships pass through. Above this tall space ran two walkways, parallel to the road below but thirty or forty metres up. The views from them were spectacular. Alex knew this because he was sitting on top of one of them, and that was spectacular too.

And high. So very high. So very, very high.

He made the mistake of glancing down, and very quickly looked away. 'Or is street magic old hat now?' he said desperately. 'Too Noughties? What do people want out of magic these days, hmm? Comedy? I could try my hand at comedy.'

'Don't talk about magic as if you actually know how to do it,' Else snapped. 'You do silly tricks. Smoke and mirrors.'

'Sexy smoke and mirrors,' he said. 'Remember that routine with the balance work, when you were Yelena? Your core muscles just amazed me.'

'I'm very flexible,' Else said.

'Yes! Wow. I mean, that move you could do with the ribbons? Just astonishing, how did you learn to do that?'

He was babbling, he knew. Because he needed to do something to stop himself gibbering with terror, but also to stall her a bit. Else wanted to throw him off the top of Tower Bridge, but not until Poppy was there, in order to truly devastate her.

At which point, he gathered she was going to try to console Poppy, because it was Poppy's chaos that had led to the tragedy. And then she would offer to take the chaos magic that was so burdensome to Poppy, and thus regain her power.

At least, that was the gist as he understood it. It was quite difficult to comprehend the plans of an evil genius when you were forty metres above sea level, with nothing but terminal velocity between you and the river.

The key element Alex had understood was that Poppy

needed to be here for Else's plan to work. And if she arrived before he was pushed – because he sure as hell was not jumping – then she'd have a plan to save him. Right?

Poppy was not going to be taken in by Else's bullshit. He had to believe that. Just like he had to believe she would actually come. She wouldn't have washed her hands of him, she wouldn't be sitting at home with Iris drinking gin and cursing him to have a significantly smaller penis, she'd come and rescue him.

Alex found himself wondering if he'd accept the smaller penis in exchange for getting to survive, and shook himself.

'That's amazing,' he said, when Else paused in her ranting. 'And – just humour me, because I'm fascinated. The whole Great Fire of London thing. That was you, right?'

Else looked at him sideways. Then she gave a little self-deprecating shrug.

'Some maidservants are so slovenly,' she said, her eyes flashing knowingly. 'They just don't clean out the embers from a fire before they go to bed.'

'And then they use their magic to spark them back into flame, am I right?' he said, grinning at her. He could charm Else. He could.

'Well, maybe just a tiny bit,' she said. 'The real genius was the wind. The prevailing wind in London is west-southwest – that's why all the really smelly industries were always in the East End. My stroke of genius was to persuade the wind it wanted to be easterly.' She made a wafting motion with her hand. 'Pfft, off it went towards the City. If it had spread east, it would have hit the Tower and then just acres of nothing, and burnt out in a hot minute. Hah, get it, a hot minute?'

Alex laughed, as if the burning of a whole city was just hilarious. He could still smell the smoke, feel the coating of ash on his skin, hear the roar of the fire, the crackle, the voracious appetite of the blaze that wanted to devour everything—

'It's truly impressive,' he said. 'So, where have you been all this time? Since you gave up your magic?'

'I didn't give it up, I hid it,' said Else sharply.

'Yes, of course, that's what I meant. Of course.' He smiled at her. 'You hid it. So clever. And then ... what? You had to pretend to be an ordinary human?'

'It was hideous,' said Else. She was standing right on the edge of the roof.

'I bet. Yeah. We are pretty hideous,' he said sympathetically. He daren't look at his watch. Why wasn't there a clock on this stupid bridge?

'Ordinary people are so ... tiny. In their heads. Just – eat, sleep, work. They fuck, but they don't even enjoy it most of the time. They squander years of their lives rearing horrible little squalling babies, and why? Because it's what everyone else does. It's madness. Don't you ever look at your own lives?'

'Totally,' said Alex. There was still traffic on the river. Maybe he could do some kind of signal...

'It's all so tawdry. I had no idea. Twenty-eight years I had to live like that. Can you even imagine?'

'No,' said Alex, who had lived roughly the same length of time and never minded his humanity one bit.

'Torture. Pure torture. And I was so weak. So weak. Could barely raise a glamour on myself. Do you have any idea what that's like?' She paused, and looked him over. 'Well, of course you do.'

Alex blinked. 'Beg pardon?'

'This.' She waved her hand at him, sitting there in his trackie bottoms and hoodie. 'Your whole … glow-up. It's what humans do instead of a glamour, isn't it?'

Alex stared, unseeing, at the magnificent river vista before him. A glamour was what magical creatures did to assume a different appearance. Else had apparently been able to maintain several, even after she'd given away so much of her power that it was undetectable. But he was an ordinary human being, and he…

…he had assumed a different appearance. Sandy Grubb had been a chubby kid with lank hair and glasses. Alex Raine had gone to the gym, cut out carbs, got laser surgery and spent a small fortune on shampoo.

Everything about you is made up and pretend. Smoke and mirrors.

'Holy shit,' he said.

'You see? A shame they all had to see through it.'

And there was something in her tone of voice that made Alex turn to look at her.

She was *gloating*.

'You did that?' he said.

Some girl who appeared to be the only person in the world who realised the hot guy from Surf Rescue *used to be the fat kid in* Collingwood High…

'What, me?' Her hand fluttered at her breast. 'Oh no, I couldn't possibly.' She rolled her eyes diabolically.

'You...' He gazed at the glittering tower of the Shard. 'You leaked that information?'

'Hmm? It was all there for someone to find. Just ... whisper in the right person's ear ... or in their comments section, at any rate – and watch the connections being made.' Else was walking along the edge of the roof, on tiptoe, quite as if it was a completely normal thing to do. 'Guess what else?'

'What?' said Alex woodenly.

'It's too funny. You know my vessel?'

He wanted to snarl at her. 'Her name is Poppy.'

'Well, whatever. That silly little party at the ship? I did consider making it float, but that's a lot of effort and I've been doing these glamours, so – anyway – her stupid cousin. The one having the party? Whose fiancé is definitely fucking one of his grooms—'

She waited until Alex looked up in shock and stage-whispered, 'I know because I'm that groom!'

'Amazing,' he managed.

'Well anyway. One of the waitresses slipped her a spliff. You'll never guess who that was!'

'No,' said Alex, staring at the lights glittering on the river. 'I never will.'

'Haha, it was delicious. I spun her a little story about adopting a – might have been a puppy? Anyway, I said the word "adoption" about fifty times. Glorious.'

She sighed happily.

Alex thought about how utterly broken Poppy had been

when she came to see him that evening, and he began to wonder if he could bring himself to actually throw Else off the bridge himself.

'I honestly thought that might tip her over, but you can't predict these things. Chaos!' trilled Else. 'Anyway, so my back-up was the Great Fire. Kind of hard work, you know, but you guys were on fire, so a brilliant conduit. I knew you could do it, *kotku*,' she said, reaching out and stroking his cheek. Alex flinched away. 'You were always a red-hot lover. Speaking of, that vessel is taking her sweet time. You want to remind me what you can do with your zip open?'

Like magic, it unfastened itself.

Alex wrenched it back up. 'I would rather,' he breathed, through clenched teeth, 'cut my own dick off than touch you ever again.'

Else shrugged. 'Suit yourself,' she said. 'I was just trying to offer you something nice. Last meal, type of thing.'

Very suddenly, she went still, her gaze fixed on the distance. Alex peered that way, but all he could see was a flock of birds.

Really large birds.

On broomsticks.

He smiled.

'What do you mean,' said Poppy, 'you have broomsticks?'

'You helped me make them,' said Iris. It sounded like she was moving fast, wind whistling through the phone speaker. Poppy was practically running, having told her parents in no uncertain terms to get a cab back to their nice safe beds.

'Yes, for the shop! As … props! Decorations!'

'Oh, those ones. Yes, those are just brooms. The ones at home, however…'

Poppy gazed at the traffic splashing through the rain on the Victoria Embankment. 'Do you mean to tell me,' she said, 'that I've been paying through the nose for my Oyster card, and hiring bikes by the mile, and all this time I could have been *flying*?'

'Well, not all the time, Pops, be reasonable,' said Iris. 'You can't go flying everywhere. You'd get hit by drones.'

'Drones,' said Poppy, to no one. 'Look, where are you? I'm looking at Cleopatra's Needle—'

'Oh, you'll see me, lovie.'

Poppy looked up. 'Won't everyone else – ohholyfuck.'

That was because Iris was zooming in towards the top of the obelisk, and drifting gently down on the river side, away from the traffic. Poppy looked around madly and sprinted down the steps to the dock where Iris was coming into land, casually pulling out her earbuds as if she'd just pulled up in a car.

'Holy shit, you can fly,' Poppy said.

'Yes, dear. What did you think I was doing?'

Poppy looked at the hovering broom. 'I – I don't think I actually believed it.'

Iris tsked at her. 'Silly girl. Now. Astride the stick, bristles to the back, that's it – for once you're wearing trousers, much better than a skirt, I can tell you – and hold it with both hands.'

'You're only using one,' Poppy said, her heart rate already rising. She tied her shawl in a firm knot around her waist, and tried to get her hair into some kind of plait. It plastered itself down against her skull, like the ears of a frightened cat.

'Yes, and when you've been flying for a hundred years maybe you will too. Now. It's simple to control – just move the stick up and down, left and right, tilt it to speed up and slow down. All right?'

'No,' said Poppy, who couldn't think of a stronger word right now. She was going to *fly*.

'Good. We've no time to spare.'

And with that, Iris reached out to Poppy's broom, and lifted it into the air alongside her own.

Poppy gripped the stick hard with both hands and her thighs clamped in a death grip, but the broom seemed very steady. Rather like riding a bike, but without all that tiresome pedalling.

In fact, as she sailed out across the Thames, Poppy felt exhilaration rise within her, and if it hadn't been for the fact Alex's life was in danger, she'd probably have been really enjoying herself.

'Stay high,' Iris called. 'People don't look up.'

Poppy supposed she should be grateful for the self-obsessed Londoner peering at their phone. She tensed as she soared over Waterloo Bridge, but nobody erupted in amazement, so she assumed Iris was probably right. Besides, they could always say it was some kind of viral stunt.

Maybe I should tell Alex. He could do some street magic while the theatre's being repaired.

And then came the pain, because Alex had lied to her. Told her he loved her, told her he missed her, and lied with every word. What did she expect? Even his name was a lie. His accent. What would she find out next, that his eyes were really brown?

It was easier to think about that than what lay ahead. Else meant to hurt Alex, although she didn't understand why. Poppy had to get there in time and save him, although she didn't know how. Because even if he was a liar and a cheat, he didn't deserve to die.

Well, probably.

Maybe I could give him some of that tea Iris gave her first husband though…

She flew past Blackfriars, the Tate Modern and swooped up high over the Millennium Bridge.

'That reminds me,' Iris said, waving at Shakespeare's Globe. 'I really must see if they're doing *Dream* next season. I can never resist messing with it a bit.'

'Iris! You, messing with magic?'

'*Lord, what fools these mortals be,*' Iris replied.

Then they were over Southwark Bridge, and Poppy's smile faded, because now she could see Tower Bridge clearly, rising above the river like the absurd confection it was. Those gothic towers, so very Victorian, and the blue and red paint for a jubilee more than forty years ago.

What would be there when they arrived? Would Alex still be alive? He had to be. Poppy wouldn't allow the alternative.

They passed London Bridge, a squat concrete affair that didn't resemble the old bridge in any way whatsoever. Chiefly, in Poppy's mind, because it wasn't on fire. And then Tower Bridge, looming ahead, as Iris drew alongside Poppy.

'Up there,' she said. 'On the walkway. Do you see?'

Poppy squinted. 'Are you sure?'

'Yes. The tide is out, so there's probably a hundred-and-fifty-foot drop to the water.'

'And it's dramatic,' came another voice alongside her, which almost made Poppy fall off her broomstick. It was Fiona, and beside her was Sylvia.

'She loves drama,' said Sylvia.

'You guys are here?'

'Of course we're here, Poppy, don't waste time stating the obvious. We made a few calls.'

'We got a few calls,' Sylvia added. 'Now. Distraction, I think, until we've got him safe?'

'Yes. It's you she wants, Poppy. Try stalling her until the cavalry's here.'

'I thought you were the cavalry?'

'Darling, you have no idea. Go on, go. If he falls from that height all his internal organs will burst upon impact.'

Alex. No.

Poppy put the nose of her broom down and flew so fast the wind blew her hair straight out behind her. She could see Alex now, getting to his feet as she approached, bracing himself against the wind. There was no sign of Else. She was almost there. Almost—

Alex suddenly jerked forward. He dropped off the top of the walkway and plummeted to the river below.

Poppy screamed. Her hair flew out wide, and a shockwave radiated out from her just as it had by the Customs House that night, and she turned the nose of her broom down and flew hard to intercept him.

The shockwave caught his falling body, and slammed it at an angle into the river, which swallowed him and kept on flowing.

Chapter Nineteen

The River Thames was dark and silty, its water nearly opaque in daylight. At night, under the shadows of the bridge, it was Stygian.

Poppy emerged from the water, her hair a sad heavy mass about her shoulders, and allowed the broomstick to take her up onto the road level. It was free of traffic, and only one person stood there.

She rushed over as soon as Poppy's feet touched the ground. Fashionable jeans, a cute little top, hair styled into bouncy curls. Elspeth.

'Oh my God! Poppy, I'm so sorry. I saw him fall. Do you think divers can recover the body?'

'The tide's going out. He'll be halfway to Tilbury by now,' said Poppy, staring dully at the river.

'It's awful. It's so terrible. Why do you think he did it?'

'Because you pushed him.'

Elspeth clapped a hand to her chest in dismay. 'What? I

was nowhere near him! You couldn't possibly see me from up there.'

'No,' said Poppy. She turned her head slowly to look at the broomstick she held. It dripped copiously onto the road. 'But you know what's strange, Elspeth?'

'What? You're in shock, Poppy, come and sit down…'

'What's strange is that you just saw me fly onto the bridge on a broomstick and you don't even seem in the slightest bit surprised.'

Elspeth stilled. Poppy could almost see the machinations going on in her head. Then she shrugged, and said, 'All right. I'm a witch too. Surprise!'

'Surprise,' Poppy echoed.

'Oh listen, I'm sorry I didn't tell you, but I didn't want to make things worse for you.'

'Worse?'

'Yes.' Elspeth pulled a face. 'It's just – you're so chaotic, Poppy. You've never really got it together. And I've been on top of my power for a long time. Look, I can do a glamour without even thinking about it.'

Her face sort of rippled, and her hair too. Her clothes marbled and reformed into a new outfit. The effect was quite nauseating.

And when Else looked back at Poppy, it was with a sharp, pale face, a pointed chin and high cheekbones. Her eyes were a pulsing violet, her hair a slithering mass that looked as if it was floating in water.

At least now I know where I get that from, Poppy thought hysterically.

'Is this your real face?' she said.

'Yes. I know how much authenticity means to you, Poppy. From now on you'll see my real face. I won't lie to you.'

All of a sudden, Poppy was reminded of the mean girls at school. One in particular, who had a marvellous way with the passive-aggressive comment, and used to say things like, 'Oh, I have to trim my hair all the time or it gets such split ends, Poppy, how do you live with them?' or 'I read this quote about religion being the opiate of the masses, but I'm sure they weren't talking about your mum, Poppy.'

And now here was Else, with the same hungry look on her face. She wanted Poppy to think about Alex, whom she'd just thrown off a bridge. She wanted her to be humiliated by Alex's betrayal. She wanted to remind Poppy of the double heartbreak she'd just suffered.

She wants to break me. Why?

'I just wish I'd been able to help,' Else was saying now, looking sadly out at the dark, rushing water. 'Help you, I mean. If you could control your magic more, maybe it wouldn't have drawn someone like Alex into your life.'

'I thought you fancied Alex rotten?' Poppy said. 'You were the one showing me his videos.'

'Yes,' said Else smoothly, 'and I regret that so much. When I think about what happened after I sold him that necklace. If only I'd known it was cursed! That whole theatre collapse, and Yelena and Jose being injured. So horrible.'

She put a hand on Poppy's sodden sleeve. 'But you

mustn't blame yourself,' she added, those violet eyes blazing with sincerity.

'For the stage accident?'

'Yes, and for cursing that pendant. What else has it gone on to do?'

You know perfectly well, because I'll bet you were behind it all, Poppy thought furiously. Her hair trembled.

'There was this mummy ghost,' she said. 'We had to banish it. And then this thing with talking figureheads—'

'Talking what? That must have been a nightmare. However did you cover it up? What did your family think?'

'I think they thought it was part of the entertainment,' Poppy said. The wind blew straight along the river, chilling her soaked clothes and wet hair. 'But then – they're not my real family, are they?'

It was a calculated risk. Poppy waited with her breath held.

'Oh, they told you, did they? I'm so sorry, Poppy. It's not how I wanted you to find out.' Else took a deep breath, looked Poppy in the eye and said, 'I'm your real mother, Poppy.'

Poppy considered pretending she didn't know this. But it was cold, and she was soaking wet, and whatever Else had done to the traffic was surely backing up all the way to the North Circular by now. So she said, 'I know.'

Else looked disappointed. 'You do? I suppose Iris told you. Interfering old besom.' Then, as if she was remembering her own role, her face softened. 'I'm so sorry, my darling. But it was too dangerous. All those other witches after me. They wanted to steal my power for their own. I couldn't keep you safe. If only I'd known...'

'Known what?'

Else contrived to look troubled. 'That your magic would grow to be so chaotic. So uncontrollable. And being raised by a vicar – oh Poppy, my darling, how did you ever bear it?'

'It had its challenges,' Poppy said.

'They called you Poppy, like opium!'

'They called me Poppy, like peace,' Poppy said.

She'd learned about poppies growing on battlefields when she was at school. They flourished in the blood-soaked grounds of Flanders precisely because of the explosives, the corpses, the chaos of war. Poppies came from chaos. They were created by it.

The clues were all there, all along.

'I bet you wished every day you could just be like all the other girls, didn't you?'

Clarity blossomed inside Poppy. That was the game then, was it?

'Other girls,' she said.

'Yes. Imagine life without all this chaos. Just waking up and knowing what the day holds. Being able to get a haircut. Going on dates that don't end in fire and screaming.'

Poppy's gaze snapped to Else's.

'Oh, I'm sorry, my darling. I shouldn't have reminded you of poor Alex. Such a tragedy. If only you hadn't driven him to such madness. I'm sure you'll find someone else soon enough, but you'll have to be so careful. So, so careful.'

Poppy tried hard to keep her face from showing its incredulity. How stupid did Else think she was?

'Really careful,' she said thoughtfully. 'More careful than you, at any rate.'

Else's sympathetic expression faltered. 'What?'

'Dates that end in fire and screaming? You were there, Else – or was it Nellie? Which, by the way, mega creepy to come onto me when you're technically my parent. Gross. So gross.'

Else looked as if she'd just been slapped.

'It's bad enough you slept with Alex. Got a kick out of that, did you?'

'I don't know what you're—'

'Else, Else. You knew the names of the two people injured in that stage accident. Yelena, maybe, I might have given you, since I might have let it slip in the shop when you were being Elspeth, but Jose? The guy she was seeing? Or – you were seeing?'

Else really wasn't that great an actor. Poppy folded her arms and watched her try to work out whether to style it out or confess.

'Oh, all right,' Else said. She spread her hands. 'You got me! I was Yelena too.'

'Right. Right. And – all that stuff earlier. About Alex? That he thinks he loves me? Nice bit of catfishing there, pretending to be Iris.'

'Modern phones don't show a number, just a name,' Else said smugly. 'And he'd brought home all that whiskey.'

Poppy shook her head. 'You nearly did it. You really, nearly did it. You had me so convinced Alex was just some player who had girl after girl and said the same old lies to them.'

'He is. He's a liar. Was. He's dead now,' Else said hurriedly. 'Because of you—'

Poppy held up her hand. 'It's probably time I told you something,' she said.

Else watched in some kind of consternation as Poppy turned to the side of the bridge and called, 'You can come up now.'

'Oh, you brought your silly little coven, did you?' Else sneered. 'Well, they couldn't subdue me last time. And I've spent thirty years growing stronger.'

'Yes, so strong you can now maintain one whole glamour,' said Alex's deep voice, and Poppy had never been so glad to hear it.

Down under the bridge, things were dark, damp, and even colder than they'd been up on the walkway roof. The wind whistled through the arch, and Alex was very glad he hadn't actually gone into the water, because he'd be worried about his extremities right now if he'd got wet. As it stood, his chances of making sweet love to Poppy ever again were already pretty low; they'd be even worse if he got frostbite of the penis.

'Can you hear a single thing they're saying?' he asked.

'No, and I don't like the way you're asking,' said Lettice Lane, from Limehouse, lately of Lancashire. She glared at him from the other end of the broom, the one without the bristles.

Alex shifted uncomfortably. A twig was poking into his right buttock. His feet were freezing, because he didn't even have shoes on. 'Sorry. And have I said how very grateful I am for the rescue?'

'Hmph. I was watching *Strictly Come Dancing*, you know. It's Hallowe'en week,' Lettice said.

'Again, apologies. I'm sure it won't be much longer.'

Lettice sniffed. She was a woman of indeterminate years and impressively awful hair. She was wearing a sort of 1950s housewife's tabard, which Alex had never seen outside of gritty mid-century dramas on TV, and her teeth and nails were nicotine-yellow.

She had caught him as he fell from the bridge's high walkway, in what had been the single most terrifying few seconds of his life – and that included having a pike thrown at his head.

Even now, sitting on the broomstick – a *broomstick*! – a few feet above the water, Alex had decided he had very definite opinions about being suspended in mid-air, and all of those opinions were negative.

'I still don't really understand what happened,' he ventured. He'd been falling, and then the broomstick had come out of nowhere, and he'd been whisked under the bridge by a woman who proceeded to complain she couldn't even have a cigarette down here 'cos the smoke would give them away. 'How come Else didn't see you rescuing me?'

Lettice rolled her eyes. ''Cos I flew up from behind, and Else's the kind of snob who forgets there's a city beyond Zone 1.' She sniffed. 'Also 'cos of the perception whatchamacallit,' she conceded. 'Young Avery whipped it up. Impressive, to do it on the fly like that.'

'Like … a glamour?' said Alex.

'Yeah. Sort of. They saw you hit the water. You heard young Poppy. She's a nice girl. Are you two an item?'

'To be decided,' muttered Alex. Poppy had come to rescue him – had flown here on a broomstick to rescue him! – and been completely distraught when she'd thought he'd gone into the water. The look on her face when she'd seen him sitting there, completely unharmed, was one that he'd treasure for the rest of his life.

And now she was up there, facing off against Yelena or Else or Elspeth or whoever she was, stalling to give the other witches time to get into position. Alex had no idea what for. None of them seemed to be much into making plans, still less telling each other what they were intending.

'Oh, hang about,' muttered Lettice, cocking her head. 'Yeah, off we go. Hold on, pretty boy.'

And with that warning, the broomstick swooped out from under the bridge to land on the road above, a feat which made Alex feel quite seasick.

But there was Poppy, inexplicably soaking wet, facing off against Else. And creeping in from other corners of the bridge, as if they'd been loitering unseen this whole time, were the other witches.

And not just the three he'd met. There was Avery from Essex – recognisable by the same chandelier earrings as before – who seemed to melt from the shadows, and a cloaked figure with a raven on its shoulder, and a grandmotherly type who looked like she could stab you to death with her knitting needles.

And there was Poppy. That was the important thing. Poppy had come for him, and Poppy was glad he was alive. They could fix everything else.

He really hoped they could fix everything else.

'Oh, you brought your silly little coven, did you?' Else sneered.

'Not a coven,' said Iris patiently.

'Well, you couldn't subdue me last time. And I've spent thirty years growing stronger.'

'Yes, so strong you can now maintain one whole glamour,' Alex said.

Else whirled around and gaped at him. 'Impossible,' she whispered.

'Very possible,' said Avery. 'You were so busy maintaining your own glamour you never stopped to think that someone else might be spinning one, too. And I'm good at them, sweetheart. I'm very good.'

As if to prove this, Poppy shook herself, and the illusion that she was soaking wet melted away.

'Good work, young … person,' said Iris to Avery. 'I really thought he had fallen until I realised Poppy would be a bit more upset.'

'Oh, I fell,' said Alex with feeling. He never ever wanted to feel like that again. He was never doing any more wire work on stage, that was for sure. Right now he had extremely mixed feelings about being any higher up than the top of a short staircase.

'But you're all right?' said Poppy quietly. She wasn't looking at him.

'I'm all right,' he said.

He wanted to go to her. He desperately, desperately wanted to go and wrap his arms around her, reassure himself she was all right, and then proceed to beg her forgiveness in any way he could think of.

But she wasn't looking at him. And she had to finish this thing with Else.

'Very touching,' said Else. 'I don't see the same concern for your own mother.'

'My mother?' said Poppy. 'My mother is a vicar called June.'

And right enough, Poppy's parents appeared, tentatively walking onto the bridge, looking extremely apprehensive.

'Hello, love,' said her mum. 'This nice lady came to collect us.'

She gestured to a tall lady with long braids, who nodded regally to the others. 'My sisters.'

'Tia Bon Amie,' said Sylvia. 'Long time no see! How was your trip to Haiti?'

'Most enlightening. But I think we have other business, Sylvie, *non*?'

'Fuck's sake, Sylvia,' Fiona muttered. 'Look, can we wrap this up? The twins have got rugby practice at eight tomorrow.'

'Look at you all!' Else said. 'A bunch of amateurs and part-timers. More concerned with holidays and children than with magic. We used to be queens. People cowered before us. Your silly little church was terrified,' she added with satisfaction.

'A dark period of our history that we're still coming to terms with,' said Poppy's mum.

'Think of what we could do,' Else urged Poppy. 'You and I. We could take their magic and be the most powerful creatures in the world.'

Poppy looked genuinely puzzled. 'But why would we want to be?'

'Fine, then give all your power to me,' said Else.

'Nice try,' said Iris.

'You really need to put more work into your planning,' said Sylvia.

'Failure to plan, plan to fail,' said Fiona.

'Oh, what do you know? I've been working on this for thirty years!'

'Twenty-eight, thank you,' said Poppy's mother. 'Which reminds me, love, will you be coming home for your birthday?'

Else rounded on her, and Alex saw all the other witches tense. Poppy raised the hand that held her broomstick, and he thought he saw small sparks along the handle.

'You touch my parents,' she said calmly, 'and I will end you.'

'Parents? What parents? These pathetic creatures? I am your parent, you silly girl! I created you! I spun you from nothing! You will be under my control! As I will it, so will it—'

'You're not my parent,' Poppy said. She advanced on Else, and Alex found himself taking a step back. 'A parent is someone who changes nappies, and sits up all night making you a costume for the school nativity, and – and remembers about the damn mushrooms in the pasta sauce! You're not my parent.' She put her face right up in Else's, and repeated firmly, 'You're not my parent.'

Alex didn't feel whatever effect that repetition had, but the other witches clearly did. He watched them react as if a strong wind had blown over them all. Else looked stunned.

'By my will,' she croaked, and slumped. Her head bowed. Her eyes closed.

'Right then,' Poppy began, turning to the others and unfastening her shawl as if it was all over.

Alex felt himself surge forward. 'It's a trap—'

He was right. Else's head came up, and she charged towards Alex. She had one hand out in front of her like a shield, and he could already feel some kind of energy coming off it, pushing him backwards, towards the edge of the bridge.

No, no, not again—

But Poppy was ready. She spun around, her eyes blazing violet and green, and threw her shawl at Else. And as it covered her face, Poppy said in a voice that could command the legions of hell, 'Duck.'

Everyone did, and Alex got the impression it hadn't been voluntary. But it was too late for him to obey, the force of Else's will already toppling him backwards over the railing of the bridge.

He had just enough time to see the shockwave radiate out from Poppy, and then he was falling down, down towards the dark water.

• • •

The shockwave threw Alex back over the edge of the bridge, but it also smashed into the one person not ducking. Else jerked as if she'd been shot, and Poppy ran towards her, grabbing her by one arm and vaulting herself onto the broomstick and over the bridge railing. The boots Avery had given her launched her into the air as if they were made of springs.

In what might have been the greatest feat of co-ordination of her life, she dropped Else, grabbed Alex, and swung the broom back into the air, landing them back on the bridge, the two of them tumbling over on the road surface before coming to a halt with Poppy sprawled on top of Alex.

Thank you, aerial ballet class.

He gazed up at her as if she did indeed hurl the moon, and Poppy allowed herself one moment to press her lips to his. Then she was up again, and racing to the outer railing, where the other witches and her parents were peering down at something thrashing in the water.

'Should we call the police?' said her mother anxiously. 'The coastguard?'

'Mum – she just tried to kill Alex. And probably you. And all of us, given half a chance, I expect.'

'Yes dear, but she's only human.'

'Not yet she isn't,' said Iris. 'Ladies – and persons of fluid gender – are we in agreement?'

'About what?' said Poppy. She glanced back at Alex, who was picking himself up off the ground and glancing distractedly at the south end of the bridge, where flashing blue lights were beginning to approach. 'What we don't have is time.'

'Else put most of her power into you, but she kept a little for herself. A very little. If we strip it, it will give us each a negligible boost, but render her as helpless as the next woman.'

'Speaking as the next woman, thanks,' said Poppy's mother.

In the water below, Else thrashed and spat and swore.

'You have my agreement,' said Tia Bon Amie.

'And mine,' said Fiona. Sylvia and Avery gave their assent.

'Thank you for the boots and shawl,' Poppy said to Avery, who shrugged graciously.

'I told you. Beldam House provides what you need.'

Iris looked around the other witches. 'Providence Chatter? Lettice Lane? Maggie Silver? Er, Maggie Silver's raven?'

Providence and Lettice nodded. The silent cloaked figure bowed its head, and the raven cawed.

'Then we have an agreement.'

'Wait,' said Poppy. 'What will happen to her?'

Iris appeared to consider it. 'She'll get old and die,' she said. 'But before that, she'll probably be arrested for holding up the traffic on Tower Bridge on a Saturday night.'

'Er, guys? The, er, police are coming,' said Alex, behind them.

'Hurry up, I'm missing *Strictly*,' said Lettice.

'Poppy, you should do it,' said Iris, and Poppy stared at

the splashing, angry creature who'd created her. Just an ordinary human.

She turned and held out her hand to Alex. 'I'm stronger when you're with me,' she said, and he looked nonplussed but came forward and took her hand.

She felt a jolt run through her, but that wasn't magic. It was just Alex. He smiled at her, and she smiled back, and for a moment there was no one else on the bridge, no one in the water, nobody in the whole world but the two of them.

Then Iris cleared her throat, and Poppy squeezed Alex's hand. She took a deep breath and let it out. Then she raised her free hand and began, 'This is my will.'

Chapter Twenty

The witches dispersed pretty quickly after the spell had been worked. Alex felt nothing, but Poppy assured him the last remnants of Else's power had been drawn from her and distributed amongst the witches.

'But nobody is staying to … talk about it?'

'Witches are like cats,' she said. 'Limited tolerance for hanging around with others.'

'Iris has a coven though.'

'Yes, who are distributed over Greater London.'

The police vehicle lights flashed blue at them, like some sombre sort of disco. Down below, the coastguard had fished Else out of the water, and Sylvia was busy telling them a terrible story about how they'd all been held hostage by this disturbed person, who should probably be evaluated by a criminal psychiatrist because honestly, she was a danger to herself as much as everyone else…

Else had been led away in handcuffs, protesting

violently but not magically. Even her weird floating hair was plastered to her sopping wet clothes.

And speaking of hair...

Alex ventured to reach out a hand, and Poppy's hair came to meet it, silken strands twining around his fingers. He peered at it, and smiled. There was some kind of algae in it.

'Are you okay?' he said.

'Am I okay? Alex, you nearly died. She threw you off the bridge.'

He shuddered. 'Yes. Don't remind me.'

Her hand squeezed his arm through his sleeve, and joy surged in him. 'Sorry. Also we hit the road pretty hard just now and I, er...' She reached up and touched his cheek, which he realised for the first time stung a little. 'I might have cut you with my hair earlier.'

He touched his own face, the face he was so vain about and had gone to such lengths to perfect. 'I hadn't noticed,' he said.

'I'm sorry,' she whispered, and he knew she wasn't just apologising for the cut.

'So am I,' he said. 'Poppy – all those things Yelena said, I mean – Else—'

'Poppy, love?'

Poppy's eyes closed briefly at the sound of her mother's voice. *Perfect timing.* 'Mum, we're kind of...' She sighed. 'Yes?'

'Oh, it's just we thought we'd get a move on. You know. It's way past our bedtime! And I've left Alan – you know, our curate – in charge but it's still a Sunday tomorrow.'

They looked so normal standing there on the bridge where, as far as Alex could tell, an apocalypse had narrowly been diverted.

Poppy glanced at Alex, then back at her parents. 'I'll take you,' she said.

'Oh no, love, you don't have to. It's not far. Where are we, Tower Bridge? I'm sure we got the train – no, the tram thing, what's it called?'

'Oh.' Her dad blew out his cheeks. 'The DRL?'

'DLR, Dad,' said Poppy. She rolled her eyes at Alex, who grinned at her.

'Is it still running? It's ever so late.'

Poppy grabbed Alex's wrist, which gave him a thrill, and peered at his watch. 'Yes, it's still running.'

'Imagine being the driver, getting home that late,' said Poppy's dad.

'There aren't any drivers, it's – never mind. Come on, I'll walk you to the station. No protests,' she said, when they began to tell her she didn't have to. 'I am a very powerful chaos witch, you know.'

Her mum leaned in and kissed her cheek. 'I know, love, and we're very proud of you.'

Poppy wrapped her shawl around herself. Alex had no idea how it had worked to prevent Else from being affected by her instruction to duck, but it had been hanging neatly on the railing when everything was over. *A gift from your Essex cousins, indeed.*

He would never understand magic.

He followed them off the bridge, down through streets

which, last time he saw them, had been full of ash and fire and panic, and past Tower Hill.

'Are you okay?' he said to Poppy. He kept his voice low, so as not to alarm her parents. They seemed mostly accepting of what Poppy had just done, but he didn't want to push things too far.

'Yeah. Are you?'

'Yes, but I'm not the one who freaked out last time we went past Tower Hill. The, er, ghosts. I know it wasn't pleasant for you.'

'Oh.' She looked surprised he remembered.

'You want to go a different way?'

'No.' Poppy looked up at him, and there was warmth in her smile. 'I've got it under control now. I think the reason I couldn't before was Else. I was never out of control, Alex. All the completely batshit stuff that happened this last week – it wasn't me. It was her.'

'But I thought she'd lost most of her power. That she'd put it into you. Was she causing all the chaos?'

Poppy screwed up her face. 'Sort of. It was more like she was manipulating my chaos. It was so gradual I hadn't realised. It crept up on me, and I thought I was the one out of control.'

'Which was what she wanted,' Alex said. 'So that you'd be so overwhelmed, so miserable, you'd give it up to her. She was gaslighting you.'

'Yeah. And then she'd use it, to, I don't know, go all comic-book villain on us.' She shook her head. 'It's amazing how free I feel now she's not influencing me. Sort of … light. Unburdened.'

Alex smiled. 'I'm really glad.'

'Come on, you two, we'll miss the tram,' called Poppy's mum.

'It's a train,' Poppy called, and groaned lightly. 'And there's one every few minutes.'

Alex smiled, and they sped up to say goodbye to her parents outside the station. Well, Poppy said goodbye. Alex hung back, unwilling to interfere with a relationship that had to have changed quite a lot in the last few hours.

'I could come back with you,' Poppy said to them. 'Make sure you get home safely.'

'What? No, don't be ridiculous. It's already too late. And how will you get back?'

'Cabs exist, Mum.'

'All that way? Cost you a fortune,' said her dad.

'And there are bikes you can – never mind. Text me when you get back to your ... convent thing.'

They both laughed. 'Convent? Oh, Poppy. It's a church retreat. You do say the funniest things.'

'Yep, I'm the one saying funny things,' said Poppy gravely. She hesitated. 'You are okay with all this, right? I mean ... I just did, like, magic. I'm a witch.'

'Yes, love. And you did ever so well. We're proud of you.'

'You will still keep your proper job though, won't you, poppet?' her dad asked anxiously. 'I mean – is there much money in witching?'

'Well,' Poppy began, and then she frowned. 'Honestly, Iris has this massive house in Highgate, so maybe. But don't you mind? I mean – you're a vicar, Mum.'

'Yes, thank you for reminding me. Poppy, I just want you to be happy. That's all either of us have ever wanted for you. Does it make you happy, this witch stuff?'

'It's who I am,' said Poppy.

'Yes, but does that make you happy? Love – if those witches could take away your power, make you ordinary, would you do it?'

Poppy recoiled. 'No,' she said immediately. 'No. I don't want to – I like being… me.'

Her parents beamed at her. 'Then that's your answer. Look, we'd better go, it's ever so late. Your dad will text you when we get back, all right? Oh, and good night, Alex. It was nice to meet you.'

Alex returned the platitude, and waved them off. It had actually been nice to meet them. To know Poppy had someone else in her corner. Alex had spent most of his life pretty sure his parents didn't like or understand any of his life choices, but if Poppy's parents could accept her being a witch, maybe his could accept him being a stage magician.

A little voice inside him said, *But do you accept it any more?*

He smiled at Poppy, but inside his head was exploding a little bit. When she turned to cross the road and walk along the edge of the park, he followed mindlessly.

Do I want to be Axl Storm any more? Do I want to spend my life being someone else? Always pretending, always faking, never being myself? Who even am I under all this?

'Alex?'

'Yeah?'

'Um, do you need to sit down or something? If you faint I'm not sure I can carry you. Broomstick or no broomstick.'

He blinked at her. Here was Poppy, who was absolutely totally herself, and he didn't even know what his name was any more.

'Okay, there's a bench,' she said, and steered him to it. A bunch of youths were approaching, but Poppy simply glanced at them and they abruptly decided to be elsewhere.

'Sit,' she said. 'You look like you're going to faint. Is it shock? It's probably shock.' She looked around, as if expecting someone to materialise and assist them. To be fair, it wasn't outside the realms of possibility. 'And you're freezing,' she said, leaning down and taking his hands in hers. 'You haven't even got any shoes on! Why don't you have shoes?'

'Because we were asleep,' he said.

Poppy stared at him. 'What?'

'When Yelena came. You put your shoes on and walked out –' he nodded at her boots, which had looked sensible but apparently made her fly '– but I still only had socks on. Because we were asleep.'

'Oh, Alex.' Poppy sat down heavily beside him.

'It's the fashionable thing around here,' he said.

'It is?' said Poppy, doubtfully.

'Yeah. Last time we were here you had no shoes on.' He frowned. 'Place was on fire, though.'

'Oh, Alex.' She rubbed his arm. He was cold, now she mentioned it. 'Your poor feet. Did you walk all this way? From Holborn?'

He shrugged. 'No. I don't know how I got here. I think

she knocked me out. And then I was on top of the bridge walkway thing.' He shuddered. 'I have decided I don't like heights. No more wire work for me.'

'Wire work?'

'In the show.' He frowned at the artfully lit walls of the Tower across the road. 'I do entrances and exits and stuff. I'm not really flying.' He gave her a bit of a smile. 'I'm not a witch.'

Poppy made a face. 'Um. No. Is that going to be a ... problem?'

'Well, we'll have to retool quite a bit of the show. Of course, I'll need a new Valkyrie anyway.'

'Hah!' said Poppy suddenly. 'Valkyrie. Ten letters, psychopomp. Even the papers were trying to tell us.'

Alex blinked at her. 'Some of those were words,' he said.

Poppy smiled and stroked his arm. 'Sorry. You were talking about your show. A new Valkyrie?'

Alex nodded, and then made a so-so motion with his hand. 'But you know what I'm thinking? I ... I don't know if I even want to be Axl Storm any more.' He ran a hand through his hair, which was still damp from the rain. He didn't know when that had stopped.

'You don't—' Poppy touched her hand to his forehead. 'Did you hit your head?' Her expression darkened. 'Did Else hit your head?'

'No. I don't think so. I'm not concussed.' He waved her hand away, then thought better of it and held it in his own. 'Poppy. Seeing you do actual real magic – not just tonight but all this week – I feel so ... fake. And I know no one really believes I'm actually doing it, but all the pouting and posing and everything… You know what that was?'

'Really kind of hot?' Poppy said.

'No. Well – yes, thank you. That was the idea. But what it actually was, underneath? I think it was that fat kid who got bullied, just wanting to prove something. Hey look, I'm really hot now.'

Her thumb stroked the back of his hand.

'And I love it, being up there in front of the crowd and everything, but … if I stopped going to the gym and ate some carbs, would anyone come to see me?'

'I would,' said Poppy.

He kissed her hand. 'You're very sweet. But you'd be the only one.'

'What a load of absolute old bollocks,' said Poppy, and he blinked at her again. 'Alex – you have so much talent and only about five per cent of it is in your abs. You're really charismatic and compelling. God knows you're charming. You could get up on that stage in a cardboard hat and cape made out of a bin bag, and do card tricks, and the audience would still be eating out of your hands. You'd be wading through groupies every night.'

Alex looked away. 'I don't want to be.'

There was a moment, stretched from seconds into hours, during which he *felt* Poppy thinking about this.

'You don't want groupies?' she said slowly.

'No. That was me proving something, too. I'm done with it. There's only one person I want, and she is definitely not a groupie.'

'She isn't?' There was enough of a smile in Poppy's voice to give him hope.

'No. Poppy,' he turned to look at her. 'I am talking about you, just to be clear.'

'I got that,' she said, and she was smiling.

'All that stuff Yelena – Else – said about other girls, that was before you. It's really important you know that.'

'I do know that.'

'And all the stuff about me telling them all I was falling in love with them – it was a lie. I don't know how she knew I'd said that to you.'

'Catfishing,' said Poppy.

'Seriously?' Alex blew out a breath. 'Well, thank God, I suppose. I thought she'd been listening at the door.'

Poppy looked revolted. 'Ew. Really? We could have been … you know.'

'Let's be grateful for small mercies,' said Alex fervently. 'Do you … do you think we might, *you know*, again?'

Poppy looked down at her lap.

'Soon?' he added hopefully.

Her shoulders began to shake.

Alex's heart broke.

'Okay,' he said. 'I see. It's okay. I will never love again,' he declared. 'How could anyone ever—'

Poppy kissed him.

Oh, thank God. Alex melted into the kiss, holding her close, his heart hammering in relief.

'And this is not to say everything's just fine and we don't have a whole load of shit to talk about,' she said, breaking for air.

'Absolutely,' said Alex, kissing her again.

'And I've got a lot to think about with my magic and where I came from and what I want to do with my life—'

'Any time you want to talk,' he assured her, and kissed her some more.

'And I'm going to have bloody words with Iris about all the stuff she didn't tell me—'

Alex put his finger over her lips. 'I don't want to think about Iris right now,' he said.

She sucked gently on his finger. Alex whimpered.

'Do you want to get a cab back to your place?' she said, and Alex leapt to his feet.

'Taxi!'

Chapter Twenty-One

'All right,' said Jonno, consulting his iPad. 'They've reset the kitchen set, and I'm assured the smoke alarm will stop wailing any minute now.'

'I did say there would be smoke,' Alex said.

'Can you blame me for being paranoid? You are not a cheap man to insure, my friend.'

'Ironic really, since it's me who's the liability.' Poppy grinned at Jonno through the mirror as her make-up was retouched. Avery had been teaching her about glamours, and Poppy thought she could do a reasonable job if she needed to, but somehow it felt like cheating, and she didn't want to end up relying on it, or looking unnatural.

Besides, it was much easier to let the make-up team do their job without explaining she was actually a witch.

'You're not a liability,' said Alex from the next chair. He took a bite of a low-carb muffin. Poppy supposed that was one step at a time. 'Can we have a bit more eyeliner? What do you think, Pops?'

She turned to look at him. 'I don't know. You don't want to be too sexy. Kids watch this.'

'So do their mums,' said Jonno. 'Do the eyeliner.'

Alex peered at himself. He'd let his beard grow a little now, and maybe his face was a little fuller, and his stomach less washboarded, but Poppy liked it. And as Jonno had pointed out, so did the female audience of their show.

'And your hair?' said Poppy's make-up person, who was clearly new. 'We could maybe curl it a bit, and have you ever thought about cutting some layers in?'

'Don't touch the hair,' Poppy and Alex said at the same time, as her hair flicked like the tail of an angry cat.

'It's a, it's like a, it's a cultural thing?' Poppy said. 'Can't cut it. Like Delilah in the Bible.'

'Samson,' murmured Alex.

'Right, yes. I mostly spent Sunday school chatting to the ghosts. Oh, that reminds me, Mum called – firstly, Cousin Sarah has filed for divorce and it's about to get really messy.'

'I thought it was bad enough that Kaspar was having an affair, let alone her too,' said Alex.

'Yes. The "I'm just being Dutch" line didn't really go down well, did it? And secondly, the churchwarden is doing Airbnb if your parents are interested? There's absolutely no pressure. She's a nice lady but she will make them say grace every time they make a cup of tea.'

'Sounds perfect,' said Alex.

'Your parents are religious?'

'Nope,' he said happily.

'Are we ready?' said Jonno, and both of them nodded

and stood.

'Alex. They're coming over. That's a big thing.' Poppy grabbed the thermos Iris always gave her on filming days, and handed it to Alex.

'I know, I know.' He sniffed the tea. 'What's in it this time?'

'Whatever Iris thinks we'll need today.' Poppy sniffed it too. 'Possibly brandy. Oh dear.'

'There's going to be another fire?'

'Iris cannot see the future,' Poppy assured him, as they left their dressing room and followed Jonno towards the kitchen set. They'd filmed their early TikToks in Iris's kitchen, but the older witch drew the line at a full film crew invading the house. She had some very sensitive new plants and Malkin had recently brought home a female cat from whom Iris had great hopes of a litter.

Poppy intended to take a couple of kittens. Alex's flat had seemed empty without a cat, but now they'd bought a house overlooking Highgate Cemetery, there was simply no excuse. Poppy was intending to train them to sit on the end of her broom.

'Yeah, Iris can't, but Avery said something about their housemate who knits the future?'

'Texeomancy,' Poppy said. She'd tried it once, and even Malkin couldn't have tangled the threads any worse. 'I am rubbish at knitting. Sylvia can tell you about it. Oh, should we have her on to do some tarot?'

'Nah, that wouldn't work unless it was live, and Poppy, I love you but we are not going live.'

'Amen to that,' said Jonno, not quite under his breath.

'Hey! I only said "fuck" once on TV.'

'It was on live national television,' said Jonno. 'At teatime.'

'I could have set the place on fire,' Poppy said sulkily. Alex grabbed her in a one-armed hug and kissed her hair, which wriggled pleasurably.

The kitchen set was heavy on bunches of hanging herbs and copper pans on the fake walls. There was a large cauldron, which Poppy always lit by magic while the cameras were rolling, and enjoyed watching the crew try desperately to figure out how she did it.

The first time Poppy had helped Alex film one of his videos, debunking common magic tricks on stage, she'd just been there to hold the camera and make sure he didn't move into shadow. And then Malkin had wandered in and knocked over the broomstick they'd been using for set decoration, and Poppy had corrected it without thinking. Neither of them had noticed until after they'd uploaded the video, which had gone viral as people tried to work out how they'd staged such a stunt at home.

Very shortly after that, *Could It Be Magic?* had officially launched, and now Alex and Poppy scripted her magic into their shows, sometimes very subtly, for the fans who absolutely loved trying to work out the tricks behind it.

'Places,' called the director, and Poppy enjoyed Alex and Jonno replying, 'Thank you, places,' like they always did. 'Final touches.'

The wardrobe person tweaked the neckline of the dress they'd provided for her, and the necklace Poppy had made herself. The hairdresser fiddled with one of Alex's braids.

She turned to Poppy, whose hair swatted her away, and retreated.

'I still don't know how you do that,' said Jonno.

'Magic,' said Poppy. She and Alex took up position behind the kitchen counter, and she turned to regard him as the clapperboard snapped.

His hair was in a messy manbun, like the first time she'd seen him. He was slightly less ripped in the abs department, but still built on the scale of a Norse god, and he had the same devastating smile. He turned it on her now, his eyes sparkling blue, and Poppy fell in love with him for about the fourth time that day.

He was still looking at her as the director called, 'Action,' so the first shot of the show was Alex gazing at her with adoration. Jonno nearly swooned in the background, because contrary to his fears, it turned out that Alex being devoted to Poppy was ratings gold, and nobody had to pretend a thing.

'Hi, everyone,' said Poppy, because Alex was gazing at her instead of introducing the show. 'I'm Poppy Thistlewood, and this is my glamorous assistant, Alex.'

He laughed. 'Hi, I'm Alex Raine, and I used to be a stage magician. This is Poppy, who is the real power behind the throne, and one day somebody will actually realise that's the truth.' He winked at her. Someone sighed happily.

'Welcome to today's episode,' said Alex, gaze swinging to the camera like a pro, 'where we're going to explore the many ways to create fire on stage.'

'Be aware this is our third attempt today and the crew hate us,' Poppy said, to general laughter.

'Thankfully, we love each other,' said Alex. 'Some day fairly soon, I'm going to work out a trick to conjure up an engagement ring.'

'He's joking, folks,' said Poppy.

'He's not,' said Alex, and his fingers just brushed hers, sending sparks of sensation right through Poppy.

For a long second, they gazed at each other. Alex's face, so beloved and familiar to her now, so handsome, so adorably honest, smiled back at Poppy.

'Holy shit,' she whispered, and in the background the director told the cameras to keep rolling as Alex kissed Poppy, there in front of the cauldron on their fake kitchen set.

'Would that be a yes, then?' he murmured.

'Yes, Alex, Axl, Sandy, Percy – whoever. Do you even have to ask?'

'Well,' said Alex. 'I figured you might object if I just booked the church without asking you.'

She laughed, and the director called for a reset, and the make-up artist had to fix Poppy's lipstick before the cameras started rolling again.

'I love you,' Poppy said, as the clapperboard sounded again.

'Not as much as I love you.'

'You poor deluded fool,' she said, and Alex laughed and turned to the camera.

'Okay, now, there's this trick I do with my hands where I make them glow, and today, I'm going to show you how I do it...'

Acknowledgments

Since writing a book is never just about writing a book, I want to thank the people who've kept me going during the occasional hour when I haven't been nose deep in broomsticks, magic amulets, and the moon phases of 1666 according to the Julian calendar:

The magnificent Naughty Kitchen (who have far too many pen names between them): Ruth, Immi, Alison, Janet, Jeev and Sheila. For Soup Or Sandwich, Periods Are Stupid, Fine And Then Wine, and so many other things, I love you. (This book is definitely soup.)

Jan, who is always there to congratulate, commiserate, and allow me to be furious. And who sends the best flowers.

Charlotte, for taking a chance on me and allowing me to say I'm going to write a nice contemporary romcom about witches and then not minding too much when I throw in the Great Fire of London.

My family, both the human and feline members. I don't know how people get through the day without a cat; happily, I've never had to find out.

It's just a bunch of hocus pocus...

Essie Winterscale lives in a huge and ever-changing house in the village of Good Winter, in deepest, darkest Essex. She lives with various witches of various ages, one of whom is still a bit salty about being hanged in the 1700s, one who keeps accidentally casting fertility spells, and one who knits things that create the future.

Into this coven of chaos stumbles gorgeous, clueless Josh, their new landlord – and he's just discovered his tenants haven't paid rent since the 1700s! As Josh is drawn further into the lives of the inhabitants of Beldam House, Essie is determined to keep him at broomstick's length. That is, until a family secret, lying hidden for centuries, puts Josh firmly under her spell...

Now available in paperback, ebook, and audio!

ONE MORE CHAPTER

YOUR NUMBER ONE STOP

FOR PAGETURNING BOOKS

The author and One More Chapter would like to thank everyone who contributed to the publication of this story...

Analytics
Emma Harvey
Maria Osa

Audio
Fionnuala Barrett
Ciara Briggs

Contracts
Georgina Hoffman
Florence Shepherd

Design
Lucy Bennett
Fiona Greenway
Holly Macdonald
Liane Payne
Dean Russell

Digital Sales
Laura Daley
Michael Davies
Georgina Ugen

Editorial
Arsalan Isa
Charlotte Ledger
Jennie Rothwell
Tony Russell
Caroline Scott-Bowden
Kimberley Young

Harper360
Emily Gerbner
Jean Marie Kelly
Juliette Pasquini
emma sullivan
Sophia Walker

International Sales
Bethan Moore

Marketing & Publicity
Chloe Cummings
Emma Petfield

Operations
Melissa Okusanya
Hannah Stamp

Production
Emily Chan
Denis Manson
Francesca Tuzzeo

Rights
Lana Beckwith
Rachel McCarron
Agnes Rigou
Hany Sheikh
Mohamed
Zoe Shine
Aisling Smyth

The HarperCollins Distribution Team

The HarperCollins Finance & Royalties Team

The HarperCollins Legal Team

The HarperCollins Technology Team

Trade Marketing
Ben Hurd

UK Sales
Yazmeen Akhtar
Laura Carpenter
Isabel Coburn
Jay Cochrane
Alice Gomer
Gemma Rayner
Erin White
Harriet Williams
Leah Woods

And every other essential link in the chain from delivery drivers to booksellers to librarians and beyond!